MASTER
OF
SOULS

ALSO BY

RENA BARRON

Kingdom of Souls
Reaper of Souls

MASTER
OF
SOULS

RENA BARRON

An Imprint of HarperCollinsPublishers

HarperTeen is an imprint of HarperCollins Publishers.

Master of Souls
Copyright © 2023 by Rena Barron
Map art copyright © 2023 by Maxime Plasse

Library of Congress Control Number: 2022949038
ISBN 978-0-06-287116-9

Typography by Jenna Stempel-Lobell
23 24 25 26 27 LBC 5 4 3 2 1

First Edition

To everyone who dares to hope in the face of
insurmountable odds,
this book is dedicated to you

. . . and to my family.

PART I

I am the puppet master,
the petulant child,
the silent bystander,
the witness to a crime.
I am my mother and my father.
I am the beginning of the end.
—Heka

PROLOGUE
DAHO

Hate me if you like, but I will not apologize for exacting revenge against the gods. I will not make excuses. I alone carved a path of destruction through time and changed the course of my fate. I have changed your fate, too. I have broken the universe.

But if it is to burn, let it burn brightly.

Every story has a beginning and an end. Whether my story will end in ruin or victory—well, that chapter has yet to be written. You may think you already know how it begins, but there have been certain omissions. Now I will tell you the truth, and when I'm done, you will understand why the gods truly fear me.

In the beginning, there were two gods: Koré, the Divine Creator, and her brother, Re'Mec, the Almighty One. We called them the Twin Kings.

There were other gods, but they were not the gods of Ilora. They molded other lands and other people from the stuff of the universe. My wife was one of these celestial beings: eternal, beautiful, and terrifying. But Dimma could do the one thing her brethren could not: she bore a child of her own flesh, and the gods despised her for it.

Their fear and envy drove them to demand that she return to the Supreme Cataclysm—the inferno that birthed them—to be unmade. Of course she refused. A goddess named Eluua sought to punish my people in retaliation. First, she murdered our children to steal away our hope. Then, with help from our endoyan cousins, she set about terrorizing our cities.

Dimma put an end to Eluua's tyranny and spun her soul into a dagger of immense power. To protect our people, Dimma offered immortality to all who had survived the attack. True, with her gift came her insatiable hunger, but we will get to that part soon enough.

My most vivid memories are of the gods' vengeance. After Eluua slaughtered my people, Koré and Re'Mec arrived to finish what she had started. They stood on a tower, overlooking the havoc their sister had wreaked upon Jiiek.

Koré had pretended to grieve, her vessel utterly still save for her hair writhing in the breeze. Her proud features seemed carved of black marble, her eyes the deepest crimson. She'd chosen to wear mourning robes of pure white—the same kind I wore the day of my coronation to honor my parents' legacy. The sword dangling from her left hand crackled with energy.

Re'Mec lingered at his sister's side, appearing as a human—one of his creatures—with bronze skin, a head of disheveled curls, and irises the color of an autumn sunrise. He gazed at me across the leagues between us, above the soaring bones of half-burned skyscrapers and wreckage in the streets. His expression was petulant, like that of a child. I'd known even then that it was a mask—one of many. He was and still is drunk on the nectar of eternity, power incarnate, rage.

I will always remember Koré and Re'Mec perched on that tower, looking down in judgment. For this was the day they destroyed my soul.

I was standing on the edge of the palace grounds when Shezmu uttered a curse that dragged my attention from the Twin Kings. He gripped a curved, double-bladed sword that would undoubtedly be no match for the gods. His snow-white hair was pulled back into a knot, his skin pale, his cheeks hollow and sunken. He'd become a shell of the man he was a month ago before Eluua killed his daughter. "We'll fight them to the end," he vowed. "Death to the gods!"

Ten thousand souls, all that remained of my subjects, waited for the attack. We were the many shades of our race, scarred and wounded and exhausted by battle. Eluua had been unrelenting in her rage. She'd left a third of my people with splintered bones where once there had been beautiful wings. But we all shared one goal: a burning desire for revenge against the gods who had betrayed us.

Though we'd forged swords and armor from blueprints taken from history books about wars long forgotten, Dimma said we must fight her brethren on their terms. It took me centuries to truly understand what she meant, but in the end, I became as ruthless as them.

Before Koré and the others arrived, Dimma had barricaded herself inside the innermost chamber of our palace, her magic shielding her so that no one, not even the gods, could enter. I'd convinced myself that I could protect her, but it was a lie.

A fog crept across the land, swallowing everything in its path and leaving behind smothering ash. The beasts and fowl of the forest surrounding the palace shrieked and howled their last breaths. The grass withered beneath our feet; the sky pulsed the colors of fresh bruises. The sun dimmed.

"They're here." I willed my words to carry across our ranks. They: the gods. I sensed hundreds of them, more than I could've ever imagined. "I will not fault anyone who wants to leave while there's still time."

"I will," Yacara declared at my side. He bore a faint resemblance to our creator's vessel, with smooth dark skin and black wings. "If you run away, I will haunt your dreams for all eternity."

Yacara's threat was empty, but no one fled. We had nowhere to go. This was our home and our fight. "We stand with you," someone muttered among the ranks.

"Kill the gods," hissed another, and soon more picked up the chant.

"Kill the gods, kill the gods, kill the gods."

"Kill them, we shall!" Shezmu answered with a manic laugh.

He, Yacara, and I held the front line as the fog tumbled to a halt, hovering an arm's length away. The gods' voices whispered in chorus, low and brooding, their words indistinguishable. Shezmu tensed with his swords ready. I clutched the dagger made of Eluua's soul.

When nothing happened, Yacara grimaced. "What are they waiting for?"

"*What are they waiting for?*" the gods mocked him in return.

For centuries, Dimma had reminded me that my body was only a vessel, but my muscles coiled in anticipation nonetheless. My heart raced and sweat dampened my brow. I knew what I had to do. Once

I killed the Twin Kings, their brethren would falter.

The fog separated into distinct shapes as the gods revealed themselves. Some were tall and hideous; others, mere flames or wisps of wind. Several had blank canvases for faces, barbed tails, or elaborate horns of polished bone.

The attack came at once. They swarmed us, ripping and shredding flesh, severing heads and limbs, spilling blood that painted our lands. They cut down demon after demon, and my fury grew until it consumed me. I became one with my dagger, driving my blade through them with no thought but killing as many as I could. With each god's death, the dagger absorbed their soul with a hunger of its own. The blade began to glow and lengthened until I was holding a sword.

I fought my way to the top of the tower, where Koré stood waiting for me. Re'Mec wasn't with her—he'd joined the battle on the palace grounds. The Divine Creator barely seemed to notice my arrival; she was too busy watching her brethren attempt to destroy what was left of my people. I'd wondered what she thought of Dimma's gift of immortality as Shezmu, Yacara, and the others rose from their broken bodies to keep fighting.

"Is this what you want, child?" Koré finally tore her eyes away from the battle to face me. "Hasn't this gone far enough?"

"How can you ask such a thing," I spat, "after you let Eluua murder my people?"

Koré tilted her head to consider the dagger, now a sword of light to match her own. "I should have acted sooner to stop her," she conceded.

"You did not act at all," I reminded her. "Dimma did."

She sniffs the air. "I will allow you to keep Eluua imprisoned. She deserves it. But you must let the others go."

"I'll only free them if you promise to leave Dimma alone," I countered.

"You know I cannot." Koré chided me almost gently. "She and your child are the beginning of the end. If they live, the Supreme Cataclysm will consume the universe and destroy us all."

I'd hoped she would finally see reason. She and Re'Mec alone had the power to stop this. "So be it."

I raised my sword high and brought it down upon the Divine Creator, but she struck first, severing my arm so cleanly that for a moment, I felt nothing. Then . . . pure, searing agony. She beckoned my sword to her with an imperious crook of her finger. The blade went willingly, but as soon as she gripped the hilt, a single shudder passed through her.

"This can't be," she whispered.

Flesh and bone materialized to replace my severed limb, but that was of no importance next to what was happening to Koré. Her skin withered and cracked. A buttery light oozed from inside her, escaping through the many fissures covering her body. So, it was true: Dimma said that only she or I could wield Eluua's power, but I hadn't guessed it would consume anyone else who touched it, especially a god.

I strolled forward and pried the sword from Koré's unresisting hand. She was mere ashes shaped into some semblance of a vessel now. As I prepared to reap her soul, the echoes of my mother's stories—of Koré's kindness and love for our people—rang in my ears. All of them lies, for our god was selfish and cruel. "Goodbye, Divine Creator."

Another sword blocked my killing blow, and Re'Mec appeared between his sister and me. He clucked his tongue. "Would you really strike down your *divine creator*?"

I gritted my teeth in frustration. Koré had already recovered—her skin smooth again, her white mourning robes pristine. Of course it wouldn't be so easy. Still, I had held out hope. Behind her, shadows converged on the palace, and inevitability carved a place in my heart. Dimma's magic was failing. I had to get back—but before I could take a step, Re'Mec pierced his sword through my belly. "You're too late," he grunted as he twisted the blade.

The impact hurtled me into the void between life and death, and my rage began to fade, replaced by the gentle beckoning of the Supreme Cataclysm. It called to my soul, enticing me to be unmade. It promised comfort. Rest. I will not lie. I was tempted.

But I wasn't ready. I refused with everything left in me, fighting against its lure until I returned to my body. When I regained consciousness, I was still holding the sword. The Twin Kings were gone.

I staggered to the edge of the tower and let myself fall, already pumping my wings hard and fast when I caught the current. "Dimma!" I screamed. "Dimma!"

My desperate calls yielded no answer, and her silence was deafening, cold, final. A part of me died with her, and the insatiable hunger was all that remained.

Now you know why I despise the gods, and why I will not rest until I destroy every last one of them.

ONE
ARRAH

I dream of a different life. I dream of kissing Rudjek in our secret place by the Serpent River underneath a shade tree, magic alighting on my skin and glowing inside me. Grinding herbs at my father's side in his shop while he tells me another story of his tribe. Watching my mother paint dancers on the wall outside my bedchamber. I dream of holding my sister's hand as we traverse the crowds of haggling patrons and eager merchants in the East Market.

This Efiya is a little girl admiring all the trinkets with wide-eyed innocence. She's not the monster who killed our parents and so many others—the monster who freed the Demon King. And my mother isn't the woman who fed children's souls to a demon in a bid to destroy the gods. My father is still alive. Sukar. Grandmother. All the others. But these dreams will never come true—they're only wishful thinking to calm the ghosts that haunt my memories.

I've sacrificed so much already. I don't doubt that I will sacrifice much more before the end.

I wish that I could bury my thoughts as easily as I push back the branches of saplings that cut across our path. We're deep in a forest on the crossroads in search of what's left of the five tribes of Heka. Sweat softens our grime-stiff clothes, and mosquitoes the size of horseflies buzz about our faces. Under different circumstances, I might close my eyes and listen to the birdsong or watch the lizards scurry across tree trunks or admire the wildflowers nestled in the underbrush. But all I can think about is Dimma.

I tell myself that I will be better than her. That I won't make her mistakes. That I will turn away from the temptation that ruined her . . . but I am very good at pretending. I am good at killing, too, or I was before she stripped me of the chieftains' magic to protect her *ama*. In a way, the Demon King was my *ama*, too, for she is a part of me. *Twenty-gods, I was her.* That much, I will concede. I was once a ruthless god who loved the Demon King. Let me clarify: Dimma still loves him despite the horrible things that he's done. I sigh at the memories of his touch, his lips against hers, the calming timbre of his voice. I am not her, but I can't deny the longing stirring inside me.

"Dare I ask what's on your mind?" Rudjek says as the still morning air gives way to the lash of the hot sun. He's keeping his distance as he walks alongside me.

I curse under my breath when we pass a familiar wizened tree stump. I can't bring myself to meet his gaze, so I stare intently at the path. "I think we've been here before."

"We should stop for a bit," Rudjek suggests, though he sounds like he has enough energy to go on for days.

His craven guardians have shifted into hawks that circle the sky, their wings occasionally offering slivers of respite from the sun. Essnai clings to her *ama*'s arm and whispers something that draws a coy smile from Kira. I try not to think about the absence of Majka, Raëke, Sukar, but a hollow ache rises in my throat nonetheless. With it comes the bitter taste of shame. I killed Sukar while trying to protect him, and then the Demon King stole his body.

"I would rather keep moving," I finally answer.

I think about the survivors we left in Tribe Zu. After we rescued them from Tyrek Sukkara, they'd settled at the head of the crossroads. They had agreed that they wouldn't run anymore and would make their stand in the Zu mountains if the demons attacked again. I promised them I would find out what happened to the rest of the tribal people, but after a month on the crossroads, we're no closer to an answer. Without the chieftains' magic, it's been nearly impossible.

Ahead of us, the path splits into forks that double back and cross over themselves in every direction. I sigh when I see a circle of white ash marking a tree. Kira drew it just this morning. She's been tracking our path through the crossroads. Somewhere I've made another wrong turn.

"We knew this wouldn't be easy," Essnai offers, her voice a soft coo. "We expected detours, but we can't give up hope. We'll find the tribes."

"It would help if I weren't leading us in circles half the time," I mutter, annoyed.

I have to believe the tribes made it to safety after Efiya and the demons attacked their lands, but my hope is beginning to dim. We've found no fresh footprints. No smoldering ashes of campfires, no bones from roasted meat, not so much as a branch crushed under a passing foot that wasn't our own. I think of Dimma again and my plan. She'd used my borrowed magic to heal Rudjek; maybe it was possible to use *her* magic to stop the Demon King. There must be someone left in the tribes who could help me unlock it while keeping her asleep. I can't stand by and let the Demon King hurt anyone else—not if I can do something to stop him.

I wish that I could trust Koré and Re'Mec, but I've seen firsthand through my own eyes and secondhand through Dimma's that things only get worse when the gods are involved.

"We've been walking for hours," Rudjek says suddenly; then he leans in close to me, knowing full well what will happen. "You look like you could use some rest."

I brace myself for the effect of his anti-magic, and it comes at once. The faint lines of the trail suddenly disappear. I bite my lip, pushing back my frustration. I don't regret making the deal with Dimma to give up the chieftains' gift to save Rudjek's life, but I hate that his anti-magic completely washes out my ability to see magic when he's this close. "I'm fine," I say, insisting on pushing ahead.

Rudjek squints and glances at me sideways. A look meant to bait me. "You're not a very good liar."

It works.

I press my hand to his cheek, tracing the bristle of the beard that has only recently cropped up. I suspect it will be as thick and curly as the hair on his head in a few years. Touching him, now that we *can* touch, always helps me not to feel so lost. Rudjek, Essnai, Kira, and even Fadyi and Jahla are my anchors. They are all I have left. I shiver when Rudjek kisses my palm—Dimma liked when Daho did that.

"You always get that dreamy look when . . . ," Rudjek murmurs, his gaze searching. He lets his words trail off, but I know what he started to say. *When you're thinking about him.* "At least when I kiss you, I won't puncture your lips."

The joke is about Daho's pointed teeth, of course. Teeth that spent countless hours delicately grazing Dimma's wrists, her neck, the hollows of her collarbone. Other places that I try not to remember.

"Are you so insecure that you think I'd waste my time fantasizing about the Demon King?"

"Yes." Rudjek looks down at me, rubbing the back of his neck. "He's taller than me, I'll give him that—and then there are those wings and glowing eyes. Oh, and that wicked blade for trapping souls."

I frown. "Now that you mention it . . ."

Rudjek pretends to stagger back, clutching his heart. Then he bats his long dark lashes and poses. "I happen to be very pretty, too, you know."

I raise an eyebrow, delighting in this playful banter. It reminds me of the way we were before things became so complicated. "I hadn't noticed."

But pretty is an understatement. Rudjek is also tall, with pale brown skin, eyes as black as a moonless night, lush dark eyebrows, and an irresistible smile. His curls have grown unruly while we've been on the road. I like it. He looks less like the Crown Prince and more like the boy I used to sneak away to meet by the river, the boy with a spark of adventure in his eyes, who couldn't have cared less what his demanding father thought of him.

Essnai laughs. I glance over my shoulder and get the feeling that she and Kira are gossiping about us. Sometimes I think it's a mistake to let my friends come with me, but I don't know how to do this alone.

"See?" Rudjek scoffs. "Even Kira and Essnai think I'm pretty."

"You wish," Kira says, making a face.

"Must you always be so insufferable, Rudjek?" Essnai asks.

"You finally see how much work it was to serve as his attendant! And then again under his command." Kira pretends to be exasperated. "He is so tiring."

"Hey!" Rudjek protests.

Kira picks up a small stone and pitches it at him, and he dodges it with ease.

I'm grateful for these moments of levity, but they don't last nearly long enough. "Now, if you don't mind, I need to get back to tracking the crossroads," I say, gesturing for Rudjek to give me more space.

He frowns, but he doesn't object when Kira hooks her arm underneath his and pulls him away. "There'll be plenty of time for frolicking later. Stop distracting her."

"I am not distracting her," he mumbles. "As usual, she's being stubborn."

Once the sting of his anti-magic fades, I seek out the lines of the crossroads again, my gaze searching over rocks and crooked tree roots and vines. I'm convinced that one day even this gift to see magic will be stripped away, leaving me with nothing. Since I was a child, it's been my one true talent, and I can't imagine losing it.

I stare so long I have to blink back tears gathering in the corners of my eyes. It helps the burning but not by much. My vision isn't what it used to be—yet another not-so-subtle side effect of trading my years in exchange for magic. Another consequence I must live with to the end of my days. I let out a soft sigh when the lines of the crossroads finally shimmer underneath the sun. The tightness eases in my chest.

Rudjek's guardians perch high in a tree, waiting for us. One is iridescent brown, the other snow white. Before I lost the chieftains' gift, I could see the way the cravens worked to hold their physical shape—their skin always moving like water washing over the hull of a ship.

My friends don't question our route as we pick up the trail again, though it loops, circles, and takes random turns through thorned bushes that sting our ankles. We cross into a thick part of the forest that offers relief from the sun. In the shadows, the magic is much more pronounced. It clings to the trees like silky moss and drifts lazily between the branches. It makes me ache for the nights when it came to me willingly.

After everything that's happened, I should be repulsed by it, but I still feel a sense of wonder like when I was a child during Imebyé in Tribe Aatiri and tried to pluck it from the air. I swallow my bitterness. If I can't tap into Dimma's gifts, the only way I can possess magic again is to trade my years. That could lead to nothing good. If recent events have taught me anything, it's that I want the chance to live my life on my own terms, for however much time I have left.

"There's something strange about the magic here," Rudjek says almost to himself. He stops in the middle of the path and slowly turns, frowning at a single sapling in a clearing bathed in the amber of the afternoon light.

I stop, too. I don't sense anything amiss, but I trust his instincts. The sun orisha made cravens to hunt down magic, so his perception of it is much stronger than mine. I look ahead at a tangle of lines on the crossroads that intersect near a tree. They pulse and writhe, but that isn't unusual. It's by design: the entire crossroads is a maze meant to keep anyone from finding the tribal people.

"What is it?" Kira asks.

Rudjek rests his hands on his hips, near the hilts of his swords. "I don't know. All I can say is that it feels *strange*."

"Maybe it's best if we keep going and not stay here." I point to the lines as if my friends can see them. "I just need some time to study the intersection."

"I think we'll scout the area," Rudjek says, but it's an excuse to give me more distance from his anti-magic. His guardians, Fadyi and Jahla, land nearby, and their shapes stretch from feathers and wings into arms and legs. Their human forms look much like the hawks': Fadyi with rich brown skin and dark hair; Jahla with paler skin, light eyes, her hair now silver instead of white.

Essnai thrusts a waterskin in my hand. "Drink this before you pass out from the heat."

I take it from her, but I hesitate, my hand shaking. The supple leather reminds me of the night when she, Sukar, Tyrek, and I sat around a campfire, sharing a wineskin and playing the drum. That was before Tyrek revealed that he was a snake. Sukar had danced with Essnai, the two of them ethereal underneath the moonlight.

Only it wasn't Sukar.

Essnai's eyes meet mine as if she knows what I am thinking. Her touch is gentle as she guides the waterskin to my lips. "Drink."

Always so bossy, Sukar used to tease her. And he was always cynical but warm and funny.

"Fine." I sigh. After taking a sip, I turn back to the path. The magic of the crossroads is clever. Sometimes it pulses like a heartbeat; sometimes it flows like water over smooth stone. I kneel and run my hand along the tangle of lines, feeling the throb of the magic.

It takes a moment, but one of the lines shimmers, suddenly standing out from the others, revealing the right path. I get to my feet. "I've found the next leg of our journey."

"Time to go," Essnai calls to the others.

Rudjek returns to the clearing with his guardians. They stay back while Kira and Essnai keep me company, chattering away. Now that we're following the shimmering line, I see the strangeness that Rudjek sensed earlier. The magic is disjointed, as though it's held together by a fraying rope.

As the sun sinks low in the sky and then finally slips below the horizon, I take a fork on the path and immediately know that something is wrong. I'm hit with a blast of rank air that twists my belly in knots. The stench is of death and decay, things that I have become intimately familiar with.

Shadows pass in front of the flickering lines of the crossroads. *Familiars*, I tell myself. Until recently, they'd been harmless—shapeless, wandering souls trapped between life and death by Dimma's hand.

But when Efiya released Daho, he commanded them to attack Rudjek. Another rush of rank air sweeps across my path, and I see staring, hollow eyes in the dark. Dozens of them, faintly glowing.

Familiars don't have eyes.

I stumble back and collide with Rudjek, and he catches me in his arms. The crossroads blink out, blocked by his anti-magic. "I take it we took a wrong turn . . . ," he says as he pulls away from me and draws his swords. His guardians flank him, searching the darkness unfolding in front of us. Essnai readies her staff.

"Demons?" Kira asks as she retrieves two of the many daggers strapped to her body.

"No," Rudjek murmurs, and Fadyi nods in agreement.

Magic swells in the forest. Sparks fly from the trees to join with the shadows, swarming like wasps, until they illuminate the faces of decaying carcasses. Dread crawls across my skin at the realization: before us stand a dozen *akkaye*.

"So much for looking forward to a moment's rest," Rudjek says as he and the cravens move between the *akkaye* and me.

"Burning fires," Kira curses. "What kind of perversion is this?"

I swallow down my horror as the *akkaye* shudder. Their long spindly arms quake, and their skeletal fingers stretch and flex as they fully awaken. Ghastly shrieks tear into the night as, one by one, the creatures lurch forward, each step smoother and faster than the last. The *akkaye* are almost inconceivably thin, with pocked, gray skin stretched tight over protruding ribs and clavicles. They heave in gulps of air, gasping before their hollow, unblinking eyes seem to find us all at once.

"We have to go." I back away from Rudjek so his anti-magic

doesn't keep me from finding the path again. I frantically search. I should see something, a glimmer, a stray spark of magic, but the crossroads have gone dark.

Too late I realize that I've led my friends into a trap meant for the demons. The *akkaye* have only one instinct: to kill. And we've been caught in their snare.

TWO
ARRAH

If *ndzumbis* are the living dead, then the *akkaye* are the undying. They were legends from a time when the tribes fought each other in vicious wars. When magic was little more than a weapon to wield against your enemy—the way my mother had wielded it against the orishas and against me.

An impression of the Litho chieftain stirs in my mind, like an echo of a memory. From the remnant of white ash on the *akkaye*'s withered faces, I can tell they had come from his tribe. Töra Eké was talented with magic that could twist souls in unimaginable ways. He had done this before Efiya killed him and the other chieftains. He sacrificed his own people.

"Are those... *corpses*?" Kira remarks, interrupting my thoughts.

These had once been people with families and friends, and Töra Eké had turned them into abominations. How could he do something so vile? This was no better than the demons—maybe it was even worse. "They *are* corpses," I say as the *akkaye* lurch forward another step. "They're more dangerous than they look."

"They look plenty dangerous to me," Essnai mumbles.

"How do we kill them?" Rudjek asks, cutting to the point.

"According to the stories, the *akkaye* cease to exist by killing the witchdoctor who made them, but that witchdoctor is already dead," I answer, rushing my words. "The only other way is to destroy their bodies, completely, so they can't draw more magic to them."

"That shouldn't be so difficult." Rudjek rotates his wrists, and moonlight shines off his curved blades. "I'm rather good at destroying things."

This is my fault. We wouldn't be facing the *akkaye* had I not made another mistake. Maybe if I retraced our last steps, I could find the path again. I scan the clearing, looking for any sign. We'd crossed it from north to south, then thrice circled the whispering tree—where the *akkaye* stand now—before doubling back. Where was the exact spot the magic had blinked out? I bite the inside of my cheek hard enough to taste blood, and an *akkaye* snaps its head in my direction. There's awareness in its hollow eyes, a keen sense of foreboding as if it can smell death clinging to me.

"Here." Kira hands me one of her knives. "In case one gets by us."

The blade is slick against my sweaty palm, its weight unfamiliar and awkward, yet I had wielded the Demon King's dagger with deadly precision. With that dagger, I had killed. Now the compulsion to reach out and snatch magic from the sky to destroy the *akkaye* overwhelms me. I can do it if I pay the price—if I offer up my years. I push that thought away. The dagger will have to be enough.

"Just what we need." Jahla utters the first words I've heard her say in well over a month. Her voice is small and raw. "More monsters who refuse to die."

Near the front of the advancing horde, an *akkaye* arches its back and brays at the sky. Spiny appendages with curved claws wiggle from between its shoulder blades, and oily black wings unfurl. More *akkaye* sprout wings as the terrible sound of splitting flesh fills the forest.

Rudjek quirks an eyebrow at me. "Well, that certainly makes things interesting."

As the *akkaye* transform, I finally catch a glimpse of the cross-roads behind them—a single spark of magic on the ground near the whispering tree. The *akkaye* watch us with sunken glowing eyes, standing between us and our path to safety.

"We have to go through them," I say desperately. "It's the only way."

Rudjek lifts his shotels, resigned. "Let's get on with it, then."

He, Fadyi, and Jahla spread out along the ragged line of *akkaye* that chitter with anticipation. Their appendages twitch, and bone scrapes against bone as they lurch forward. But when Rudjek signals his guardians to stop, so do the *akkaye*. It's a grotesque game of jack-als and hounds. Who will strike first?

"They're protecting the crossroads!" I shout. "They won't venture away from the trap."

"Then we'll hold them off while you find the path," Rudjek says a split second before he, Fadyi, and Jahla disappear. The place where they stood is empty, and I experience a jolt of horror before they reappear behind the *akkaye*. Rudjek's ability to bend time and space, even if temporarily, still leaves me breathless.

The changes in the *akkaye* are instant, their bodies straightening like threads pulled taut. Leathery lips stretch across jagged teeth as they swarm Rudjek and his guardians. Rudjek roars in pain as a claw slices open his chest. He slams the *akkaye* into the whispering tree so hard that flesh is torn from its body, left to hang from the bark. He relieves another *akkaye* of its head and acrid green blood sprays on his arm. His skin sizzles and smokes. The smell taints the air and turns my stomach—but in seconds, his wounds have healed.

Fadyi and Jahla let go of their physical shapes, becoming two gray amorphous masses that race through the *akkaye*, twisting into sharp edges that cut and sever and impale. The cravens slip from the creatures' grasp with ease. When the *akkaye* are nothing more than a heap of rotting corpses spread about the ground, Fadyi and Jahla return to their human forms.

"Well, that was a nice distraction," Rudjek says with a deep sigh.

But his relief is short-lived as magic alights on the *akkaye*. Roots spring up from the ground and weave together to replace their missing heads, limbs, and wings. New grotesque creatures rise from their broken bodies, and Jahla lets out a growl.

Rudjek shrugs. "And here I thought it would be easy."

The *akkaye* attack again, and a narrow gap opens between them and the crossroads. "There's our chance," I tell Essnai and Kira, and we dash toward the whispering tree. I keep my gaze on the single spark of magic, desperate not to lose sight of it as Essnai and Kira fight off a handful of *akkaye* who have peeled away from Rudjek and his guardians.

When we reach the spark of magic, my breathing slows and my eyes slip out of focus. Another spark careening in the air descends and lands in front of me. Light spreads out along the ground, seeping into the undergrowth, around the rocks and exposed roots, illuminating the path again.

"Here!" I yell, but as I turn to the others, an *akkaye* sinks its teeth into my shoulder. Hot, searing pain cuts through me, and I scream. The creature stares in confusion as if there's some shred of consciousness left inside it. Blood oozes around its mouth, but the *akkaye* doesn't let go. Finding my strength, I manage to stab it in the neck. Kira's blade glows—imbued with the sun orisha's magic. The *akkaye* stumbles back, my flesh still between its teeth.

"We're not the enemy," I whisper.

Essnai splits the *akkaye* across the skull with her staff. "Arrah, watch out!"

Too late, I see the shadow sweeping down from the sky. An *akkaye* slams into me, and Kira's dagger slips from my hand. I stare at the blood soaking through my tunic—at the claws clutching my sides. The world is a blur as the *akkaye* takes flight, hauling me with it.

The wind howls in my ears, and tree branches sting my skin. I struggle to free myself, but it's no use. We land in another part of the forest, separated from the others. The *akkaye* pins me to the ground, and a thin, rank string of drool drips from its mouth.

I scream again, succumbing to pain and frustration. Only a small trade, and I could have magic again. I could call upon it to destroy the *akkaye*—but instead, I'm reduced to sheer terror. Without Kira's dagger, I have no other means to defend myself. The orishas never intended for mortal kind to possess magic, and I've begun to understand why. We twist it in horrible, horrible ways, just like Töra Eké did with his own people.

I brace myself for the *akkaye*'s next move, but it only perches on my chest, clicking its teeth and sniffing the air. I can't die, not after coming this far. Not before I've found a way to use Dimma's magic to stop Daho. *Gods.* If I die, she'll be free.

The *akkaye* cocks its head and stretches its long neck. It's listening intently but to what? The forest is quiet except for the fighting in the distance. While it's distracted, I run my hand across the dirt until I find a rock. When I raise my arm to strike, the *akkaye* lowers its face to mine, leering at me through the fetid fog of its breath. Its hollow eyes pierce my soul. But like the first *akkaye* that attacked me, a flicker of uncertainty crosses its face.

Another *akkaye* crawls toward us, mouth open in anticipation. I grit my teeth and choke out a desperate cry. "Don't!"

Magic shudders in the trees, eager to come to me. I resist calling it, even as the temptation grows stronger. The *akkaye* both stop at my command, but something else has their attention. A gush of warm air; a shift in the space around us. Bending shadows. I follow their gaze and stare into the darkest part of the forest. My heart leaps in my chest, summoning an image of beautiful, outstretched wings the color of a snow dove. I push down the longing that stirs inside me, but I can never fully suppress Dimma's yearning for her *ama*. Then the shadows shift again, leaving cold emptiness in their wake.

Rudjek suddenly appears behind the *akkaye* pinning me to the ground. The creature shrieks as he plunges his shotel through its chest. Blood splashes on my face and sears my cheek, but the *akkaye* stiffens, its skin turning papery. Rudjek's anti-magic pours off him like the hot lash of the sun. In moments, the *akkaye* turns into ashes. No amount of magic will bring it back this time.

The second *akkaye* moves to attack, but I yell, "Stop!"

Again, it freezes in place.

Rudjek frowns at me, but I can't explain it, either. I sag against the ground, deflated and relieved that it hadn't come to trading my years. I swallow hard as I issue another command to the creature. "Sleep."

The *akkaye* tilts its face to the sky and brays, then more cries ring out across the forest. The *akkaye* backs away until it's swallowed whole by shadows. "They're fleeing," Rudjek stutters. He narrows his eyes, looking at me suspiciously. "Did you . . . ?"

"No," I say, inhaling a breath that's cut off by the pain in my sides. The best I can guess is the *akkaye* had sensed that Töra Eké's *ka* once resided inside me, the same way I knew that he had made them. "What took you so long to rescue me?"

Rudjek leans over me, mischief dancing in his dark eyes. "I'll be faster next time."

"See that you are," I say, but there's no bite in my words.

He reaches for my wounds, but he hesitates. I press my palm against his chest. Not so long ago, we could have killed each other with one touch. He smiles down at me as he slides his hands to my waist, his calloused fingers ever so careful.

I go slack, comforted by the warmth of his embrace. He smells of blood and sweat and rot, but I don't care. I can feel my skin responding. I can *feel* him. At first, my body resists his anti-magic, but soon the tide turns, and a soothing tingling spreads through me . . . and the pain recedes.

He quirks an eyebrow. "To think that I've been hoping to get you alone for weeks."

"And now here we are," I say with as much dignity as one can muster while wallowing in dirt and blood.

He smiles. "This is nice."

"I'm bleeding to death, and all you have to say is 'this is nice'?"

"We're alive, Arrah," he says quietly, and I don't miss the layers of meaning in his words. *We're alive, and our friends are dead. We're alive, and we don't know how much time we have left.* "I plan to keep us that way."

It's a promise that I want so desperately to believe will come true, and even though I know better, I let myself bask in this moment. Rudjek makes to pull away once my wounds are healed, but I grab his arm. I can't let this chance go by like all the others. It isn't as I imagined it—I'm not as I imagined, with my hair graying and my missing tooth, the cost of trading my years. But I am beyond caring about things I cannot change. "Are you sure we're alive?"

Rudjek grins, and he lowers his lips to mine. "There's only one way to find out."

THREE
EFIYA

I am not meant to be idle. I need to do something—anything—that isn't wasting away in this barren land. I am meant for greatness.

How can the demons call this pathetic place home? The sun is a burning eyesore, and the twin moons bleed across the sky at night. My father expects *me* to stay in Ilora while *he* waits for the Demon King to move against the orishas.

He clearly doesn't know me very well.

Since I cannot stand another moment cooped up in the palace without setting it on fire in a fit of rage, today I've decided to take a stroll. I wander through a scattering of dwellings in what was once Jiiek. The soil is ash against my bare feet, which only annoys me more. I don't get why these demons even bother to put on this charade. They should crush these relics from the past and build something new. Better yet, they should stop licking their wounds and make the orishas pay. That's what I would do.

My father and the Demon King control the gate between worlds;

they can take their people away from here. There must be any number of homes the orishas made for their little pets that we can claim for ourselves. I personally prefer Zöran. I have a few scores to settle there.

I pause when I come upon a sickly tree with festering wounds in its gray bark. It's been dying for a very long time. "Did you do this, *Ugeniou?*" I whisper. The many souls I've consumed stir inside me. Their anger and despair rise to the edges of my thoughts. I rather enjoy their protests. It reminds me of my power. Ugeniou—the harvester—is only one such soul that lingers within me now. "You would have needed Nana's help—your counterpart, the mother of the land. She poisoned the soil first, and you poisoned the plants. . . . That was rather nasty of you both but quite clever. Though I might have done something more . . . *exciting.*"

Ugeniou doesn't answer. He can't. He's very much dead—not that he was particularly hard to kill. What is left of him is only an impression, a compulsion. I press my hand against the tree, and its bark crumbles. A sadness passes over me. Regret. "It hurt you to destroy your harvest," I realize. "But you still did as Re'Mec and Koré asked like a good little sibling."

Bitterness rises in my throat. My sister wanted me to obey her, too.

I slowly turn around the tree, scraping my nails across the bark. I'm keenly aware that I have an audience. The demons that I freed from Kefu know me—they're grateful, but the demons that have been trapped on Ilora for five thousand years treat me like an outsider even after everything I did for them. I alone reunited their people and freed their king. My hand begins to pulse with light as I pour magic into the tree. The poison resists my efforts, but in the end, it succumbs to my will. Everything always does.

The bark grows firmer underneath my touch, and it turns from sickly gray to a rich black. The roots writhe in the dead soil as my magic brings life back to them. Pink buds blossom on the bare limbs. I am filled with a profound sense of pride, but I snatch my hand away. I don't care about this tree. All I care about is my revenge, and I'm tired of waiting.

I take back my magic and leech the last bit of life from the tree. I smile when the demons watching me slink away in the shadows. It seems that I have given them something to talk about.

I storm back across the dead land to the palace. Perhaps I'll pull apart the bones of Dimma's throne and make something new of them. But when I reach the chamber, I feel even more restless than before my stroll. I slump into the throne, which sits on a raised platform above the chamber. Light filters through the stained-glass sky dome and shimmers against my skin. I conjure a mirror on the wall to see myself. I look marvelous, truly, considering that my sister destroyed my vessel and forced my soul into the Demon King's dagger. I shudder, remembering that dark, lonely place.

After the Demon King released me, I remade my body, just as it was before, in all its perfection and glory. I can't wait until the moment Arrah sees it. She's going to be beside herself to learn that her efforts were for nothing. I'm still mad that she wouldn't let me out of the dagger, but I'm looking forward to our reunion. I've missed her.

To think that she once sat upon this throne, back when she was Dimma. Her presence lingers here even now, impressions from the day she died. I smooth my palm across the armrest made of bones that have long ago turned to crystal. The design of the throne is morbid, even for my taste. Dimma's grief still chokes the air. If you ask me, this palace could use a spiritual cleansing—too many sad memories. I wonder what will happen if Arrah returns here. Will she become Dimma again—or will she still be my sister?

My forearms tingle: the gate between worlds is about to open. The air shifts to make space for it. I sense my father's overbearing presence at once and roll my eyes. The Demon King isn't with him, so he must still be on Zöran pining after my sister when he should be putting an end to the orishas. Spending five millennia in their prison has made him feeble. Like this decaying world, the gods are relics, too, that must be put down.

My father says I should abandon my quarrel with them now that I've freed the Demon King. I guess he wants only to keep me safe, but he doesn't get it. I like games, and I'm not done playing.

When the Demon King is here, he spends most of his time at the frozen lake in the little cabin waiting for Arrah . . . *Dimma*. Whatever. What an absolute fool he is—a complete and utter tragedy. I sigh and lean my head back against the throne. His people, our people, still love him, even after he helped my sister kill the demons loyal to me.

That was an unfortunate mistake.

"Efiya!" Shezmu shouts from the base of the throne, as if I'm a child he can order around when I'm the one who helped him regain his strength. "Come down from there."

"I'm busy, Papa." I play along for now. A spoiled child left too long to her own devices. "I'm paying my respects to your beloved queen." I don't bother hiding the contempt in my voice.

I can tell from Shezmu's silence that he's flustered, but when he speaks again, it's obvious that he's trying not to show it. "Will you please come down, daughter?" He is so restrained—the pillar of patience.

I soften at the gentle plea in his voice. If there is a weakness in me, it's this—I'm vulnerable to the occasional show of kindness, even though I know it can't be trusted. Mother never asked; she only demanded. Nothing I did was ever good enough for her.

But Shezmu is different. He doesn't demand anything of me. I step to the edge of the raised platform and peer down at him. In appearance, he could be the Demon King's distant cousin. They both have white wings that shimmer silver in the right light and silvery skin, though the Demon King's has purple undertones. His hair is dark and wavy, while my father's snow-white locks are pulled back into a perfect knot at the nape of his neck. The Demon King is single-minded when he wants something, but my father is clever. He is always planning and watching, biding his time. I must take after him, for I am biding my time, too, sizing up the players in the game. The vengeful Demon King. The wrathful orishas. The enigmatic Heka. And, of course, my traitorous sister, Arrah.

"Is *your king* still avoiding me?" I ask nonchalantly.

Shezmu answers my question with one of his own, his wings twitching. "Why would Daho avoid you? He owes you a debt of gratitude for freeing him from Koré's prison."

I hate how the orishas have immortalized the Demon King. They filled their scribes' heads with visions of his great evils, so much that people have told stories about him for countless generations. Whether he deserves it or not, the Demon King has become a legend. I wonder if people are telling stories about me in Zöran. They should. I am far more capable than he will ever be.

"Perhaps because I disobeyed him." I shrug. "He warned me not to challenge my sister, but I did anyway. I tried to kill the vessel that holds his precious Dimma's soul."

"We all have done awful things, Efiya," Shezmu says, his eyes the same shade of glowing emerald as mine. "I don't make excuses for my mistakes, and neither should you. We can't linger in the past. Our queen is alive."

Your queen, not mine, I think spitefully, but know better than to say it. He is loyal to the Demon King and Dimma to a fault.

"Don't you regret eating those children's souls?" I ask, aiming a strike at his heart. He shrinks into himself, and he looks so small down there, so powerless. I almost feel bad. Almost.

"I do," Shezmu answers, and his voice falters. "I have to live with my decision to help Arti, but I do not regret you. You—" He pauses to search for the right words. "You are my second chance, Efiya. You are all that matters to me now."

It does feel nice to be cherished. But it won't last. Eventually, I will disappoint him just like I disappointed Mother.

I step off the edge of the platform, intending to take my sweet time drifting down to him, but instead, a sharp pain cuts through my belly, and I plunge toward the floor. My father is swift as he catches me in his arms, his grip too tight. Even if I could die from a frivolous accident, he would never let me, not after everything he's sacrificed. I am his one and only child. A true miracle—the first demon born in a very long time. Everyone says I'm special.

He is shaking as he cradles me in his arms, and I bury my face against his shoulder. He is warm, and I know I will always be safe with him. "Is it the pain again?"

"Yes," I admit. "It's getting worse."

"You need to rest, daughter," Shezmu says. "You're still weak from the dagger."

It's true that I haven't felt like myself since the Demon King brought me back. I am pretty sure that one of the orishas I ate is attempting to poison me. I can't tell which one, but no matter what, I won't give in. I always win.

"Take me to my chamber." Shezmu tenses at my not-so-subtle command, so I add a gentle, "Please, Papa."

My father carries me through the cavernous halls of the Demon King's palace. The Iloran demons have kept it pristine over the millennia, but it's plain compared to the palace in the Almighty Kingdom. Veins of silver and gold run through the marble walls. The large windows that once overlooked a lush forest open onto a barren wasteland.

When we pass demons in the halls, they step aside with heads bent in respect. Already, they are drawn to me despite their trepidation: the beautiful daughter of Shezmu, the beloved first general to their king. It's only a matter of time before they love me, too.

While the Demon King is still moping around, pining for Dimma, there is a hunger inside these people. They crave revenge. In the right hands, that appetite can be stoked and strengthened.

I can give them the vengeance they deserve.

I let myself imagine how they might address me. So many possibilities . . . Beloved Queen, The Divine, The Goddess.

Shezmu carries me up two flights of stairs, and my chamber door opens before we reach it. Like the Demon King, my father is talented with his gifts—much more talented than most of the other demons. I suppose it's because of all the souls he ate.

I climb from his arms. "I can walk from here."

"Of course." Shezmu releases me. "I'll come back this evening to check on you."

"I'm sure I'll be much better by then." I give him a reassuring smile. Otherwise, he won't leave, and I really need him to go.

Shezmu hesitates, his eyes searching mine. "Stay out of trouble, Efiya. I know that look."

I stand on my tiptoes and hug him. "Of course, Papa."

Once in my bedchamber, I drop to my knees. The souls inside me simmer with rage. They're trying to claw their way out as if that were ever possible. I ignore the echoes of their pleas. Instead, I focus on the one soul that doesn't yearn for revenge—the one that only yearns for me. Then I heave and heave until a cold tendril reaches up through my throat and emerges from my mouth. It's a difficult and demanding task, this disgorging, and I am left shaking as the soul settles into a shivering gray puddle on the floor.

I've always known that I could release the souls inside me, but I haven't had a reason to. Until now.

I sit with my knees drawn to my chest, watching the soul begin to float up, caught in the Supreme Cataclysm's compulsion to be unmade. I feel that pull occasionally, but it's easy enough to dismiss. I draw on my magic to weave a new vessel and force the soul inside it. When I'm done, a familiar body is balled up on the floor, naked and trembling, drawing in shallow breaths.

He is as beautiful as the first time I visited him in the desert—dark skin, perfectly symmetrical features, eyes that dance with mischief. "My queen," Tyrek gasps. "How I have longed for this day."

I sigh, bored. Couldn't he come up with something more original? *My queen*—there is a note of possessiveness in the way he says it, as if he wants me to belong to him. But I belong to no one. He should've realized that already.

The Demon King would have never freed him from the dagger after what he did to Arrah, so he's lucky that I took the precaution of eating his soul for safekeeping. That doesn't mean I've forgotten.

I glare at him. "You hurt my sister."

"I am sorry, Efiya." Tyrek sits up finally, but he doesn't look sorry at all. He looks quite proud of himself. "Wasn't that why you gave me a piece of your soul? So that I could save you?" When I narrow my eyes, he clears his throat. "I couldn't do that without hurting Arrah . . . a little bit. I did it for you. I would do anything for you."

"That might be true," I say, not ready to let him off the hook, "but you failed."

"I underestimated her," Tyrek admits, not bothering to mask his frustration. "We both did. Your sister is quite the trickster."

That little jab should be of no consequence to me, but I don't like it when others speak of Arrah that way. She's still my sister. "We'll see who the trickster is in the end."

Tyrek gives me a lazy smile. His overconfidence is still going to be a thorn in my side, I see. "I do appreciate you rescuing me," he says, "but I could use some clothes."

He can wrap a bedsheet around himself for all I care.

Another sharp pain cuts across my belly, but I return his smile with one of my own. I can't let Tyrek see my weakness. He worships me, and I intend to keep it that way. I need him if I'm going to win this game. There's nothing worse than playing without an audience.

FOUR
ARRAH

The forest is so dark that we must tread carefully. My eyes are tired from tracking the crossroads all day and now from trying to see by the weak moonlight shining through the canopy. Rudjek takes point, having no problem navigating through the darkness, but every snap of twig underfoot and every rustle in the bushes put my nerves on edge. Frogs croak in the trees, and somewhere hyenas cackle with hunger. I'm anxious to get back to the clearing, back to Essnai, Kira, and the others.

The smell of rotten corpses chokes the air, making it difficult to breathe, a not-so-gentle reminder of the *akkaye*. It was a gamble trying to control them. They could easily have killed me. Next time, I might not be so lucky. Next time, we might encounter something that will not hesitate.

I peer into the wall of shadows ahead of us. "Are you sure this is the right direction?"

Rudjek squeezes my hand as he leads me around a tangle of bushes. "Yes—I can hear them. Kira was hurt during the fight. Jahla is healing her while Essnai attempts to distract her from the pain. Fadyi is standing guard."

"You can hear all of that?" Not for the first time, I wonder how much of my own hearing I've lost from trading my years. "From *here*?"

"I suppose my superior craven senses are useful for something," he says, and I scoff at the smile in his voice.

He's dismissive of his anti-magic like it's nothing special. When I still had my magic, we could never touch, never kiss, never be more than friends. The only reason we can be this close is because I gave up the chieftains' gift. I dread having to reveal the truth to the tribal people if we ever make it off this gods-awful crossroads. How could I look into their eyes—knowing how much they've sacrificed and tell them that I willingly let the souls of their beloved chieftains go? They won't understand why I did it—they won't care. I can't bring myself to guess how they might react to the news. Then again, if Daho keeps his promise to me, maybe they don't have to know.

"I still don't understand how you were able to control the *akkaye*," Rudjek muses.

"It's complicated," I say, knowing that the answer will fuel a long-standing argument between us. "They recognized me, or at least I think they did."

"Recognized *you*." Rudjek stops when we reach the edge of the clearing. "That's interesting."

A wave of rot washes over us on the breeze. I tense, bracing for more trouble, but the smell is fleeting, like a brush of death. I'm relieved to see that our friends are okay—and a tad annoyed that they are as Rudjek described. Standing watch, Fadyi spots our return first and nods in our direction. Kira sits with her back against a tree. Her trousers have been shredded into bloody strips, but Jahla has healed her wounds. Essnai is next to her *ama*, stroking her hair.

"Perhaps not as interesting as you think." I lower my voice, even though I know that his guardians can still hear me. "I believe that the former chieftain of Tribe Litho, Töra Eké, created the *akkaye*. If he was their master, they must have sensed that his *ka* once resided within me."

Rudjek cocks an eyebrow. "What is it with Tribe Litho? As if *Ka*-Priest Ren Eké wasn't bad enough. He used his magic in such depraved ways to hurt people." It's not the real reason for his curious expression—nor the real question he wants to ask.

"You mean he used his magic to violate the minds of his victims," I say, not dancing around the subject. My mother. Ty. Nezi. Countless others. I bite back my dread, my disgust. In the end, he got what he deserved. I walk toward our friends, ready to put any conversation about the former *Ka*-Priest behind us. "At any rate, the Litho have an affinity for magic that afflicts the soul."

"Those things were already dead," Kira says, overhearing the last bit of our conversation. "How could they have souls?"

"Remember what I told you about *ndzumbis*?" Essnai tells her. "Some witchdoctors could force people to serve them—something that was considered unconscionable even in the five tribes. It was no different with the dead. A powerful witchdoctor could stop a person's soul from ascending into the afterlife and infuse their corpse with magic."

Rudjek crosses his arms. "You mean to say a witchdoctor would have to commit murder to make these *akkaye*?"

"We don't know that for sure," I interject, an edge of uncertainty creeping into my voice. "They could've already been dying before Töra Eké bound their souls."

"You know the Litho chieftain best," Rudjek says. "Was he capable of such a deed?"

Before I can answer, Kira groans, frustrated. "The tribal people could've sent *akkaye* to the North to help us fend off the demons. If they had, our friends would still be alive." She locks eyes with Jahla, and I wonder if they both are thinking about Majka. "But no, they set up booby traps in forests to protect only themselves."

"Do you still think the tribal people should sit out this war?" Rudjek asks, looking pointedly at me.

He says it as if I could decide such a thing—as if it were up to me. Daho had promised to spare the tribal people if they didn't side with the orishas against his army. That'd been two months ago, and we'd spent half of the time since then navigating the crossroads with no word from the outside world. But I know Daho, or at least Dimma knew him. If he hasn't attacked the orishas yet, it's only because he's biding his time. Can I really trust that he'll convince *all* of his people to leave the tribes alone—when so many of the demons have already proven themselves to be treacherous? "What I think doesn't matter."

"Doesn't it, though?" Rudjek argues. "You once carried the souls of their chieftains, and as we saw with the *akkaye*, that means something. You could convince them to act."

"What will it mean when they find out that I *gave up* those souls?" I shoot back. *It would mean that I failed—that I chose you over them.* I turn away from him.

"We don't even know what's going on back home," Kira

grumbles. "The Kingdom could be in ashes by now if the demons have attacked again."

"They haven't," Jahla interjects quietly. "Lord Re'Mec would have sent a message."

"Not if he's dead," Essnai says.

"Jahla's right," Rudjek chimes in. "As much as Re'Mec is an annoying pest, he would come to fetch us himself if he needed our anti-magic. One can only assume that the Demon King hasn't made his move for some reason."

I have to wonder, too, why Daho hasn't kept his promise to lay waste to the orishas. He has his army again and Fram's children at his command. I shudder, remembering the shadows that had emerged from Fram the moment Daho killed them. *The reapers*, Koré had called them. *The destroyers of worlds.* They had leeched life from everything they touched. Daho already has the advantage. He only needs to take it. It's too much to hope that he actually listened to me—that he will turn away from his never-ending quest for revenge.

Fadyi clears his throat. "Perhaps this is a conversation we should continue elsewhere. We cannot be sure the *akkaye* won't return, and I would prefer we find another place on the crossroads to settle down for the night."

"I'm in agreement," Jahla adds with a deep sigh. "Besides, it stinks here."

"I don't think anyone can argue with that," Kira adds.

Rudjek shifts on his heels as he meets my gaze again. "I'll give you some space." I don't miss the emphasis on *I*—not we. *I'll give you some space.*

He and his guardians move to the far side of the clearing, leaving

Essnai, Kira, and me near the tree where I'd seen a glimmer of magic that marked the trail. Now it stands out in grass slicked with blood and bowel from the *akkaye*. I stare long enough for my eyes to adjust, and the magic flows like water across stone. I follow it until I reach a patch of lines that's shifted from the original pattern. I can't untangle it. Soon my eyes begin to burn again, and my vision blurs.

Magic alights on the tree branches as if waiting to be plucked like ripe plums. I press my hand against the bark, remembering my first ritual—how the vines had grown from the sacred Gaer tree, where the first *Ka*-Priest of the Kingdom had died and taken up root. They'd snaked under my skin and stretched through my body. *Gods*. The pain. It was unbearable, but it had seemed worth it at the time.

The chieftains left me with one gift after Dimma forced me to let go of their souls. I know thousands of rituals in meticulous detail, including several that could help me navigate the crossroads. I could make a compass of animal bones and my blood or make a blood medicine with herbs common enough in the forest. The temptation will always be there, but now I would have to sacrifice more years to possess such power. I turn away from the tree. The price is too high.

Essnai yawns while eyeing me. "*Akkaye* or not, I'm tired."

She knows that I can't find the right path—not in my current state, and she's saving me the embarrassment of having to say it. Kira grumbles, but otherwise, no one protests. We find a place upwind from the carnage for the night. With no streams nearby, we wipe away some of the grime from the day with dry rags. No one has an appetite, so we forgo eating from our dwindling supplies.

"You should rest," Rudjek says once Essnai and Kira are sound asleep across from the fire. With Fadyi and Jahla prowling the forest in case of more trouble, we have a semiprivate moment. "It's not every day you almost get eaten by the undying."

I crack a smile. "I'm sure I would've given the *akkaye* terrible indigestion."

"I'd always imagined that you'd taste sweet," he remarks.

I quirk an eyebrow at him, and we both blush. But I need his levity, his humor, and his awkward attempts at flirting. I don't want to discourage it, not when I want more of this and more of him. "To answer your question from earlier," I say, "I don't know if the tribal people should keep hiding or fight. I just want this nightmare to be over."

"The orishas are convinced that it will take all of Zöran to have a chance against the Demon King's army," Rudjek reminds me. "And I'm inclined to believe them. If we don't stand together, the demons will pick us off one by one. You saw the devastation that Efiya and only a third of his army inflicted in just a few months. Think of the advantage we'd have if we had tribal magic on our side."

"If I had stood against Daho, we wouldn't be in this predicament."

"I don't think Dimma would have let you," Rudjek says, glancing at his shotels next to him, "but one way or another, this war will end, and I don't intend to lose."

I ache, remembering on the battlefield when Dimma had surged forward in my mind. She hadn't broken free of her chains, but she had bent them enough to take control of my magic to protect Daho from the orishas—and perhaps from me. Could I have really killed him? I thought I could then, but now I'm not so sure.

Rudjek isn't the only one counting on the tribal people. I need their help if I want Dimma's magic. "Whatever happens, we cannot let her wake. We know what she's capable of, and I don't trust her to do what's right." I don't even trust myself.

Her choices might've been warped by terrible loss, but I have no such excuses. When I misused the chieftains' gift, it was deliberate. I broke Princess Veeka's glass out of jealousy after she made a pass at Rudjek. I turned a man into a *ndzumbi* to do my bidding because I couldn't control my rage. I showed no mercy when I killed the assassins who tried to murder me, even though they were only following Suran Omari's orders.

Gods. I recoil now, thinking of the dozens of souls I reaped with Daho's dagger.

"Maybe it's for the best that I don't have magic anymore," I say, second-guessing myself, but I don't know if I believe it. For all the wrongs I've done, without magic, I will be powerless if Daho's army attacks Zöran.

"You're not like her, Arrah," Rudjek insists. As usual, I cannot hide my thoughts from him. "Dimma should have known the consequences of making the demons immortal—the devastation it would cause."

I almost laugh—he still doesn't understand. Dimma knew what would happen. She knew that her brethren wouldn't stand for it. Yet, she'd still done it to protect the people she loved.

I should count myself lucky that I didn't do more damage when I had magic. But I can never escape the unpleasant knowledge that I am no better than Dimma. I gave up my magic to save Rudjek. How was my decision any different from hers? I wonder if I'm repeating her mistakes. We're cut from the same cloth, the two of us. "I don't know who I am," I admit bleakly. "I'm not a whole person, not really.

I'm just a shadow of a dead god."

"I can't accept that. . . . I've known you too long." Rudjek is so earnest, so certain. "You are a whole person, with your own mind and your own life, even if she's inside you. I . . . I know it's not the same, but I'm still getting used to what I am."

I peer up at his face bathed in moonlight. "You mean your anti-magic?"

"Yes." He gestures helplessly in the forest. "Look, maybe I'm less human than I originally thought, but that doesn't make me any less of a person."

"Rudjek." I draw his attention back to me. I need to say this now in case there isn't another chance. "If I die before I can find a way to keep Dimma asleep, promise me that you won't trust her."

He presses his hand to his heart. "Do you take me for a man who can be wooed so easily?"

I glare at him, but I can't keep a straight face. "I'm serious."

"I know you are." Rudjek grins. "I promise I will be on my guard against your alter ego."

"Good," I say. "Now, we should get some rest."

"Wait," he says, digging in his pocket. He pulls out a silver chain with a stone that glimmers in the half light. "I've been meaning to give you this. I picked it out to celebrate your coming of age before I left for the North."

"You got me a gift?" I can feel my face warming. I don't know what to say. My birth day came and went while he was still on the edge of death, just days after we got back to Zöran. I've been seventeen for two months now and have barely given it a thought.

Rudjek cups my hand and drops the chain in my palm. The black stone is cool to the touch and pulses like a heartbeat. "It's a wishing stone."

I smile up at him. "It's beautiful."

"I got it when we couldn't touch. I thought . . . if we both had one, we could wish together." He pulls a matching chain from underneath his tunic. "I hope I wasn't too presumptuous."

"Can you put it on me?" I'm moved that he remembered my birth day and that after all this time, he hasn't given up. I clutch the smooth stone in my hand, hoping that some way . . . somehow it will mean a future for us.

As he joins the clasp, his fingers brush my collarbone and send pleasant thrills through me. Once the cool stone settles against my chest, I lean into him, and he buries his face in my hair. I don't care that we both smell atrocious. I sink into his arms anyway. But when I close my eyes, I hear *his* voice. Daho's. The memory is a stubborn wound that refuses to heal.

What happened to our forever and always?

Even though the words were meant for someone else, they still find their mark. They drag up deep longing and regret. Since I let go of the chieftains' magic, Daho hasn't been able to reach my mind. I'd be lying if I said that I don't miss our connection, the lull of his company. But I do my best to push aside my uncertainty as Rudjek holds me tight. He is *my* forever and always, at least for the time I have left.

DAHO

Time has no meaning, no substance, no shape, yet it is my greatest enemy and my most trusted friend. It is the only prison I can never escape—one without walls and chains. It has not healed my wounds, only sharpened my resolve into a finely honed blade.

There are moments across time that define what I eventually became. Choices and consequences that set me on a singular path from which I have never deviated. It began with Dimma's death. I sit at the foot of the throne, clinging to the empty vessel that once held my wife's soul. There is nothing left of her—no spark of her warmth, her scent, her smile. Her body is a discarded husk. In my arms, it melts into tiny orbs of light that hold the shape of her until they pull apart and scatter through the palace walls.

She once told me that the energy of the universe is an endless canvas that could be painted over again and again according to our desires. When the energy has served its purpose, it returns to a state of magic. She'd been so clinical when she explained it, so detached. Nothing wasted, nothing lost.

Here's what I know. Once the Supreme Cataclysm unmakes my

love, she will become something new, something not *her*.

Echoes of Dimma's last moments, her desperation and anguish, press against my soul. I was a fool to let Koré and Re'Mec lure me away from the palace—away from her. I walked right into their trap while the custodian of life and death came for my wife. I should have died by Fram's hand, not her. Not our son.

I would die a thousand times if I could bring them back.

Moments turn into hours, then days, then weeks. Still, I sit.

Shezmu whisks into the throne room. He is dressed in white mourning robes, his hair pulled into a knot. He takes a seat on the platform next to me with his legs hanging over the ledge.

"I won't lie to you," he says. "The best you can hope for is learning to cope with it. The pain will never go away."

"Cope?" I echo. "You expect me to cope with an eternity without her?"

Shezmu stares at the streams of light filtering in from the sky dome. "You have no other choice."

I can't be angry with him. He's in the same purgatory.

"Not a day goes by that I don't wish that I had spent more time with my daughter." Shezmu picks at a loose thread on his robe. His voice is raw. "Ta'la was brilliant at strategy games, you know? We would play for hours."

"She inherited that from her father." This kindness is the least I can give him, though I am out of practice at conversation. Words feel wrong on my tongue.

"I'd like to think so," Shezmu says with a sigh. "I've assumed your duties until you return from your period of mourning."

"Thank you," I say, but in truth, I am only half listening.

He squeezes my shoulder and says something else, but my mind has drifted away. After some time, I realize that he's left the throne room, and I sink back into my private mausoleum.

As Dimma told me centuries ago when she made me immortal, I no longer need to eat, breathe, or sleep, so I shed these mortal constraints. I become a shell, hollowed out. More than once, I consider giving in to the constant pull from the Supreme Cataclysm to be unmade, but I can't abandon my people. I can't let them down again.

One morning I leave the throne room. I walk through the palace, shadows crawling in my wake. "The king has fallen," they taunt. "The pretty queen is dead."

I leave them behind and go to the arboretum. It's overgrown now with weeds and vines and blanketed in decaying leaves. So many of Dimma's cherished plants have died, though the bristletwine is still alive, its crooked branches studded with a smattering of golden leaves.

A shapeless form slithers across a dying bush and lets out a whisper of a laugh. This shadow—this *familiar*—is what's left of Minister Godanya, the endoyan ambassador who broke bread at my table more times than I can remember. The minister that betrayed my people.

"I was in morning prayer near the dahlias that fateful day the Divine Creator came to visit Dimma," he says. "You both were warned—yet you would not give up the abomination growing in her belly. One might even say that she got what was coming to her."

I kneel in the flower bed and begin to pull up weeds, remembering the night that Dimma became with child. I felt a prick against my consciousness that woke me from my sleep.

Is this real, or am I dreaming? I'd asked her, my eyes on her belly.
How is this possible?

"Do you remember my grandfather Anth Godanya?" The
minister's question cuts through my thoughts. "Of course you do.
You've lived a very long time. Longer than anyone has the right to
live." When I don't answer, he continues. "Grandfather worshipped
you. He believed that we were more than your distant cousins—he
believed we needed you to survive. As you can imagine, that view
did not go over well with most endoyans. We saw you and Dimma
as unnatural, you see. But of course, I could not risk the trade agreement between our nations."

"Why are you telling me this?" I spit.

"You need to understand why I convinced my people to side with
Eluua. That day in the arboretum, I saw the look in your eyes, what
you had decided to do. You'd become obsessed, and it had stolen
your reason. You were willing to sacrifice the world for one child."

"And you saw an opportunity," I say, clearing away dead leaves.

"Indeed," Godanya admits.

"It must be difficult for you," I say, feigning pity. "You worshipped Koré, but where was your Divine Creator when Dimma was
destroying your people? She turned her back on the endoyans when
she could easily have spared you. Don't you ever wonder why?"

Godanya is silent. I much prefer having the upper hand, but he
doesn't stay quiet for long. "It's true—we have a common enemy," he
says. "The gods betrayed us both."

A spark of something vile and vengeful begins to grow in my
mind.

"Release my people from your queen's curse," Godanya begs. "Let us die in peace."

"I'll release you, yes . . . in due time," I say, "but before then, you will do what Dimma intended. You will serve me faithfully."

Godanya's shadow quivers with fury, but I'm already thinking ahead. As if he'd sensed it, Shezmu enters into the half light of the arboretum. Seeing the minister, he wrinkles his nose in disgust. "You should not consort with those foul things, especially that one." He leans against the bristletwine, and Godanya hisses at him.

"Find out everything you can about the gods," I say to Godanya. "Do not return until you have information that will help us destroy them."

Compelled to obey, his shadowy form slinks over the edge of the balcony and disappears.

"How did you let the arboretum fall into such shambles?"

Shezmu shrugs. "I was too busy running the country while you moped around the palace. I am more than happy to give you the job back."

"I have a score to settle with the gods first." Hearing myself say the words, I feel a renewed surge of fire in my veins. "It's time to destroy every last one of them."

FIVE
ARRAH

In the morning, I feel whole again, restored, as though someone has handed me a cup of sweet nectar after a long journey through the desert. Rudjek is curled around me, his anti-magic warm against my skin like the first kiss of a sunrise. He always does this—soothes my aches and heals my bruises while I'm sleeping. I listen to the birds chirping in the trees and small animals rustling in the bushes. I revel in these moments of peace, knowing that they won't last.

"Shall we get up, or shall we sleep until midday?" Rudjek breathes into my hair. "I vote for the latter."

I turn on my back and crack my eyes against the breaking dawn. "Careful, Crown Prince. Your father most certainly would not approve."

"Ah, so we should definitely sleep all day, then," he declares. "Anything to draw my father's ire."

I'm tempted, but early morning is the best time to travel before the brunt of the heat settles in and the sun washes out the trail. Besides, I'm anxious to keep moving. Until last night we hadn't encountered anything like the *akkaye* on the crossroads. If the tribal people protected this leg of the path, it must mean that we're close to the end. Close to reaching them. "We have to keep going," I say to Rudjek as I sit up.

After a quick bite to eat, I return to the clearing, where the trail picks up again. The air is foul and flies buzz around the blood-soaked ground, but the magic's still there, waiting to be followed. I inhale a sharp breath, stilling myself against yesterday's failure. Again, Rudjek and the cravens keep their distance as we start down the trail, so their anti-magic doesn't block out my ability to see the sparks of magic.

"For the love of all that's holy and sacred, let there be a stream on the path today," Kira says. "What I wouldn't give to wash my hair."

Essnai fans flies away. "I'll take a muddy watering hole at this point."

"Speak for yourselves," Rudjek calls from behind us. "I want nothing less than a prestigious bathhouse complete with perfumed oils and rose petals."

"And an attendant with a tray of sweetcakes," I add.

"Who eats sweetcakes in a bath?" Kira scoffs.

Even Fadyi, who's never one for small talk, chimes in. "I'd much rather a swim in the ocean. It's been too long since I last took the shape of a whale."

I'm glad that my friends still have their senses of humor after yesterday, but I'm nervous as I study the crossroads. There are hundreds of lines reaching in every direction. Nearly all of them are dead ends, loops, or perhaps traps like the one last night. It takes a moment for me to find the string of magic that isn't pulsing or vibrating like the others. It's an unassuming braid of light, perfectly deceptive, easily dismissed. It *almost* looks like a dozen other strings. But when I focus on the braid, the hum of its magic grows louder. It sounds like a sweet lullaby, lulling me into a sense of peace, but I don't let my guard down.

Another string flickers and catches my attention. It isn't like the others, and this is the first time I've seen it on the crossroads. It pulses twice, then dims, before thrice more. The compulsion to touch it is overwhelming, and I bend down, well aware that my friends are watching me. I run my hand across fibers of silver and evergreen sparks woven together. Silver like his skin, evergreen like his eyes. Two pulses for him and Dimma, then three pulses for the family that would never be.

It's an invitation, a map, a plea. If I follow it, I know what I'll find at the end.

I inhale a sharp breath, remembering the almost-kiss in Tyrek's tent. When Daho had been pretending to be Sukar. "Arrah," he'd whispered, his mouth against my neck. "I can't, not like this."

He'd caressed my cheek and smiled, hope filling his eyes. Delirious from the anti-magic poisoning my body, I'd wanted him to kiss me, needed it. I wanted everything I thought I could never have with Rudjek. Later, when Daho revealed himself, I realized that it wasn't *me* he wanted. Sometimes, I still forget that.

The irony of it. Him hiding in Sukar's body, and Dimma hiding in mine.

"More tricks and false trails," I say lightly, ignoring the bread crumb that Daho's left for me. I stand up and brush my palms against my tunic.

Sparks of magic buzz around my face as I start down the right path with my friends on my heels. Now that I've rested, some of the false trails and detours and loops are a little more obvious. Still, I move carefully, taking my time, stopping whenever I am unsure. Occasionally, I can even sense the *akkaye* sleeping deep in the forest, waiting for me to wake them. I don't know how long this clarity will last before I tire again and make another mistake.

The crossroads changes into a desert, our footfalls sinking into sand, the sun bearing down on our backs. Next, there is an icy trail along the edge of a cliff. I almost lose my footing at one point, but Essnai is there to grab my arm and pull me back. My doubts grow. So does my fear. Sweat pours down my forehead and soaks through my tunic. My whole body shakes as I try desperately to hold on to the trail. If I lose it, we could get lost or encounter another nasty surprise.

Soon enough, the path changes again, and we enter a rocky plain. It is late afternoon, and the day has caught up with me. More than once, my legs almost give out, and there is a new ache in my bones. The sharpness of my senses has faded, and my vision grows blurry. Even Rudjek's power to heal my wounds cannot replace what I've lost from trading my years.

Magic takes from all.

A few paces along the rocky plain, the path changes once more. A boy sits on the ground in front of us, his eyes glowing, his knees drawn to his chest. He jumps to his feet, startled by our appearance.

The boy raises his hands, palms facing out. The sting of his magic hits me in the chest, and I stumble into Essnai and Kira. Rudjek and his guardians quickly move to the front. But I recover quickly. The magic isn't particularly strong.

"Wait." Rudjek steps forward, and the boy's magic winks out. "We're friends." Rudjek points to himself. *Friends.*

Shadows suddenly swarm around us and settle into faces. I am speechless; tears fill my eyes. The warriors have their staffs and spears pointed at our throats, but I don't care.

Essnai bursts into hysterical laughter, and she shoots me a look. "You found them, and they want to kill us. Sounds about right."

"I am Arrah N'yar, granddaughter of Mnekka, the Aatiri chieftain, daughter of Oshhe," I say in tribal common tongue, wistfulness tinting my words, my voice shaking. My grandmother and my father are long gone now, their memories the only thing I have left.

"Arrah?" A girl pushes her way through the crowd. I could weep with joy—it's my cousin Semma, dressed in a gold-and-blue kaftan with flowers trimmed in silver. She throws her arms around my neck and hugs me. "It's really you!"

I sink against her, my legs going slack with joy and exhaustion. I almost think that I'm dreaming—that this is another trick of the crossroads, another trap. Maybe Semma will turn into a winged beast that will bite off my head. But as we hold each other, my doubts melt away, replaced by the weight of the moment. We've reached the end of the crossroads. We've found the tribes.

The moment is surreal as I blink back tears. There were times when I'd almost given up hope. "I thought that I would never see you again."

Nenii stands behind her sister with her hands on her hips. Her hair has grown longer, her braids loose around her shoulders. The sisters are both taller than when I last saw them at the Blood Moon

Festival. "Aren't you a sight for sore eyes." Nenii hugs me, too, the three of us holding each other.

"Is she dead?" Semma asks, her voice pitched low.

I tense in my cousins' arms, going still. I can't bring myself to say the words, so I nod.

"Efiya is dead!" Nenii shouts to the crowd in common tongue, her voice projecting with ease over the growing whispers. "Praise be to my cousin Arrah. She has returned to us with the might of the chieftains!"

The tribal people begin to cheer, but my heart sinks. I open my mouth to say . . . what, I don't know. That I failed to stop Efiya from releasing the Demon King. That I gave up the chieftains' magic. I don't deserve their praise.

I glance desperately at Essnai, who gives me a slight shake of her head. Perhaps she knows I'm on the verge of admitting everything. But now is not the time to tell the tribal people that Daho is free—that he plans to lay siege to Zöran, that without the chieftains' magic, I cannot protect them if the demons come to eat their souls.

SIX
ARRAH

Golden evening light stretches across the valley as the tribal people crowd around me to get a closer look. Their laughter and excited chatter ring in my ears, and it's hard to catch my breath. People press their hands to their hearts and whisper thanks. Others reach out to touch my arms, my shoulders, my hair, and I burn with shame. Their fingers are like flames threatening to set me on fire. They speak mostly in the tribal common tongue, a combination of Mulani, Aatiri, Zu, Litho, and Kes.

Is it really her?

The blessed one.

I see Töra Eké in her eyes.

No, it's a shadow of Mnekka.

Despite my trepidation, I am immensely relieved that the tribal people have survived. I wipe away my tears, wishing that Sukar could be here to see the tribes—to see the Zu warriors with their masks pushed to the tops of their heads now that they're certain there is no battle to fight today. He would say something profoundly ridiculous to make everyone either roll their eyes or laugh.

"Tell us how you defeated the demon witch," someone asks.

The words have an instant sobering effect, and the crowd falls silent. The answer is complicated. Efiya is inside Daho's dagger. He wouldn't be foolish enough to release her—not after she disobeyed him. He might want revenge against the orishas, but he must know that he could never truly control my sister.

"I . . ." My voice is soft, broken. The crowd stares at me so expectantly that I wish I could crawl under a rock. "I trapped her soul."

"Ah, Litho magic," someone muses.

"Praise the mother and father," another person cheers. "Praise Heka!"

I cringe at the declaration. Heka gave a piece of himself so that Efiya could possess unimaginable power. He stood by and did nothing when she attacked the tribal people, who looked to him for protection. They worshipped him—welcomed his return every Blood Moon. Yet he turned his back on them . . . *on me* . . . when we needed him the most. He let my sister and her demons slaughter them. He was no better than the other gods—selfish with no regard for mortal life.

"We left survivors back in Tribe Zu—nearly two hundred," I tell the crowd. "People from all five tribes." I fumble in my sack and take out a scroll. "We have names."

Excitement ripples through the valley, and everyone starts to talk at once. I take some small satisfaction in bringing them this news, though it's not without a price. Some of them won't find their missing loved ones on the parchment.

"Gather the chieftains and give them the list," Semma says to a tall Aatiri man with a shaved head.

He nods to my cousin, and I hand over the list. In a strange way, it's a relief, as if a burden has been lifted from my shoulders. "It's been a long journey," I say, weary. "We could use some rest."

Semma claps her hands twice. "There will be much celebration to come, but we must let my cousin and her companions retire for now." When the crowd doesn't immediately make room for us, Semma begins to push people out of the way.

"Don't be rude," Nenii yells on my opposite side. "Show some respect to the *blessed one*, or she'll curse you something ugly where you stand."

When we finally break free of the crowd, I take in the scatter of tents across the valley and the surrounding hills. Wisps of smoke wreathe into the sky as people prepare their evening meals. A creeping sense of panic rises inside me. "This can't be everyone?"

Semma shakes her head. "Those of us who live in this valley protect the crossroads in case of trouble. It's the only way on or off the island. The rest of the tribes live in villages from here all the way to the coasts."

I ease out a breath, relieved that despite everything, the tribes had survived my sister's wrath. Someone among them must be powerful enough to help me tap into Dimma's magic. It would mean that I wasn't the last witchdoctor—that the tribes might one day flourish again.

"We're on an island," Rudjek comments. "That would explain why it smells like the sea."

Semma narrows her eyes at him. "And who are you?"

"Forgive me." I rub the back of my aching neck. My cousins know

Essnai but not the others. "Allow me to introduce Crown Prince Rudjek Omari of the Almighty Kingdom, honored commandant in the Almighty Army, heir apparent to House Omari." Rudjek touches his forehead and performs a slight bow to my cousins. "His guardians, Fadyi and Jahla, and Captain Kira Ny, daughter of Guildmaster Ny, head of the Scribes' Guild of the Almighty Kingdom."

"Ah, so this is the boy you were always talking about." Nenii giggles, eyeing Rudjek. "He *is* quite handsome."

My cheeks warm as Rudjek gives me a sidelong smile. I will never hear the end of this.

"Such pretty, useless titles," Semma says, less welcoming. "Why has the Crown Prince of the Almighty Kingdom come to us?"

"I'm here because of Arrah." Rudjek clears his throat. "And I thought I might have a word with your leaders." He leaves it at that, but I know what he wants. He hasn't explicitly said so, but I wouldn't put it past him to try to convince the tribes to join the fight against the demons. I can never forget that he's the son of a politician—a ruthless one who will do whatever it takes to accomplish his goals. As much as I'm against the tribes fighting, they deserve to make their own decision.

"Tomorrow," Semma says. "The chieftains will want to see the *blessed one* first."

Rudjek gives another slight bow. "Of course."

"Essnai, you're more delectable every time I see you," Nenii blurts out, blushing.

"My *ama* tells me so every day," Essnai says, smiling at Kira.

Undeterred, Nenii lets out a squeal. "She's quite delectable, too."

Semma pulls me ahead of the others. "You never mentioned that your Rudjek was a *dshatu*." She glances over her shoulder. "He and his guardians."

The tribal common tongue for cravens. *Dshatu*. Ghost of the forest. "It's a very long story."

"Nenii, perhaps you can take the others to the stream," Semma says. "They look in need of a bath."

"That would be wonderful," Kira remarks.

"Hmm," Rudjek scoffs. "I didn't think we were that bad off."

Nenii escorts my friends, but Semma leads me back to the tent that she and Nenii share with two of our younger cousins. A girl of about nine or ten sits inside, humming as she braids her little brother's hair. Semma tells me that they were orphaned, like so many other children, after the demons attacked the tribes. The boy wiggles on his pillow, his eyes full of wonder as he palms a wooden toy. I'm taken aback by the moment, that after so much death, so much loss, they still can find some semblance of joy. Watching them, I push down the rising ache in the hollow place in my heart.

"Leave us," Semma says to the children. "I need to talk to the *blessed one* alone."

I cringe as the siblings scamper out of the tent. I wish that Semma and the others would stop calling me that. I am not blessed. I am cursed. With the children gone, sparks of magic surge into the tent at Semma's command, sealing the canvas edges. "Now we have privacy."

She sets out a large bowl of warm water and gives me a pretty, embroidered kaftan to change into once I'm done washing. I flinch at the sight of the kaftan. I am not a witchdoctor. I don't deserve to wear it, but I don't have a choice. If I refuse, I will have to explain why.

Semma sits on a pillow while I bathe, her back to me. "Did your friend Sukar stay behind with the survivors in Tribe Zu?"

"Why do you ask?" I stutter, caught off guard.

"I had a dream about him. It was strange. He had the same face, but he was someone else." Semma's voice shifts uncertainly. She has the gift of vision, although it's never been as strong as Grandmother's foresight.

I scrub the rag across my arms, leaving trails of heat. "Sukar died at Heka's Temple when we fought Efiya and her army."

"May his soul return to the mother and father in peace." Semma whispers her condolences. She waits a moment before asking, "Efiya isn't truly dead, is she?"

"No," I admit, "but she is trapped inside the Demon King's dagger."

My cousin lets out a deep sigh. "That's just as well."

Neither of us speaks again until I'm finished with my bath and dressed. I settle on a cushion across from her, and Semma gives me a curious look. "You've changed, cousin," she tells me, frowning. "You're not only Arrah anymore. . . . Maybe it's because of the chieftains' *kas.*"

I can't bring myself to tell her the truth—that it's not the chieftains' souls she senses inside me. "That's another long story." I massage my temples. Too many long stories.

My cousin has changed, too. She is more self-assured now, more confident. She wears her hair in a crown of locs like Grandmother; her cheekbones are broad, her gaze intense. Long gone is the girl who spent nights giggling with her sister and me about tribal gossip and the objects of our affections.

"I've dreamed about the Demon King, too." Semma squeezes her hands together. "He's standing over your broken body, but that will never happen now that you stopped Efiya from releasing his *ka*."

Semma recalls the vision with such certainty that it cuts deep. If it's true, it would mean that despite Daho's promises, he will eventually kill me to get Dimma back. "When did you have this dream?"

"A few months ago—perhaps it was before you imprisoned Efiya," she offers, hopeful.

I don't want to believe that Semma's given me a glimpse into my fate, but I have to consider it. I'll only be able to protect the tribes and myself if I can control Dimma's magic, and perhaps it will lead to my undoing. I have no doubt that my path will cross with Daho again, and I must be prepared. But if I am to die by his hand, I won't make it easy. I will deal him a blow of my own.

SEVEN
EFIYA

There was a time when I could split myself into bits and pieces and be many places at once. It was very convenient. One day when I was taking a bath in a spring, I was also looking for the Demon King's soul, leading an attack on the Dark Forest, and convincing Tyrek to betray his entire family. And before my sister trapped me in that wretched dagger, I destroyed the five tribes of Heka and killed a few orishas. No one can deny that my accomplishments are many and my failures are few.

Since I've been back, though, things have changed. I haven't been able to split myself infinitely. The dagger has weakened me, and it's all Arrah's fault. I will never truly forgive her for that. I'd still be trapped inside Eluua's womb if it were up to her. Arrah could've let me go, but she turned her back on me. She said that I couldn't be trusted. She was right, of course.

While I'm lying in the garden under one of the only trees in Ilora that survived the gods' wrath, I'm also eavesdropping on Shezmu. He's pacing in the library on the other side of the palace, talking to himself again. "We've almost come full circle now, haven't we?" he says. "I cannot trust that this isn't another trick. The gods are full of treachery, but we're better than that. I will not let them divide us—not after all we've gone through together."

Sometimes his musings are more entertaining, but today, he's such a bore. Staring up at the leaves on the tree, I have a sudden compulsion to visit the dying sun. This arboretum is only possible because of magic, but what if I can undo Re'Mec's nasty little curse? Then I could bring life back to all the flowers and trees in Ilora. We could use some color to spice things up a bit. Maybe that'll inspire the demons to have some fire in their bellies and regain some shred of dignity.

I close my eyes and concentrate on cleaving myself again, but the magic catches, and I am stuck in an empty void. I grit my teeth, attempting to push past the blockage, but the effort only exhausts me. I growl and call back the part of myself eavesdropping on Shezmu. This is so frustrating and so limiting. No matter how many times I've tried, I can only split myself in two now.

With the dying sun forgotten, I storm out of the gardens. I have no time for these frivolous games anyway. If I'm to restore my full strength, I must consume more souls. Who better than the orishas? But I can't do that if the Demon King insists on keeping me in Ilora.

I return to the only tolerable place in the palace: the throne room. I drop down cross-legged on the floor, staring at the spiraling staircase that leads to the sky dome. From here, the crystal throne bathed in sunlight looks as if it's floating among the clouds.

I can only imagine what the Demon King saw when he gazed upon his queen. Pity that she died and squandered the full potential of her gift. On the other hand, if she hadn't, I wouldn't be here now.

I hardly notice that Evelyn and Jasym, two of the demons who have lived in the palace since before the Demon King's imprisonment, are also in the chamber. The siblings are sitting in a grand window that overlooks the wasteland that once was a forest. Jasym wears a black silk tunic and green pants patterned with writhing vines, while their sister wears a gown of the same style. They always coordinate their clothes. I suppose they have to do *something* to entertain themselves.

"Hello," I say, smiling at the pair.

Evelyn is tall, with a splash of freckles across her nose and white wings covered in brown spots. She returns my smile, revealing teeth with pointed edges. I've thought about reshaping myself to look more like the demons but decided against it. I am rather fond of my face. Besides, let it remind them of the humans the gods so love.

Jasym's expression remains neutral as they peer around the throne room without meeting my eyes. Their skin is the perfection of a polished stone, their eyes small and wary. Where Evelyn keeps her hair braided in cornrows that trail down her back, Jasym's hair is a poof of inky black curls a shade darker than their wings. They seem more skeptical of me than Evelyn, but I'll win them over eventually.

"Why do you come here?" Jasym asks. "You visit the throne room every day."

I am delighted by their lack of pretense. Straight to the point. "I suppose I do," I say. "It's very lonely in the palace, and I like how bright it is here."

"There's no harm in that." Evelyn gives her sibling a sidelong look. "Goodness knows this place hasn't been used in many years."

"What was she like before . . . your queen?" I glance up at the throne and let my voice trail off. "I've only ever known the shadow of her that lives within my sister."

Evelyn flinches at the mention of Dimma, but Jasym answers thoughtfully. "She was . . . contemplative. Never really talked all that much, but when she looked upon you—I mean when she really *noticed* you, it was like being bathed in warm light."

Jasym ducks their chin, embarrassed, but it's fascinating to hear how much the demons loved their queen—as they should have. A queen must be adored, just as a god such as myself must be feared.

"That sounds nice," I say quietly.

Encouraged, Jasym continues. "She found wonder in the simplest of things. They say the first time she encountered a clock, she became fascinated with it and studied how it worked for the better half of a century. I mostly remember that she spent much time in the arboretum, and she liked to wander around at all hours."

I let a moment pass before blurting out, "No one loves me the way you loved Dimma." I dab at my eyes, though I can't bring myself to conjure up tears. "In Zöran, I had to do a lot of bad things to free your king. Maybe I deserve to be despised."

Evelyn glances at her sibling as if there is a secret language between them. "You did what no other before you could, Efiya," she says earnestly. "If you had to hurt the gods and their spawn in the process, well, so be it. They are not blameless. They stood by and did nothing when Eluua and the endoyans murdered our children. Then they tried to kill us, many times. You'll find no sympathy for the gods here. We know best what they're capable of."

So there is still fire in their bellies after all. Good. Finally, I have something to work with.

"To keep both Daho and Dimma imprisoned for five thousand years, to trap your brethren in the void and you on a dying world, that's beyond cruel," I say, hugging myself. "How can they call themselves gods when they condemn their own children?"

I pretend not to notice as more demons slip into the throne room, keeping to the outer edges. I weave a magnificent story of how the gods shower affection on the humans and cravens in Zöran. How powerful the endoyans who fled Ilora became once they began to breed with humans. I tell them about the worlds that I visited while searching for the Demon King's soul—how they had flourished while Ilora lay in ruin. Some of what I've told them is true, some I made up. It doesn't matter which parts.

Once I'm satisfied that I have planted my first seed, I add a warning. "What the gods did to you was awful, and it's only a matter of time before they come back to finish what Eluua started." I look around the room at my audience, finally shedding a few tears. "Never forget that they still have your queen, and if given a chance, they will use her against you. I've seen firsthand how much the gods hate us."

I leave the demons with that haunting revelation and retire to my rooms. Let them think on it long and hard; let it fester in their minds. They deserve their revenge against the gods as much as I do. Once back in my bedchamber, I perch on the narrow window ledge with my knees drawn to my chest while Tyrek drones on about the Demon King.

"Show his people that he's ungrateful after all you've done for him," he says, lounging on my bed. "Make it so he can't avoid you any longer. He'll have to confront you if you stir up enough trouble.

Burning skies, he really should be on his knees kissing your feet."

I'd forgotten how annoying Tyrek's voice can be.

"You could always seduce him. If your father has any inkling that the Demon King has been inappropriate with you, he'll turn against his friend." Tyrek laughs, clearly thinking himself clever. "This is perfect, Efiya. Don't you see? We can get rid of them both, and you'll control the power of the gate between worlds. Who will stand in your way then?"

It isn't as if I haven't thought about the Demon King in that way. He's infuriating, yes, but he's also intriguing. I admire that his people are still loyal to him, but I despise him, too. How can I forget Mother's disappointed face every time I searched for her precious master's soul and came back empty-handed? She never truly loved me—not the way she loved Arrah. I was only created to serve *him*. Whenever I've imagined myself in his bed, it always ends with me eating his soul. The temptation would be too great to resist.

As for who would stand in my way, it should be obvious—the Twin Kings. I need the Demon King to help me kill Re'Mec and Koré. Once I consume their souls, then I will regain my full strength. There is an order of things that Tyrek doesn't see from his limited perspective. If I'm to be the one and only god of the universe, I must be patient, which, admittedly, is not one of my strengths. "I'll think on it, my little prince," I tell Tyrek.

"I'm sick of sitting around waiting for you to do something." He slumps dramatically against the headboard. "You were fun before, but now you're playing it safe." He pauses at that, his eyes growing brighter. "I think you're afraid that the Demon King will reject you, just like my dear cousin Rudjek did."

Suddenly a bout of anger and shame encroaches on my thoughts. I wonder if it belongs to one of the souls or if it's mine. I smile to keep from ripping Tyrek's heart from his chest. While I was trapped inside the dagger in my own little purgatory, I had plenty of time to reflect on my deeds. I've crossed lines that can't be uncrossed. I've made mistakes.

"I grow tired of you," I snap, leaping from the window to my feet. "I have somewhere else I need to be."

Tyrek gives me a sly wink. "Did I strike a nerve?"

I don't know why I'm annoyed with him, but I am. Most of the time, I find him mildly entertaining and full of schemes that rival even my own, but he was wrong about Rudjek. I was wrong. That said, I have to look to my future. If I am to achieve the greatness waiting for me, I must put aside all doubt and seize my destiny. For all my gripes with Tyrek, he's right about turning the demons against their king. I need to know that when the time comes, they will stand with me.

I push down the uneasiness growing inside me. "Not at all, little prince."

EIGHT
ARRAH

My cousin keeps staring at me with a questioning expression like she wants to say more, but she holds her tongue. I squeeze my hands between my knees, willing myself to be brave. I'm afraid of how she'll react if I tell her the truth about the chieftains' *kas*, but it's Semma. She and Nenii have always been kind to me. They treated me like a true daughter of Aatiri when others had doubts. "After I trapped my sister in the Demon King's dagger, I discovered that I share a soul with the Unnamed orisha," I start tentatively, testing the waters. "She was punished for disobeying her brethren. Her name is Dimma."

"The Demon King's *ama*," Semma says quietly. "I have seen her in my dreams, too. A tall girl with dark veins running down her forehead like the Kes and the people from the North. She has iridescent brown eyes almost the color of midnight." My cousin hesitates. "She's the strangeness I feel inside you."

When I don't answer, Semma frowns. "Arrah," she says deliberately. "Is there something else you're not telling me?"

I realize too late that I'm not ready to have this conversation—I will never be ready. It hits me all over again—that the chieftains are gone. I gave them up. "I don't carry Grandmother's soul or the others' anymore. They've ascended."

My cousin looks beyond her eighteen years as she gasps. She takes a good long time to find her voice, and when she does, it's shaky. "How did it happen?"

"That part doesn't matter," I offer pathetically.

Semma closes her eyes and pinches the bridge of her nose. "There are no witchdoctors left, Arrah. Some of us can do little more than call the rain or heal small ailments. Life on the island has been difficult. We kept going on our hope that one day you'd find us—that you would cure the blight ravishing our crops and convince Heka to come back." Her voice falters. "If . . . if you deliver this news, cousin, you will send a wave of panic through the tribes."

I wrap my arms around myself, trembling. Her words ring in my ears. No witchdoctors. I swallow the bitterness on my tongue. I think about Daho's promise to spare the tribes. I want badly to trust him. "There is something else you should know," I say, finding my courage. "Efiya freed the Demon King before I could stop her."

Semma goes still again, and the silence that stretches between us is deafening until she finally breaks it. "Oh, Heka."

"It's fine." I rush my words, but she only frowns. I swallow the lump in my throat. "No—I mean, it's not fine, but the Demon King agreed not to attack the tribes as long as they do not aid the orishas." I hear how hollow my words sound—how completely unlikely. "I made a deal with him."

"Is that how you lost the chieftains' *kas* . . . because of him?" Semma presses.

I glance away, unable to hold her gaze. "The Demon King attacked Rudjek, and he was dying. Dimma had the knowledge to save him. She agreed to heal Rudjek if I gave up the chieftains' magic."

Semma's eyes narrow, her face going from disbelief to anger. "The chieftains sacrificed their lives so that the tribes would have a chance to survive—and you're telling me that you willingly threw away their gifts to save one boy?"

"That boy lost people, too," I say, almost a plea. "He fought hard to push the demons back to their world. Without him—"

"Don't." Semma climbs to her feet.

I need her to understand. "Dimma gave me no choice."

"You had a choice," Semma says. "You should've let him die."

Her words sting like a slap to the face. "You don't mean that."

"Yes, I do. You were the chieftains' last hope. How could you give up their magic when you knew the Demon King was free? Grandmother said that you would protect the tribes, but instead, you have condemned us."

I sink into myself, deflating. My cousin has always had a sharp tongue, but I deserve her anger. I couldn't just let Rudjek die, and some part of me still believes that Daho will keep his word. "If I can access Dimma's magic, I can protect the tribes," I say desperately. "She gave the demons their power. Maybe I . . . maybe I can take it away." The thought just occurs to me. With Dimma's magic, could I undo the demons' immortality? Can I take back her gift?

Semma stares at me, her gaze so piercing that I look away. "I might know someone who can help you, but we must tread carefully. Not all is peaceful among the tribes. Do not tell anyone else about the chieftains' *kas* or Dimma yet. I'll see what I can find out."

I don't know what to make of this news—and it only drains what little energy I have left.

Nenii walks into the tent, fiddling with the tail end of her tunic as if she doesn't know what to do with her hands. "What did I miss?"

"The Demon King is free," Semma says bluntly. She raises an eyebrow, making it clear that I am not to reveal my secrets even to her sister.

"You've met him, *haven't you?*" Nenii asks me. "What's he like? Is he as handsome as the Crown Prince?"

What's he like? He is kind, loyal, vindictive, and dangerous. He is a breath of fresh air. He is the shadow of an impending storm. But I don't say those things; I say nothing at all. I am out of words.

"Nenii." Semma lets out a frustrated breath now that the first wave of her anger has receded. "What's important is that Arrah has convinced him to leave the tribes out of his war with the orishas."

"And what about the rest of Zöran?" Nenii argues. "What will happen to them?"

"Where were they when Efiya and her demons slaughtered our people?" Semma snaps. "Grandmother and the other chieftains got word to the Kingdom begging the Almighty One to send his soldiers to help us, but he ignored their messages. Where were the *dshatu*? What about the Northern city-states or Ghujiek or Siihi? No one came."

"It's more complicated than that," I explain. "I can't speak for the North, but by the time the demons attacked the tribes, Efiya had already turned the Kingdom against itself. She collaborated with the youngest Sukkara prince, Tyrek, to kill his father and take the throne." I massage the sharp pain building between my eyes. The list of betrayals is so long. "The cravens—the *dshatu*—had to defend themselves against both Kingdom soldiers and demons."

"Perhaps you can talk to the Demon King again—get him to spare all of Zöran," Semma says, an edge to her voice. "If he's not amenable to that, well, so be it."

Nenii crosses her arms. "When did you become so selfish, sister?"

Semma glares at her, but then her face softens. "We were lucky in Aatiri. We sent the children with the first group on the crossroads, but some of the other tribes weren't so fortunate. The demons ate their children's *kas* to strengthen themselves. So forgive me if I don't care what happens to the rest of Zöran."

I am stricken. Horrified. Daho has so much blood on his hands, but he would never hurt children. It's Efiya who's responsible for what happened to the tribal people. She alone should bear the blame.

Nenii lets out a noisy exhalation. "Fine, so let's stand around and sulk instead of celebrating the *blessed one*'s return."

Semma sighs, and Nenii lays her head on her shoulder. "Choose your words wisely when you speak with the chieftains, cousin."

Nenii frowns, perhaps sensing that her sister is intentionally being vague.

"I'll tell them what they need to hear," I decide.

"We should go," Nenii says. "They will be expecting you."

Outside, musicians start a slow beat on the djembe drums. Nenii hooks her arm through mine. "Tell me, cousin," she presses. "Do you think I would have a chance with Essnai? Kira doesn't seem like the sharing type, but you never know."

I smile at her. Somehow, she hasn't changed one bit through everything that has happened, while Semma has become the iron will of our grandmother. The strength of the tribal people shines in both of my cousins, which gives me hope. Instead of answering her question, I shake my head, which I guess is an answer in itself.

As we walk, people stare at me. Some of them whisper and point. They look hopeful when I just want to hide my face, embarrassed by all the attention. When they press their hands to their hearts or sweep their palms across their foreheads in a show of respect, I want to blurt out that I don't deserve it. The worst is when they begin to weep and pray for me, as though I am the savior they have been waiting for.

I have never felt more like one of the charlatans in the East Market. A fraud, a pretender, a fake. What will these people think if they discover that I no longer hold their beloved chieftains' *kas*? Semma's right—I have to be careful.

Up ahead, I spot Rudjek and the cravens in the crowd. The tribal people give them a wide berth, sensing their anti-magic. Rudjek sees me, and his dark eyes shine in the torchlight. I start toward him without thinking, but Semma holds me back. He gives me a crooked grin and shrugs as if to say there is nothing he can do.

My cousins guide me toward a large white tent at the center of camp and fall back when we reach the opening. I look at them, uncertain, but Nenii offers me an encouraging smile. With an unsteady hand, I lift the flap to find the five chieftains sitting on a row of pillows. Their conversation stops abruptly. The golden light of oil lamps glows against their faces, revealing expressions that range from skeptical to surprise.

I kneel in front of the new chieftains, resting my hands on my lap. After spending months with the memories of the former chieftains in

my head, whispering their secrets, the moment is surreal. Icarata of
Tribe Mulani, U'metu of Tribe Kes, Beka of Tribe Zu, Töra Eké of
Tribe Litho. My grandmother, Mnekka of Tribe Aatiri. They're all
gone, but these chieftains in front of me still feel like impostors. I
don't recognize any of them, which only makes Semma's warning
feel even more important.

No one speaks as they take their time appraising me like I'm
something to auction off at a market. One of the chieftains grumbles, another nods, and yet another narrows their eyes. Magic buzzes
in the tent, and an awareness flits around the edges of my mind.
Someone is trying to see my thoughts, to lift the curtains on my most
cherished secrets.

I swallow the uneasiness building inside me—determined not to
cower in front of them. Before Grandmother and the other chieftains
tied their souls to mine, my only natural gifts had been the ability
to see magic and to protect my mind from it. Whichever chieftain is
trying to read my thoughts will fail. I take small satisfaction in that.

"We were glad to hear the news of the survivors in the Zu mountains," says the Mulani chieftain. She has golden eyes like all the
people of her tribe and wears her hair cropped close to her scalp. "It's
a shame that none of them are witchdoctors."

Before my sister, there had been a hundred witchdoctors across
the five tribes. They'd shown a mastery of magic above all others
and earned the honorable appointment. I still can't believe they're
all gone. "The survivors may not be witchdoctors, but they stood
against the demons and lived to tell the story."

The Litho chieftain, a squat man with an angular face, leans close to the Aatiri chieftain. "This is truly a granddaughter of Mnekka?" he asks in disbelief. "She looks Mulani."

The Mulani woman glowers at the disdain in his voice. "She is a daughter of my tribe, too, as it should be. We are Heka's first chosen."

"And the first to betray him," says the Litho chieftain under his breath. "Let's not forget the deeds of this girl's mother. A Mulani woman unlike yourself, though—one with Heka's gifts."

Magic spins around the Mulani chieftain in a frenzy, but if she's calling for it, it does not come. She grits her teeth in frustration, and the magic flutters away. Again I notice the oil lamps set about the tent. Grandmother and the former chieftains never needed such conveniences. They could string sparks of magic together to give them light.

"Enough bickering," says the Zu chieftain. She wears the *ado* upon her head—a horned headpiece that once belonged to Beka, her predecessor. "This is supposed to be a time of celebration. The *blessed one* has returned to us."

"We are at your service, Arrah N'yar," the Mulani chieftain says, lowering her gaze.

The Aatiri chieftain shifts on his pillow. His shoulders are stooped, and his eyes bloodshot. I cringe at how different he is from Grandmother, who presided with an air of unwavering confidence, pride, and kindness. I don't like the way this man looks down his nose at me or the hardness in his eyes, but I can't judge him. After what they've had to endure, I can't judge any of them. "Before we turn over the fate of our tribes to this girl, we should know if she is worthy."

I frown at his declaration. What does he mean? The Mulani and Zu chieftains smile at me. The others do not. "I don't understand," I say finally.

"There is nothing to understand," the Litho chieftain snaps. "It was our predecessors' wish that should you survive the demon witch, you would unite our people and lead them." He leans forward on his pillow as he studies my face. "You carry their *kas*. You should know this already."

I have a chance to tell the truth now—to get it off my chest— but I hold back. Both the Aatiri and Litho chieftains sit perched like leopards ready to leap at the first sign of weakness. Whatever I thought it would be like to meet the new chieftains, this isn't it. There is too much suspicion in the tent, too much distrust. Is this what has become of the tribes—a parting gift from my sister? "I can assure you that I am not worthy of the honor of leading the tribes," I say without pretense. "The Demon King is free."

A wave of collective dread passes through the chieftains, and they fidget on their pillows, whispering curses and prayers.

"So you failed?" the Aatiri chieftain barks, his voice too loud for the tent. "It was all for nothing."

"It was not for nothing if she stopped Efiya," the Mulani chieftain says calmly. "She is the one who attacked our people, not this Demon King."

"Don't be a fool," the Aatiri chides her. "It is only a matter of time before he comes to eat our souls, and we're not strong enough to defend ourselves."

"He won't attack the tribes if you do not side with the orishas," I say, my voice sharper than intended.

The Aatiri chieftain clucks his tongue. "And how do you know that, girl?"

"I made a deal with him," I say.

Magic swirls in the tent, eager to be called. It gravitates closest to the Aatiri and Litho chieftains—the two who seem to like me the least. The Zu chieftain twitches in agitation while the Mulani whispers a prayer. The Kes chieftain, who hasn't said one word since I arrived, clears his throat.

"Interesting," the Litho chieftain remarks.

"This could be an advantage for us," the Zu chieftain muses almost to herself.

"Or our damnation," the Aatiri adds.

"Go rest, child," the Mulani chieftain says. "You do not look well from your travels."

The Litho man narrows his eyes at me. "A most curious thing for one with so much magic."

"One more question before you leave," the Kes chieftain says, finally breaking his silence. "Heka did not return during the last Blood Moon. There are some who believe he has abandoned us. What do you know of this?"

"It's true," I say, dread coursing through my veins. "He has."

The tent falls silent except for the crackle of the fire. The chieftains stare at me in disbelief, but they do not utter another word. Semma was right to tell me to be careful. I don't trust them. I dip my head and take my leave.

Rudjek is outside waiting for me, alone. "That was awkward to say the least."

"Did you eavesdrop on the entire conversation?" I say as the drums and laughter from the gathering crowd almost drown out my voice.

"It wasn't particularly hard." He clears his throat. "I noticed you left out some details."

"For now," I tell him. "Until I know who I can trust."

"They aren't at all what you expected, are they?" he asks quietly. "The chieftains."

I shake my head as chills crawl up my spine. The new chieftains are nothing like Grandmother and the others. They don't seem to be committed to working together for a single goal. Instead, they're too busy bickering and trading petty slights. "I'm sorry," I say after a moment.

Rudjek cocks an eyebrow. "Sorry for what?"

For failing over and over again. For thinking that I could be better than my mother or my sister or Dimma for that matter. For what I am about to do tonight. But I don't tell him any of that. After the fraught conversations with my cousin and the chieftains, I've realized I can't wait for Daho to make his move. I must act first. "For everything."

Before he can respond, Nenii appears out of the shadows. "There you are, Crown Prince!" she proclaims as she grabs his arm. When he startles, she adds, "Not to worry, I'm a *ben'ik*—I have no magic to react to your anti-magic."

He scratches the back of his neck. "It's not that. I—"

She cuts him off cheerfully. "We've found a tent for you and your *dshatu* friends—far away from those with magic. Let me show you."

"I'll join you soon," I call after them, and set off in a different direction before either of them can protest.

I keep far away from where the crowds are gathered around fires, celebrating. It's the only way for me to avoid everyone. Let them think that I'm still talking to the chieftains.

I retrace my steps back to the start of the crossroads. It takes only a few moments to spot the thread of silver-and-evergreen magic meant only for my eyes—the trail that Daho left for me. *Burning fires.* I cannot deny the anticipation and longing at the chance of seeing him again.

DAHO

My prison of time has taught me patience. When one is immortal, there is no rush, no urgency, no need for ticking clocks. Perhaps that is why Dimma was fascinated with the idea of time, for it always stood still for her as it does for me now. To that end, my revenge against the gods unfurls across the span of centuries, or is it a millennium? That particular detail matters not.

Shezmu and I are in the library with the game board set up on the table in front of the bay windows. The three tiers form a glass tower that obscures our view of each other. He takes great delight in the complicated rules of the game, its many pieces. Strategy has been one of his obsessions since before he became immortal. I play only to humor him.

The twin moons hang heavy in the sky and bathe the bookshelves in buttery light. Tonight, I will kill my first god, or he will kill me.

"Black or gold?" Shezmu asks as he unpacks the game pieces from a bronze box.

"You always play black," I say, surprised.

"I've never asked your preference." This is a revelation to no one but him. He turns over the black empress in his hand, running his thumb across her crown. "Technically, we should switch every round."

"You're realizing this after playing Paradigm with me for how long?" I ask. "Why this sudden mood of self-reflection?"

"I couldn't risk you dying thinking that I was a selfish toad."

I lean back against my chair and squint at him. "I'll play gold."

Shezmu shrugs and opens with one of his usual bold attacks—always straight to the offense. Laughter rises from beyond the closed doors. Our people are celebrating the Day of Remembrance. It used to be a solemn occasion, but in recent years it's changed to a day of indulgence meant to spite the gods. I made my obligatory appearances earlier, reciting speeches that Shezmu wrote.

My mind isn't on the game. I am eager to meet my target. He calls himself the Collector. He spends his time stealing people and building monuments of their bones. He takes hundreds at a time. People of all ages and all walks of life. His collection spans hundreds of worlds.

His brethren do nothing to stop him from siphoning off the lives of their children—just as Koré did not protect my people from Eluua. He isn't the only vile god I have watched for the better half of a century, but he is the most isolated. That is why I've chosen to kill him first.

Shezmu quietly makes his next move on the game board. "There are those among our people who inquire about your well-being. Some even wonder about . . . with *whom* you spend your time."

I grimace. "Neither of which is anyone's concern but my own."

"Of course, my king," Shezmu says in that sly way of his. "But I thought you should know the latest gossip."

"I'd rather not."

It isn't long before he has reached the ascension square at the center of the first tier of the board. He takes four of my footmen before placing his empress on the second tier.

"You *are* a selfish toad," I observe. "Always playing to decimate me."

"And you are selfish for not letting me come with you," Shezmu says as my footmen change from gold to black, denoting that they now serve him.

Ah—here we are. I have come to expect no less from him. "Who would care for our people if we both die at the hands of the Collector?" I advance my magician on the board two spaces to corner his goddess. "You offer our people some sense of normalcy, of hope. All I can offer is desperation and a reminder that I couldn't protect them when they needed me."

"They are tired of going through the motions," Shezmu counters. "They await the revenge that you promised against the gods."

"Our time will come, brother," I say as he advances the twin to his goddess—the horned god—to block my magician, "but I must take this first step alone."

"Well, at least if you die, I'll have a reason to lead a crusade against the gods and take all your glory," Shezmu says, resigned.

I offer him a smile. "That's the spirit."

"All the same, I hope you will be safe." There is tenderness in his voice as his empress advances to the echelon, the third and final tier. The game is over. He's won.

* * *

After the orishas killed Dimma, Iben—the god of time—did not close the gate that connects Ilora to the other worlds. It is a mistake that will aid my cause. The gate looks like a singular ring of pulsing light, standing in the city that once belonged to both my people and our endoyan cousins. Sometimes it appears as the mouth of an inferno or a doorway into an abyss. I enter the stream of light and search thread after thread until I find the one I'm looking for.

I land on a barren landscape covered in crystallized bones. While my senses come back into focus, I think about the first soul I ever consumed. It was the day that Dimma made me immortal—the day I took my vengeance against Yaneki, the man who killed my parents and stole my throne.

With Dimma's gift came an insatiable hunger—an undying yearning. I do not need to devour more souls to remain immortal, but the hunger has never left. Yaneki's soul had been marked by unwavering focus and discipline, and to my surprise, those things had become a part of me. I fear what will happen when I consume the Collector, but my apprehension isn't enough to stop me.

I find him dragging a pile of fresh corpses to the foot of a new monument. He appears as a stooped creature with a hunched back—the form he takes when hunting to terrorize his prey, but it does not scare me.

"We have company," the Collector says, his voice like shattering glass. "We did not invite you."

He was at the front of the cloud of fog that had descended upon Jiiek the day that Fram killed Dimma. I will make him pay for that.

I remove the dagger from the sheath at my waist. "Do you remember me?"

"You are the abomination." His mouth is a black hole; it's hard not to stare into it. "Koré said that you would not be a problem. Re'Mec thought differently."

The dagger thrums in my hand, lengthening into a sword. "Re'Mec was right." I descend upon the god in a fury of wind, but he becomes a blur, an afterthought, a mirage just out of my reach.

"I am older than time," he whispers as he evades my attacks. "Older than most of this universe."

"Is that supposed to mean something to me?" I roar in frustration.

"You will be the first of your kind I collect, but you won't be the last." His voice is a soft purr. "I will build with the bones of your people."

The Collector dips in and out of the shadows, always appearing in the corners of my eyes. I stop cold, gripping the sword. He must think his threat will deter me, but it's only fueling my determination. I'm standing in the heart of his many towers of crystalized bones, some so translucent that they glow. This is his domain. His safe haven.

"Have you given up already?" he taunts. "I'm disappointed."

I swing the sword of light again and set out to decimate everything that he's built. The Collector shrieks as if in agony, then he makes the fatal mistake of coming too close to me. I rake my blade across his vessel. Light seeps out of his wound. The blade yearns to drink up the substance of him, but I squeeze the hilt to stop it.

The Collector stumbles over bones as he backs away. I relish the fear in his eyes as I strike again and again. When he's sufficiently weakened, I grab his throat and force him to his knees. "No," he pleads. "It cannot be."

"Goodbye, Collector." The organ underneath my tongue stretches and stretches, my jaw opens impossibly wide.

He resists, but it is no use. His soul drifts into my mouth and scrapes across my tongue like shards of ice before sinking into the organ. I snap my mouth shut, feeling him unraveling inside me.

The gods aren't invincible after all. I bellow with laughter, but my joy is short-lived: sharp pain doubles me over. I drop the sword; the light blinks out. It's a dagger again, lying amidst the shattered glass bones. I collapse to the ground.

Footsteps approach, two sets. Koré and Re'Mec? They must have sensed that I killed one of their brethren. Despite my agony, I roll on my back to face my execution.

"This is what happens when you insist upon being stubborn." Shezmu glares down at me. "Thankfully, we never listen to you."

Yacara, my second-in-command, is at his side, his face twisted in shock. "You actually killed one of them—you killed a god."

PART II

When my mother told me to hide,
I hid inside the Supreme Cataclysm.
When I emerged a thousand years later,
the gods thought that I was one of them.
Koré had imprisoned my father while
my mother exists frozen in the throes of death.
I kept quiet and soon the gods forgot me.
Oh, but I did not forget about them.
—Heka

NINE
ARRAH

I once considered demon magic invasive and overwhelming. But in this moment, it feels like a warm embrace, an invitation, an offer, an escape. I follow the path Daho has set out for me as it veers from the crossroads and weaves through mossy underbrush. It flows like a trickle of water that divides when it meets an obstacle and pools in the hollows of the earth.

I tell myself that I am not betraying Rudjek and my friends by seeking out Daho. I am not naive. I have a plan. Daho wants Dimma, and I want to stop a war. Not only for the tribal people—for Zöran. There's been enough bloodshed. Perhaps I am a fool, but I believe that he can be reasonable—that he'll at least hear me out. I got to know him, not just as Dimma, but when he was hiding in Sukar's body. He was by my side for months. I laughed with him, cried, slept in his arms.

I know I'm close when the path suddenly pitches me forward, my feet barely touching the ground. I see the gate ahead of me. It's a pool of darkness, humming with magic. I pause, my heart racing in my chest. I've come too far to turn back. This is what I want. I step into the mouth of the darkness, and the gate pulls me apart. I become strings of light and flickering shadows, gently careening along. The feeling is so familiar. Dimma had done this countless times.

When I land on the other side, I'm dizzy, but only for a moment. He's there, standing in a clearing lit by pale light with no discernible source—tall, beautiful, winged. He inhales a sharp breath, his glowing evergreen eyes wide with relief. Something inside me twists when I realize how much he'd been hoping I would come—and fearing that I wouldn't. It isn't his history with Dimma that draws me to him—it's more than that. I'm supposed to think that he's a monster, but perhaps I'm the monster hiding in plain sight.

I force myself to keep some distance between us. I will not succumb to Dimma's memories and emotions. Daho is my enemy; I can never forget that. I steady myself, planting my feet firmly on the ground. His shoulders relax, and he holds himself completely still.

"You came," he whispers, his voice ancient, tender.

I do not lift my eyes to his. Instead, I watch the grass ruffling even though there's no wind. The trees are covered in violet buds that pulse with light, and the air is as sweetly cloying as summer wine. One of Dimma's memories crawls to the surface of my mind. She and Daho lying in this field, watching stars shoot across the sky. This is not Ilora. This is another world—a place they used to visit on occasion. "You knew that I would."

"And yet, not even a thank-you?" *Such sarcasm*—and I remember how changeable his moods are. He reminds me a bit of Sukar, which I suppose was how he'd been able to completely fool me when he took my friend's body. If I'm being honest, I like this part of him, the unpredictability. The snark.

"A thank-you?" I scoff. "For what?"

"For sending you back to Zöran with your *beloved* prince." He doesn't bother hiding his contempt. "I see that he's as right as rain."

On the crossroads, after the *akkaye* had pinned me against the ground, I'd seen shifting shadows in the belly of the forest. It had seemed as if they, too, had noticed something amiss. I'd dismissed it as wishful thinking . . . but it wasn't. "You were in the forest."

Daho stares down his nose at me. "You forget that Dimma and I are connected. Through her, I know when you are in trouble. I couldn't be sure if the gods had finally turned against you."

"I didn't need your help."

"As they inevitably will," he barrels on, ignoring my declaration. "The gods, that is. And don't fool yourself—I wouldn't have come if some part of you hadn't called to me. Whether you're willing to admit it or not."

"Don't pretend you know my heart." I hurl the words in anger, even though what I feel is more like defeat. I may no longer hear his whispers in my mind without the chieftains' magic, but he isn't wrong. There is an invisible tether that binds us. It led me back to the crossroads to seek him out—that and to plead with him to leave Zöran alone. I think of when I was still sick from anti-magic in Tyrek's tent, and Daho had kept me alive. He could have easily let me die.

"I might not know your heart," he replies, his voice infuriatingly calm, "but I do know your soul." His words are an entire desert of sand smothering the breath from me. I want to run from them, to deny them, to rage against them. But no one made me come here. It wasn't Dimma's urging that brought me, either. I came because I wanted to.

That moment in the tent when I asked him to kiss me and he had almost given in to my request—when he was still pretending to be Sukar—I have never felt a yearning so strong. The need between us was real, as real as the awkward silence between us now. Here is the part that I can hardly bear to admit: *I wanted him even more after I realized the truth.*

"We need to talk," I say, forcing a change in the conversation.

"And here I thought we were talking, *Arrah?*"

My name sounds so odd when he speaks it, as though he has been practicing so he doesn't call me Dimma again. This is a step in the right direction. There was a time when he was convinced that we were one and the same.

"You recall our agreement," I say. "You will spare the tribal people should it come to another war against the orishas."

"I remember."

"Do you?" I press. "What assurance do I have?"

"What assurance do you need?" He is suddenly standing inches away, so close I can see the silver flecks in the depths of his eyes. "I have already given you my word. Is that not good enough?"

"No," I murmur. "If your army attacks Zöran, you will not be able to control their thirst for souls. Eventually, they will come for the tribal people. They did it before under Efiya's command."

"And you and I dealt with them, did we not?" Daho says, frustrated. "Do you think it was easy for me to let you trap my people in the dagger—after everything they've been through?"

"I reaped the souls of murderers of children," I snap. "They deserved worse."

"True," he concedes, turning away from me. "But the rest of my people do not deserve to be punished for the actions of a few."

"And what about the rest of Zöran?" I say quietly. "Will you spare them, too?"

"Yes," he answers without pause. "So long as they stay out of my way; though I can't speak to what will happen if they side with the gods."

As we turn circles in the field, both staying far from each other, a flutter of glowing butterflies drifts up from the grass. I close my eyes, remembering when he and Dimma danced here, her body pressed against his, his hands warm against her back, the bottoms of their feet swaying above the grass.

"Is there anything else I can do for you?" Daho quirks an eyebrow. "Or was this only an excuse to see me again?"

"You think too highly of yourself." I wish I could cut Dimma's memories out of my head and burn them until there's nothing left but ashes that scatter on the wind. Maybe then I wouldn't be at their mercy, nor would I feel the constant pull of the tether that binds me to him. "It was cruel to bring me here of all places."

"It's crueler that, after five thousand years, my wife is mere steps from me, yet she's still out of my reach," he says with a bitter edge. "I supposed in a sense you're her jailer, and she is your prisoner, even if not by choice."

Semma's premonition of him standing over my broken body crawls its way to the forefront of my mind. What if tonight he decides to end my life—this very moment or the next? He could do it without any effort at all, yet I can't bring myself to fear him. Not because I don't think he's capable of it, but because I'm tired of being afraid. "Are you willing to kill me to get her back?" I blurt out the question unintentionally.

Daho stares at me contemplatively, then he says, "No—that truly would be cruel given the circumstances."

I think about all the times I offered up my years for a taste of power. Each trade left me with new scars—the missing tooth, the gray hair, poorer eyesight, more aches and pains. "You know how much time I have left." It's a statement, not a question.

"Please don't ask," he says with a deep sigh. "It would do no good for you to possess such knowledge."

My chest feels hollow as the truth settles upon my shoulders. It was always inevitable, wasn't it? Sooner or later. But why should *he* of all people know when I would meet my end? Was that what Semma saw in her vision? Perhaps Daho won't kill me, but he'll be with me when my heart finally stops beating and my bones snap. "I'm sure you're counting down the days until Dimma returns." I don't hide my bitterness.

"I am," he says unapologetically, then he pauses. "But I find myself conflicted." He faces me from across the field again, more butterflies scattering between us. "I've come to know you, Arrah, and you are brash and impulsive, but you're also kind, loyal, and resilient. I don't want to see harm come to you."

His eyes are guilty—of what I do not want to know. Guilty of seeing me as someone more than Dimma's shadow or guilty of something else?

"Is that why you haven't attacked Zöran and the orishas yet?"

I ask. "You're waiting for me to die first so you can reunite with Dimma?"

"Don't be so morbid," he says. "Is it hard to believe that I'm tired of this war, too?"

I narrow my eyes, not at all convinced. It's too easy. "Why the sudden change of heart?"

Daho sighs, and I see the years on his face—not the effect of time that mortals suffer but a weariness that has taken eons to settle into his ageless features. "My priorities have changed since I consumed Fram's soul." He stares at the shadows at the edges of the field as if summoning all his strength for whatever it is he wants to say to me. His nostrils flare and the black veins along his temples stand out starkly against his silver skin. Yet nothing could have prepared me for his next words. "Did Dimma kill our child?"

I can't believe what he's asking. I look at my hands—remembering Dimma's hands, and the spark of light they once held. My fists clench and unclench. I remember the child's joy, his curiosity, his fear— Dimma's love for him.

Then Fram had appeared in shades of light and dark. *Oh, Dimma.* The dual voices of the orisha of life and death had cut through her soul, and I tremble beneath the weight of them even now. *What have you done?* The rest of the memory comes to me in bits and pieces that don't make any sense.

This is a puzzle that I cannot begin to solve, so I settle on the truth. "I don't know."

Daho massages his temples like he has been bracing for the worst. "I have Iben's ability to travel the threads of time," he tells me. "I've revisited Dimma's last moment over and over. I see Fram breaking through her defenses and entering the throne room, and then the moment skips ahead to when—" His voice goes quiet. "To when Fram's ribbons strike Dimma. I believe Iben erased what happened between those two points in time to spite me."

Koré had erased her memory of where she hid the box imprisoning his soul. But this was different. He thinks that Iben cut out a piece of time itself. I couldn't pretend to understand how that could be possible, even for Dimma's brethren. "You believe there's a way to get it back."

"If there is," Daho says, his eyes burning into mine, "you are the key. I am here to ask for your help. You have Dimma's memories, and I'm hoping that they are still intact."

"Why not ask her yourself once I'm dead?"

"Even my patience has limits, Arrah," he answers. "If you're willing, seek me out again, and we will learn the truth together."

He's waited until now to ask, knowing that I won't refuse—not when he's still offering to spare the tribes and all of Zöran should the others choose not to aid the gods. But what if Dimma did kill their child? What if she struck a deal with Fram in a desperate bid to save herself? Would he kill me for her crimes—*could he*? Will the answer he seeks be the thing that makes Semma's vision come true. I ease out a sigh. In the end, curiosity outweighs my apprehension. "I'll come tomorrow night."

Daho nods and turns to walk away. His wings unfurl, and then he is gone. I should be satisfied. For now, Zöran is safe. But I feel like I've swallowed a pot of ashes that is slowly poisoning me to death.

TEN
ARRAH

I stumble back to the settlement with Daho's voice ringing in my ears. Once, I wondered out loud how Dimma's memory of him could be so different from the stories, and Essnai had said that both could be true. I am not a fool. Daho is mercy, and he is vengeance. He is a man, and he *is* a monster. For now, I have the ear of the man.

Tonight had gone better than I could ever dream. His desperation to find out what happened to his child is greater than his hatred for the orishas—now I have to keep it that way for as long as I can.

"Ah, there you are." Rudjek steps out of the shadows in front of me. He glances across my shoulder at the crossroads, his hands on the hilts of his shotels. "Are you okay?"

Does he know where I've been? Can he smell the cloying scent from the field or the remnants of demon magic? "Yes," I answer, "but today has certainly been trying."

"For all of us," Rudjek agrees, relaxing his hands. "We've had an incident already."

I frown. "Do I even want to know?"

"A Litho man tried to cast a curse on Fadyi, and it rebounded." Rudjek shrugs. "All the man's teeth fell out, but Nenii said there was a healer in the camp who might be able to regrow them. Apparently, it's an excruciating process."

"Serves him right for being such an ass."

"You look tired," Rudjek says, dropping the attempt at light conversation.

I want no more secrets between us, but I don't know where to start. There is too much to tell him. "I do need to rest, but first, can we talk in private?"

"There's no one in my tent, and I have been dying to get you alone." Rudjek shifts on his heels, uneasy, as if he has an inkling that I have something to say he won't like. He gestures for me to follow him. "Jahla and Fadyi left to survey the rest of the island; they needed a little space from the constant assault of magic. It really is overwhelming."

"I can only imagine," I say quietly, but my mind is elsewhere.

"But I am playing the role of the perfect Crown Prince," Rudjek assures me as we pass a group of Mulani youth gathered around a fire with bowls of blood medicine. He flashes them a smile, and they cluck their tongues at him.

A girl pats the ground next to her. "Come join us, pretty Kingdom boy."

"Maybe tomorrow," he tells her coyly as we continue on our way. "See, I'm winning over the tribal people with my good looks and irresistible charm."

That makes me laugh, despite myself. "Oh, is that what you're doing?"

I brush my fingers across his calloused palm. I will make the best of the time I have left with him. He lifts my hand and presses it to his mouth. His lips are warm, steady, gentle. They make me feel safe.

Once we reach the tent, we slip off our shoes, and he pulls back the flap to let me enter. A small fire crackles at the center of the tent, the smoke curling through an opening at the top. The tent is lined with furs and pillows, made comfortable for Rudjek and his guardians.

He removes his sword belt and sets it on a low table. "We'll have the tent to ourselves all night."

"Do my ears deceive me, Crown Prince," I murmur, "or are you propositioning me?"

"I have no idea what you're suggesting. Though if you should want to share my . . . um, *pallet*, I would not be opposed to such an arrangement."

We are standing so close that I can feel the warmth rising from his skin. I'm in danger of getting lost in the reflection of the light in his obsidian eyes. It's too easy to fall back into our usual banter, but I have to think beyond the here and now. He deserves to know the truth. I take a seat close to the fire. "I have something to confess."

Rudjek arches an eyebrow, trying to decide if he likes the sound of that. Possibly, he's been waiting for this moment, too. We've never spoken much about what happened when I was alone with Daho after Essnai fled the demon attack and I killed Tyrek. He lowers himself to the cushion next to mine. "Don't look so nervous," he says gently. "I am your friend first and always."

My stomach twists. "I don't deserve such loyalty from you, Rudjek. In the past . . . well, I haven't always been truthful, and I'm sorry."

"We've both lied by omission." He offers me a smile. "I'd call us even."

I stare into the fire dancing across the logs, wishing that were true, but I'm carrying too many secrets. I could die soon—and I don't want anything left unsaid between us.

"I almost kissed *him*," I blurt out. "At the time, I believed it was Sukar, and I was delirious from anti-magic poisoning. I was mad at you. I thought that you'd sent Raëke to spy on me . . . that you didn't trust me."

Rudjek takes in my words, his face grim. "To be honest, I suspected that something happened between the two of you. Somehow the fact that you believed he was Sukar makes it worse."

I cringe at the pain in Rudjek's voice. "I had convinced myself that with your anti-magic and my magic, we would never be together. I was reckless and lonely." I pause to brace myself. "But that's not the worst part." There—I've said it, and now I'm committed.

Rudjek arranges his features into an expression of careful neutrality and waits. Why does he have to be so perfect when I am so flawed? So calm when all I want to do is scream to the top of my lungs?

I force myself to get out the rest. "After I realized who Daho was . . . after he'd shown his true face . . . I still wanted him." I wrap my arms protectively around my shoulders—warding off the chill in my bones despite the fire. "I had Dimma's memories in my head. I was confused . . . Maybe I still am. . . ." My words hang between us as if time itself has stopped to linger on the moment. Seeing Daho again tonight, I realize that, yes, I am drawn to his intrigue and mystery. That much I can't deny.

Rudjek swallows hard, his mask slipping. His body goes rigid next to me, his anti-magic flaring like hot lashes. "Are you saying that you want to be with him?"

I squeeze my shaking hands between my knees. Telling the truth has only made me more miserable when I had hoped that it would set me free of this guilt. "I carry Dimma's memories of her life with Daho. Seven hundred years' worth. I can't put them aside, as much as I want to. . . . I can't wish them away. But no, I don't want him—I'm just still trying to discern her feelings from mine."

"I don't pretend to know what you're going through, Arrah." Rudjek leans forward, digging his knuckles into his forehead. "It's just that—how am I supposed to compete with someone like him? *Like them?* They had lifetimes together."

I take his hands and lay them against my chest. "Can you feel that?"

He nods as he stares into my eyes.

"You already have my heart, Rudjek." I lean into him so that our foreheads touch. "You're my best friend, and I want there to be more when we're ready."

"Yet, you went to see him tonight." Rudjek pulls away from me. His voice is so matter of fact, so cold. I should have known he would realize where I'd been. He was practically waiting for me as soon as I stepped off the crossroads. Not that I was planning to hide it from him.

"Yes," I admit.

I expect him to recoil, to stand up and start pacing, but Rudjek surprises me by staying perfectly still. "Did he give you an ultimatum, then? You in exchange for peace?"

"Gods, no—he's not like that."

"'He's not like that,'" Rudjek repeats, sliding away from me. "How can you say such a thing? Have you forgotten that he restrained you with craven bones only months ago? He killed countless people in his war with the gods. Don't tell me that he's 'not like that.'"

"You're right," I say hastily. "That was a poor choice of words, and I'm sorry. What I meant was, he's agreed to leave Zöran be—all of Zöran—if we stay out of his fight with the orishas. And he's asked me a favor . . . one that will require that I visit him again."

Even in the firelight, I can see the flush in Rudjek's cheeks. The dark vein pulses at his temple. "I'm going to kill him. You're not a piece in a game, Arrah. He doesn't get to have his way with you in exchange for peace."

I'm horrified to realize what he thinks. "You've got the wrong idea. He wants me to help him find out what happened to his child with Dimma."

"Of course, it'll start with that," Rudjek says with a mocking smile that doesn't conceal his anguish. "Don't you see what he's doing? He'll earn your trust, and then you'll let your guard down."

"Then what, Rudjek?" I ask, coming to my feet. "You think I'll fall into his bed. I've told you how I feel about you . . . that I want a future for us . . . however short that may be. I'm not going to do anything to jeopardize that. But if meeting with Daho can help keep him distracted from starting another senseless war, then I will do it."

"How will we have a future when I know you're spending time with him?" Rudjek says, his voice breaking. "At what point will Dimma's urges become your own?"

"I have no right to, but I'm asking you to trust me," I say quietly.

"Forgive me if I don't share your trust in him," Rudjek says. "If it's all the same to you, I will still make a formal request to the chieftains to ally the tribes with the rest of Zöran. If your attempt to keep that beast at bay fails, then we'll be stronger together."

I know that I can't dissuade him any more than he can change my mind about seeing Daho again, so I let it be.

Outside, the sounds of the dying celebration finally fade. "When you're tired," Rudjek says, his voice softening, "the color of your eyes darkens. They're her eyes, aren't they?"

I nod, all the fire burned out of me. I think about Semma's vision of Daho standing over my dead body and of him saying that I don't have much time left. One way or another, my life will end and Dimma's will begin anew. "When I die, Rudjek, I hope that some part of Dimma will love you, too, in her own way."

Rudjek smiles through his misery. "At least I'll have that."

ELEVEN
EFIYA

I wait for the Demon King in the cabin on the dreadfully cold mountain. I've been told it's off-limits to anyone but him. Therefore, I simply had to come. It's where he likes to open the gate when he returns from trying to woo my sister. I bet that he's brought her here already. Seems like the kind of thing he'd do out of some pathetic attempt to awaken his dead wife. I suppose he must be a romantic.

The cabin is modest but cozy in its own way. A bed, a fireplace, a stove, a table, a chamber to wash, nothing more. I run my fingers across the miniature wood carvings on the table. They're a nice touch to this illusion of the past. I particularly like the figurine of a bear standing on his hind legs with his claws raised, and I've decided to keep it for myself.

I settle on the rug in front of the fireplace and wait. It's much too dull here so I've changed into something more appropriate. I wear a black chiffon dress woven with flames. The diadem might be a bit much, but it fits me perfectly. I'm impressed that there's not a speck of dust or decay in the cabin. Dimma's magic has held fast over the years, which is a testament to her powers. I would like to have known her. Though I doubt we'd get along.

When I feel the first tingle against my skin, a sign that the gate is about to open, I arrange the spread of my chiffon dress tastefully around me and ashes float up from the smothering flames.

The Demon King startles when he sees me. Good. I like getting under his skin.

"Hello," I say as he takes in my elaborate dress and perhaps my intentions. "I thought we should have a little chat."

His wings ruffle against his back. "Did your father not explain the rules to you? No one is to visit here under any circumstances."

I don't much like rules, but it's best that I don't voice that particular opinion. I must be careful with my words for now. "Oh, I'm sorry," I say. "But you've been avoiding me, and like I said, we need to talk."

The Demon King clears his throat. He really is gorgeous. Who could resist his boyish immortal face, his tortured expression, his unwavering will? Well, I can, but I'm not just anyone. "What do you want?"

"Ah, you don't even deny avoiding me," I say, aghast. "After everything we've been through *together*. . . . Or have you forgotten that you wouldn't be here if I hadn't helped you?"

He frowns, his eyes shining with brilliant light. "I'm not in the mood for your games, Efiya. I thank you for freeing me from Koré's eternal prison, but you are a child and should act as such. Your father would be very disappointed to see you here like this."

I laugh as I get to my feet, the layers of chiffon ruffling, smoke rising from my dress. I can't believe how ungrateful he is after my mother bred me with the sole purpose of serving him. After I searched the depths of the oceans and the bowels of volcanoes in search of his soul. After I freed his people while he was still rotting away in a box. "Why would I ever think that I am more than your faithful servant?" I ask, keeping my face pleasant. "I only have life because you needed someone to do your bidding."

The Demon King lets out a noisy breath like he's lost his patience with me. "You are not my servant—you're my best friend's daughter." He relents, and I see the moment he's decided to change his approach. He's so predictable. "You are free to live your life as you wish in service of no one but yourself. Not that I expect you to do anything other than that."

"Where—in this purgatory you call home?" I snap. Now I've lost my patience. "Do you expect me to stay here forever and rot?"

"Of course not," he says. "In time, I'll find a better place for our people after this mess with the gods is over."

"And when will this mess be over if you do not let us take our revenge?" I ask, raising my voice. "I have a score to settle with the Twin Kings as much as you. They turned my sister against me."

"You did that yourself," the Demon King says, his face twisted into disgust. "You tried to kill her twice." He opens the door and steps aside. "You've done so many unforgivable, despicable things. For that, you deserve death. Be thankful that I have shown you mercy."

Be thankful. Thankful? To him of all people. The souls writhe in my belly, and I grit my teeth. I have an urge to shred him into tiny pieces. But that won't satisfy my rage. That would be too easy, and I never do things the easy way. "You're right." I glance at my feet. It isn't like I don't know that I've done awful things. I do. There are things that I wish that I could undo, things that I avoid thinking about. "I have made mistakes, yes, but I'm willing to do better. I don't know how to explain it . . . but I'm changing." I swallow hard, embarrassed. I hadn't meant to say that last part aloud. I don't want him to think I'm weak. "I'm not a child anymore."

"You are still a child in every way that counts," he says. "You can have a second chance at life with a father who adores you. You need only give him a chance."

"This isn't about Papa and me." I cut straight to the point. "This is about you stopping me from going after the orishas. Are you afraid of what I'll do to Arrah if you let me leave Ilora?"

The Demon King turns on his heels and glares down at me. For a moment, I think he's going to pull the dagger from his waist and plunge it into my heart. I admit, the idea excites me. If he thinks he can beat me, let him try. I might have let my sister get the best of me, but I will not repeat that mistake.

"You are not returning to Zöran, and you will never see Arrah again," he says, his voice the picture of practiced calm. "Do you understand?"

I force another smile. I'm doing that a lot these days. "I didn't come here to fight." I head for the door with the flames of my dress trailing behind me. "But I can see that you're not ready for this conversation."

"And what conversation is that, Efiya?"

I gather my skirts up to keep them from dragging in the snow outside the cabin. "I want to know why you're stalling instead of mounting an attack on the orishas."

"I'm not accustomed to having a child questioning my decisions." The Demon King frowns as if truly seeing me for the first time. "You must learn patience, Efiya, for it will serve you well."

Oh, but I have learned patience over these past few months locked away on Ilora. Had I not, I would have died of boredom already or done something more drastic like burn down his ugly palace or rip apart Dimma's throne like I have thought about doing dozens of times. I'm in this for the long game, and he doesn't even know it. "Maybe you're right." I step closer to him. He keeps his eyes on my face, ignoring that my dress has changed from black to fiery red. Why does he have to be so dull? I've known trees with more personality than him. "But understand this, *Daho*, for I will say it once more. I am not a child, and I will not allow you to treat me like one."

"I shall keep that in mind," he says, but I can tell that he isn't taking me seriously. He's wearing an annoying little smirk. "Now, if you would excuse me."

With that, he gestures for me to leave. He is by far the most infuriating person I have ever met, but it's so annoying that I still need him for now. I step through the door, one foot landing in the snow and the next landing on the soft grass of the arboretum where my father is waiting for me. In the process, I have changed my dress into something more subtle—a loose sheath with long sleeves and a high neckline.

"We were supposed to meet at midday," Shezmu says, his back to me. He is standing at the edge of the terrace, overlooking the dead land beyond the gardens. "You're late."

"Sorry, Papa," I say sweetly. "I was with the Demon King in his cabin."

Shezmu turns around slowly, his shoulders stiff. "Why were you there?" he asks, his voice an instrument strung too tight. "You have no reason to be visiting with him."

"And why shouldn't I visit him?" I cross my arms. "You have no say in who I spend my time with."

Shezmu's silver skin flushes. "Efiya, what were you doing at his cabin?" he repeats, each word drawn out.

I burst into tears and turn away from my father. I'm still fuming from seeing the Demon King. How could he treat me like a child after everything I've done for him? He should worship me. I'm his savior.

Shezmu is there, pulling me in his arms. He gently strokes my hair as he holds me tight against him. He is shaking with rage. "Please, daughter, tell me. Did he hurt you?"

I feel safe for the first time in my life. One of the souls inside me pulses with love, too, and I remember that, even while cursed, Oshhe still loved Arrah despite all her flaws. Maybe Shezmu loves me the same way. I decide that I could never kill him as Tyrek suggested to gain control of the gate. It wouldn't be right.

"No, but he won't listen to me," I say through my sobs. "I wanted to talk to him and find out why we're stuck in this awful place while he gets to travel freely. He wouldn't even hear me out! It isn't fair, Papa."

Shezmu gently pulls away and looks down at me, his expression one of calm again. "Oh, Efiya, is that why you're upset?" When I nod, he adds, "He only wants to keep us all safe."

No, Papa, he only wants to keep Arrah safe and take the orishas' souls for himself. That much is clear.

"You want to leave Ilora, yes?" Shezmu asks in earnest.

Ah, could it really be this simple? I'd never thought to just ask him. I assumed that he'd say no, but how could he deny the daughter he so adores? I swipe at the tears on my cheeks and look up at him. "Very much so, Papa," I say eagerly. "I miss seeing flowers and trees and blue skies. I miss seeing ducks floating in ponds and watching boats idle down the Serpent River. I miss home. This place is so dreadful."

After a moment, Shezmu decides. "How about I take you to another world? Not Zöran but one that is even more beautiful. I used to visit it on occasion many moons ago."

It's not the answer I was hoping for, but it's a start. "Are we going through the gate?"

"Yes, yes, of course," Shezmu says with a laugh. "I see no reason why we can't visit another world while Daho is busy making his plans for the gods. We'll go tomorrow, just you and me."

I smile as I stare into my father's eyes. He's giving me exactly what I need: access to the gate. Once he opens it, I will split myself into two and go to Zöran to see what the Demon King has been up to all these months. And I think I'll pay my sister a little visit. It's long overdue.

Shezmu insists on walking me back to my chambers like I'll get lost on the way. I have to admit that it feels nice to have someone care. I lean into his side as we stroll down the corridors with gold vines carved into the arched ceilings. As usual, the palace is eerily silent. "Tell me about Ta'la?" I've never asked him about the daughter that Eluua and the endoyans killed. In truth, I've never really thought about her or what she might have been like. Now I'm curious.

My father shudders next to me, his skin going cold. It takes him a moment before he can speak. "She was a curious child. When the other children were running in the palace halls, she studied star charts and maps. She always dreamed of seeing more worlds, but she never got the chance."

"I want to explore other worlds too, Papa," I say, not to be outdone.

"We will, daughter," he says as he reaches my chambers and opens the door.

I roll my eyes when I see Tyrek standing in my salon. I had forgotten to warn him that we were on the way, so he could hide. I guess my secret's out now. Oh well.

Tyrek stops midpace when his eyes land on Shezmu, then he grins. "Ah, we have a visitor. Lovely."

"Efiya," Shezmu growls, making no effort to keep his temper under control as he barges into my salon. "Explain."

"Explain what, Papa?" I say innocently, my gaze meeting Tyrek's wicked smile.

"Him!" Shezmu erupts. "Why is Tyrek Sukkara in your chambers?"

"Have a little grace, man." Tyrek sighs, shaking his head. "I made sure the gods never found the dagger with Efiya's soul inside— and this is your welcome?"

"I'll show you grace!" Shezmu snarls through gritted teeth. He is much taller than Tyrek, but to the prince's credit, he doesn't flinch.

"Efiya." Tyrek manages to sound bored. "Can you please clear up this misunderstanding?"

On another day, it might be amusing to watch Tyrek and my

father bicker, but I'm not in the mood. I am about to insist they both leave when I feel a tingle down my spine. Moments later, the Demon King storms into my chambers without knocking. His eyes are wild, his jaw clenched. When his gaze finds me, I shrink back. Shezmu steps between us, and Tyrek casts me a meaningful look. This is what he wants: to drive a wedge between the king and his best friend.

"Do you forget yourself, charging in here unannounced?" Shezmu snaps.

My mood instantly improves.

In one step, the Demon King passes my father and pins Tyrek against a wall, his dagger to the prince's throat. "Give me one reason not to kill you where you stand."

Tyrek swallows, glancing down at the dagger. But he keeps his languid tone. "I can give you several."

"You tried to kill me." The Demon King pushes the dagger dangerously close to drawing blood.

Tyrek switches to groveling. No one could ever accuse him of losing sight of his own agenda. "In fairness, I had no clue you'd taken over Sukar's body. Had you revealed yourself to me, of course I would have loved to work together to restore Efiya's soul."

"Work with you?" the Demon King spits, his eyes filled with rage. "After what you did to Arrah?"

"That was . . . a misfortune." Tyrek looks pained. "I am deeply sorry for hurting her, but she gave me no choice."

"Arrah?" Evelyn muses. "Isn't that Dimma's new vessel?"

I resist the urge to roll my eyes a second time. My salon is becoming as crowded as a public bathhouse. When did *she* so rudely invite herself in?

The fire goes out of the Demon King. "Not exactly." He lowers the dagger and drops Tyrek to the floor. "Dimma is inside her, but Arrah is not Dimma."

After all that's happened—all I've done—they are still treating me like a child. How dare they barge into *my* chambers, boss *my* servant around, then talk about *my* sister like I'm not even here? Someday, they will realize how grave a mistake it is to underestimate me. Without a word, I turn on my heels and push open the doors to my bedchamber so hard they slam into the walls. I am sick of the lot of them.

Evelyn follows me, shielding me from the chaos. Over her shoulder, I watch Papa grab Tyrek by the back of his neck and drag him out of the salon into the corridor. Evelyn closes the doors on a flustered Demon King, who growls and storms away.

"Don't you worry about them," she reassures me. "No reason why you can't have a human plaything. Life on Ilora is terribly boring at times."

"So true," I say with a laugh as I drop on my bed. Maybe I've misjudged Evelyn. At least she's not trying to order me around. When she prepares to leave, I surprise myself. "Can you stay with me for a little while?"

"Of course," she answers with a smile. "Shezmu and Daho can be overbearing." Evelyn takes a seat in an oversized chair opposite my bed. "But I have to ask—why did you free that boy in particular?"

"He's good for some fun now and again," I admit, feeling faintly embarrassed.

"Starting tomorrow, we'll get you out of the palace more," Evelyn says like I'm her new pet project. "You can mingle with our people.

No need for you to spend all your time with him."

"Can I tell you a secret?" I ask, changing the subject.

"Yes," Evelyn answers too quickly, and leans forward.

"I believe the gods are using Dimma to distract the Demon King," I confide in her. "I haven't shared my suspicions with my father yet."

Evelyn frowns. "I would be lying if I said I didn't suspect the same. He's not been the same since he's been back. He's distant and moody. Well, moodier than usual."

I take a breath, knowing I've reached a delicate point. "I have made mistakes, but I'm not a horrible person. That's more than I can say for Re'Mec and Koré—they are vile creatures, petty and selfish. Why should they decide who lives or dies? Why should we sit here waiting for them to come back and finish what they started?"

Evelyn slowly stands and wraps an arm around her belly. She has the look of a caged animal, desperate to be free. "Let me show you something."

She says it like she's about to reveal a secret of her own, and I do like secrets. I raise an eyebrow and practically bounce on my toes. "Of course," I say, tempering my enthusiasm. Best not to seem too excited.

Evelyn leads me through the dreadfully boring corridors until we stop in front of a pair of gilded doors. I haven't explored this wing of the palace. No one ever comes here, so I didn't think it was worth my time.

"This is the great hall," Evelyn said, choking back tears. "It's a place of sorrow, but it wasn't always so." She glances up at the vaulted ceiling. "We used to have grand parties here that would go on for days if you could believe it. Here was where I—" Her voice is full of longing. "That part doesn't matter."

I push the doors open, and dust flutters in our faces as the hinges moan in protest. It's still early afternoon, but hardly any light reaches the hall through the floor-length windows. At first, I don't know what I'm looking at, but the scene comes into focus. The hall is filled with statues of demons. No, not statues—real people.

I watch as a man clutches and unclutches his fists. A woman reaches in front of her to grab something, draws her hand back, then does it again. Another demon's wings unfurl, only to close a moment later. Someone is whispering the same word over and over. *Yethe. Yethe. Yethe.* They're all stuck in time, reliving the same moment.

"His name was Kalen," Evelyn explains, nodding at the man. "He's saying 'the end.'"

But I understand him just fine.

"What happened to these people?" I ask in awe.

"The gods are what happened," Evelyn spits. "They did this."

"The Demon King can't release them." I already know the answer.

Evelyn shakes her head. "Dimma and her siblings have done so much harm to our people."

When her sibling had talked so fondly about Dimma in the throne room, I hadn't missed the hesitation in Evelyn. I knew there would be others who hated Dimma, just like the demons I freed in Zöran. In fact, I had counted on it. I let my magic slip around the edges of the minds of the demons in the great hall. They can hear us talking, though they can't speak. The gods have poisoned their souls and bodies. For now, I won't tell Evelyn that I can release them from their eternal prison. The moment isn't right. Instead, I say, "I can make the gods pay . . . if given the chance."

Evelyn reaches for my hand, and I hesitate. Everyone I've ever known has wanted something from me, but Evelyn smiles, and I am surprised by how easily I smile back. Maybe we can be real friends, like my sister and I never were. "You do not know how long I've waited to hear those very words," she says. "Let the gods know our pain and suffering. Let them know that the very children they have forsaken will be the end of them."

TWELVE
ARRAH

I wake to Rudjek's gentle snoring vibrating in the hollow of my neck. He's curled around me, his intoxicating scent of woodsmoke and lilac filling the tent. The light seeping through the seams of the flap is pale, and the air is crisp, but his body is warm. I nestle more deeply into his arms, not quite believing that we have this quiet moment together.

Rudjek stirs and buries his face against my hair. I squeeze my eyes shut and ease out a breath. I could spend eternity like this—with him. But I don't have eternity. I don't have much time at all. I've given up so much already.

"I had the most exquisite dream," Rudjek murmurs. "Delightful, really."

"I thought you didn't need to sleep," I tease, glad to think about something other than my impending death.

"Yes, but when a beautiful girl sleeps in your arms, how can one resist?"

My heart hitches on his words. It's hard to think about how I looked not so long ago. People would see my golden eyes, the slope of my nose, the curve of my lips, and say that I was the spitting image of my mother. But I have my father's Aatiri cheekbones, his proud chin. Coily hair like my grandmother. Even with her skin softened by time, she'd been one of the most striking women I have ever met. But the signs of age in my body are all wrong. I didn't earn them, and they've brought me no wisdom. Rudjek can pretend not to notice, but we both know what they mean.

I don't let those thoughts spoil the moment. "What did you dream about? I'm sure it was wicked."

"Quite wicked," Rudjek admits. "I'm not sure I ought to tell you. It wouldn't be proper."

"Proper?" I repeat, bemused. I shift my position so I'm leaning on my elbow. "I suppose you must concern yourself with propriety now, Crown Prince. Does this mean no more gambling on the docks?"

Rudjek cringes, and I realize my mistake almost immediately. He, Kira, and Majka used to sneak away from his father's villa at night to visit the docks—the three of them inseparable. I cup Rudjek's face as he stares at the ashes of the dying fire, feeling the warmth fleeing from his skin. "I miss him so much," he says. "Pompous ass that he was—Majka was my brother."

It hits me all over again like the jagged edge of a kobachi knife digging into my belly. Our friends will never come back. No amount of magic or trading years can change that. The Supreme Cataclysm will make their souls into something new. Maybe it already had. "It won't be the same without them."

Rudjek glances up from the ashes, and he clears his throat. I know before he speaks that he will fall back on humor, as he so often does when retreating inside himself. He gives me a comically haughty look, every bit the prince. "It's a travesty that Majka will never hear the songs written about me. How after I united three armies to fight the demons, I stood bravely against the Demon King himself, who is quite unimpressive in person. Rudjek—the descendant of Caster of the Eldest Clan—the craven who killed Oshin Omari, assumed his identity, and infiltrated the Almighty Kingdom." He stares at his hands, and a bitter edge creeps into his voice. "Crown Prince and future Almighty One."

"And yet, when I first met you, you didn't know how to cast a fishing line." I try to cheer him up, but I know his sadness cuts deep, even if he hides it beneath his humor most of the time. "So many accolades for a boy who lacks basic survival skills."

"Ouch." Rudjek smacks his forehead. "What must I do to impress you?"

"Learn to be useful," I say with a smile.

"As if killing demons isn't useful." He is sitting up now, the furs twisted at his waist, his bare chest exposed. I try not to stare, but I am utterly failing. He grins to himself as he reaches for his tunic, pretending not to notice. "I have been granted an audience with the chieftains this morning. Will you come with me as the voice of the Almighty Temple? I would feel more comfortable if you were there."

It seems so long ago that I stood against Rudjek's father in the coliseum, thrust into the spotlight. The head Temple attendant, Emere, had insisted upon me taking my mother's place. I had agreed to do it only to stop Suran Omari from claiming the tribal lands and banning magic in the Kingdom. "As long as you know that I intend to tell the chieftains of my new deal with Daho."

"Hmm," he grumbles, climbing to his feet. "What makes you think they'll believe him any more than I do?"

The chieftains had not exactly been welcoming, but I have an advantage. They still think I carry the souls of their predecessors. I only have to make sure they don't find out otherwise. "They'll believe me."

Once we're dressed, Rudjek and I make our way toward the chieftains' tent. Now that it's morning and the shadows have lifted, I can see the layout of the camp and the distant hills beyond it. We traverse the colorful Aatiri tents, flanked by a small Kes encampment. The Kes have hung pouches of burning eeru pepper, bloodroot, and ginger on stakes between their tents.

The smell burns my nose, but it reminds me of the days I used to help my father make potions and blood medicines. It seems so long ago that we'd settle down for tea and milk candies after toiling away in his shop. I would give anything to have him back. I miss his stories, his smile, his calming presence. What's worse is that his soul will never ascend or know peace because of my sister. I ball my hands into fists, and my nails dig into my palms. I hope she's rotting in her eternal prison.

I press ahead, trying not to linger on the past. The Mulani white tents stretch to the west of us, opposite the Zu tents shrouded in animal hide and crowns of antlers to the east. The Litho tents sit on a bluff overlooking the valley, separated by sheets draped across wire.

People busy themselves washing and hanging clothes, tending pots on fires, cleaning bones, crushing herbs. The air has a strong smell of broiled meat, spices, and blood medicine. Children run past me, chasing each other. Mothers hush their crying babies; people whisper their morning prayers. It seems that life has mostly moved on for the tribal people, but it's not the same. Silence threads through the tents as steadily as the frigid breeze. Some people stare at us with somber faces, the excitement from last night gone. I can't bear to meet their eyes.

"There isn't much magic," Rudjek comments.

I nod as my gaze tracks the stray sparks flitting sporadically in the air around the tents. I haven't felt any strong magic since we left the crossroads. These people might've been spared the battle with the demons, but they still have their wounds. I hope that Semma's right, and there's someone left powerful enough to help me gain control of Dimma's magic. Even with Daho's promise, I'd feel better if I could protect the tribal people. It's what Grandmother and the others would have wanted.

"Arrah." Rudjek pauses on my name. He cocks his head, and I can tell that he's eavesdropping on conversations that I cannot hear. "These people . . . they think you're here to lead them."

I swallow the sudden lump in my throat. I couldn't even lead a horse to water, let alone them. My cousin thought that sharing the news that I no longer have the chieftains' *kas* would devastate the tribes. They need hope and knowing the truth would take that away. But how can I be their hope when I've failed them, failed everyone I've ever loved? It's a responsibility I never wanted, one I cannot bear. "Thankfully for them, the chieftains do not agree, nor do I."

As we draw closer to the center of the valley, I spot Nenii with a group of women cleaning pestles and mortars. Their hands are stained with flecks of herb paste. Aunt Zee sits on a squat stool among the women, doing more talking than cleaning. In the morning light, she looks so much like Grandmother—the same proud forehead and high cheekbones—that I have to push back tears. As annoying as she's always been with all her gossiping, I'm glad to see that she made it here with the rest of the tribes.

"It's true." Nenii raises her voice for our benefit. "The Crown Prince of the Almighty Kingdom is madly in love with Arrah."

"Nenii!" I chide her, biting back my annoyance.

But she is unashamed. She gives me a big grin. Rudjek lets out an amused little huff at my side, but he doesn't correct her. My whole face flushes with heat. He doesn't deny it, not that he could any more than I can deny my feelings for him.

Aunt Zee looks unsurprised—and unimpressed. "Surely you're not as foolish as your mama, girl?"

After all this time, this is the first thing she has to say to my face. I'm not shocked. She's her usual belligerent self. Always criticizing and insisting that she knows what's best for everyone. One of the other women clicks her tongue.

Aunt Zee doesn't bother to hide the fact that she's looking me up and down. When I don't answer, she tries again. "Haven't you learned from Arti's mistakes? Have you forgotten that my sister sacrificed everything for you?"

I am not the girl I used to be. I will not let her push me around anymore. I level my gaze at her, keeping my chin high. "I do my best to disappoint you at every opportunity, auntie."

Her eyes go wide but only for a moment. "Is she really fixing her mouth to sass *me*?" Aunt Zee asks the woman next to her. "If she didn't carry Mnekka's *ka*, I swear."

Nenii catches my eye and shrugs. "We're very fortunate that Arrah has Grandmother's fire. Wouldn't you say?"

Aunt Zee purses her lips, full of indignation, but the other women murmur their agreement.

It's praise that I don't deserve, but I smile anyway before Rudjek and I continue on our way. "I think those women were doing their best to pretend that I wasn't standing right there?" he says.

I nudge his side jokingly. "Not everyone is impressed by your titles, Crown Prince."

"Ah," Rudjek muses, scratching his face. "I take satisfaction in knowing that I don't have to be a puppet on a string here, not like back home."

When we reach the chieftains' tent, an attendant beckons for us to enter. As soon as we're inside, shadows flicker in and out of our line of vision. A wisp of cold brushes against my back, and a familiar sense of malice laces the air. And then I see him: Re'Mec in his human form, with bronze skin, sky-blue eyes, and a tangle of golden hair. Once, I knew him as Tam, a scribe at the Almighty Temple— but that was only his alias to keep an eye on Rudjek.

"It seems we have drawn some unwanted attention, sister," the sun orisha says as he perches on a cushion. Koré sits next to him, hair wriggling against her shoulders, and if I didn't know better, I'd think she looked happy to see me.

"What are you doing here?" I direct my glare at Re'Mec. I still haven't forgiven him for trying to kill me.

Koré flicks a glance at me. "We were invited."

"And truly, it's long overdue that we extend a hand of friendship to the tribal people," Re'Mec adds, his eyes bright. "It is a shame really that your god abandoned you." He's relishing in the moment, twisting the blade.

"Heka has not abandoned our people," the Mulani chieftain says through a thin smile. "He is testing the strength of our faith."

I don't have the patience to correct her or to snatch away what little hope she has that he will return. I know the truth.

"We did not ask you here to debate faith," the Litho man says. "We called upon you to be certain that the Crown Prince speaks for you and the Almighty Kingdom. And frankly, we do not trust your intentions, either."

Burning fires. This cannot be happening. Rudjek quirks an eyebrow as if the news is amusing, but this isn't anything to take lightly. The chieftains went behind both our backs. Now their actions have jeopardized everything I worked for. I can't keep the tribal people out of the demons' path if they ally themselves with the orishas. Rudjek should be on my side, but he just stands there, seemingly unfazed by this turn of events.

"I see not much has changed over the generations," Re'Mec says with a sigh. "You still expect us to prove ourselves to you. Too long you have forgotten that you are my children. It is my fault for sparing the rod." He leans closer to his sister. "I suppose they're still less of a disappointment than your children, though."

Koré only stares at her brother, resigned.

Rudjek clears his throat as he steps farther into the tent. "You must forgive the sun god, for he's too ancient and cranky to have much cause for manners and decency. I may be only a prince, but I am determined to unite our two peoples against our common enemy."

The Kes chieftain gestures for us to take a seat, and Rudjek moves to sit next to Koré. He eyes Re'Mec the entire time as if expecting trouble. Re'Mec only scoffs as he casts me a wicked grin. I realize then that Rudjek is careful to position himself between the orishas and me. He doesn't trust that Re'Mec won't try to kill me again. He and Daho at least have that in common.

"Those are fine words, Crown Prince, but where was the Almighty Kingdom when Efiya and the demons attacked our homes?" the Zu woman snaps. "We sent messages asking for help that went unanswered."

Instead of going into a long story and offering hollow excuses, Rudjek says, "The Sukkara family made many mistakes, and in the end, it will be a lasting stain on their legacy. I do not intend to follow in their footsteps. I have fought the demons many times, including in the tribal lands at what was once Heka's Temple."

He takes a dramatic pause and smiles at me. "I led a Kingdom army alongside my craven—excuse me, *dshatu* cousins and the Zeknorians to push the demons back through the gate between worlds. Since then, the Delenians, Estherians, and Galkians have also allied themselves with the Kingdom with one goal: to end the demon threat for good."

Rudjek radiates unwavering confidence as his voice rings in the tent. He's changed so much. From reluctant prince to skilled orator. Long gone is the boy who shied away from public attention. He'll make a good king one day, better than his father will ever be. But he's painted a picture that's only partly true.

"More fine words, Crown Prince," I say, interrupting his speech. "I believe that you mean them, but your father, Suran Omari, only months ago declared his intentions to claim the tribal lands for the Kingdom. That is not an act of goodwill."

Rudjek grimaces like he hadn't expected me to bring up his father's latest schemes as if they should have no bearing on the chieftains' decision. "A mistake that he regrets, I assure you," he says. "My father was under the impression that the tribal lands had been abandoned."

"More like he saw an opportunity to seize the tribal lands and steal their resources," I remark. "So much of the Kingdom's precious metal comes from the caves in Aatiri. Dyes from the Mulani, spices from the Kes . . . shall I go on?"

Re'Mec watches the exchange in silent bemusement, but Koré's attention seems to be elsewhere.

"Your point is well taken and valid," Rudjek continues, undeterred. "My father made a foolish decision. I'm not too proud to admit that. But he never sent the Almighty army into the tribal lands."

"If you have already fared well against the Demon King," the Aatiri chieftain asks, "why do you need us?"

"If we are truly to defeat the demons, then strategy will be key," Rudjek says, clearly in his element. "The craven people are anti-magic, but the sheer number of demons would still overwhelm our forces. We need your magic to help keep their souls contained in their bodies, which is when they are the most vulnerable."

"Just this morning you said there wasn't much magic left among the tribes," I interject. "What good would they be to you if not to add to the death toll?"

Rudjek looks completely caught off guard for once. I've dealt him a blow, but he recovers with ease. "Any magic is better than none at all, wouldn't you say?" He glances at his hands, embarrassed to have crossed that particular line. The faint black veins stand out against his forehead like they always do when his emotions are high. "I . . . I didn't mean it *that* way."

The chieftains don't seem to notice the unspoken words, but I'm speechless. *Twenty-gods.* This couldn't possibly get any worse. I never thought we'd be on opposing sides.

"And what will the orishas be doing if we choose to fight their enemies?" the Mulani asks, cutting her eyes at Koré and Re'Mec.

"I will not lie to you," Koré says, her expression still distant. "My children are nearly immortal—some as powerful as we are, but they have limitations that we can exploit. In truth, we are too few to expect to win against them alone."

"Had you adequately punished them the first time, we wouldn't be in this situation, sister," Re'Mec says unhelpfully. "You should never have shown mercy to that boy." He looks back to the chieftains. "This time, with the cravens and your magic to assist, we'll divide and conquer the abominations. Then my siblings and I will drag their filthy souls to the Supreme Cataclysm to meet with their deaths. One could only hope that they'll be made into something more palpable next time."

The chieftains exchange glances with each other as they consider Rudjek and the orishas' proposal. The Zu and Mulani chieftains look skeptical, the Kes man appears undecided, and the Aatiri and Litho seem committed to fighting. I don't understand how they could actually be considering this even after knowing that Daho promised to spare the tribes.

"How many of us will die in another senseless war?" I ask

quietly. "Efiya almost destroyed the tribal lands with a third of the Demon King's forces—what will happen now that his army has been reunited?" I pause, letting them take in my words. "The Demon King killed Fram, the orisha of life and death, only months ago. Were they not one of the most powerful among your brethren?" I direct my question to the Twin Kings.

"They were," Koré answers simply, but Re'Mec only wrinkles his nose.

"The Demon King did this after being imprisoned for five thousand years," I say. "That should tell you what you're up against."

"Ah, interesting," Rudjek says, feigning calmness, but he's wearing a mask again to hide his emotions. "This morning, you were calling him by his name . . . *Daho*. Now you're using his title again. Such a change in the tides in the mere span of hours." He gives me a look riddled with guilt. He wouldn't dare, would he? "You know what I think, Arrah?" Rudjek presses on without pause. "Perhaps carrying his dead wife's soul is clouding your judgment. How can we trust that you have the tribespeople or any of our best interest at heart? I for one cannot say."

The chieftains stare at me in horror. They act like I've grown three heads before their eyes. "What did you say, prince?" the Aatiri chieftain whispers. "Do my ears deceive me?"

"You must be mistaken," says the Mulani.

I open my mouth, but to do what? Protest, deny it? I never thought he'd stoop so low, but I can't ever forget that he has his agenda, and I have mine. Our feelings for each other will not get in the way. But is that what he really thinks—that Dimma is influencing my decisions? After I poured my heart out to him last night, after my reassurances?

Koré's hair falls still as she meets my gaze. "You hadn't intended to tell them."

It isn't a question. She already has her answer.

Re'Mec doubles over laughing, and when he recovers from acting like a complete ass, he turns to Rudjek. "Well played, Crown Prince, well played."

"I told you there was something wrong with her," the Litho man spits at the other chieftains. "If she carries the soul of the god who made the demons immortal, why would she want to see them destroyed?"

Re'Mec breaks into a slow smile. "The most dangerous enemy to your people is sitting across from you, hiding in plain sight. Our sister is a menace. She mustn't be allowed to reunite with the Demon King."

"I couldn't agree more," I say, finding my voice again. I have to make this right. I have to salvage what I can before the chieftains make a mistake that will destroy the tribes. "They can never be allowed to reunite, but for now, my carrying Dimma's soul gives me an advantage over the Demon King." I look each of the chieftains in the eye. I have to make them listen despite their suspicions. "I met with him last night, and he has given me his word that as long as we do not aid the orishas, he will leave *all of* Zöran alone."

"Consorting with the Demon King himself." Re'Mec throws up his hands. "The young prince here is right. She's not to be trusted. Perhaps she should tell you how the Demon King came to be so powerful. Now, that is a story worth telling—a tragedy really."

"I suspected he'd been visiting you," Koré says. "We've felt the gate open several times in recent days."

"I met with him *once*," I say, annoyed with the Twin Kings. "If you do not go after his people, then there is no further need for bloodshed. And perhaps you should tell the story of how you started this war out of pettiness and jealousy. I wonder if the chieftains will find that story tragic as well, or maybe they'll see how the gods who pretend to love their children turn against them as soon as they become an inconvenience."

Re'Mec scoffs. "Jealousy? Be serious."

He doesn't deny the pettiness. He couldn't even if he tried. He and Koré could've let Dimma and Daho live their lives. If they had, Dimma would have never made the demons immortal.

"Why should we believe the one who carries his *ama*'s soul?" the Aatiri chieftain snaps at me. "I agree with the orisha. I do not trust you, girl."

I brace myself for my next words—words I don't have any right to say, but I'm desperate to convince them. This is the only thing I have left. "Your predecessors bound their souls to mine and bestowed their gifts upon me for a reason—do not forget that. You said it yourself. I am their chosen leader to rule over the five tribes. If you trusted them, then you must trust me now. I say that we mustn't strike against the demon army as long as there is peace."

I see the moment Rudjek's jaw twists—the shadows in his eyes. He's on the verge of revealing this secret, too. Dread pulses through my veins, but to my relief, he presses his lips into a hard line and glances away.

Re'Mec yawns and says offhandedly, "Not that any of that matters when you don't carry the former chieftains' souls anymore."

The chieftains gasp in surprise; they curse. They all speak at once, bombarding me with questions and insults and more questions. Their reaction is as bad as I expected. Had I really thought I could get away with not telling them? Had I thought I could be so clever after failing at everything else? I've just lost the one advantage I had. They won't listen to me now. If it's up to the Aatiri and Litho chieftains, they'll join the fight against Daho's army, and the tribes will perish.

Re'Mec winks at me as shadows suddenly shroud him. "Our work here is done, *sister.*"

Soon the Twin Kings have disappeared, leaving me to deal with the aftermath.

DAHO

The first soul I ever consumed had been full of determination, purpose, and unwavering discipline. Those things became a part of me. I think of this as I writhe on a bed of bones in agony with the Collector's soul burning in my belly. I may have miscalculated.

This soul rages like shards of glass slicing and shredding me from the inside out. The Collector bleats in my mind, spewing depravity and greed and lust. *Kill, collect, kill, collect, kill, collect*—his single compulsion since the Supreme Cataclysm birthed him. This is his nature. *Kill just enough not to anger the others. Just enough. Kill, collect.* I scream, and he laughs. *I will collect you, boy. So young, so sweet.*

My muscles seize with spasms, and my bones stiffen until there is a crack in my spine, then another. Half-delirious, I attempt to shed my physical form, but I'm too weak.

It's a great effort to keep my eyes open. Two faces blur in front of me—one brown, one silver.

"What have you done, brother?" Shezmu is kneeling next to me.

He moves in and out of focus, his white hair tangled by the wind.

I struggle to answer him, but my belly and throat burn. Ash flakes from my skin. The soul of the god I ate is consuming me—how fitting.

Pain shoots through my vessel as Shezmu and Yacara lift me from the bones. There's not much left of me, and my mind breaks its tethers and seeks Dimma. I find her sitting on the side of the frozen lake, her bare feet digging into a drift of snow.

It's so familiar, a memory out of reach.

You may call me Dimma, she says, *but I am not terrifying, nor am I death.*

Yacara's voice cuts through my thoughts. "We can't take him through the gate like this. What if it makes things worse?"

"We don't have a choice," Shezmu grunts.

I linger on the edge of consciousness as they drag me into the gate. Muscles and bones and sinew turn into ribbons of light. The Collector screams, and his pain tastes both bitter and sweet. He isn't invincible. Even immortality has its limits. It can be transformed. What Dimma did to Eluua, I will do to the Collector—if he doesn't consume me first.

When I open my eyes again, I'm resting on a mound of pillows and blankets in my own bed—a bed that's cold. I haven't slept here in a very long time. Moonlight streams through the curtains, and shadows flicker in the chamber, cast by the fire crackling in the grate. My body is so hot—my skin is on fire. I try and fail to move.

"He's finally awake, little one," I hear Dimma say.

My heart races, and I make a renewed effort to get up. I fight the stiffness, the lethargy, with everything I have until I crest the surface, gasping.

"Dimma." Her name scrapes my throat, emerging as a croak. I taste blood. I despise my physical constraints, the indignity of bleeding.

A shadow falls across the bed. She's cradling a baby in her arms. I blink back tears. This isn't real. . . . *It isn't.*

"You need more rest, my love," Dimma says. "Soon, you will be well again."

The baby gurgles. Dimma is gazing down at his little face. He resembles her save for his nose and the color of his eyes—they're mine.

"How is this possible?"

"This is your solace, Daho," Dimma tells me. "Everything is possible here."

My solace. She means that I'm dreaming, but there is something more. There has to be. It feels like I've been living another life all along, in a world where the gods didn't kill her.

Dimma smiles at our son. "Isn't he beautiful?"

"He's dead, Dimma," I whisper. "You are, too."

She looks up at me in surprise. "What does it mean to be dead for someone like me?"

"I . . . I don't know." I summon all my strength to speak. "You told me once that everything returns to the Supreme Cataclysm to be unmade and made into something new. Maybe that's what death is."

"I wonder what I shall become," Dimma muses thoughtfully.

I say nothing. She will be made into something not *her.*

Dimma leans over and kisses me, her lips cool against mine. "I will always be a part of you, my love. Do you not feel me tucked inside your heart?"

"I do feel you, Dimma, so strongly." So many times, it has been almost like I could reach out and touch her soul. "Sometimes it feels like you never left."

"But I am gone." Dimma sighs and caresses my face. "You must accept that."

I reach for her, but she is already fading. The baby hiccups and turns into a glowing orb of light. I remember that I am on the verge of death—that the Collector is destroying me from the inside. Dimma and our son disappear as my hand falls to the bed.

"You are looking better." Her voice is strange, but I don't care. She's come back to me.

I take her hand and press it to my lips, reveling in her warmth. "My love . . . I've missed you."

A moment passes before she says, "I didn't think you were interested."

I open my eyes, startled to see Evelyn sitting on my bed, grinning.

I ease my hand from hers. "What . . . what are you doing?"

"I'm taking care of you, of course," she says. "You've been delirious for a long time."

I struggle to sit up, and she helps me. "Where are Shezmu and Yacara?"

Evelyn shrugs. "You're not to worry about that. Shezmu has things under control."

"How long has it been?"

"Three months."

Three months. Belatedly, I realize that the Collector hasn't killed me. Almost at the same moment, I feel a pang of hunger. I'm ravenous.

"Get Shezmu." I want Evelyn gone. Too late, I remember that without her, I might not have survived. "Thank you for taking care of me," I add.

Evelyn is already halfway to the door, but she stops. "Did you know that since Dimma changed us, not a single child has been born?" She steals a glance at me.

"I'm sorry." I lower my gaze. Had Dimma been aware that her gift of immortality would rob our people of children . . . ? I want to think that she would've made a different choice. The truth is that I don't know.

"I wonder if you ever might consider taking a companion," Evelyn says. This time her back is to me. "Eternity is a very long time to be alone."

THIRTEEN
ARRAH

The Litho and Aatiri chieftains sling insults at me long after the ori-shas are gone. They call me charlatan, *ben'ik*, liar, fool, among more colorful names. I bite my tongue and swallow my pride when all I want is to remind them that they are, in fact, piss-poor excuses for witchdoctors. They argue with the other chieftains, and soon their bickering turns into more insults—this time wielded at each other. These five are supposed to lead their people, help them rebuild after so much devastation? I shake my head in disbelief. They're going to tear what's left of the tribes apart.

"The girl does not carry the *kas*," the Litho chieftain spits. "She is useless to us."

"Watch your tongue," the Mulani chieftain says. "She is a daughter of my tribe, with or without magic. You shall show some respect."

I'm surprised that she's come to my defense, even after finding out my secrets. I'd never been close to my mother's tribe, but perhaps, I have judged them too harshly.

The Aatiri bares his teeth at the Mulani woman. "You dare

demand respect, *ben'ik*? You with no magic. If you're the best the Mulani can offer, it must be a sign that Heka will never return."

"Small words coming from a pathetic replacement for Mnekka," the Mulani retorts. "She was a great woman, a true leader, but you lack wisdom *and* her prowess with magic. You'll only lead the Aatiri to their deaths."

"Not before you burn on the pyre along with that traitor," the Aatiri says, jabbing a finger at me.

His threat is insignificant, so small that I almost laugh. I will not cower before him or anyone else. Death is the least of my concerns.

"We can't possibly stand against the demons," the Zu chieftain says to no one in particular.

"Have you not heard a word I've said?" I groan. "I can still protect the tribes."

But they're not listening—they're too busy squabbling like small children. I watch the Kes chieftain, who has the least to say. He tugs at the hairs on his chin as if he's in deep thought. I can't tell if he's more inclined to side with the Zu and Mulani against fighting or if the news has pushed him to agree with the Litho and Aatiri chieftains.

"Please, calm yourself!" Rudjek shouts. His tone is brimming with so much authority that the chieftains finally fall silent. "This is not the time to turn against each other. You'll only be giving the demons what they want. Don't you see that if we stay divided, they'll destroy us one by one?"

"The path is clear," the Litho man says. "If we join the orishas, we have a better chance of defeating the Demon King."

The Zu chieftain shakes her head in disagreement. "They couldn't kill him before, and I doubt they will this time."

The Mulani woman turns to me. "If, as you say, we are protected, then that gives us time to properly consider all our options. You only need remain on good terms with the Demon King."

"Are you on good terms with him?" Rudjek asks, casting me a sideways glance.

I push down my frustration. I don't know what I expected. He's hurt and angry and lashing out. That doesn't make it right, but I understand. I'd done the same when the princess from Galke had flirted with him. That wasn't right, either. I inhale a deep breath. "I'll do whatever it takes to prevent more deaths."

"Don't you think I want the same?" Rudjek says. "The difference is that I'm thinking about the long game. You may appease the Demon King for now, Arrah, but you won't always be here. Why should—?" He stops speaking abruptly, then lowers his voice so only I can hear him. "Why should he get to spend time with you when you've already given up so many of your years?"

There—he's said it. No more dancing around the tension between us. Maybe he doesn't know how many years I have left like Daho, but he's the one who heals my aches and pains every night. He knows better than anyone else that my body is falling into disrepair. I reach for his hand, and he takes my offering. "This is much bigger than you or me."

He stares at me, unblinking, and runs his thumb soothingly across my palm. "I know."

"We must put to a vote the matter of whether to join our forces with the Kingdom and the orishas," the Aatiri chieftain announces. The magic in the tent pales as if suddenly drained of its vitality.

The Kes chieftain strokes his beard thoughtfully. "I would like to consult the other leaders of my tribe before I give my answer."

"Of course you would," the Litho chieftain scoffs. "But now is the time to be quick and decisive." The Mulani and Zu women nod in agreement.

"No point in waiting," the Aatiri says. "I will start the vote in favor of joining with the rest of Zöran and taking the fight to the Demon King."

"On behalf of my people, I vote against," the Mulani chieftain says.

"I also vote against," says the Zu woman.

"Cowards," murmurs the Litho. "I vote in favor."

The vote is down to the Kes chieftain, who grimaces like he'd rather be anywhere else but in the tent. He's furiously pulling at the hairs on his chin now as his eyes flit between Rudjek and me. He has to see reason—see that I'm giving them a chance to save what's left of the tribes. I rock gently on my cushion, though it does nothing to calm the creeping sense of dread that's come over me. "I'm not anxious to thrust my people into another war," the Kes chieftain says reluctantly. "We've already suffered too many losses. I vote . . . against."

Rudjek lets out a little sigh beside me, but some of the tension eases from my shoulders. *It's the right decision*, I tell myself. He would see that, too, if he didn't hate Daho so much.

The Litho and Aatiri chieftains glare at the others, but the Mulani chirps, "It's settled. The tribes will not join the Kingdom. This is our final decision, Crown Prince."

Rudjek doesn't allow them the satisfaction of seeing him look disappointed. Instead, he comes to his feet and sweeps his hand across his forehead in a show of respect. "If you should change your minds, you know where to find me." He turns on his heels and leaves quickly, and I follow.

"Rudjek," I call after him. His name on my tongue is sugar laced with bitter poison.

He stops with his back to me, his hands on his hips. He takes several breaths before he stiffly turns around. His eyes are endless depths of sadness and despair that threaten to swallow me whole. I almost glance away. "You once told me that you tried to kill the Demon King, and Dimma stopped you," he says. "I saw for myself on the battlefield when you and he fought Re'Mec and the others, you became something more. . . . She was with you."

I wrap my arms around my shoulders. "What does that have to do with anything?"

Rudjek's shifts his weight. The cool breeze tangles in his wild curls. "If Dimma was able to take control of you and your magic before, we have to consider the possibility that she's influencing your decisions now." He pauses, his gaze roaming over the rows of tents. "And let's not forget your own history with the Demon King."

It's a slap in the face, a reminder of my treacherous heart, of my mistakes. I tremble as I remember how Daho had held me tenderly when I was on the verge of death. In that moment, despite everything that happened with Tyrek and the search for the tribal people, he'd made me feel safe. I glare at Rudjek, but I don't know if my fury is at him or myself. "You're being ridiculous." Even as I say the words, uneasiness settles in my bones. "Dimma is asleep, and for the last time, there isn't anything between Daho and me."

"Are you sure?" Rudjek asks, his voice measured, careful.

I narrow my eyes as if that can protect me from his accusation. "Am I sure about what exactly?"

"Are you sure that Dimma is asleep?" he says, enunciating each word slowly.

"Yes." I stare down at my hands—hands that once wielded magic with the ease of lifting a finger, hands that look so small now. I can't really blame him for questioning, but he's wrong. I've known each time Dimma pushed against the chains that bind her. And for better or worse, I believe that she won't interfere now that I've given up my borrowed magic. "You had no right telling the chieftains about her."

"Twenty-gods, Arrah," Rudjek says. "You can't keep something like that secret."

"Why not?" I snap. "You've kept your craven heritage a secret from all of Tamar, including your parents."

Rudjek pinches the bridge of his nose. "My father is an ass. We both know that he'd use the knowledge to his advantage. I cannot allow that—not while the alliance between nations is still so fragile."

I massage my temples, exhausted by this conversation. What's done is done. At least I don't have to keep pretending I'm something I'm not. I'm just relieved that the tribes will stay out of the orishas' war with Daho.

"Are you going to see him tonight?" Rudjek asks me suddenly.

"Yes," I say, my voice a single, sharp note.

"I thought so," Rudjek replies before he turns to leave. He takes one step and stops. "Be careful, Arrah. I don't trust his intentions."

"I will," I whisper as he walks away.

I almost ask him to stay, but I know we both need space. I'm still standing outside of the chieftains' tent in a daze when I see Semma hurrying my way. I can tell by the way she wrings her hands that she's nervous. When she reaches me, she casts a fleeting glance at the chieftains' tent, then she takes my arm and pulls me with her.

"Tell me you have good news," I beg.

"I do." She smiles ruefully. "I have a friend who believes they can help you tap into Dimma's magic. It should take only a few days for them to prepare for the ritual."

I allow myself a small smile, too, as I lean against my cousin's shoulder. She wraps an arm around me and pulls me into an embrace like she knows what I need. Finally, things are going right for once.

I spend my afternoon worrying. I worry that word will spread through the tribes that I no longer carry the chieftains' *kas* and the panic it will set in motion. I worry about whether the ritual to control Dimma's magic will work. I worry about what I will discover tonight.

Rudjek, Fadyi, and Jahla spend the day making plans to return to the Kingdom. But I'm not ready to think about leaving here, not after we've only just found the tribal people. Nenii keeps Essnai and Kira company while I help Semma with her chores.

Semma tells me that many of the Aatiri do not like their chieftain—that some went as far as despising him. "He shames Grandmother," she says as we wash clothes beside the river. It's a small, ordinary task, but it feels good to do something useful. The ice-cold water is a shock to my hands. It reminds me that I'm still alive. "She wouldn't abide the way he conspires with the Litho chieftain to undermine the others."

"His claim as chieftain should be challenged," I say. "There must be someone better to lead the tribe."

"There has been talk," Semma says quietly. "But it's just talk."

It's nightfall when I'm done helping her. My friends gather with the rest of the tribes while I sneak away to meet Daho. Before I reach the crossroads, a new awareness pricks against my back. I glance over my shoulder to see magic dancing excitedly under the stars in brilliant shades of color. Maybe Heka has abandoned the tribal people, but for now, there's still magic lingering in the sky, alighting on tree branches, tucking itself under pillows at night. But I know that the magic is finite. One day, it'll be used up, and the mortal world will be as the gods intended: magicless.

For the first time in my life, I am content to watch magic from a distance instead of wishing that I had it. It isn't that my desires are gone, but I feel more at peace with my lack of gifts. I'll probably feel different when the aches and pains settle in again, when my vision blurs, or if my plan to control Dimma's magic works. It's a strange contradiction to reconcile within myself.

Once I'm on the crossroads, the path winds down a hillside and across a valley until I am only a few steps from reaching the forest. I hesitate at the threshold, another prick at my back. This time when I whirl around, the magic is coalescing. Bright sparks swarm together in a frenzy. A chill crawls up my spine, but a moment later, the magic scatters.

I reach the gate between worlds. It appears as an arch of shifting shadows that give me pause, but I've committed to this path. When I cross to the other side, Daho is waiting for me in the clearing. Butterflies swarm around him, though he seems not to notice. My feet sink into the mossy grass that sweeps against my ankles. I remind myself that this is not a social call. I am here with a purpose.

"It's beautiful, isn't it?" he says. "Dimma and I explored every corner of these lands. You should see the waterfalls and the lakes the color of a starless night."

"There are no people here?"

He hesitates. "They were gone long before we came."

I frown. "Did they all die?"

Daho strolls to the edge of the field, with its view of the distant mountains through the trees. I get the sense he's stalling. Calculating. "There was a god who called himself the Collector," he finally says. "He became obsessed with the people who lived here."

I crush the fabric of my tunic in my hands, knowing that I'm not going to like what comes next. "Go on."

"He stole them—hundreds every single night. He stripped the flesh from their bodies and kept only the bones, which he used to build monuments to himself."

Daho glances at me, but I can read nothing from his expression. "When the gods discovered what the Collector had done, they argued for centuries about what to do with him before deciding to let him off with a warning. He learned to temper his appetite, make do with fewer people at a time, and spread his thefts over many worlds. The gods were not pleased, but they still allowed him to continue."

As far as I know, there is no mention of the Collector in the holy script at the Almighty Temple. "What happened to him?"

"He was the first god I consumed," Daho says. "I'm telling you this so you truly understand that the gods do not think like us. Their actions have little to do with mortal notions of right or wrong."

I understand what he's saying—that Koré and Re'Mec only care about their children when it suits them. "The Collector was on Ilora, wasn't he? When Fram killed Dimma?"

Daho frowns as if he's surprised I've made the connection. "Yes— the god who stole countless people was among those who sought to kill my child."

"Dimma's brethren believed that your son's existence was destroying the universe."

Daho lets out a long sigh. "Yet, my son is dead, and the universe is still dying."

"What do you want from me?" I ask finally.

"I believe if we go back in time together, we'll be able to find a loophole in Iben's magic," Daho says.

"Go back . . . in time?" I say, shocked. "Are you serious?"

He quirks an eyebrow, looking amused. "Of course."

"I'm starting to regret agreeing to help you."

Daho smiles as he holds out his hand. "I am in your debt."

I don't know if I can go through with this. What if Dimma did kill their son to appease the gods? Can I live with knowing that she was capable of such a thing? What will Daho do if it's true? Against my better judgment, I step forward and take his hand. In the end, I can't live with not knowing, either, no matter the consequences.

Grayness bleeds across my vision, and something tugs at my back. It feels like I'm in the gate again, unraveling like a spool of thread. I am floating up while my body is standing completely still in the clearing, eyes unblinking. My *ka* has separated from it.

"This is the only way. We can't travel through time in physical forms—there are rules we must observe. Trust me, Arrah," he says when I hesitate. "I promise to return you safely to your prince."

I don't trust him—I'll never trust him, I tell myself. But that isn't true. I'm still holding on to him when the tether between my body and soul snaps. I squeeze my eyes shut. The earth spins and turns upside down. Despite everything, I know that I am safe.

We land on the cusp of a battle. Demons surround a palace of smooth white sandstone, and we're in the middle of their ranks. Wings quiver nervously against backs. Feathers ruffle. I recognize this moment immediately, and a sense of longing and sadness comes over me.

"We'll fight them to the end," I hear a familiar voice scream behind me. I turn to see a silver-skinned, white-haired demon flanking Daho—the Daho from the past. It's Shezmu—Efiya's father, the monster who ate children's souls and killed Majka. "Death to the gods!"

I burn with fury, seeing him, but he is only a memory. Beyond the front line, a menacing fog rolls closer to the palace. The demons move around me, marching to meet it.

"That's never happened," Daho says at my side.

Dread fills my belly. "What?"

Before he answers, I realize that the demons aren't moving around him—they're walking through his *ka*. "In all the times I've traveled to this moment, it always plays out the same," he tells me. "You've changed it simply by being here."

I don't miss the hope in his voice. He truly believes that my presence matters, and maybe he's right. I can feel Dimma uncoiling inside me like a serpent waking from a great sleep. She knows why we've come, and soon we'll see the truth.

We ascend the palace steps and walk through the closed doors.

Once at the threshold of the throne room, I hold back, dread coursing through my soul. I sense Dimma's power permeating the space, pulsing, stretching, threatening. My awareness latches on to her, and everything else about the memory fades. I'm drawn to her like a moth to a flame.

"I've never seen this moment fully—only a glimpse of it," Daho says, barely above a whisper.

Inside the chamber, Dimma sits upon a bone throne inlaid with jewels. When I was underneath Heka's Temple with Rudjek searching for Daho's dagger, I saw myself on this same throne. I was wearing the red dress that Dimma is wearing now. "This isn't right—the throne isn't supposed to be here."

"A gift from Iben," Daho murmurs, his gaze transfixed on Dimma. "I built that throne using the bones from the Collector's monuments after I killed him. Iben pulled the strings of time and moved it here as a reminder so that I could always see my two beginnings: the day the gods killed Dimma and the day I truly became a devourer of souls. He must've known that I would find a way to recover the missing slice of time."

I float up to Dimma without willing it, and her thoughts begin to bleed into my own. I don't fight it—not that I can. Her words spill from my mouth, answers to questions I have yet to ask.

"Of my brethren's creations, time has always been the most difficult for me to accept," I say. "All these years, it's been slippery on my fingertips. Now time is running out for me. It ticks down to the moment of my first death and the day the war between my brethren and Daho began in earnest."

"Arrah." Daho ascends between me and the throne. "What are you saying?"

I frown. "I'm repeating her last thoughts."

Dimma shows no sign that she is aware of our presence. She cradles her belly.

"*My son, you are the beginning of the end,*" I say. "*I know that now. That is why my brethren are afraid.*"

Dimma reaches into her vessel, her hand passing through her flesh like a phantom, and takes the child. My own body moves in concert. I can't control it—I barely notice. All my attention is on her.

The child is a tiny beam of light. He has her true form and Daho's kind heart. She—we—sense it pulsing in him. He is stronger than any of her brethren. Stronger than Daho. Stronger even than Dimma herself.

Daho has gone still beside me as he watches the moment happen. He's waited so long to learn the truth.

"*He is more like the Supreme Cataclysm than I could've ever imagined.*" I'm speaking Dimma's thoughts again. "*I don't know how this is possible, and I would like to understand if there was time. But my brethren are moments away from breaking through the shield I have made around the throne.*"

Dimma holds the spark of light, and then the memory slips over nothingness. It happens so quickly that I almost miss it. Tears streak down Dimma's face; I feel them against my own phantom form. Darkness bleeds into the room, swallowing the sunlight and the sounds of the battle. One of Dimma's siblings has slipped past the other Daho and his army and broken through her defenses.

It's Fram, the custodian of life and death. The child disappears from Dimma's hands.

I gasp at the realization. "There is a hole in her memory—right before Fram arrives."

"Are you sure?" Daho asks, his voice shattering.

I don't answer him as Dimma looks up from her empty hands and stares straight at me. "You shouldn't be here," we say in unison. We are locked in a moment together, only the two of us. This shouldn't be possible, but I am interacting with the past—with her.

"I've . . . I've seen this before." Daho hesitates. "I've seen this exact moment."

"Why are you here?" Dimma and I say at the same time. Her gaze pins me in place.

"What happened to your son?" I ask, finding my own voice at last. "Did you kill him?"

"No," Dimma answers—and then her attention is tugged back to the events of the past.

Fram is suddenly in front of Dimma—their two bodies light and dark, night and day. "Oh, Dimma—what have you done?"

"I don't understand," Daho says, his voice anguished. "She didn't kill our child, but Fram was convinced she did."

Iben might've manipulated a piece of time, but Dimma erased her own memories. If she didn't kill their son, then what is she hiding? For now, I won't tell Daho of my suspicions—not until I know for sure. "Take me back," I say—a command, not a request. I'm exhausted, too tired to fully process any of this.

It takes a moment for him to collect himself. I don't think he'll be satisfied with what he's seen in Dimma's memories. There are only more unanswered questions. He reaches for my hand, and the past fades as we return to the present.

When we're in the clearing again, I drop to my knees, back in my body. He's at my side, staring at me, his eyes haunting. He must be realizing now that Dimma is as deceitful and devious as her brethren. Maybe he knows that I'm hiding something or that Dimma is keeping a secret from the both of us—a secret she's made sure no one will ever find out.

FOURTEEN
ARRAH

Daho paces in the clearing, reeling from the experience of seeing Dimma's memory of her last moments. His eyes glow with hope, though the feeling is tempered by the reality that we still do not know what happened to his child. The gods do not play by any rules, that much I'm sure of. Koré and Re'Mec would do anything to accomplish what they want, no matter the cost, and Dimma is no different.

"I've never been able to affect the past," Daho says, his voice as bright as a summer day. "I thought it impossible. Time is linear. A straight line. But what if it's not? What if it's more of a curve? If we can influence the past, maybe we can change the future."

His musings only make me think about the things that I wish I could change. I would stop my mother from cursing my father and stop my sister from killing him. I would save Sukar, Majka, and the others. I would protect the tribal lands and the Kingdom from the demons. I would spend more time with Grandmother. "You have your answer," I say quietly. Unlike him, I don't believe that we can change the past. We can only look forward and hope not to repeat the same mistakes. "Dimma didn't kill your son."

"No—but she is hiding something."

"Does it matter?" I shift on my heels.

"In truth, I don't know," he answers thoughtfully.

"I should go." I glance over my shoulder. "My friends will be worried about me."

"You mean Rudjek will be worried about you," Daho says, his tone changing to amusement. "Knowing that you're here with me."

"You assume that I told him."

Daho only smiles slyly. "I assume you tell him everything."

Dimma hadn't told you everything. Maybe if she had, you wouldn't have spent your entire life consumed by revenge. "At any rate, it's none of your business."

He cuts his eyes away from me. "I've made mistakes with you, Arrah," he says. "I know that now, and I'm sorry." He strolls almost silently through the mossy grass. "I can see her in you . . . in your eyes, the way you care deeply for those around you, and of course your sharp tongue." He stops, keeping his distance again. "But you aren't her, and to be honest, I'm relieved. Better that than the idea that she's fallen in love with someone else." The gate materializes at the edge of the field, taking on the appearance of an arch of butterflies. "Thank you for your help tonight. As I said before, I am in your debt."

"I'll hold you to it for as long as I live," I say, "which I suppose isn't very long at all." He glances back at me again, guiltily, and I cringe at the pity in his eyes. "It must give you solace to know that Dimma will return soon," I say, unleashing my frustration. "What was it that you called me? Her jailer, I believe."

"Solace and torment," he admits. "With Fram's soul, I can feel the impending death of every person near me, not accounting for unnatural causes. It's a strange thing to contemplate now, having tasted immortality. Life is too short for your people, and especially for you. Try to make the best of it."

"I'll keep that in mind." I turn away from him. "Now that you know the truth, what will you do?" My shoulders tense. I'm afraid of what he will say.

After a long pause, Daho answers, "I haven't decided yet."

The more time I spend with him, the less I know him, like becoming reacquainted with a childhood friend that you can only vaguely remember. There's familiarity between us but also strangeness and apprehension.

I start toward the gate but stop cold as a flush of magic washes over me. I remember, then, that when the gate is open, it connects all worlds at once. Chills crawl up my spine as, one by one, Dimma's brethren begin to appear around us. Koré and Re'Mec. Mouran, the roar of the sea; Sisi, the breath of fire. Essi, the sky god; Oma, the dreamer; Yookulu, the weaver of seasons. And then I spot Rudjek stepping through the gate behind them, flanked by Fadyi and Jahla, looking miserable.

I curse under my breath. They followed me here to get to Daho. They're going to ruin everything just when he'd finally agreed not to attack Zöran. I can't let this happen, not after coming this far.

I whirl around as Daho reaches for the dagger. "Return to Ilora— let me fix this."

But he pushes me aside and pulls the blade. It quickly grows into a sword of pure light. "You never learn, do you?" he addresses the Twin Kings. "Arrah convinced me to spare you, but I see that was a mistake.

She thought that you could be reasoned with—she was wrong. One cannot reason with the likes of your kind. It's just as well."

Re'Mec is wielding two swords that hum with magic, his eyes blazing suns. Koré's hair has morphed into writhing shadows that bleed against the night. Mouran's barbed tail curls like a viper ready to strike. Sisi is a blaze of fire shaped into a semblance of a body. Essi is shifting shadows moving across the stars. Yookulu wears a crown of thorns. Oma is something otherworldly, like pieces of a dream put together all wrong. Some of Dimma's brethren are not here tonight, and I count that as a small blessing.

"How can we reason with you?" Re'Mec roars. "You, who single-handedly killed so many of our siblings—how many now?"

"Too many to count." Daho pats his belly. "But I do have room for a few more if you care to join them."

Koré steps in front of her brother, holding a wooden box, the chains around it pulsing with light. The place that she'd kept Daho imprisoned for five millennia. I tremble as I look into the hollow darkness inside it, the eternal sorrow, the nothingness, the echo of broken promises. "I cannot let you ruin more innocent lives, my child."

Daho inhales a sharp breath at her words, his wings convulsing. I can almost see the fear moving through him, the way it darkens his face and sharpens his determination. "Arrah," he mutters, "leave now before it's too late."

Instead, I move in front of him and face the Twin Kings. I will not let this happen—not again. "Is this what you want?" I yell. "More bloodshed, more death? We can end this now."

"That's the point," Re'Mec hisses.

I turn to Daho again and whisper, "Please."

He backs away as the gate changes position so that it's directly behind him. The sword returns to its dagger form, and he waves it at the orishas. "Be thankful for Arrah—she has saved your pathetic lives tonight."

"Well, not quite," I hear a singsong voice say.

Then I see her.

Dread almost brings me to my knees. *No, no, no.*

Burning fire. No.

My sister descends from the night sky, long tendrils of scarlet smoke billowing around her. She's exactly how I remember. Breathtakingly beautiful, with our mother's golden-brown skin, loose curls, and Shezmu's glowing emerald eyes. When her feet touch the ground, the tendrils lash out like vipers, catching Yookulu in her snare. The god of seasons turns to ashes. It happens so quickly that I can barely trust my eyes. She's killed him.

Efiya yawns and stretches like a lazy cat playing with a mouse. She scans the field until she finds me and smiles. "Hello, sister. Did you miss me?"

I gasp, my voice a small croak. I look at Daho, but he won't meet my gaze. How could he . . . how could he release her? Rudjek is by my side in an instant, his shotels ready. "She's . . ." I glance at Efiya again, my whole body shaking. "She's . . ." I can't finish my thought.

"I know," Rudjek says somberly. "I know."

Koré howls a sound so horrible that it withers the grass beneath our feet. She drops the box and launches herself at Efiya with two daggers to fight at close range. But my sister dodges Koré's blows. Efiya tangles the moon orisha in scarlet tendrils of smoke and holds her suspended in the air like a rag doll.

"You bitch," Koré spits.

"It's nice to see you again, too, Koré," Efiya says. "You are a pesky little thing, aren't you? This time I'll make sure I finish what I started."

"Kill them," I hear one of the gods say.

Suddenly I'm whisked off my feet, and a scream tears from my lungs as the world spins around me. I'm hurtling toward the thicket of trees on the edge of the field—then I hear the sound of frantic wingbeats, glimpse a flash of silver. Daho knocks me clear. My face is on fire as I slam into something that yields on impact—not a tree. Rudjek. He's bent space to reach me in time. We collapse into a heap of arms and legs.

I'm delirious and confused, my head spinning. The orishas set a trap for Daho and my sister . . . my sister who is very much alive. My face feels like it's melting, and I can't see out of one eye. "We have to stop them from fighting."

"It's too late for that," Rudjek says, and the fear in his voice goes right through me.

The battle echoes around us as the rest of the orishas attack Daho. They rip and shred and tear and burn. He strikes back with swords as dark as obsidian. He isn't wielding the dagger. It must've fallen when he rushed to save me.

"We can't let this happen," I plead as Rudjek helps me to my feet.

He squeezes my arm. "Arrah, it was always going to be like this."

I don't believe that—things could've been different. But now, it's starting again. When Dimma comes back, she will wage war on her brethren. It'll be a never-ending cycle of death and revenge. When Dimma comes back, it'll mean that I'm . . . I'm dead.

Daho slashes Mouran's tail with one of his swords, severing it in two. The sea orisha shrieks, but Re'Mec uses the distraction to plunge his own sword into Daho's chest. Sisi, Essi, and Oma surround Daho, their magic pinning him in place. He falls to his knees.

"Why aren't you dead yet?" Efiya yells at the moon orisha.

"I should be asking the same of you," Koré says as her shadows strike Efiya.

"Ouch, that hurts," she pouts.

Fadyi and Jahla join the fight against my sister. Even from this distance, their anti-magic feels like a thousand bee stings. Efiya screams, but she doesn't let go of Koré. It's still not enough.

"Stay here," Rudjek says, pulling his shotels. He races to help Fadyi and Jahla. For the moment, it seems to be working. They're at a standstill, neither with an advantage.

"This time, I'll toss you into the Supreme Cataclysm myself," Re'Mec says as he and the other orishas weave strings of golden light around Daho. "This is a mercy, really—you deserve so much worse."

Shadows gather at the forest's edge, and a sense of dread aches in my bone. I don't have time to second-guess; I have to do something. I open myself to the bridge I forged when I traded my years for magic the first time. It feels like a lifetime ago, but I try anyway, even if I'm breaking my promise to myself. I glance up at the night sky, willing magic to answer my call, but nothing happens. There's no magic here—not like back home.

I scream, defeated, just as a demon with white wings speckled with brown spots steps from the gate. She sweeps across the field in a fiery rage, wielding a broadsword. I remember that her name is Evelyn—she is the daughter of one of Daho's advisers.

Evelyn stalks toward me, but before she's even halfway, Rudjek bends space again and his swords clash with hers. The force deflects her blade and sends her spinning, her white-and-brown wings a blur. She recovers, but he blocks her next blow and the next.

Behind Evelyn, Shezmu flies from the gate. I stumble back, remembering when he greedily ate the children's souls. This time he isn't a memory—he's here. Re'Mec peels away from the fight with Daho and lets out a vicious laugh. He attacks Shezmu, and the two of them scorch across the sky.

I search for Daho's dagger. If I can't call magic, it's the only way to put an end to my sister. I stumble through the battle. Perhaps the rest of them have forgotten about me for the time being, but it serves my purpose now. I see a glint of silver in the high grass and pick the dagger up. It hums against my hand, but I don't let it draw my soul inside. I know how to use it—I know that I can, though it will still kill me.

Evelyn slashes Rudjek across the chest, and he counters with quick thrusts, one to the shoulder and the other across her belly. "I can do this all night," Evelyn howls.

"Oh, good," Rudjek says. "I'm just getting started."

"Evelyn!" I yell. She turns to face me. "Don't!"

"You're Arrah," she says in a tone that makes it clear how little she thinks of me. She doesn't hide her contempt as she adds, "*You carry Dimma's soul?*"

"Yes."

Evelyn stares at the dagger in my hand, and her eyes narrow. Her disgust swells into hatred. "You would betray him after everything he's done to save Dimma? Everything we sacrificed for her?" She spits on the ground. "You're no better than the rest of your kind."

"I haven't betrayed him—I'm trying to help," I say, willing her to understand. "Take Daho and leave."

Evelyn looks as if she has something else to say, but she backs away and races to Daho. I'm relieved that she's listening to reason. She swings her sword and cuts the chains of light binding him. "I'm here, my king," she cries—and I don't miss the tenderness in her voice. Had it always been there, even before Dimma died?

Daho rises from the ground, his shoulders heaving. His skin is ghastly pale. He takes one step and stumbles. Evelyn grabs his arm to keep him from falling.

Efiya is hunched over, weakened from fighting Koré and the anti-magic. Shezmu shrugs off Re'Mec and sends him hurtling backward. Then he's at Efiya's side. "Come, daughter." He grabs her arm, but she resists.

"Let me go," she demands.

"No," Shezmu says, his voice a sharp note that leaves no room for argument.

Efiya glances around and, perhaps realizing they're outnumbered and losing, groans. She's not as strong as before. My sister isn't invincible. "I'll see you again soon," she tells Koré as though they are friends parting at the end of a celebration. "Perhaps for the last time."

Daho glances at the dagger in my hand, but he makes no move to take it from me. Instead, he heads for the gate, along with Evelyn, Shezmu, and Efiya. My sister glances over her shoulder at me before they disappear across the threshold. I am left grasping the dagger so tightly that my knuckles burn. They'll be back. That much I know.

This is the beginning of the end.

FIFTEEN
EFIYA

When Papa closes the gate behind us, I'm still giddy from the thrill of the fight. I almost laugh out loud, thinking about how Koré had wailed when I destroyed Yookulu's vessel and devoured his soul. Not the one I wanted, but he'll do for now. I catch a glimpse of Papa's face, and my mood sours. We should've stayed and finished off the orishas. I could have done it. He only wanted to retreat to save his friend.

I can't say that I was particularly pleased with Arrah's reaction to seeing me, either, after all this time. From the way she was gawking, you'd think I'd grown a wart on my face. After everything we've been through together, I expected better from her. I know I've messed up some things, but we're still sisters, and she should act like it. I can't put my finger on it, but somehow, she's different.

"Letting the girl keep your dagger is a mistake," Evelyn tells the Demon King.

"She needs it more than I," he says, winded. "Now the gods will think twice before attacking her again."

The Demon King is so sentimental, which, if you ask me, will be his downfall. He doesn't know my sister as well as he thinks. She'll turn the blade on both of us if it suits her mood. She can't be allowed to keep it. Maybe I can talk some sense into her before she does something she'll regret. "She seemed quite fine to me—just half of her face burned to a crisp," I mumble to myself. "She'll live."

We're in front of the palace, where Jasym and another dozen demons are standing, waiting for the fight we haven't brought back with us. They wouldn't leave Ilora without the Demon King's order.

"What happened?" Jasym asks their sister.

"Exactly what Efiya said would happen," Evelyn answers, projecting her voice. "The gods used the girl to strike at our king."

The Demon King says nothing as we stalk up the palace's steps. He ignores the outright whispers and stares. It feels nice that everyone knows that I was right—again. I'm always right.

"I'm not so sure the girl wasn't planning to use the dagger on one of us," Evelyn continues. "She's surely capable of it."

"I should know," I chime in grimly. "She's tried to kill me more than once."

I keep my eyes on Jasym's and the other demons' reactions. Their faces fall, their weariness giving way to resignation. Their doubts about Dimma are growing. Good. She doesn't deserve their love.

"Let's not jump to conclusions," Shezmu says, in a voice that's tempered and brimming with authority. It has a calming effect on everyone in earshot. I need to learn that trick. "Had Arrah wanted to turn against us, she could have made her move. But she didn't, and that counts for something. She carries our queen's soul. We mustn't forget that."

I scoff and quickly cover it with a cough. "I suppose."

"What are we going to do now that the gods have sent a message of their own?" Evelyn asks. "We cannot let this attack go unanswered."

"You can't expect us to keep hiding behind the gate," I add.

"Enough!" the Demon King snaps. "We do nothing until I say so." Done with the conversation, he strolls away with my father on his heels like a lapdog.

"You'd think he'd be more grateful that we saved his life," Evelyn grumbles.

I squeeze her shoulder gently as we step inside the palace. Evelyn was a lucky find—she is making this too easy. I leave her, Jasym, and the others, confident that they will spread the news of what transpired between the orishas and us. Then I retire to my chamber.

Since Papa forbade Tyrek from staying with me, he has his own rooms. I need to see him now, though. Who else will listen to how I single-handedly—well, *almost* single-handedly saved the Demon King and killed another orisha to boot? I tune my mind into the sounds of the palace and snort when I find him in the arboretum with a woman with long raven hair. Same old Tyrek: if there's a beautiful girl to catch his eye, he'll do his best to bed her.

"I was stripped of my titles for helping Efiya," he says, peeking under his lashes to see how his sob story is going over. "Beaten, tortured, imprisoned. I'm lucky I didn't die—another man probably would have. But I never gave up hope, you see."

The woman practically swoons. "Efiya was lucky to find a human not corrupted by the gods."

"That's very true, sadly. There are so few of us." He clears his throat. "Of course, one mustn't overlook the advantage of my convictions. I was the one who ordered the destruction of the orisha statues in the Almighty Kingdom. I did that on my own. Even when the odds were against me, I alone hid the dagger that held her soul from the gods so that she might be restored to her full glory."

I roll my eyes and leave them to it—no point in wasting my time with him. As soon as I close the doors to my salon, I'm seized with pain so sharp that I collapse against the wall. With the addition of Yookulu, the souls inside me are misbehaving again.

I stagger to my bedchamber but pause at the threshold. Something is amiss. Everything is the same, yet the room feels strangely hollow and cavernous.

I listen for a moment, but there is nothing to hear, so I step inside, and the space changes to a starry night. Shadows stir not far from me and come together to form the shape of a person.

"Who are you?" I demand, readying my magic to strike.

The shadows shudder and coalesce into—me, or rather, an exact mirror image. An altar shimmers into existence between us. Oshhe is lying on top of it, and Arti is standing over him. A soul—Shezmu's— twists as it moves to Oshhe's open mouth. Off to the side, Arrah cowers against a stone wall slicked with mildew.

The scene is the moment of my creation, and I have to admit it's a neat trick. "Ah, this is quite a surprise, Heka," I say. "Or should I call you Father and Mother?"

Arti looks up from the soul in her hands. "In your case, neither."

I scoff, not pleased to be corrected. "Why visit me now? What have I done to pique your interest after all this time?"

"The end is near," he answers in Arrah's voice.

"Maybe for you and the other gods," I say, "but I am just beginning."

Oshhe speaks next, but his mouth is the only thing that moves and not much. "The war, the pain, the suffering, the injustices, the revenge," he chants. "You are the key, Efiya."

I beam, taking his words to heart. I have always known that I was special. That I was meant for great things. My mother told me, but by then, I already knew. I was born knowing.

"You didn't come all this way to tell me that, did you?" I give him my most charming smile. "There's something more."

Through Arti's eyes, Heka gazes at my belly, where the souls twist and writhe inside, wanting to break free. He answers my question through her. "I'm here for the souls. I am their keeper."

"Their keeper?" I laugh. "What a thing to say. In what way?"

"They are my charge," Arrah says with a frown, like Heka is having a hard time explaining what he means.

I don't like how he talks in riddles, and I've grown tired of him already. "Too bad," I spit. "These souls belong to me. Go get your own."

It strikes me that when I'm done with the orishas, I will have to deal with him. I can't have him making demands of me and looking over my shoulder all the time. I have some of his power, but I want all of it.

"They will eventually kill you if you don't let them go," Arrah says.

"Ah, you've just answered a question that I have been pondering for months," I muse. "None of the other demons can release a soul once they consume it, but I can. Was that one of your gifts?"

"As I said, I am their keeper," Heka repeats through Oshhe.

"The Demon King ate many souls, including gods, and he's still alive. Come to think of it, why don't you take his souls? He probably doesn't need so many."

"Daho is of Dimma," Arrah says. "I cannot interfere."

"You can't interfere?" I repeat, raising an eyebrow. "Why is that?"

Arrah frowns as if it should be obvious, and I have to remind myself that it isn't my sister but Heka. "They are the beginning and the end, the constant in a story that must play to its conclusion. I am the watcher, the one who must bear witness."

"And why should you bear witness to what happens to them?" I ask. "What's it to you?"

"I am the petulant child," Oshhe answers. "The silent bystander."

Heka is more infuriating than the orishas and my sister combined. He's making no sense. "If it's all the same to you, I don't care how petulant you are," I say. "I will keep every single soul I've eaten."

Arrah glances at the altar, her eyes sad. "You will beg for my help before the end."

"I doubt that." I turn my back to Heka. "By the way, you're not so silent—you talk too much."

In the blink of an eye, I'm in my bedchamber again. The illusions and starry night are gone.

"Efiya?" Shezmu clears his throat from my salon. He's let himself in, which I find very annoying. Evelyn's right: I deserve more privacy. "Are you all right?"

I storm into the salon and find him standing idly beside a chaise. "Did you even bother to knock?"

"I did, but you didn't answer," he says. "I was worried about you."

I'm still thinking over the conversation with Heka. Who is he to ask me to give up my souls? They're mine—I defeated every single person I consumed. I've grown even stronger than the Demon King himself, and I won't let anyone control me again, not like my mother did. Those days are over. "I'm fine."

"Daho is asking for you." Shezmu frowns. He takes a step forward and hesitates. "Are you sure you're all right? You look unwell."

"I said I'm fine." I peer out the window. The eyesore of a sun is high in the sky, and I realize that it's been a full day since I came up to my rooms. I've lost a whole day. I grit my teeth. This is Heka's fault for wasting my time. "Shall we go?" I'm not especially happy to be beckoned like a servant. I need time to think more about my encounter with Heka. I don't know why he was really here, but I intend to find out.

The Demon King is waiting for us in the library in a high-back chair, looking worn and tired. He's robed in a white tunic. White is the color of mourning among the demons, but if you ask me, it's of questionable taste for him to be wearing it after I delivered such a victorious blow against the orishas.

Evelyn is perched on a windowsill. I'm sure she's been coddling the Demon King, waiting on him hand and foot.

"Leave us," the Demon King says, looking at no one in particular.

"Whatever you have to say to my daughter should be said in front of me," Shezmu tells him coldly.

The Demon King looks up in surprise. "Fair enough."

"I would like to stay as well." Evelyn gives me a sympathetic smile. "Efiya shouldn't have to face down the both of you without someone to support her."

"I *support* her all the time," Shezmu says indignantly. "I'm her father, in case you've forgotten." Still, neither of them tells her to leave.

The Demon King massages his forehead and comes to the point. "I forbade you to leave Ilora and you went against my wishes."

I pretend to be shocked and look at Papa and Evelyn to see if they, too, can believe this is why he asked to see me.

"Efiya is the only reason you're alive right now," Shezmu says. "She sensed something wrong and led us straight to you."

"You know better." The Demon King jerks his head around and stares at my father in disbelief. "The only way you could've found me that quickly is if Efiya knew where I was."

"We were lucky," Shezmu argues.

"Furthermore," the Demon King continues like my father hasn't spoken, his attention back to me, "I've heard rumors that you've been spreading doubt among my people of Dimma's loyalty to them."

Evelyn gives him a cutting look. She's outraged; bless her. "How could you make such an accusation against this girl?"

"I've done nothing of the sort!" I say, defending myself. In truth, I'm delighted that the news has made it back to his ears, but I do my best to appear wounded. It's not a natural look for me. "Why would I ever do such a thing?"

Daho's eyes gleam with fury. "You're lying."

"That's enough, brother," Shezmu snaps. Finally. "You have no right to talk to my daughter like that. She's been nothing but loyal to you, as have I."

"Efiya has never been loyal to anyone but herself," the Demon King remarks.

"This is ridiculous!" Evelyn's voice is shrill. "The gods almost imprisoned you again, and Efiya helped us save you. And now you have the nerve to accuse her of spreading doubt and being disloyal? Your concerns should rest with the one who carries Dimma's soul."

The Demon King frowns and shadows deepen the lines of his face. "You would say that, Evelyn, since you have been helping spread her lies."

"You really have lost all perspective . . . and over a girl you barely know," Evelyn spits. "You said it yourself; she isn't Dimma."

"I trust Arrah," the Demon King says as if that's the end of it.

Shezmu puts his arm around me, all too happy to play the caring father. "We've heard enough of this nonsense." He shakes his head in disgust. "You need to get your mind right, brother, before you lose the last people who truly care about you."

"*Get my mind right?*" the Demon King snaps, leaning forward in his chair. "You who ate the souls of children? I must live with that shame . . . that you would do something so despicable . . . for all eternity. Those children's deaths are on my conscious."

My father's arms drop limply to his sides. His wings quiver as he stares with hollow eyes at his friend. Shezmu is clinging to life by a thread. He's done a good job of hiding it, but I have known it for some time. I just haven't wanted to admit it. Magic burns across my skin, and it takes every ounce of self-control not to strike the Demon King down where he sits. Can't he see how much pain Shezmu is in—that he's suffering? He sees it all right, but he only cares about himself.

"I did it for you," Shezmu mumbles, pushing back a sob. "I'd do anything for you."

"I know, brother," the Demon King relents, "but I wish you hadn't."

Shezmu presses his lips together tightly and turns his face away. The Demon King doesn't deserve his loyalty or his friendship. I take my father's hand to pull him from the library, but I stop to glance at the Demon King one last time. He's slumped against his chair, looking quite miserable. It doesn't matter if he ever comes to his senses about the orishas or Arrah. After that little skirmish, we saw how weak he is. In fact, I'm beginning to think that we don't need him at all. He meets my eyes, and I smile.

SIXTEEN
ARRAH

I stand in the aftermath of the battle, still shaking and in shock. Rudjek keeps telling me that everything will be okay, but it won't. It'll never be okay, not with Efiya back. Daho, I could reason with, but my sister only wants to destroy everything in her path. She is fury and vengeance and chaos. My sister—who has done so many awful, unforgivable things—has been given a second chance, when in reality, she deserves to burn in a fiery pit for all eternity. Everything that I've done to stop her, it's all been for nothing. She'll come for me soon enough—I'm sure of it. She'll want revenge. I clutch the dagger so hard that it digs into my palm. She'll come, and I'll be ready.

As Re'Mec climbs from the broken tree trunks, bark and dirt fall away from his vessel. By the time he's taken two steps, the trees right themselves like giants rising from shallow graves. "That didn't go as well as we'd hoped," he grumbles. "It didn't go well at all, but it's only a minor setback."

"Efiya is free," Koré says as shadows peel away from her face. "I'd call that more than minor."

"The girl is vulnerable," says Mouran as he grows another barbed tail that whips around his feet.

"Something's wrong with her," says Essi. "I can smell it."

"She was still strong enough to take Yookulu," Koré snaps. For once, her hair isn't writhing; it's fallen still. "We've underestimated the situation."

"That *is* quite unfortunate," Re'Mec says. The usual arrogance and spite that weave between his words have melted away. His face looks at once too young and too old—a paradox inside a contradiction.

"We have the dagger," says a voice that comes from all around us that sets my teeth on edge. It's an orisha who hasn't taken physical form—and I'm not sure who it is. It's unsettling to know they're right there, and I can't see them. I haven't so quickly forgotten that one of Dimma's brethren attacked me.

"Give me the dagger, Arrah," Koré demands, thrusting out her hand.

I laugh, my voice a shriek in the night. My fear and exhaustion are giving way to hysteria. "No, and if any of you try to take it from me, I'll reap your soul with it myself."

"Ah, she shows her true nature," Re'Mec says, his smugness returned.

"Arrah is under my protection," Rudjek proclaims in a tone that makes me want to giggle, which is how I know I'm close to falling apart. "Leave her alone or deal with me."

Fadyi and Jahla stand in the mouth of the gate, their anti-magic keeping it from closing. "I suggest we have this conversation once we're safely back in Zöran," Fadyi says.

"Are you serious?" Re'Mec spits, ignoring Rudjek's guardian. "We haven't the time for games."

"No games," Rudjek says with an imperious smile. "You've done enough damage tonight."

"Let's not make another costly mistake," Koré says, resigned. "We shall talk again soon."

Re'Mec opens his mouth to protest but instead lets out an exaggerated sigh. One by one, the orishas disappear into the gate until only Rudjek, Fadyi, Jahla, and I are left in the field.

"I promise I didn't lead the orishas here," Rudjek confesses. "When Re'Mec told me of their plan, I came because of you."

Whatever our differences, I trust Rudjek, and I don't question his word now. I nod.

"We should go, too," he says.

I don't move—I can't. Exhaustion snaps what little strength I have left. Rudjek takes my hand, and I lean against his side, succumbing to the searing pain in my face.

Already his anti-magic is washing over me, healing my wounds. I want so badly to sleep, curl up in a ball and forget this night. I hold on to Rudjek as we step through the gate, back to Zöran. We follow the crossroads again to the camp. I take in the sight of the tents, but the stars seem to shift and blur before everything goes dark.

Then I sleep, but I find no rest, no solace waiting for me, only nightmares.

I dream of Daho on his knees in the grassy field. I see the orishas circling him, coming closer and closer, their expressions gleeful. I dream of him standing over my broken body, waiting for Dimma to emerge while Rudjek is holding me. I wake with my hand clutching the dagger, swaddled in cloth I tore from my tunic. I haven't let go of it all night.

I stare at the top of the tent, replaying what happened in the clearing. Koré would've put Daho back in her box. She would have imprisoned him for another five thousand years, ten thousand, for eternity.

Only a month ago, I would have betrayed him. Even now, I would gladly shove his soul in Koré's box myself if I thought it would save the people I love, but Efiya is the real threat. My mother had been right. My sister will destroy Zöran if we don't stop her.

I can't fathom why Daho would be foolish enough to release her from the dagger—unless all of his promises to me were lies. I was so quick to hope that he meant what he said about ending this war. But he had made his terms clear. As long as the orishas left him alone, he would not attack Zöran. We're so far beyond that now.

Rudjek comes into the tent with firewood. Essnai and Kira are curled up on a pallet under a mound of furs. I can only assume that Fadyi and Jahla are nearby. We're together again, watching each other's backs as we'd done for so many nights on the crossroads.

"Good, you're awake," he says. "I had to walk to the edge of camp to find wood. The tribal people have been less than friendly since our return."

"I supposed they've all heard that I'm not their *blessed one* anymore," I say, sarcasm lacing my words.

"Yes, courtesy of the chieftains." Rudjek stacks the wood on top of the pit of ashes. "They're not happy to hear about Efiya."

He stares at the wood, a beat too long. I don't pretend to understand what he's feeling right now, knowing that she's back. I might have my doubts about Daho, but Efiya is despicable, vile. She's done nothing but hurt people and will do it again if given the chance.

I clutch the hilt of the dagger so hard that it digs into my flesh. "I never had a choice." I remember the vision that Heka showed me so long ago of a mountain of broken bodies and raging rivers of blood. "This was always how it was supposed to end. Me against her."

Rudjek puts his hand on top of my mine. His touch is at once gentle, reassuring, and strong. "I don't believe that—you were given a second chance, Arrah. You can't just throw that away. . . . You know what will happen if you use the dagger. It'll kill you."

I meet his gaze. "Dimma is the lesser of two evils."

"Do you know that for sure?"

I inhale a breath, pondering his question. When I die, I will become a part of Dimma. I have to believe that despite everything, she'll be better than Efiya. But I don't know. "I hope."

"We'll find another way, okay?" Rudjek says.

"Okay," I recite, but my heart isn't in it.

Rudjek turns back to the wood, his brow furrowed like he's trying to figure out a complicated puzzle.

I tuck the dagger into the waist of my tunic. I'm conscious of it pressed against my body, all too aware of what hangs in the balance. I refuse to let it out of my sight, even for a moment. I have to be ready for when . . . when Efiya makes her move. "You don't know how to start a fire, do you?"

He gives me a sheepish shrug. "Not really."

"It used to be Majka or me if no one else was around." Kira sighs as she rolls onto her back and stretches. "When we were in the North, we had attendants who did all the domestic work."

I can only assume she'd heard our entire conversation, but she makes no mention of it.

"Don't need to drag my name through the mud, Kira," Rudjek mumbles through gritted teeth. "I'm putting my best effort into it."

Essnai groans as Kira climbs from their bedroll and takes a sachet of flint from her traveling sack. "How many times did I warn you that you need basic survival skills? Perhaps if you'd actually gone through military training, you'd know a thing or two that's useful."

Kira's ponytail has come undone, and her inky-black hair spills around her face. It takes her only a few moments to get the fire started while Rudjek crouches next to her, watching. She shoves the extra flint at him. "Think you can remember that?"

"Probably not," he muses. "I'm really only good for killing demons and defying gods."

This draws a chorus of groans from Kira, Essnai, and me.

"Quite the reputation you're building for yourself," Kira teases. "You make Oshin Omari look like a sloppy drunk."

"The real Oshin *was* a sloppy drunk," Rudjek confirms with a grin.

I'm grateful for the distraction, but I can't stop thinking about last night. "There are worse things one can be."

Rudjek clears his throat as he brushes wood dust from his hands. "I need to head back to the Kingdom soon. If the tribal people are determined to sit this one out, there's no reason for me to stay any longer."

"It's a mistake." Essnai sits up in her bedroll. "The Demon King might have agreed to leave them be, but I doubt we can expect the same from Efiya. He can't control her—no one can."

I had been so convinced that the tribal people had already taken too many losses. Abandoned by their god, driven from their homes, hunted down, and killed. There are so few of them left, none of them true witchdoctors. And maybe one day magic will be gone, too. But in my desperation, I had made the mistake of thinking there could be an easy answer. I trusted Daho, and he conveniently left out the part about releasing my sister from the dagger. "Efiya won't care about our deal—and after last night, I doubt even Daho will honor it."

"If it's all the same, we should plan to leave soon if you're up for traveling." Rudjek stares at me from across the fire. "When the Demon King and Efiya return, they'll want revenge against the orishas. It's not far-fetched to believe they'll strike at the heart of the Kingdom first."

He's right. Re'Mec has shown favor to the Almighty Kingdom for countless generations. The capital city, Tamar, is an homage to one of his names. Before the demons attacked, no other nation had stood against the Kingdom in nearly a hundred years because of his blessings.

Fadyi quietly slips into the tent. "The chieftains would like to speak with you, Arrah."

"Me?" I frown, surprised. I would've thought I'd be the last person they wanted to see. "For what reason, I wonder."

Fadyi shakes his head. "The messenger did not say."

I climb to my feet, still clutching the dagger. With the news about Efiya, maybe they're reconsidering their choice not to join the Kingdom. After last night, I'm not so sure it was the right decision either. "This should be interesting."

"I'll come with you," Rudjek says. "It wouldn't hurt to have my notorious charm in the mix."

Essnai yawns. "I will come, too—I would like to meet this new Aatiri chieftain. Semma and Nenii think very little of him."

I grimace, not particularly excited about seeing him again.

By midmorning, the three of us—Essnai, Rudjek, and I—are standing outside the chieftains' tent. Unlike before when we visited, warriors have been stationed around it. Some of them spit at their feet when their eyes land on me.

"I'm here to see the chieftains," I say, forcing my voice to stay strong.

"They asked to see you alone, *ben'ik*," says a Litho warrior, looking down his nose at me. "Though I'm sure it's a waste of their time."

Rudjek tenses beside me at the way the man throws around the word, but I only step closer. "This *ben'ik* is the key to saving your neck, so either let us pass or witness the consequences if you don't." It's an empty threat, but my words hit their mark.

The man looks at the other warriors, and one nods toward the tent. The Litho groans as he pulls back the curtains and enters. When he returns, he barks, "They will see you and the Aatiri. No outsiders."

"What a surprise," Rudjek murmurs. He leans in close to me. "I'll be listening, and if there's any sign of trouble . . ."

"I know," I said, smiling at him.

Inside the tent, the five chieftains sit on their pillows, their backs stiff, their faces stern. I have a feeling they have as much to say to me as I do to them.

"You're the reason the Demon King is free and Efiya is still alive," the Aatiri chieftain spits.

"She's also the reason none of you are dead," Essnai says in her calm way. "You'd do well to remember that."

"Do you still have the Demon King's favor?" the Mulani chieftain asks, nervously kneading her knuckles together. "Are the tribes safe?"

"No," I answer honestly.

The Zu chieftain scoffs. "You told us we'd be safe if we didn't fight."

"From the Demon King and his army, yes," I say. "The same doesn't apply to my sister."

"We should have never agreed to hide behind the crossroads to start with," says the Litho chieftain. "It's made us weak."

"You forget that the crossroads is all the protection most of us have," the Kes chieftain says.

I swallow hard, thinking about how Efiya had convinced the demons in Kefu to follow her. Daho doesn't know how persuasive she can be. She is a festering disease that will spread among his people. "Things are different now."

"You know firsthand what Efiya is capable of," Essnai says. "Do you trust that she will honor a deal between Arrah and the Demon King should she hunger for more souls?"

"No," the Kes chieftain says, furiously stroking his chin.

The Aatiri man nods at the dagger at my waist. "All is not lost. You have that."

I don't miss the desperation in his voice and how they're all staring at the blade. I place a hand over the hilt. "I plan to use it against my sister when the time comes."

"But not against the Demon King himself?" The Aatiri man laughs. "Of course not. You carry the soul of his *ama*."

"We'll come to the point, Arrah," the Litho chieftain says. "We want the dagger."

I shake my head. "It stays with me."

"You're under the impression that we're asking," the Aatiri man says as magic alights on his skin, and his eyes begin to glow.

I start to back away, but a force holds me in place. Essnai struggles beside me. I'd thought all of the chieftains were weak in magic, but I've misjudged them. Outside, I can hear a scuffle. The warriors must have attacked Rudjek.

"What are you doing?" the Zu chieftain asks, but the Litho blows dust in her face. She screams, her body twitching and contorting.

"You treacherous cowards," the Mulani chokes out before she and the Kes succumb to the same fate.

Essnai and I fight against the magic as the Aatiri and Zu chieftains rise to their feet. I strain to reach for the dagger, but it's no use. My fingers twist and bend in unnatural ways. The pain is excruciating.

The Litho chieftain smiles at me, and I think he's about to take the knife, but he yanks me by my arm instead. "You are the key to controlling the Demon King."

"Let me go!" I scream.

"Hush, child," he says. "When this is over, your soul will be bound to mine to do my bidding."

Essnai growls and lets out a slew of curses, but I am frozen in horror. The Litho chieftain means to turn me into a *ndzumbi* so he has control over the Demon King's dagger and Dimma's soul.

He kicks aside the cushion that he'd been perched on only a moment ago, revealing a trail of magic like the crossroads. One moment we're in the tent, and the next, he and the Aatiri are dragging me through a shady forest, where there's no one to hear my cries.

DAHO

There are moments when I retreat inside myself and savor the sweet memories of years long gone, but there are other times when I am adrift in a sea of nothingness, lost in my grief. I am becoming something I don't recognize, and I have no desire to fight the process. If I want to beat the gods, I must do it on their terms and play by their rules.

Once I find a way to appease the Collector's impulses, the pain from consuming his soul slowly dissipates. I don't have to kill to sate his appetite. He's left behind enough bones to build monuments for several lifetimes. With him, I have learned an important lesson about a god's nature. It cannot be denied.

The bones clank when I drop the sack on the floor in the throne room. The sound echoes against the marble walls, their eerie vibrations sweet music to my ears. I look up at the elevated throne where Dimma used to watch the sky, at the twin moons rising high above Jiiek, through a prism of reflected colors.

The moons are a constant reminder of our Divine Creator, Koré. Of her betrayal, her disregard for my people.

I select a femur from the sack. It has long ago transformed into a crystal with nearly translucent sapphire veins. It's beautiful—a true work of art.

It's taken much time on that wretched red world, sifting through piles of bones, to find the perfect ones for the new throne. I set about the work in the corner of the room. I've assembled an array of chisels, scalpels, and hammers. Though I'm clumsy at first, my hands soon remember how to carve and cut and file, like my father taught me when I was a boy.

I work without interruption for countless days—the passage of time measured only by the shifting shadows of the skylight. Evelyn stops by on occasion to bring me food and drink.

"Just because we don't need to eat, it doesn't mean we should stop indulging in that which brings us pleasure." She's holding a tray of strange fruit that only remind me that Ilora has been dying for a very long time. "Yacara and his men brought these back after their last forage through the gate."

"By all means, indulge," I say. I've built the throne seat and polished the skulls that will be its handrests. It's coming together nicely.

"Would you care to join me?" Evelyn asks pointedly. "I could use the company."

I turn my full attention to her, trying to be polite, but she's distracting me from my work. She wears a black silk gown peppered in pink rose petals. Her hair is braided in an elaborate style and her face powdered in rich colors. She's beautiful with or without the extra effort. "Another time."

She gives me a disappointed smile and takes her leave. I'd thought that she would have found someone else to occupy her time by now, but she is persistent.

My people do their best to pretend that we are something that we are not—many of them still live as if they're mortals. They eat and drink and celebrate. They build houses from material brought through the gate. They master instruments, hobbies, and languages long forgotten—anything to pass eternity. But I feel less and less the need to pretend.

They ask me when we will seek revenge against the gods, and I always say in due time. But I have already begun.

I almost miss Minister Godanya's shapeless form slithering along the wall near my head. He moves like a stray beast, always on the hunt for prey. He has come alone. He is the only one of the familiars I will speak with.

It's been many years since I sent him away to spy on the gods. I don't think of his people as endoyans anymore. They haven't been corporeal or even truly alive for a very long time.

"What news do you bring?" I ask as I polish the arch of the throne.

"I've been gone for more than two decades, and this is how you greet your old friend?" Godanya wheezes. "I, for one, haven't missed your moping around feeling sorry for yourself, but I see you have found a new way to spend your time."

The years have not made him any more tolerable. "Answer the question."

"Of course," Godanya says, picking up on my tone. "We have tracked down a hundred and fifty-two gods, although I suspect there are more hiding in the mouth of the Supreme Cataclysm. You'll recall we cannot go there because of your queen's curse."

"Stick to the facts."

"There are many worlds across the universe, most connected by the gate," Godanya says. He'll never give a short answer when a long one will do. "It seems that the gods use it to travel great distances, though some of them have shunned it all together. Many of the gods do not associate with each other, which gives you an advantage."

"Where are Koré and Re'Mec?" I ask, forcing him to the point.

"Re'Mec is napping in a cave. He and Koré had a falling-out after orchestrating the attack that killed your queen."

Godanya adds that last bit to strike at my heart, but I will not give him the satisfaction. "Where is the Divine Creator?" Saying her name out loud stirs the rage within me.

"Koré spends her days sulking in a volcano," Godanya says. "The gods are peculiar, aren't they? More like children sometimes."

"I take it that they're bored."

"I think they regret standing by while Eluua destroyed your people and Dimma destroyed mine." Godanya seems pleased with his analysis. "But I say to hell with their regrets."

I frown. "Hell? What is that?"

"Just a place that one of the gods made in their spare time," Godanya says. "I don't recommend visiting—it's quite dreadful."

"Find Yacara and Shezmu and give them a list of all the gods," I order him. I'm tired of having to sort through his nonsense. "Their names, their natures, where they spend their time. We'll consume the ones we find useful. The rest, I will reap with my dagger."

"Yes, *master*," Godanya says mockingly. "Most of them aren't as strong as the Twin Kings. They shouldn't give you too much trouble . . . in theory."

After all these years, I've grown tired of Godanya and the other familiars lurking in the shadows, but I'm not quite ready to release them from their eternal servitude. He and those like him helped Eluua kill my people while the rest of the endoyans fled to Zöran to move on with their lives. We were robbed of that chance. "Once we destroy the gods, I will grant you and the other your freedom."

"That is all we wish for," he says before slithering underneath the door.

Another day passes, and Yacara and Shezmu enter the throne room. Yacara carries a ledger and a pen. Shezmu looks at the mess around me.

"How long are you going to dwell in here like some hermit?" Shezmu demands. "You're beginning to grow mold on your face."

I rub my fingers along the bridge of my nose before realizing that he's joking. "I am almost finished," I tell him, looking up at my masterpiece floating above us. The bones shimmer in the shifting light. "The back could use a few more ribs."

Shezmu says nothing, and Yacara clears his throat. I know that they have been strategizing how best to get me out of this room.

I shave down the edge of another bone. "You think my pastime strange."

Shezmu rocks on his heels, considering the piles of bits and pieces of bone. "I don't understand this new obsession of yours, that's all."

"You will soon." I wonder how he and the others will handle consuming a god and their nature.

"Thanks to Godanya, we have valuable information about the

gods' whereabouts," Yacara interrupts. "We can target the most isolated ones first. With luck, the others will be caught unaware."

I can feel my pulse quickening in anticipation for the first time in ages. "You have my permission to start the hunt, but keep to the shadows," I tell them. "I do not want to tip off the Twin Kings. Leave Koré, Re'Mec, and Iben to me."

"I'll start sending out scouts today." Yacara bows and turns on his heels to leave.

Once Shezmu and I are alone, I say, "I need your help to kill Iben. He lives in the between-space, the void. If I am correct, he has the power to undo the past."

"It would be my honor to help you, brother," Shezmu says. "It's about time that you ask. I'm tired of taking on your royal responsibilities while you get to have all the fun."

I glare at him reprovingly. "I've spent months building a chair out of some poor bastard's bones. I'd hardly call that fun."

Shezmu narrows his eyes. "But . . . you must prefer it to presiding over ceremonies that none of us believe in anymore."

"True enough." I get up from my worktable and clasp his shoulder. I've missed him. "We'll go in a few days after I'm done with the throne."

Once Shezmu and I travel to the gate, we shed our vessels. We do not find the god of time the first night, the second, or the tenth. We don't find him on the hundredth or the thousandth. It takes a quarter of a century to track him down in the vast emptiness of the void, and when we finally stumble upon him, it's entirely by chance.

"I've seen this moment countless times," he tells us, folding himself into a writing shadow with a thousand appendages. "And yet I find I'm still fascinated by my end. Shall I tell you how this will go, or do you want to experience it for yourself?"

"We're not here to listen to your riddles," I say. "I have one question for you."

"You want to know if there is a way to walk the threads of time to save Dimma and your child," Iben says.

Of course he'd known what I would ask. He's seen this moment. I have to steady myself—afraid of what he'll say.

"Some things cannot be undone without destroying the fabric of the universe," Iben says. "To answer your question more directly, no. You can't undo the past, though you can influence it on occasion, as you will one day discover. Your time would be better spent making decisions that will shape the future."

His words wash over me in a fiery haze. In truth, I don't believe him—I can't. To believe him would mean that I've given up hope. I step closer to his writing shadow. "You're lying."

"I have no reason to lie," Iben says. "My death will be the most anticlimactic of all your kills. We will battle for a very long time until you get the best of me, then you will split my soul in two and consume it. You shall both control my gate."

Shezmu and I exchange a glance, not quite sure what to make of Iben. I do not know if we're walking into a trap, but it doesn't matter. I have committed to this path. I will see it through.

"Before we begin, I would like to show you a glimpse of what's to come," Iben says as the space around him shifts into images. "Both of you will see the exact same moment, but your perspectives will differ. Your future is not set in stone, so to speak, though I do not doubt that this future will come to pass. For at some point, the ties that bind you to each other will untether and your paths divert."

In all the years since that moment, I have never shared with Shezmu what Iben showed me, and he has never told me what he saw. Some things are best left unsaid. I convinced myself that the god of time had only wanted to divide us, but his premonition had been an omen of what would eventually be our downfall.

PART III

I am the custodian of souls.
I am their keeper, their protector.
Death isn't light or dark.
It is a prism.
Only when true death is obtained
will the story come to an end.
—Heka

SEVENTEEN
ARRAH

I twist my way free of the Litho chieftain's grasp, but I don't get far before his magic slams into my back and knocks the wind from my lungs. I fall facedown in the grass, heaving, the soil cool and bitter in my mouth. He's going to turn me into a *ndzumbi* to serve him for what few years I have left, and I don't even know his name.

"Are you really so eager to die today?" I spit, glaring at him and the Aatiri chieftain. I shove down my fear—they'd only use it to their advantage. "My friends won't let you get away with this. That's if the Demon King doesn't reap your souls first."

"You truly have no idea the gift you gave up when you let the chieftains' *kas* go," the Litho man snarls. "You could have had all of Zöran at your feet, but you threw it away."

"And did you think you and Semma could plan to tap into the orisha's magic without my knowing about it?" the Aatiri chieftain says next to him. "I found out about your plans—and took it upon myself to eliminate that option."

I stare up at his gaunt face in horror. "You wouldn't. . . ."

"Your coconspirator will live, but they can no longer help you."
The Aatiri pats the bag slung across his shoulder. "Thankfully, I
have everything needed to complete the ritual."

Magic winds around my wrists and ankles, keeping me pinned
firmly in place. "Do you think you'll be able to control the Demon
King's *ama*—a god? When I die, she will make you suffer for all
eternity."

The Litho pulls a dagger from his waist and cuts off one of my
braids. Sparks of magic alight on the hair and it shrivels in his palm
until there's nothing but ashes left. "But you won't die, child. If you
truly understood Töra Eké's gift, you would know that there is a way
to tie your *ka* to mine at the exact moment your body dies. You will
survive, and you will serve me."

I shrink in on myself. I'd thought he meant to make me a
ndzumbi, but what he intends is irreversible. He's planning to turn
me into an *akkaye*—the undying. This is so much worse. He'll have
Dimma's power at his fingertips. "You do this, and you risk your
own destruction along with the five tribes. Do you really want to
take that chance?"

"Whoever controls you controls the Demon King's dagger and
the Demon King himself," the Litho answers as if it should be obvious. "When you first suggested that we not join with the Almighty
Kingdom against the demons, I thought you a fool. You saw what
your demon witch sister did to the tribes, yet you expected us to sit
around and wait to be slaughtered again."

I glance toward the trees, hoping—no, praying—that Daho will
come. Can he sense the danger through our bond like before with
the *akkaye*? Or has he decided to leave me to my fate? "Do you truly

think such a petty act would sway a man who's dedicated his entire immortal life to revenge against the gods? I mean nothing to the Demon King."

The Aatiri chieftain mixes herbs and oil hastily and begins to crush them into a paste. He sets a fire, puts the bowl on it, and stirs.

The Litho man cuts his palm and adds his blood and the ashes from my hair to complete the blood medicine. "Don't you see, Arrah? You are the perfect solution to our problem. You can protect us against the demons and gods alike and give us magic beyond our wildest dreams. As for the Demon King, I'm willing to bet that he would do anything to keep his *ama* safe."

"You can stop staring at the forest, girl," the Aatiri says with a smirk. "No one is coming to save you. Only another *djeli* can follow the lines of the crossroads, and the only one left is a boy still in training. He will not be able to lead your friends to you in time."

The *djeli*: the keepers of stories. They could see the true path of the crossroads and not be tricked by the detours and traps. Yet, I had followed the crossroads just the same, even if not perfectly.

The Litho chieftain begins chanting in his native tongue, and I catch only snippets of words. He says my name, Arrah N'yar, and his own name, Kura Tajé. I laugh. He's not even an eké, a designation given to the head of his family. He's a tajé, a person of age without distinction.

"You're a pretender playing a game you don't understand," I taunt him. Maybe it's a mistake, but I have nothing else to lose. My anger and frustration boil to the surface, and with them, my bitterness, my pain, my need to strike back. "You're going to suffer a slow and painful death."

"So many empty threats," says the Aatiri. "You have no power. You gave that up."

I dig my nails into the dirt, wanting desperately to slap that smug look from his face. He is nothing like Grandmother. She would never participate in something so vile. "You're going to die with him."

In response, the Aatiri chieftain forces my mouth open and pours the blood medicine down my throat. I choke and try to spit it out, but in the end, I swallow. *Twenty-gods*, it burns like a raging firestorm. He passes the bowl to the Litho man, who tips it up to his lips. I feel the tug almost immediately, an untethering between my soul and body. This can't be happening, not after I survived my sister and the demons—not after I've lost so much.

Tears slip out of the corners of my eyes as I stare into the depths of the forest again, but there are no shifting shadows, no movement at all. Daho isn't coming to save me. I can't ponder what that means right now. Rudjek and my friends aren't coming, either. No one's coming.

"Argh," the Litho chieftain—Kura Tajé—groans through gritted teeth. "She's resisting."

"How is that possible?" the Aatiri man asks. "She has no magic."

"Give me your knife," Kura Tajé demands. "Let me try scrivener magic."

My body convulses, and I'm on the verge of passing out. Sharp pains shoot up from the tips of my fingers and my toes. They travel through my chest and legs and gather in my belly. I do not know how they think I'm resisting when it feels like I'm being ripped apart at the seams.

Kura Tajé pushes up my tunic to expose my belly, and then he wastes no time carving a serpent into my flesh as my mother had done so long ago. I scream in rage. I would rather die and let the world burn than do someone else's bidding again. Some part of me realizes that this is justice for what I did to the assassin on the Barat Mountains when I stole away his will and bound him to me.

Sweat beads on Kura Tajé's forehead. It streaks in his eyes. Smoke rises from his skin where more magic alights. He's struggling to complete the ritual. Even though I might be on the verge of becoming some twisted monstrosity, I feel vindicated that I hadn't misjudged him and the other chieftains. Only the most powerful witchdoctors can make a *ndzumbi* or an *akkaye*, and he is weak. I want to taunt him again, but there's too much pain. I am slowly coming undone.

When he's finished carving the serpent, magic clings to the wound, burning into my flesh. Kura Tajé leans over me, his black eyes glowing with light. "You belong to me, Arrah N'yar."

Again, I think of the *akkaye* we encountered on the crossroads and the one who had pinned me against the ground, its gray face staring down at me, looking curious and confused. *Confused.* It'd sensed Töra Eké had once been a part of me. I'd used that connection to send the *akkaye* away.

Could I use it to bring them back?

"I belong to no one," I bark as I concentrate on the *akkaye*.

Come to me. At first, I only say it in my mind, but my pleas quickly grow more desperate. "Come to me!" I scream, and the Litho and Aatiri men both startle. "Come . . . to . . . me!"

I taste blood in my mouth. It permeates the air, burns my nose.

Something snaps inside me, and Kura Tajé staggers. The magic fades from his eyes.

"What's wrong?" the Aatiri asks, looking back and forth between us.

Kura Tajé doesn't answer as he backs away, but it's too late. I can feel the *akkaye* stirring in the forest, their creaking bones, the twitching of their appendages, their low hisses. The sounds are so sweet.

"No," Kura Tajé moans, shaking his head.

The hold he has over me breaks as the first of the *akkaye* appear at the edges of the trees. They lumber forward—their murderous eyes fixed on the chieftains.

I heave in a breath and pull myself to my feet, clutching the wound on my belly. "I believe I promised you a slow and painful death," I say. "It's time for me to make good on it." Rage consumes me as I beckon the *akkaye* forward. "Take them."

The *akkaye* descend upon the chieftains, their claws and appendages snapping at them. I raise one hand, tempering my fury, barely. "I should kill you where you stand," I say. "But you deserve to face the people you betrayed."

"How are you controlling the *akkaye*?" Kura Tajé grumbles, aghast. "They belong to Töra Eké, and he is no longer with you."

"Ironic, isn't it? That this *ben'ik*, with no real magic to speak of, still outwitted you." I break into a cold smile. "Now take us back to the camp, or I'll have the *akkaye* shred you into little pieces." This time my threat isn't empty. I mean every word of it. When the Aatiri chieftain resists, one of the *akkaye* sinks its teeth into his shoulder and leaves behind a gaping, bloody mess. He screams. "Do try something else if you are so bold."

Kura Tajé curses and spits on the ground, but he leads us to the trail. I command the *akkaye* to stand down, except for the two guarding the chieftains. We march through the crossroads and land in what was once the chieftains' tent, but it's nothing but rubble now. I dig my nails into my palms, imagining the fight that went on here after we left. Some two dozen warriors lay sprawled out, moaning and tending their wounds. I'm relieved when I see Rudjek and our friends standing on the edge of a gathering crowd with my cousins and the boy we saw when we first found the camp. He must be the young *djeli* the Aatiri chieftain spoke of.

They all startle at our sudden arrival. Rudjek lets out a sharp whistle. "You are full of surprises, aren't you?"

I wish I had something clever to say, but I'm bone-tired, and there's still the matter of what to do with the two treacherous chieftains. Some part of me wants the *akkaye to* kill them, but I don't need any more blood on my hands.

EIGHTEEN
ARRAH

I want nothing more than to rest, but the Zu, Kes, and Mulani chieftains insist upon immediately handing down judgment against Kura Tajé and Etoiine, the Aatiri chieftain. As the afternoon gives way to early evening, they set a public trial in the spot where their tent had once been. People from across the island gather, firelight flickering from their torches. It's begun to snow, and the children run in circles to catch it. Despite everything, I smile. There is still hope in the world; even if it's a fleeting flame, it still burns bright against the dark hour.

Magic dances among the people, flirting with some but ignoring most. It reminds me of when I was a girl at Imebyé when my father knelt to put a string of teeth around my neck. He was proud of me, even when my magic never came. *Be still, Little Priestess.* After all these years, his words never cease to make my heart sing and ache. I miss him so much, and not a day goes by that I don't wish he was here.

"Fadyi and Jahla think this island is close to Siihi," Rudjek says, making small talk.

"That explains why it's snowing if we're that far south," I say absently as a series of chimes rings. Warriors push Kura Tajé and Etoiine through the crowd. The chieftains' hands are bound and their feet shackled in chains of braided magic. People spit and curse at them.

Only a few days ago, the relations between the five tribes had been fraught with mistrust, most people keeping to their own tribe. Tonight they've put aside their differences, even if only for a short time, like they did when my friends and I first arrived.

When the warriors force Kura Tajé and Etoiine onto their knees in front of the Mulani, Zu, and Kes chieftains, the crowd falls silent. It isn't all at once, rather a rippling effect that travels across the valley like a wave.

"Many generations ago, our people were at war with each other," says the Mulani chieftain, projecting her voice. "We killed one another over petty differences, border disputes, and limited resources. Then Heka appeared in the night sky and gave the five tribes a new purpose. His gift of magic united us but not at first. In the beginning, we committed horrible crimes against each other. Only when the chieftains came together to set aside our differences did our people begin to heal."

"And with that momentous first meeting between the chieftains came rules that govern how we use magic, which have stood the test of time," continues the Zu woman next to her.

"We are here tonight to hand down a swift punishment that fits the severity of the crime," adds the Kes chieftain. "Kura Tajé and Etoiine have broken one of our most sacred laws."

"Where did the *akkaye* come from?" someone asks from the

crowd. "We saw the girl control them. Is that not a crime now?"

The tribal people stare at me, but this time I'm ready for the unwanted attention. I do not shrink under their gazes that range from suspicious to hostile to hopeful. Essnai meets my eye. She was there when I turned the assassin into a *ndzumbi* on the Barat Mountains months ago. She subtly taps a finger against her lips as if to encourage me not to bring up long-buried secrets. "Töra Eké made the *akkaye*," I say reluctantly. "Since his *ka* once resided within me, I can command them."

"Lies!" someone hisses as the crowd descends into argument.

"The former chieftains sanctioned it," the Zu leader says, raising her hand to calm the murmurs. "Only a few people knew. The warriors were all on the verge of death and volunteered to be transformed to protect us."

Töra Eké's soul was with me only briefly, and he struck me as a man with an affinity for death and what lies in the afterlife. I shied away from exploring his memories too deeply for that reason, but I feel a shred of relief that he hadn't done this desperate act against the warriors' wishes.

"We must focus on the matter at hand," the Mulani chieftain says, redirecting the conversation. "Kura Tajé and Etoiine must be punished. Who will speak for their tribes?" She searches face after face to no avail.

"You should do it," Nenii coaxes her sister.

Semma begins to shake her head, but others add their voices of support. I beam at my cousin. She reminds me a lot of Grandmother. I do not doubt that she would be just in her decision. After much encouragement, she walks forward, her head held high. "I will speak for Aatiri."

Several people from Tribe Litho start to argue over who should represent them until finally a decision is made.

As the trial starts, I lose the stomach to see it through. I'd been so desperate to find the tribal people that I hadn't considered how *desperate* some of them would be. I make no excuses for what the chieftains did, but I understand how fear can lead people to make awful choices.

"I'm going back to the tent to rest," I tell Rudjek.

"Can you wait until after the trial . . . ? You shouldn't go alone," he says. "The Mulani chieftain asked Fadyi, Jahla, and me to stay nearby in case anyone attempts to use their magic to help the Aatiri and Litho chieftains."

He's worried about Efiya—so am I, but I'm sick of living in fear. My sister will come for me either way, and the truth is, it would be best if I'm alone. I pat the dagger beneath my tunic. "I'm not as helpless as I look."

Rudjek quirks an eyebrow, but he doesn't insist. "Of that, I'm sure."

I squeeze his shoulder and set off for our tent. It's been a full day since the orishas ambushed Daho and he escaped with Efiya through the gate. Twenty-gods. He knows as well as I do what she's capable of. In all his talks of peace, he conveniently never mentioned that he released my sister. To think that I was starting to trust him.

I'm at the edge of the Aatiri camp when sparks of magic gather on the path before me. Dread almost brings me to my knees as they merge into a bright light. I sense her presence before her face comes into focus like the sting of a thousand bees. I figured she'd come sooner rather than later, though perhaps not this quickly.

Efiya bursts into laughter, pure joy, as she gazes upon me. "I've missed you, sister."

She steps forward, and I stumble back, my legs stiff. A croak rises in my throat, but I don't know what it is I want to say. My sister is here . . . my worst nightmare come true. We are alone. That's a small blessing. I don't want her to hurt anyone else.

"Well, say something." Efiya catches snow on her fingertips. "Aren't you glad to see me?"

"You shouldn't be here," I snap, realizing how wholly inadequate my words are.

"You sound like *him*," she whines. "Always telling me what I should and shouldn't do."

Her voice is full of contempt. I don't know if she's talking about Daho or Shezmu, but I don't bother asking. I can't trust anything she says. She steps closer, her movements timid and unsure. This time I hold my ground and ease my hand underneath my tunic to find the hilt of the dagger. But before I can retrieve the blade, she dashes forward and throws herself against me in an embrace.

"We've made so many mistakes, sister." She sobs on my shoulder. "We have to make things right between us. Come with me—we can leave it all behind. We can start again."

I am speechless as I stand with my arms at my sides, a shiver wracking through my body. I want to yell at her and say, *You're the one who made mistakes*, but I close my eyes. I let myself forget the past, if only for this moment. Under different circumstances, we could've been good to each other. We would've spent afternoons in our father's shop sipping tea and crushing herbs. Or she'd help him make blood medicine to heal the sick. Perhaps she'd paint dancers on the wall at home with our mother. But none of these things will ever come to be. I can't forget that she turned children into *ndzumbi* and all the people she hurt. Yet I can't bring myself to unsheathe the dagger, not while she's holding me like this. I hate myself for it.

I pull away, coming to my senses. "Why are you here, Efiya? I want the truth."

"For you, sister," she says with a sigh. She stares at the tents lining the valley, her bottom lip quivering. "I have come to realize that all the pain and suffering we've both endured are because of the gods. Mother always said they were a plague, and she was right."

I back away from her in disbelief. She's serious. "You can't blame the gods for what you did to the tribes," I spit. "What you did to the Kingdom, to our parents, to Rudjek." My voice falters.

Efiya meets my gaze again, and her eyes are glassy with tears. "As I said, I have made some mistakes," she mumbles. "But I am not mistaken about the orishas. There can only be one god, Arrah."

"And who would that be?" I already know her answer.

"I'm the only suitable choice." She squints at me and wrinkles her nose. "You don't have the chieftains' magic anymore. I thought I sensed something different about you. That's why the Demon King forbade me from coming back to Zöran—not that he could ever stop me. He was afraid that you couldn't protect yourself."

I grab the dagger, and my hand freezes on the hilt. Efiya's eyes are sad as her magic seizes me in place. "I'll take that," she says. "I need it."

"No," I hiss, but I can't break free of her hold.

When she reaches for the dagger, an *akkaye* steps out of the shadows and sweeps its claws across her chest. The cuts are deep enough to kill any normal person, but Efiya only stumbles, clutching her wounds. She looks between the *akkaye* and me, her face twisted in shock. More of *the undying* appear in the shadows, surrounding us. I may not have magic anymore, but I have them.

"You would dare attack me," Efiya says through tears. "After I offered you my heart." She kneads her knuckles into her temples as if she's trying to sort something out.

I expect her to retaliate, but she seems unsure of herself again as the wounds across her chest slowly heal. I remember what Essi, the sky god, said in the field. *Something's wrong with her. I can smell it.*

My sister's emerald eyes change into liquid fire as she backs away. She takes one step, two, then pauses. "I'll be seeing you again, Arrah, and next time it won't be so pleasant. Remember that I tried to make it right between us." Her magic finally releases me, and on the third step, she disappears.

Efiya doesn't just want the orishas dead. She wants to play another game, but this time there will be no more mistakes. This time, one of us will meet our final death.

NINETEEN
EFIYA

I should have known that my sister would be unreasonable. And people say that I'm the spoiled one. Would it be so much for her to give up the Demon King's dagger? Maybe she could have wielded such immense power when she possessed the chieftains' souls, but now she should know her place. Foolish, foolish girl. Did she believe I would let her send me back to that cold, dark prison? Perhaps I'm the fool for thinking that she would come with me, that we could be on the same side for once in our lives.

So be it. I shove down my tears as I leave my sister with those dreadful creatures lurking in the shadows around her. She really ought to be more careful about the company she's keeping these days. I can accept it if Arrah wants nothing to do with me, but she still wants me dead. To think that I was going to spare her life.

I am in two places once again. Here in Zöran, drifting on the wind between the tents, and with Shezmu, visiting a world ripe with forests so lush that the underbelly is dark and damp. As we walk through thickets of vines, listening to birdsong, he calls this place *paradise.* I run my hand across tree bark, letting my fingers dip into the ridges and grooves, reveling in its texture. A spider crawls on my arm, its legs delightfully tickling my skin.

I laugh, and Papa smiles at me. "We could stay," he says quietly. "Spend our days exploring the secrets of the forest. There must be hundreds of different animals here."

"Thousands," I correct him. I can hear them all, their beautiful chorus. They watch from the tops of trees, behind leaves and bushes, from the shadows. They want to come to me, but I won't let them. I cannot lose myself in the desire to play with them when I have so many concerns to occupy my mind. Besides, I only have this urge because of Fayouma's soul. She *was* the mother of beast and fowl after all.

As Papa and I continue our stroll, I wince at the pain in my belly. This time it's dull and rolls through me in waves. It's different from when the souls are protesting. I turn my attention back to the camp with the tribal people, my sister, and . . . Rudjek. I materialize in the shadows near a crowd.

I peer across shoulders to see what the fuss is about. Two men are on their knees. Rudjek stands nearby with his arms crossed. He's with Essnai, Kira, and the cravens. It's strange to see them all again. Well, not all. I killed the craven twins quite some time ago at Heka's Temple. Tyrek had another one killed. I tried to kill Sukar, but Arrah did that on her own. Shezmu killed Rudjek's friend Majka. I don't even know some of their names—not that it matters. It's a pity that they got in the way.

A woman with an elaborate headpiece announces, "For your crimes, we have ruled that you, Kura Tajé and Etoiine, will be stripped of your place in your tribe and spend the rest of your lives in exile."

I wonder what they did, but in truth, I don't really care. Suddenly Rudjek moves his hands to the hilts of his swords. He glances around the crowd, his face panicked. I remember that look. It's the same one that haunts my dreams. I back away; it's time to go.

I stumble to the edge of the camp, where a boy is sitting in front of the crossroads that the tribes made to hide from my army—my army that the Demon King destroyed. Several of the souls inside me explode in fury, ripping at my mind. The pain is so intense that I am forced to keep moving.

"Stop it," I hiss when I'm clear of the valley. "I wasn't going to hurt the child."

The souls inside me can't speak, but when they are in agreement, their emotions are strong enough for me to sense. They are afraid that I will do something horrible. I don't have the best track record, to be fair, but how was I to know the demons would kill the children when I sent them after the tribes? I didn't mean for that to happen, but as usual, it doesn't matter what I intended. My sister will never believe me.

I have a prickle of awareness, a single beat of a moth's wing against my soul, before something plunges into my back and pierces through to my chest. I scream, but the sound I make is only a whimper. In my agony, one of the souls claws its way out of my mouth and dissipates before my eyes. I collapse to the ground.

Rudjek stands over me. He's holding one of his swords, the blade red with my blood. His eyes are black pools of tar filled with contempt, rage, and pure hate.

"What have you done with Arrah?" His voice cuts me deeper than his blade as his anti-magic assaults my body. My skin begins to flake away. He's trying to unravel my soul and shred me into so many tiny pieces that I can't come back.

Too late, I realize that splitting myself across two places has weakened me. I hold up my hands in submission. "Wait," I plead.

"Where is Arrah?" he demands again.

"I only saw her briefly," I wheeze around my punctured lungs and crushed windpipe. "She's . . . quite fine."

Rudjek is visibly relieved by the news, but he looks skeptical. "Why have you come?"

I'm appalled that he even has to ask. "To see my sister, of course."

His anti-magic is working quickly, and it's hard to keep myself together. My consciousness shifts back to the forest where I'm with my father. I'm leaning against a tree that smells like sweet perfume and heaving in gulps of air.

Shezmu hovers nearby, protectively. "What's wrong, daughter?"

His eyes are filled with worry and fear. He loves me despite my flaws and my mistakes. I wonder what things would be like if he'd been looking out for me in the beginning like he does now. Would my life be better? I bite down my pain and smile for him. "I'm fine, Papa," I say brightly. "I'm just a bit tired. Can you open the gate so we can go home?"

I need to reunite my two halves to have my full strength to fight the anti-magic.

Back on Zöran, now that I'm face-to-face with Rudjek, I find myself lost for words. "I meant what I said before at Heka's Temple. I don't expect you to believe me, and I don't deserve your mercy."

"Nor will you get it, you conniving bitch," he spits.

Emotions that I don't recognize crowd in on me, making it hard to breathe. If I let them, they will be the death of me. I remember Tyrek's words, whispered in my ear. *If you want to hurt your sister, make him love you. I'll show you how.* He laughed when I told him that it didn't work, that Rudjek hated me. I have no one to blame but myself. I won't be anyone else's pawn ever again. Not the Demon King's nor the gods'. Certainly not Tyrek's.

"I am sorry, Rudjek." That will be my final word about it. I have nothing else to give.

He only laughs. It's a cold, spiteful laugh. I deserve worse, but before his anti-magic gets the best of me, I move away from him, drawn to the gate that Shezmu has opened again. I don't have the stomach to stay and talk to Rudjek any longer, and I must get back before my father realizes I've snuck off to Zöran again.

I enter the gate in two places: Zöran and the forest in another world with Papa. When we return to Ilora, I am whole again. One person. "Why do you insist upon defying Daho's order, daughter?" Shezmu asks. "Do you think I didn't know that you've been splitting your soul?"

I blink up at my father, peering into his knowing eyes. He has that way about him like he can see right through me. And here I thought I'd been fooling him all along.

I sink against his chest and listen to the steady beat of his heart. For the first time, I think just maybe someone understands me. I look down at the seedlings I've brought back through the gate from the forest world. "I should go plant these in the arboretum."

"Efiya," he says, not letting me off the hook that easily. He's using his stern voice now.

I pull away from him and cross my arms. "It's not fair. He shouldn't tell us what to do."

"I don't always agree with Daho's methods." He glances away. "But he wants what's best for us."

"He wants what's best for him and Dimma."

Shezmu lets out a tired sigh, knowing that I'm right. I leave him with those words to think about and find Evelyn walking barefoot in the garden. She wears a long gown of the finest silk that seems to trail in her wake, but it's only a trick of the eye. Magic weaved into fabric.

"Why keep this place alive when everything else has gone to waste?" I ask her. I'm torn between loving every moment I spend in the arboretum and hating that I have a compulsion to come here because of Ugeniou's soul inside me. "Why don't you and the others pool your magic so you can heal the rest of Ilora?"

"Do you think we haven't tried?" Evelyn looks across the balcony at the forest of bare trees and the ashes stirring around their dead roots. "The gods were thorough. I will give them that."

My rage rises again—my truest friend and my most useful tool. I can help the demon people. I can make things right. "We don't have to live here," I point out. "We could leave, find a new world, make a better home."

"When *our king* sees fit for us to leave, then we will," she says sarcastically.

Mother once told me that I make messes purely for the joy of wreaking havoc. It was the thing that exasperated her the most about me. But she never understood how confined I felt by all her rules, her requirements, her demands. "Why should he get to decide when we can come and go?" I say now. "We do not have to suffer at the hands of the terrible gods anymore. We're stronger than them."

Evelyn inhales a deep breath, her wings adjusting ever so slightly. "I don't like the way he treats you," she says thoughtfully. "And what he said to Shezmu was uncalled for. We've all done things we're not proud of to survive. He forgets that for a very long time after the gods destroyed our lands, Shezmu gave us hope. Your father helped us find some semblance of a life while Daho was mourning his queen. It . . . it wasn't like we weren't all mourning. Jasym and I lost our entire family when Eluua and the endoyans attacked Jiiek."

I'm relieved that Evelyn finally sees the truth: the Demon King is ungrateful and selfish. I'm confident that she'll help me convince the others that he isn't worthy of their loyalty. "I could have guessed as much about Papa—he would do anything to protect us."

I wince at a sudden dull pain in my belly and fold an arm around my waist. Evelyn frowns at me, then her gaze drifts down. She gasps with wide eyes. I look, too, and see blood staining my sheath. It's trickling from between my legs. "What's wrong with me?"

Evelyn clasps a hand over her mouth. "Is this the first time?"

"Is what the first time?" I ask, confused. "What does this mean?"

"Oh, Efiya," Evelyn says, tears in her eyes. "You do not have our curse."

I bite down the fear wrapping around my throat. "I don't understand."

"Don't you see? This means that, one day, you might bear children of your own if you like."

"That's what this is?" I look down at myself again, aghast.

She goes on to tell me about the blood cycle. The details are fascinating. Even though Evelyn and I have become friends, I wish that I was hearing about this from my sister. It should be her place to explain these things to me. "Do you want a child?" I ask Evelyn, sensing a deep yearning in her.

Her hand goes to her belly, her eyes hollow. "It does not matter what I want."

I already know the story behind her words—how Dimma's gift cursed the demons. They can't have children. That is something that even I can't fix. I smile at her and show her the seedlings. We can plant them together. Of course, Evelyn will never replace my sister, but I find myself enjoying her company. I feel less alone when I'm with her.

TWENTY
ARRAH

I pace back and forth inside the tent, waiting for Efiya. I know my sister, and she would not give up so easily. If she wants the dagger, she will take it from me, even if it means prying it from my dead body. I'm clutching the hilt tightly, but it brings me no solace. There is no peace to be had for me. I've accepted that.

When I hear shuffling outside, I crouch, ready. Rudjek bursts into the tent with both his shotels out. Blood drips from one of them. I stare at him, my heart racing. He answers my unasked question.

"Efiya," he says with a deep sigh.

"Did she hurt you?"

"No." Rudjek shakes his head, grimacing. "Are you okay?"

I bite back the anger building inside me. "She tried to take the dagger. If not for the *akkaye*, she would have."

"Do you need further convincing that she and the Demon King plan to attack Zöran?" Rudjek asks, frustrated. "You can't still believe his lies."

"I don't know what I believe," I say, annoyed at myself for not trapping my sister when I had the chance. "Daho wouldn't have sent Efiya to retrieve his dagger—that much I know is true. And you saw how he hesitated after the orishas ambushed us. He could have let me die to bring Dimma back."

"I supposed he saved you out of some twisted sense of honor. He is the reason—" Rudjek shifts on his heels. "He's the reason you lost your family."

"Maybe," I say reluctantly, but immediately regret it. I don't really know Daho—only the stories that stand in stark contrast to Dimma's memories. But that isn't true, either. Dimma has her history with him, and I have mine. I frown, pushing the thoughts away. "Essi was right about Efiya—she's weaker than before. I don't know how or why, but we have to use that to our advantage."

"We're in agreement on that point," Rudjek says with a scowl. He sheaths his swords. "I never told you what she said to me on the battlefield at Heka's Temple."

I glance down now, afraid to hear his words, but I force myself to meet his eyes again. He deserves my full attention, no matter how much shame I might feel.

"She said that she thought I would love her—that he told her that I would. At the time, I thought she meant the Demon King, but now, I'm thinking it must have been my cousin, Tyrek. He's always been cruel, even when we were children." Rudjek pauses, tucking his thumbs in and out of his sword belt. "She went on to tell me that she'd make a mistake, that if she could live her life again, she would run away with you."

I don't know how to take any of this news. My first impulse is to dismiss what she told him. She'd say anything to make herself look innocent when she is the greatest monster the world has ever known. But Efiya *had* asked me to run away with her tonight as if we could pretend that nothing has ever happened between us. "That's . . . a lot to process," I say, unsure of myself.

"Yeah," Rudjek agrees. I know now why it's taken him so long to tell me. "We should leave first thing in the morning."

Now that the Aatiri chieftain has destroyed my only hope for tapping into Dimma's magic, I have no reason to stay. Efiya wants the dagger; if I leave, she'll forget about the tribes—at least for now, I hope. I nod my agreement.

Semma announces herself outside the tent. "Come," I say.

My cousin is still wearing the green-and-purple kaftan from earlier, and her eyes are bloodshot. I wonder if she's here to deliver some bad news. I don't think I can take any more of that tonight. She looks at me, her brows set in a deep frown. "There was a meeting after the trial—and the elders have asked me to speak for our tribe. I . . . I've been chosen as the new Aatiri chieftain."

I read the uncertainty and doubt on Semma's face. She's so young—only a year older than me, but she's one of the few left with formidable magic in the tribe. The Mulani may have chosen a chieftain without magic, but the Aatiri never would. "Is this something you want?"

"I don't know, but I'll do my best," Semma says quietly.

"You will lead with a steady hand," I reassure her.

Rudjek cuts his eyes at me. Chills creep down my spine. We have to tell her about my sister.

Semma frowns, studying my face. "What is it, cousin?"

I bite back my nerves. "It's Efiya. . . . She was here tonight."

"I see," Semma says, calmer than anyone has a right to be. "So we have no protection at all now?" She groans and her hard exterior shatters. I see the fear in her eyes. "Not even behind the crossroads?"

I shake my head, and it takes a moment too long to gather my courage to speak again. "I'm sorry." I'm sorry for so many things.

"The tribes will be stronger if you join us," Rudjek interjects. He hasn't given up. I knew that he wouldn't. "My father has made some mistakes, but I promise you, after we defeat the demons, I will stop him if he tries to take your lands."

Rudjek means well, but he's too much of an idealist and he's over-confident. He has no doubt that we can win a war against Daho and Efiya, but I have enough doubts for the both of us. As for his father, Suran will never be reasonable, no matter what Rudjek thinks. "The *akkaye* will protect the tribal people against all threats, demons or otherwise, whether you remain here or return to your lands," I say, grateful for that small grace. "Though it's still worth considering his offer."

"We will think on it," Semma says, then she hugs me tightly. "I'm sorry we couldn't help you, either." There is finality in her words as if she already knows we will never see each other again.

During the first days of our journey home, nobody talks much. I'd been so happy to find the tribes, but nothing had gone as expected. I was sure the tribes should stay out of the fight with the demons. I was wrong about that. In the end, neither Rudjek nor I got what we wanted. He didn't get the chieftains to agree to help. I didn't get Dimma's magic. By unspoken agreement, we don't mention our abrupt departure. Outside of my last conversation with Semma, there were no real goodbyes.

On the fourth day, after climbing a steep, rocky path that seems as though it goes on forever, we crest the top and find ourselves at the edge of a pristine mountain lake, the placid blue of the sky. Its surface is as smooth as glass until a fish jumps, sending ripples across the surface.

Kira and Essnai swim in the cold water, shrieking and splashing, while Rudjek and the cravens fish for our dinner on the far end. I sit on a bluff overlooking the scene, watching as my friends let their guards down for the first time I can remember in a long while.

"This is how your life should've been," I hear myself whisper, only the words aren't mine.

Ribbons of white light drift around me like tendrils of smoke. I'm still overlooking the lake, watching my friends, but it feels as if I'm far away. The ribbons reshape themselves into people. Rudjek, Sukar, Efiya, and me. "Heka," I breathe, barely believing it.

"You remember me?" he says through Rudjek.

I push down my burning rage and the urge to scream. "How can I forget the god who let my sister almost destroy the world?"

Rudjek glances down, his look one of disappointment. "Of course."

"You said that you would never return to the tribal lands," I remind him, seething.

"This isn't the tribal lands," Heka says through Efiya as if that's all the explanation required.

I frown, already frustrated with him. "Why are you here now?"

"To see you," he says through Sukar.

My tears come at once, blurring my sight. Heka looks exactly how I remember Sukar, his tattoos faintly glowing, that cynical quirk of his mouth, his head shaven. He would be here now if not for me, instead of this sham of an illusion. "Why?" I whisper. The question is twofold. Why show me Sukar? Why come to see me? "Why come back after you abandoned the people who believed in you?"

"There was a promise made," he answers through Rudjek. "It binds me."

Memories from the night my mother compelled him to do her bidding pour into my mind. Her words echo all around me. *As the rightful heir to your temple in the tribal lands, I'm the only one who can ask that your debt be repaid in full*, she'd said. *In return for sharing our souls, you promised us the full glory of your magic. I, Arti, of Tribe Mulani, hold you to your pact bound by your magic. It's time for you to keep your promise.*

I remember how afraid I'd been during the ritual—how I'd balled up in a corner in that dank, cold tomb. How I'd watched my friend Kofi and the other children die and done nothing. I'm not that girl anymore—yes, I'm still afraid, but I won't let fear control me. And I won't let it make me cower—not even before Heka. "How could a mortal bind a god in a promise?" I bristle at how unlikely it sounds. "I've met your siblings: Koré, Re'Mec, Mouran, Sisi, Dimma. None of them seem to care much for mortal rules."

The Arrah next to me goes rigid. "They are not my siblings."

"Trust me, they feel the same way," I mutter. Re'Mec had practically disowned Heka.

All of the versions of Heka smile, as if he's delighted to know that the feeling is mutual. "A promise binds me," he says in Efiya's voice, "but I can . . . bend the rules."

"What are you saying?" I ask, my heart racing. "Can you stop my sister . . . and Daho if he joins her against the orishas?"

"I cannot interfere," he says in Rudjek's form.

I groan and slam my fist into the grass. "Then what can you do?"

As Sukar, he frowns at me. "I have helped in my own way."

I laugh. It's bitter and sharp. "And what way is that? You let demons kill off most of the tribal people and bring Zöran to its knees. Your help isn't worth speaking of."

"Do not despair," he says. "I will soon collect the souls of the people who died because of my promise. Efiya will give them to me willingly."

I don't know what I find more appalling: that he plans on possessing their souls when he could've prevented their deaths in the first place or that he really believes my sister will give them up. Nothing good could come of either. "Listen to me." I swallow down my panic. "Efiya wants to kill all of the gods. That includes you."

"I know," he says in my sister's voice. "Let us hope that I have bent the rules precisely."

This is a waste of time. He isn't making any sense. "What does that mean?"

"Have patience, Arrah," he says in Rudjek's deep timbre, his eyes bright. "All will be revealed when it is time to return to the Supreme Cataclysm."

"You mean when I die," I say, defeated.

"Yes," he says in my voice. "When you die."

I can't believe I'd spent so long hoping, wishing, dreaming that Heka would bestow his gift of magic upon me. That seems like a lifetime ago. Instead, every time I see him, he's delivering some bad news. I'm starting to think that he's enjoying this. "You've come all the way to tell me this?" I laugh again.

"In truth, I have told you more than I thought possible," he says. "I am pleased."

"Burning fires!" I scream, jumping to my feet. "You've done nothing but cause pain and suffering, and you're pleased? You're no better than the rest of the gods."

The other version of me tilts her head thoughtfully. "Perhaps that's true."

"Are you here because of Dimma?" All the other gods only care what happens to her, so why not Heka, too?

"That's an odd question," he says in Sukar's voice. "I am here because of you."

I close my eyes, not knowing what to say to that. It doesn't even matter.

Now Heka sighs like he's grown tired of me. "I will see you once more before the end. Then you will understand."

"Understand what?"

"Everything," he says as the illusions dissipate into ribbons of light.

I blink, and he's gone. I'm back in the moment, sitting on a bluff near the lake. Rudjek is squatting near the water with a net of fish while Essnai and Kira cuddle near the fire, drying off from their swim. Jahla and Fadyi have left Rudjek to take the first watch.

Later, when we're eating around the fire, I tell my friends of Heka's visit. Essnai thinks it's a good omen, but Rudjek is suspicious of the tribal god's intentions. Kira theorizes that he's come back to help the orishas, but I'm not so sure. Heka had a reason for coming. He'd talked in riddles, but there was a hidden meaning beneath his words—something I'm supposed to figure out. The problem is I'm tired of playing these games.

DAHO

The gods are enigmas, full of contradictions and obsessions. Some see their own nature as a gift from the Supreme Cataclysm; others see it as a curse. They spend their entire existence in service to whims they cannot control. They will never be free of their compulsions, as I will never be free of my desire to destroy them.

Shezmu has been unwell since he consumed half of the god of time's soul. He's out of bed tonight, though not fully recovered. Iben's soul hadn't affected me nearly as much. I assume because he is not my first kill.

Starlight pours through the windows as the musicians fill the great hall with a soothing melody. I've never enjoyed these things. I stand off to the side, watching as my people converse and dance. They are more experienced than I at pretending that Ilora will one day return to its former glory.

Yacara and the others, five hundred in all, have yet to come back from their mission. I know I must be patient. Yacara knows what he's doing.

"It's a sight, isn't it?" Shezmu leans against a tall table for support. He isn't a small man, but he's been wan and fragile since our encounter with Iben. "Despite all that the gods have done, we're still *thriving*."

I can appreciate the underlying sarcasm beneath his words. "Will we be thriving after the gods discover that we're hunting them?"

"Perhaps not, but I take comfort in knowing they will be made to suffer as much as we have," Shezmu says.

"When I was tracking the Collector, he never noticed me. Like I was a gnat, a petty annoyance."

Shezmu wipes the sweat from his brow. "Did that offend you?"

"Not at all," I say with a smile. "That is our greatest weapon against them. They underestimate us."

I follow Shezmu's gaze to see Evelyn swaying in a dress that shimmers with golden light. It hugs her curves and accentuates her graceful neckline. She's taken to wearing her hair in tight coils. "She still speaks fondly of you," Shezmu says.

"So I've heard," I groan.

He grins, and his eyes are full of conspiracy. "Have you considered asking for a dance?"

"Why does she have to wear her hair like that?" I say crossly, ignoring his question.

"You don't like it?"

I like it very much. It reminds me of Dimma's curls. "No."

"Hasn't your bed grown cold yet?" Shezmu asks bluntly.

I tense at what he's suggesting. I have no desire for another mate, not when my wounds from losing my wife are still so fresh. It's been the better half of a millennium, yet I would be lying if I said I'm not lonely. "Evelyn is a fine woman, but she could never replace Dimma."

"Nor do I think she wants to," Shezmu comments. "It's not a crime for you to have a companion, brother. Dimma would have wanted it."

I do not know what possesses me to entertain this idea, but as Evelyn said before, eternity is a very long time to be alone. "Perhaps I will partake in one dance," I say after a while.

"That's the wisest decision you've made in decades," Shezmu says.

I stroll across the floor, couples moving out of my way, their eyes on me. I remember my last dance with Dimma—her tucked against me as we floated in the night sky. Evelyn pretends not to see me as she whispers something to her partner. I approach them feeling self-conscious, but her partner makes himself scarce before I can utter a single word.

I reach for Evelyn's hand, and she slips into my arms. "I see you've finally found your courage."

"It's only a dance," I tell her. "Dimma will always have my heart."

"I only ask for a little piece of it," Evelyn says with a wink.

Her eyes are paler than my wife's. Dimma's were the deep brown of night pearls—Evelyn's are like the bright green flowers that once pushed through the snow in the spring before the gods poisoned our lands. "I can never be yours, Evelyn. I need you to know that."

"I do," she says, unconcerned.

We dance all night. Long after the crowds thin, we are the only two left twirling and swaying across the empty hall to silent music. I find that I miss the way two bodies fit together and move in harmony. I miss the warmth of hands cupped inside my own.

"Ah," Evelyn moans against my chest. "I wouldn't have guessed that you'd be so graceful."

"It's almost dawn," I say as the first light seeps through the windows.

"It doesn't matter," Evelyn says lazily. "We don't need to sleep."

"True enough," I say. "Would you like to go to the arboretum? The vines are long overdue for a trimming."

"You call that a proper outing?" Evelyn says. "It sounds like work to me."

I scratch my head. "It's a start."

"Shall we go, then?" Evelyn says with a flourishing bow.

As we stroll out of the great hall and down the corridor, I'm feeling out of sorts. I remember when her father was elected to my advisory board. She'd attended his inauguration. It seems like yesterday, but that was several lifetimes ago. Evelyn is quiet, which only makes me more nervous. I don't know what to do with my hands, so I clasp them behind my back.

When we arrive, she settles on a bench near the vines. Her skirts fan out around her. "Sit with me," she says. "I promise to behave."

I sit, and she breaks her promise almost immediately. She runs a finger across the back of my hand. "We should take things slow," I say.

She arches an eyebrow. "It took centuries for you to ask me to dance. How much slower shall we go?"

"Evelyn," I say, exasperated.

"As you wish, *my king*," she relents.

I squirm on the bench. When Shezmu says "my king," it's dripping with sarcasm and always in jest. When she says it, there are longing and anticipation threaded between her words. "How long have you . . . um, had these feelings?" I am utterly unequipped for this conversation.

"Since before it was wholly appropriate," she admits with a laugh. "Who didn't have a crush on the immortal king or his ethereal queen? You both were so elusive. You hardly appeared in public outside of royal ceremonies, but when you did, it was all anyone talked about. Demons and endoyans alike were captivated by anything to do with you. We called it the *Daneer effect*."

I haven't heard my family's name spoken aloud in many years. It sounds strange to my ears. "I wouldn't know. I've never kept up with the latest gossip."

"Well, now you do," she says.

I kiss her, surprising even myself. I'm not one for spontaneity, but the mood seems right for it. Heavens, help me. Her lips taste sweet and inviting. In the first time I can remember, every muscle in my body relaxes. Perhaps sensing the change in me, Evelyn leans in closer, her mouth greedy, her tongue exploring, her teeth eager. I breathe in her intoxicating scent. She's not Dimma—she can never be Dimma, but that doesn't stop me from wanting her in this moment.

Evelyn pulls away and giggles in delight. "That was well worth the wait."

"I should've taken you up on your offer long ago," I say.

"I don't disagree."

We are interrupted by a commotion, running footsteps, and the sound of Yacara yelling. I get to my feet quickly, and Evelyn does as well. Her eyes are full of fear as she searches my face, but I can offer her no reassurances. "I'll be back," I say before rushing from the arboretum.

What I find are anguish and suffering. Some of the soldiers who'd gone with Yacara to hunt the gods lie writhing in pain on the floor. Before the day is over, a third of them die along with the gods they consumed. I grieve for my people, but at least they haven't died in vain.

Some of the soldiers do not die. They become something else. They turn into statues, their movements jerky; their skin and muscles are as hard as marble.

"It's some kind of stasis meant to preserve the gods," I surmise as I studied those afflicted. This is my fault. I thought I understood the gods, but this time it's I who have underestimated them. I kneel at the side of Kalen, one of the afflicted, and take his hand. He's trembling. His skin is ice-cold. He looks at me, the color gone from his eyes. I've known him since he was a boy.

"Yethe. Yethe. Yethe," Kalen says. *The end. The end. The end.*

"Some of us started to get sick shortly after consuming the gods, as expected," Yacara bemoans. "We had to split their souls into pieces to destroy some of them. Others got away. Then I saw that my men weren't getting better, so we returned. There's no way we can hide this from the Twin Kings now."

I look at the others afflicted, and I can see no pattern to why some have ended up in such dire conditions. I count myself lucky that Shezmu and I hadn't experienced worse. "We need to go after the god of life and death," I decide. "Once we stop them, we will control who gets to live and who dies."

"I know where they are," Yacara says, surprising me.

"We'll leave at once."

Shezmu, Yacara, and I find Fram dangling from the side of a building shrouded in shadow in Uthura—a world that Dimma had visited long ago. This is where she discovered a people with the ability to harvest the unused years from a soul before it returned to the Supreme Cataclysm.

We waste no time attacking Fram, but it's apparent from the first blow that we're outmatched. They're faster and stronger than I could have ever imagined. But there's another problem that keeps me from making any headway. Whenever I get close to them, my head starts to pound, and I become dizzy. It's Dimma—I can feel her. It makes no sense, but I sense her with Fram.

"You are very clever," Fram tells me in their twin voices. "Too clever for your own good."

"Dimma's alive?" I sob. "She's been alive all this time?"

"She is not alive, no," Fram says. "She isn't dead either."

"You haven't told Koré, Re'Mec, and the others?" I surmise.

"It is my secret to keep," Fram says. "Now it is yours. If my siblings find out, they'll feed Dimma to the Supreme Cataclysm themselves."

"My son?" I ask, desperate, but I don't sense his soul.

"Very much dead." Fram's voices sweep over me. They are fire and ice, chaos and peace. The duality is too much to bear.

I settle in my anguish and pain, for it will always be there. As long as Dimma exists in any form, I will never give up. But I can't continue this fight—not like this. I can't risk accidentally hurting

Dimma. Reluctantly, I give the order to retreat. My thoughts spin and multiply on the way back to Ilora, and by the time we reach the palace, I know what I must do. I must destroy the god of life and death to free my wife, but I must tread carefully.

Evelyn is waiting for me in the great hall. She takes two steps in my direction, and I tell her excitedly, "I know how to get Dimma back."

She smiles at me, but her eyes are brimming with tears.

So ends our short-lived romance.

TWENTY-ONE
ARRAH

We're back to where we started, at the head of the crossroads on a grassy bluff overlooking Tribe Zu. The last time I was here, we performed a burial rite for Sukar and bid farewell to all the friends we'd lost. He used to say the Zu were small but mighty. Now the mountain has become home to the people we freed from Tyrek and the demons loyal to my sister. I scan their faces and see survivors from each of the five tribes.

We're spotted almost immediately, and word of our arrival travels through the village. Some two hundred people wait for news of the fate of the tribes. I swallow my trepidation as I tell them the truth. "The rest of the tribes made it to safety. They're considering if they will join the Kingdom against the demons."

Whispers spread through the crowds. They ask if any witchdoctors survived, and I shake my head. "They have a *djeli* who can navigate the crossroads. I'm sure they'll come for you once they have made their decision."

"We will no longer hide," says the woman who'd become their

unofficial chieftain. She wears a vest of rawhide painted bright red and a crown of antlers. She's Kes, with rich brown skin, veins along her temples, and her hair in cornrows. "Whether they come or not, we've decided to take the Crown Prince's offer to join with the Kingdom against the demons."

Rudjek bristles beside me, and I swear he breathes a sigh of relief. "I'm glad to hear it—together, we will end the threat to Zöran."

"We have already made arrangements with the *dshatu*," says the chieftain. "Elder Ro has sent for a second ship to take us back to the Kingdom."

"You will be in good hands," Rudjek says, satisfied.

Jahla and Fadyi shift into hawks and take flight for the ship anchored off the coast beyond the mountains. At Rudjek's command, the craven ship had been waiting for us the entire time. It had taken us from the North after the battle against the demon, and now it'll take us home.

I can't help but lament that once we're back in the Kingdom, Rudjek will return to his life as Crown Prince and future Almighty One in everything he does and how he's treated. It's something that neither of us has talked about and not by accident.

"You look wistful," he tells me as we descend the bluff.

Kira and Essnai are ahead of us, having a private moment of their own.

I glance up at him. "Do I?"

"Wistful and in much need of a bath," Rudjek adds with a quirk of his eyebrow.

"You should talk," I say accusingly. "I have a lot on my mind."

"Such as . . . ?" he prods.

"Just that things will be different once you're at the Almighty Palace."

Rudjek pauses, midstride, his expression darkening. "My father will no longer be a problem, nor will I let him come between us."

I want to believe him, but Suran Omari has proven that he cannot be trusted. He is the same man who banished my family, sent assassins to hunt me down, and seized power when the opportunity presented itself. I don't believe for a moment that he won't find a way to strike again, only this time, I won't have magic to protect me.

Our conversation ends abruptly when several tribal people approach with more questions. Although we're tired from our journey, we spend the day with them. They ask about their friends and family, rattling off name after name well into the night. I tell them about Efiya, which casts a shadow over the good news about the tribes.

"When we're close to the Kingdom, Fadyi will fly ahead to announce our impending arrival," Rudjek explains the next morning as we set off for the ship. "I'm sure my father will be most pleased to hear of my return."

"He's sure to be overjoyed, too, that you brought the tribal witch along," I say.

"I'm glad you haven't lost your sense of humor."

The craven ship is an impressive sight, carved from dark wood, looking almost like a mirage against the sunrise. At the water's edge, we walk in the spray and breathe in the scents of salt and kelp and fish. Along with Fadyi and Jahla, two cravens in white robes—an older woman with long gray hair and a man with inky black hair—stand on the beach waiting for us. Elder Ro, the ship's captain, and her second-in-command.

"Rudjek of the Eldest Clan," Ro says in a voice that sounds like the first notes of a song. She looks him over before glancing at me, then Essnai and Kira. It's the most acknowledgment we'll get from her. At last, she gives Rudjek a brief bow. "It is good to see you well after your journey."

Rudjek returns the gesture. "It is good to see you, too, Ro of the Elder Clan."

"We're ready to set sail." Ro raises a hand to indicate that we should board. She doesn't move, and I realize that she's waiting.

There's some hierarchy of authority at play among the cravens that I still don't understand, but it seems to come naturally to Rudjek. He helps me into the boat first before climbing aboard. Everyone else follows in a scripted choreography: Elder Ro and her second-in-command, then our friends.

The boat pitches forward, catching most of us off balance. Jahla narrows her eyes, her brow furrowed in concentration as she trails her fingers in the water.

Soon the boat picks up speed toward the ship, kicking up a spray in our wake, powered only by whatever Jahla is doing with her hand. I watch as the shore grows smaller and feel a pang of reluctance. I take in the rocky shore and the fog-shrouded mountains beyond, hoping that one day it will be teeming with life once more. Only I won't be around to see it. I will never lay eyes upon the tribal lands ever again.

Elder Ro tilts her chin up and addresses Rudjek. "In your absence, your cousins sent replacements for your fallen guardians. Though, of course, you are free to choose new guardians from any of the cravens under my command. All of them are willing and well-trained. It would be an honor for them to serve the Eldest Clan."

"If it's all the same to you, I do not want new guardians," Rudjek says tightly. "Ezaric, Tzaric, and Raëke were my friends."

The boat lifts on a swell, only to slam down again. Jahla adjusts her position, half-turning away from us. Strands of her silver hair blow across her face, masking her expression. They were her friends, too, and Elder Ro is making them seem easily replaceable. I think about Sukar and Majka. We've lost so many.

"It would be a breach of protocol not to accept guardians. In your precarious position, it may be wise to avoid giving offense," Elder Ro insists. "The alliance between our people and the humans is a fragmented one. Your victory in the North is well regarded, but many of us are still wary of the humans and what they might do if they find out your true identity."

"It didn't feel like a victory," Rudjek says under his breath. He runs a hand over his hair, buzzing with nervous energy. "But of course, you're right. I'll consider a list of the candidates."

Once we've boarded the ship, Elder Ro and her second-in-command move to line up with the rows of cravens standing at attention. To an unpracticed eye, they resemble Tamarans, tribal people, Estherians, Northerners, Yöomi. But some of them have not yet perfected their ability to mimic humans. Some have eyes too large, heads too round, torsos too lean, and faces too symmetrical. "Rudjek of the Eldest Clan." Elder Ro dips her chin. "We are yours to command."

Rudjek begins his remarks, his every word careful, practiced. "The day that Caster of the Eldest Clan foresaw is upon us." He squeezes the grips of his shotels. "The demons control the gate between worlds. I will not lie to you: they're determined to destroy Zöran. If we are to have a chance against them, it will take humans and cravens working together with the orishas. We must defeat two powerful enemies: the Demon King and Efiya."

Though the cravens remain silent at the news of my sister's return, hesitation cuts through their ranks.

"There's no love lost between you and the Almighty Kingdom, I know. But I will do everything in my power to unite Zöran for one cause—and that is our very survival. What we do now will determine the future of our world."

Elder Ro lowers her head again. "No truer words, Eldest."

I still can't believe Daho released Efiya from the dagger. I'd just started to trust him, but maybe Rudjek's right, and I'm letting Dimma influence me. For all I know, Daho is plotting his revenge against the orishas right now, with Efiya whispering in his ear. But I know my sister. Daho might want revenge, but Efiya wants power, and she's not going to share it with him.

After we've set sail, Rudjek goes belowdecks with Elder Ro, Fadyi, Jahla, and several craven leaders. They stay there for hours, presumably discussing strategy. Kira and Essnai point up at the mast, watching the cravens work a sophisticated system of gears that speeds the ship's progress.

"It's thought that the people of Tribe Kes migrated from the North on ships as large as this one," Kira tells Essnai. "Which is interesting since, to my knowledge, the Kes have never been known for seafaring. Though one can't deny that they favor the people of the North."

"They have endoyan ancestry," I say quietly. "The people of the North and the Kes." I wrap an arm around my waist, remembering the day Dimma killed all the endoyans who had helped Eluua attack Jiiek. "Some of the endoyans fled Ilora and settled in Zöran."

"That certainly changes everything, doesn't it?" Kira says, not missing a beat. "For generations, scholars have theorized about the Northerners' diaphanous skin, but there is no mention of endoyan ancestry in any of the ancient texts."

"As the orishas intended, I'm sure," Essnai comments.

I slide my hand into my pocket and palm my mother's ring. I've not been without it since discovering that Ty, the matron of my family's villa, had slipped it into the money pouch all those months ago. The ring had belonged to the vile *Ka*-Priest Ren Eké before my mother owned it. Now it belongs to me. I've never worn it, and the stone has remained clear, tinted with the faint color of smoke. My heart throbs in my chest as I remember Arti stalking the child in the alley, one of many she sacrificed to Shezmu. That night, the gemstone appeared sickly green.

After Arti's death, Emere, the head attendant of the Almighty Temple, had asked me to become the voice of the Temple to keep Suran Omari in check. I don't have magic now, but Suran doesn't know that. For the first time, I slip on the ring, and the color of the stone changes from clear to midnight blue with specks of starlight.

"I never thought I would see that on your finger." Rudjek's voice comes from behind me. It's hard to miss the note of sadness in it.

I yank off the ring and stuff it back in my pocket before facing him. Everywhere I look, the sea stretches around us, almost as dark as the stone. We step away from Essnai and Kira and lean against the bow.

"I thought it was lost after I used it in the ritual to break my mother's curse. So I was surprised when Ty gave it to me." Our matron had been fiercely loyal to Arti—something that I still have a hard time reconciling. Arti had taken Ty and our porter, Nezi, into our family after the former *Ka*-Priest had hurt them. It kills me that the harm she caused in the end will always outweigh the good and be her lasting legacy. "Maybe Ty thought I should have something of my mother's, but it only reminds me of the terrible things she did."

"There's no shame in wanting to keep a memento of her," Rudjek says. "But I think I know how you feel. I'm ashamed of my father's deeds, what he did to you and your mother, and your entire family." He frowns before adding, "I intend to set him straight about you, but that doesn't absolve him of his crimes."

"It won't matter what you say." This is something I've resigned myself to already. "Your father made up his mind the moment he saw me. I am my mother's daughter, and for better or worse, that is all he will ever see when he looks at me." I pull the ring out of my pocket for the second time. It's turned the color of black opal, and I watch the sunlight try to reach into its depths.

Rudjek stares at it with open disdain. "What are you saying?"

"I intend to become the *Ka*-Priestess of the Kingdom," I confess, though inside, I am not sure I am doing the right thing. "That is, assuming Emere hasn't already found another suitable candidate."

"Arrah, I don't think that's a good idea." Rudjek shifts his weight on his heels. "You're only going to agitate my father."

After all the underhanded things Suran Omari's done, I don't care about agitating him. I wish I could do worse. "Seems like reason enough to do it."

"Be sensible here," Rudjek pleads. "If you become *Ka*-Priestess, he'll see it as a direct challenge to his authority."

"Sensible?" I repeat, and the dark veins in his forehead deepen in color.

He glances down, looking embarrassed. "You know what I mean."

"I'm not afraid of your father." I cross my arms.

"Perhaps if you had magic to protect yourself, then things would be different."

I cringe inside, thinking about that moment in the field when the orishas attacked Daho. I'd broken my promise to myself. I'd been desperate and willing to trade more years of my life for magic, though some part of me is relieved that I failed. But this I can do. "As far as I'm concerned, we're on equal footing now," I say, knowing it's not true.

"You can't be serious." Rudjek starts to laugh but thinks better of it. "You *are*, aren't you?"

"I need to make sure that your father's decisions are for the good of the entire Kingdom, and he stays out of the tribal lands."

"And how do you intend to do that?" Rudjek grumbles.

"There are still many in the Kingdom loyal to the Temple," I say. "Prince Derane is one of them. Your father stole his throne, after all. People like him will stand against Suran Omari with me if it comes to that."

Rudjek throws up his arms in frustration. "You're the most stubborn person I know."

"Second only to your father," I retort.

"I can't argue what that," he concedes.

After a moment, Rudjek puts his arm around me, and we both stare at the waves crashing against the ship's haul. "We could be quite the pair, you know. The Crown Prince and the *Ka*-Priestess."

He's only partly joking, but I can only think about my mother's love affair with her own Crown Prince and how it led to so much suffering and death.

After a few days at sea, the craven ship approaches the Southern coast of the Almighty Kingdom. Bells peal unceasingly from the watchtowers on the cliffs, alerting the city guard of our arrival. It's midday and the sun glimmers against the rocky shores and the row of warships in the harbor. I recognize some of the flags: Estheria's shrike, Zeknor's crossed swords, Galke's stallion, and Delene's fox. The Kingdom ships bear white banners with a lion's head stitched in gold—the Omari family crest.

"No ships from Fyaran," Rudjek notes, disappointed. "Or Ghujiek or Siihi. As much as I hate to admit it, Fyaran has a formidable military. We need them."

"Maybe they haven't arrived yet." I'm hopeful, but the bad blood between the Kingdom and Fyaran has lasted for generations.

Everything happened so fast after we pushed the demons back months ago. He wrote to heads of state across all of Zöran, detailing the threat and pleading with them to convene a delegation in the Kingdom to discuss an alliance. His final letter was to his father, outlining his intention to help me look for the tribal people.

Rudjek orders the craven vessel to stop at a respectful distance as a Kingdom naval ship speeds toward us. He curses when the ship is off our starboard. "Of course it would be you." Across the water stands a tall, broad-shouldered man with a patch covering his left eye. His short gray hair is almost silver against his ebony skin. "Captain Dakte."

I recognize the soldier—he was at Tyrek's trial. Rudjek said that Dakte had constantly undermined his authority against the demons and nearly started a war with the Zeknorians.

"Commandant Dakte," the man corrects Rudjek, after waiting too long to speak. "I received a promotion for my act of valor in the line of duty."

You could hear a pin drop aboard our ship; I imagine the same is true on Dakte's. Rudjek's fists clench at his sides, but when he speaks, he projects an air of serenity. "Then congratulations are in order, Commandant. It is fortunate that you lost only a third of our contingency in the North, since you might not have received your promotion otherwise."

"Ever the diplomat, Crown Prince," Dakte says dryly. "It is good to see you alive and well after so many close calls. We feared the worst when you chose not to return to the Kingdom immediately." He lets his gaze sweep from one end of the row of cravens standing at attention to the other. "I see that you are surrounded by your mysterious friends from the South."

"I haven't the time for this conversation," Rudjek says, ignoring the subtle accusation. "I carry important news for my father."

"Of course, Crown Prince." Dakte bows stiffly. "I am most honored to deliver you and the leaders of *this* Southern delegation to the palace."

Dakte orders a bridge extended between the two ships. Kira, along with Fadyi and Jahla posing as gendars, crosses first with

Rudjek. I hadn't even seen Fadyi slip back into our ranks. The craven delegates, five in all with Elder Ro leading them, board the Kingdom ship next. Essnai and I take up the rear.

Soon we're on the way to shore. An unusually large flock of seagulls keeps pace with the Kingdom ship. Another congregates along the rock face, watching our approach. I can still feel the subtle sting of the cravens' anti-magic from afar as they follow us inland.

Once we disembark, Rudjek pulls me aside. "Are you sure about this business with the Temple?"

"Yes," I answer, annoyed that he's still trying to change my mind. "It's best that I get it over with now."

Rudjek smiles sheepishly. "Jahla will accompany you and Essnai, along with two dozen cravens hidden in plain sight." He takes my hand and kisses my palm. "I'll send a messenger once I straighten some things out with my father."

"Until then, Crown Prince," I say, dipping my head.

We watch as Captain Dakte and his men lead Rudjek and the delegates to the litters awaiting them. Kira turns to wink at her *ama*. "I miss her already," Essnai says, her expression dreamy. "Who will lecture me on seafaring or the mechanics of irrigation for the sheer torture of it?"

"When we were on our way to Zeknor, she once spent an entire evening explaining the history of the spice trade between Estheria and the Kingdom," Jahla recalls. "It was quite . . . riveting."

Essnai and I exchange a glance, and I shove down a fit of giggles. I can't tell if Jahla truly found spice trading interesting or if that was her attempt at humor. Either way, she's been so closed off since losing Majka and Raëke, it's good to hear her voice more.

We board a wagon waiting for us, and the driver snaps the reins, leaving the docks in our wake. We cross a neighborhood still mostly in ruin from when Tyrek had punished people who refused to renounce the orishas. Half-burned row houses stand in stark contrast to the richer parts of the city that had been rebuilt after Suran Omari took over the Kingdom.

Farther inland, we cut through the East Market. The crowds are so dense that we slow to a crawl. Even with the prospect of war looming, the streets burst with color and commerce, lively conversation and haggling. Merchants sell their wares, from shoes to knives to mysterious concoctions in jars. Musicians play on corners for copper coins while thieves eye their marks.

"If I close my eyes, I can almost believe that things will be okay," I say quietly.

"Almost," Essnai remarks, looking at the crowd.

I long for the days I could lose myself in the East Market, when I was comforted by the knowledge that no one cared if you had magic. They didn't argue about pedigrees or bother with family crests. They didn't have to worry about demons or my sister.

"How am I supposed to take my cows out to graze with a Yöomi caravan on their feed grounds?" I hear a man telling his friend on the side of a less busy street. "And the City Guard keeps ignoring my pleas to make them move."

"A few beggars may soon be the least of your concerns," the friend says. "Pray the demons don't come back."

There is a bitter edge to their voices, an edge that I share. It's my fault for not stopping Efiya. No, my guilt is deeper and more profound than that. Dimma hadn't considered the consequences of making the demons immortal, yet as much as I want to condemn her, I understand why she did it. I might have done the same.

We pass a group of Northerners wearing veils. There's no way to tell what country they're from, but they all share the same diaphanous skin. We see Estherians with dark eyes and silky hair like Kira's. Yöomi with hair ranging from kinky blond to inky black and eyes in shades of blue or green or speckled brown. People of tribal descent. Some tall with ebony skin, some pale brown with eyes the color of ice. So many different faces, and eventually, they melt into a cacophony of hues.

Gendars in red uniforms roam the streets in addition to the armed City Guard. So many more than I remember, and it's not my imagination that some of the soldiers look barely older than me.

It's nearly nightfall when we arrive at the bottom of the hill that leads up to the Almighty Temple. The path is too narrow for anything larger than carts and litters, so we join a swarm of people pressing forward to climb on foot. The crowd hums with quiet tension that threatens to breach the surface. I fear what will happen if it does.

At the gate, attendants in gray robes try to create order among the scores of people begging to enter. "Go home!" they shout. "The Temple is already full."

Jahla, Essnai, and I attempt to pass through the gate, but another attendant stops us. "I'm sorry, but the Temple is . . ." Her mouth drops open in surprise. "Arrah, you're back?"

"I need to see Emere." There's no time for pleasantries. "Is she here?"

"In the Hall of Orishas," the attendant says, "holding prayer."

We cross the courtyard, and I'm assaulted with memories. Rudjek lying on the cobblestones, nearly dead. Sukar shirtless, kneeling in the gardens some time before he revealed himself to be Daho. How could I have not known? It should have been obvious from the way he looked at me.

I push through the double doors to enter the hall. Cool air from the stone walls washes over me. So do the familiar smells. Sukar, Essnai, and I played here as children, weaving between pillars when no one was around to shoo us away. The memory almost brings a smile to my lips.

Among the shifting shadows of the orisha statues, hundreds of people pray. Emere and several temple attendants sit in silence at the far end of the cavernous hall. We slip around to the narrow service corridor behind the statues of Koré, Fram, Nana, and Essi. Now when I look at the orishas, I feel betrayed, but I also feel Dimma's longing. She loved her siblings for better or worse. Even after one of them tried to kill me, I can't bring myself to hate them. I wish I could find a way to end their feud with Daho—though that won't be possible with Efiya back.

By the time we reach Emere, one of the attendants has alerted her to our presence. A ripple of shock goes through the temple as I hear my name whispered on many lips. Emere wastes no time showing us to a private room. Her hair is wrapped in a sheer white gauze that trails down her back, a style favored by those devoted to Koré. As soon as Essnai and I are alone with her, she pulls me into a hug, beaming. "Arrah, praise the gods. Where's Sukar?"

"He's gone," Essnai answers for me.

The smile vanishes from Emere's face, and I can see her working up to ask how, but I change the subject before the pain of his death snatches away my words. "How have things been here?"

"Difficult," she says, pressing her fingers against her temples. "Suran Omari has banned magic and imprisoned anyone who dared to defy him. He's using the presence of the delegations in the city as justification, saying that magic endangers the alliance between nations."

"What's the point?" Essnai asks, frustrated. "So few people had magic to start, and even fewer do now. Surely no one is a threat to him."

It's a petty act suited to Suran's temperament. There needn't be a threat. I should've known that, with no one to challenge his authority, he'd try to outlaw magic as soon as I left. No matter how bad things get, he always finds a way to twist them to his own purpose.

"Emere," I say uneasily. I'm still not sure if this is the right decision, but I have to do whatever I can to help the tribal people. No matter what some of them think of me for releasing the former chieftains' *kas*, I haven't given up on them. This is the least I can do to honor Grandmother, my father, and all the people my sister and the demons murdered. After all these years of not wanting to be like my mother, I'm committed to following in her footsteps and become the *Ka*-Priestess of the Almighty Kingdom, even if it's only for the little time I have left. I remove the ring from my pocket and hold it out. "I've reconsidered your proposition. If you still need a new *Ka*-Priestess . . ."

Emere stares at the ring, her eyes filling with tears. "Oh, Arrah. We do."

"I need to tell you, though," I say, swallowing hard. "I don't have magic anymore."

"Magic isn't our only weapon." Emere grips my hand with the ring enclosed inside. "All you need is the will to fight. And that, child, you have always had . . . no matter who has stood in your way."

I think about Grandmother's words, which seem like a lifetime time ago. *Our greatest power lies not in our magic but in our hearts.* I haven't ever given up, not against my mother, my sister, or Suran. I won't give up in the face of war or my own death. I am more like Dimma than I care to admit.

Emere is right. Magic didn't save my friends, my father, or the tribal people. In the end, it won't save me, nor will it save our world, at least not alone. It's taken me far too long to accept that it isn't the answer to my problems. If I'm honest with myself, it's the cause of many of them.

I rub my eyes, exhausted from the journey. "What do I need to do?"

"I'll perform the ceremony tonight," Emere says. "We mustn't give Suran Omari time to intervene."

I might not have magic to help stop the demons if they attack, but I can do this. I'll put an end to Suran Omari's schemes. It's the least I can do after he helped destroy my family.

TWENTY-TWO
ARRAH

Emere escorts us to Sukar's old room to rest before my coronation tonight. Jahla takes up guard in the corridors outside the chambers as Essnai and I push through the heavy door. This room never really belonged to Sukar. It was Daho who came back with us from the tribal lands and pretended to be my friend. He never bothered unpacking Sukar's things that Emere had relocated from his old quarters to this one many months ago. I'm not prepared for the guilt that hits me.

I lean against a chair, suddenly too hot and short of breath. I am a hostage as the moment of Sukar's death unfolds in my mind, but I am also the perpetrator. I watch as I fling my magic to push him out of the way of Efiya's wrath. Sukar crashes into a pillar. His body slumps to the ground. He is so still. I would do anything to bring him back. Anything.

"I miss him," Essnai says, snapping me out of the memory.

She walks to a small table, where Sukar's ceremonial masks are still packed in their crate. She gently runs her fingers across a plain black one with slits for eyes, the curve of a nose, and a hollow mouth.

His uncle had wood imported from the tribal lands, and Sukar carved the mask himself, as is the Zu tradition.

"His first mask," Essnai says fondly. "The one he wore for his Coming of Age."

"He was such a brat that day." I attempt to match her bright tone, but I'm choking back tears.

She laughs softly. "To be fair, we were all brats for hiding in the Temple kitchens."

"It was his idea," I remind her. My words are feeble, and I know that this pain will never go away. *Good, that's what you get for killing me*, I imagine Sukar would say. *By the way, your singing at my burial rite was terrible, just so you know.* "I . . . I miss him, too."

"He would give me a good tongue-lashing for touching his mask, but I'd gladly take it if it meant that . . . if it meant that he was still here with us." Essnai's voice drops to barely above a whisper. "I don't want to lose any more friends."

I hear the plea in her words, the desperation, the resignation. *I don't want to lose you, too.*

I can't promise her that things will be okay, that we'll always have each other. "You have me now, and I have you. That's all that matters."

Essnai glares at me, her eyes bloodshot from exhaustion. "That's not good enough. I want to see you grow old and cranky."

"You're the cranky one," I say, but my words fall flat. I sigh, remembering all the times I thought I could do this on my own, and Essnai and Sukar had proved me wrong. I will never grow old and cranky, and I can't keep that secret from her any longer. I'm not afraid of dying, but I'm afraid of this. I don't want to hurt another one of my friends. I've done enough of that already. "When I met Daho that first time I followed his trail on the crossroads. . . ." I pause, and it hits me all at once. The weight of it settles in. There's no getting around it now. "He told me that I didn't have long before . . . before I die."

Tears slip down her cheeks. "It's not fair."

"I know," I say, putting on a brave face. "I want to make good use of the time I have left."

Essnai forces a smile. "Well, in that case, we must make sure you're stunning for your coronation tonight." I'm thankful that she doesn't linger on the news. "When I'm done with you, you'll be the most beautiful *Ka*-Priestess the Kingdom has ever known."

"I didn't know that beauty was a requirement for the position."

"Think of how much it will anger Suran Omari when you become the object of everyone's attention," she offers. "He will be beside himself."

"Since you put it that way . . . ," I relent with a devious smile of my own. "How can I resist?"

Essnai pokes her head out of the door and calls for an attendant. "We need shea butter, coconut oil, combs, clips, pins, kohl, gold dust— No, wait, I need a whole color palette for her makeup, something bold and uncompromising." Essnai gasps as if an idea strikes her. "We'll have to find a sheath befitting the occasion." She grabs the attendant by the arm. "Come with me. We haven't much time." She turns sharply and jabs a finger at me. "You, get some sleep. I'll be back soon."

I don't bother protesting. Jahla stands on guard with befuddled amusement as Essnai closes the door and leaves me alone.

I sit on the bed and stare at the gold threads in the marble floor shaped into a sundial, a symbol that represents the sun orisha. Where are Re'Mec and his sister now? Are they plotting their next move against Daho and Efiya after the last one failed so miserably? Neither side will give up until one destroys the other.

I don't think it's possible, but almost the moment I rest my head on the pillow, I fall into a dream. I am in a hall filled with demons afflicted by magic. They wear elaborate gowns and tunics frothed with lace and chiffon, but their faces are blank, and they move in small jerks, repeating the same motions. One man clenches and unclenches his fists, only to do it again. A woman reaches to the heavens; her mouth opens in a silent scream. Another person digs a knife into their belly, revealing a soul that doesn't belong to them. Another's wings unfold, close, and unfold again. I am frozen, too, my palms turned up in subjugation.

Daho walks into the hall and looks around, studying face after face. He squeezes a man on the shoulder. "I'm sorry, brother," he says, his voice full of anguish. "I will find a way to free all of you one day."

He comes to me next. "It's time, my love." He unsheathes the jeweled-hilt dagger from his waist. "This will hurt."

I wake with a startle from the dream and immediately know that I'm not alone. "Who's there?"

A shapeless shadow slithers across the bedpost. I haven't seen a Familiar in months. If one is around, usually trouble soon follows.

"Long live the dead queen," comes a hoarse whisper.

I jump from the bed and back away. The Familiars have never

spoken to me, but I recognize this one instantly. It's Minister Godanya, the endoyan who helped organize the attack against the demons, or at least, what's left of him.

"What do you want?" I hesitate. "Did Daho send you?"

"Oh, he rarely has any use for us these days," Godanya laments. "Yet he hasn't seen fit to release my people from your curse."

"I'm not Dimma," I say quickly.

Godanya laughs. "Is that what you tell yourself to sleep at night, or is that what he told you? It shouldn't be a surprise to you that I do eavesdrop on occasion."

I wrap my arms around my shoulders as if I can ward off his words. I know who I am, but I can't push aside my lingering doubt. "Why are you here?"

"Why do you think?" Godanya spits. "We have served your king faithfully as you required. Now we must rest, if you see fit to finally let us die in peace."

I don't miss the desperation in his voice, the longing, but this is the same man who ordered the execution of millions of people, including children. I think about how the Familiars had slithered like maggots in the East Market the day my friend Kofi disappeared, too, and the memory turns my stomach. "Perhaps you should ask Daho to release you."

Godanya hisses at me. "I see you haven't changed."

"Leave," I say as my head begins to pound.

He sulks before slinking away without another word—and I realize that he's only listening to me because . . . because to him, I am Dimma. I remember the day she punished the endoyans. "*You will live this way for eternity as a reminder of your crimes.*" I repeat her words with anguish filling my belly. *"You will be at our mercy until the day my love deems your punishment just. Until then, you will serve the demons when they call upon you."* I'm shaking when Essnai bursts into the chamber a moment later. I do my best to hide it—I can't consider what it means that Godanya is convinced that I'm Dimma.

"That took longer than expected," Essnai says, juggling pouches and small boxes.

Jahla follows her, carrying layers of dresses of all colors. She drapes them across the chair and then slowly backs away. "I'll be returning to my post now."

"Don't you dare leave!" Essnai proclaims as she arranges her color palette. "The coronation is in three hours, and I need help."

I'm lost in a blur of beads and lace and silk and ribbons. After my bath, Essnai fusses with my hair, redoing my braids along the edges and the front while weaving in decorative silver rings and cupping individual braids in thinly spun gold charms. Jahla fumbles to keep up with Essnai's demands. "No, not that red, the bold one." "Not the powder; give me the cream." "That's not blue. It's teal."

I offer Jahla an apologetic shrug, but she looks only increasingly amused. While Essnai is murmuring to herself about color coordination, Jahla asks, "Is she always this . . . ?"

"Bossy?" I finish with a smile.

"Determined," Jahla says.

"This midnight blue is perfect," Essnai decides as she thrusts the palette for me to see. "What do you think?"

I look down at my finger. "It matches the *Ka*-Priestess's ring."

"Exactly," Essnai says, excited. "It's a subtle statement but powerful."

I would be lost without Essnai brightening the moment. When she's done prodding and poking and adjusting, I stand in front of the mirror in a gold dress that shimmers whenever I make the slightest movement. It's high-necked and fitted through the waist, only to spread out like a budding flower when it hits my hips. The style is more Estherian than Kingdom, but I don't mind. For a little while, I can ignore the signs of decay that trading my years has caused me: the missing tooth, poorer sight, gray hair, the aches and pains.

Along with the midnight-blue shadow rimming my eyes, Essnai's accented my cheeks with a light dusting of powder paired with bright red for my lips. I stare into golden eyes that look like my mother's, but I am not her. She made her own mistakes, and I have made mine. I am not stepping into her shadow; I am casting my own.

I inhale a sharp breath when Emere and three other Temple attendants arrive in their sweeping gray robes. "It's time, Arrah," she says, her gaze lowered. "We'll perform the coronation in the Hall of Orishas so that we may honor the gods."

They turn for me to follow them, but I hesitate. The *Ka*-Priestess has always served as the head of the Almighty Temple and the voice of the orishas. I don't know how the Twin Kings will take what I'm about to do. Perhaps I should've considered it more carefully, but I don't pretend to know their hearts. I do know that Dimma loved them, even at the end of her life.

Six cravens posing as guards stand at attention in the corridor, their anti-magic hot against my skin. They appear to wear red gendar uniforms and helmets with their faceplates shoved back, but it's an illusion—a very convincing one at that. "I'd rather we be extra cautious," Jahla explains while I'm still standing in the middle of the room, frozen in place. "The Crown Prince left you under my protection."

"I wish he were here," I say quietly, but no one hears me. Emere and the other attendants lead us toward the hall with half of the cravens in tow.

"It is custom that we seek the blessing of the Almighty One and that he should attend, but in this case, we thought it best only to inform Prince Derane," Emere tells me. "He's loyal to the Temple and hopes to win back his throne. He talked to the families of influence sympathetic to our cause, who will be in attendance as well."

I swallow the lump in my throat. I'm feeling self-conscious as my dress sweeps across the floor. I wasn't expecting an audience, let alone some of the most powerful families in the Kingdom. If Emere thinks that Suran Omari doesn't know about our plans, she has greatly underestimated him. Rudjek says his father has spies across the Kingdom and all of Zöran. No doubt that means they are at the Temple, too. But it won't matter once the ceremony is over. I'll have people on my side willing to stand up to Suran. Some of them will be families he won't want to cross.

When the attendants push open the inner doors to the Hall of Orishas, I am beseeched by a hum of excited chatter that echoes against the high ceilings. I falter on the threshold, my nerves finally getting the best of me. I hadn't expected more than a few people, but hundreds have come. They stand everywhere, even between the shifting shadows of the orisha statues that blur under the moonlight pouring through the windows. The Hall is bursting at the seams.

"So many," I whisper.

"At last count, there were close to two thousand people on the Temple grounds and outside the gates," Emere says, pleased. "They came as soon as we spread the word of your coronation."

I take another step forward—this time, my legs are less steady. I make it a point not to meet anyone's eyes; instead, I look slightly above their heads or off to the side. Prince Derane stands out in a black silk elara, both the tunic and matching trousers trimmed in gold, his fingers lined with opulent rings of diamonds and opals and sapphires. He's surrounded by other Sukkaras equally as decked out in their fine clothes.

Always radiant, former queen Estelle Sukkara—Tyrek's mother—stands at the center of the Ohakims in a plum-colored sheath that complements her dark skin. Her braided hair is even more bejeweled than my own and arranged into a crown atop her head. She lost her position, too, when Rudjek's father arrested her son and named himself Almighty One. I wonder how many other enemies of Suran Omari have come tonight.

"We are here to witness the rise of a new *Ka*-Priestess." Emere projects her voice over the crowd. Her unwavering conviction only puts me that much more on edge. How could she have such confidence in me when I doubt myself? "Despite the sins of her mother, the gods have spoken to Arrah N'yar. They have guided her so that she may lead us in these uncertain times. For we know that taking up arms alone will not defeat our enemies. Our faith will be our salvation."

I listen as Emere meticulously speaks of my deeds, the good and the bad. It feels like I'm on trial, waiting for judgment to be passed. But soon, her words grow distant, and the people watching suddenly turn into smoke. I frown as everything and everyone fade away.

I am alone in the cavernous hall, and I brace myself for the worst. Has my sister come back to finish what she started? I reach to my waist. Daho's dagger is hidden under the layers of cloth.

Something moves in the shadows, and I whirl around to face the sun orisha's statue, with its crown of ostrich feathers and pearls between ram horns. I stare so long that the shadows begin to bleed into my vision. I blink, and Re'Mec himself replaces the statue. He's taken his human form, Tam, a boy with kinky golden hair, sky-blue eyes, and bronze skin set against Tamaran features. "I am quite the sight, am I not?" he says with a wicked grin.

The other orishas appear in place of their statues, too. Koré with the face of an Aatiri woman and long braids writhing across her shoulders. Mouran with pointed teeth like the demons and a barbed tail. Sisi becomes the breath of fire. Kiva, a child with bright eyes and toys scattered about his feet. Oma is shrouded in ribbons of light. Kekiyé has a face covered in many eyes. Essi is a shadow, and Nana is molded of clay.

They're all here—the last of Dimma's brethren, out of the hundreds that once existed. Tears prickle against my eyes, and a deep yearning burns through my belly. I don't know what to make of their presence. I have no doubt that some of them still want to kill me, but I don't cower—the same way I refused to cower in front of Heka.

"This is unexpected, to say the least," Koré muses as she turns a slow circle around me. "Hello, Arrah." I don't miss the pointed way she says my name. It's like I'm suddenly seeing how they all treat me.

Daho, the gods, and Godanya, like I'm glass on the verge of shattering into a thousand pieces.

"The girl who carries our sister's soul wants to become the priestess of our Temple," Kiva says in his childlike voice. "How wonderful."

"It is one of Dimma's schemes," hisses Oma. "We cannot trust it."

"What is the point of such a scheme?" Kekiyé asks, blinking some of his eyes.

"Enough of this, Dimma," says Sisi as her blazing flames cool to blue. "Stop hiding and embrace your nature."

"I'm not—" I can't bring myself to say it. *I'm not Dimma.* It's becoming less and less true somehow, and I wonder if it's because I'm so close to dying. Dimma never learned her nature before Fram killed her. I part my lips to speak again, but I don't know what to say. I look to Koré as if she has the answers. She'd once been there to guide Dimma a very long time ago.

Koré gives me a sympathetic smile, her eyes the color of the blood moon. "It's never taken this long for any of our kind to figure themselves out." There's a hint of bemusement in her voice, and it only reminds me of what Daho said: the gods don't think like us. I see nothing funny about any of this. They're saying . . . they think . . . they think that I am her. I frown, my uneasiness growing. *Am I?* I hate that I'm doubting myself.

"I've long thought your nature has something to do with transformation." Koré finally stops circling and settles in front of me. "You've become Arrah, haven't you? It's not like me—I'm only wearing a face. This is a vessel. It is not the essence of who I am, but you've become someone else completely. It's fascinating."

"You wouldn't be the first to need help discovering their nature," croaks Nana.

I'm shaking again, folding in on myself. I'm at once shrinking and growing larger at the same time. Silence stretches out in long, drawn-out beats, giving us all the time in the world to dwell on the moment.

"Oh, come on!" Re'Mec groans, breaking the stillness in the hall. "This isn't a family reunion. We should be dragging Dimma off to the Supreme Cataclysm right now so she can be unmade for good." Re'Mec puts his hands on his hips. "One less enemy to deal with."

"I am not your enemy," I say. I hope this time they'll listen. For now, it doesn't matter if they see me as Arrah or Dimma; in their minds, there is no difference. There are more important things to work out. "Your petty bickering has almost destroyed the universe." I pause to quell my rising anger. "I don't pretend to understand the will of the Supreme Cataclysm, but you've fought for millennia to ensure your immortality, and now look at you. So few left, and you're still fighting. There has to be another way."

"What are you proposing?" Koré asks.

"Does it matter?" Re'Mec snaps.

Koré glares at him. "Brother, you can be such an ass sometimes."

The sun orisha brushes his fingers across his forehead and bows. "I do try."

"I'm offering a way to bridge the divide between us, to begin to heal old wounds," I blurt out, desperate. "No matter who you think I am, the person you see before you will die soon, and Dimma will return. You will need her help to stop my sister."

"Then we should kill you now," Mouran suggests, his tail curled at his ankles. "What's the point of waiting?"

"No." Koré narrows her eyes at him. "I don't believe it's that simple. There is more at play here than we know—some unseen force."

"I have sensed so as well," Nana says quietly.

Murmurs of agreement pass through the gods, except for Re'Mec, who only scowls at me. "I still don't trust you."

"The feeling is mutual," I remind him, "but answer me this: what would happen if Efiya consumed your soul? Or Koré's or Dimma's?"

"We would either destroy her or make her powerful beyond her dreams." He shrugs like it's something he hasn't considered, but his eyes darken with fear. "I see your point."

I look at the last of Dimma's siblings, overwhelmed by the sheer magic filling the air around me. At once, it feels like a wild storm, a hot lash, a cool breeze, the tang of the sea. Any moment they could rain down their wrath on me, but I also sense that they're tired, too, and want to return to their natures rather than fight an endless war.

"We will accept you as our *Ka*-Priestess, Arrah," Koré says finally. "As we will accept Dimma when she emerges again, if she is agreeable."

"'If she is agreeable,'" Re'Mec repeats mockingly. "You have too much faith in our sister."

"And you have too little," Kiva says, sitting on the floor, tinkering with his toys.

Suddenly the hall is again filled with people, and the orishas are gone. Emere guides me to kneel between the Twin Kings' statues. Tamarans watch with bated breath, waiting to see what will happen. They whisper to each other, but before their doubt can settle, the shadows shift around Re'Mec's and Koré's statues, then light pours from the orishas' eyes down on me. The hall bursts into joy as people chant, "*Ka*-Priestess, *Ka*-Priestess, *Ka*-Priestess."

The next morning, Essnai sets off before sunrise with two of the craven guards to check on her family after being gone so long. I can't stop thinking about last night. The orishas believe that Dimma has undergone some kind of transformation to become me. It doesn't make any sense. I saw her in my mind when Rudjek almost died. I talked to her, for gods' sake. Or maybe I was talking to myself. I am pacing around the bedchamber, still reeling from my conversation with the orishas, when there is a knock at the door.

I stop midstride. "Come."

"An attendant from the palace is here to see you," Jahla says, then enters, accompanied by a stout woman. The attendant lowers her gaze as she thrusts a letter into my hand. "A message from the Almighty One to the new *Ka*-Priestess."

Once the woman leaves, I break the seal: a lion's head in black wax. Like its author, the writing is pretentious, with sharp edges and bold strokes that refuse to stay straight.

I have made some grave missteps, its reads. *I would like to make them right. Please join me at the palace at midday.*

Suran Omari is arrogant to presume that he could ever make up for his deeds. It's too late for that. But did I not just extend a hand to the orishas to mend a much worse wrong?

I give the letter to Jahla, and she lifts the parchment to her nose, employing her craven senses.

"Fake?" I say hopefully.

"It indeed smells of Suran Omari," she confirms.

"This is . . . unexpected."

"Shall I seek out Rudjek?" Jahla asks. "He might not know that his father sent you a message."

I feel a twinge of annoyance. I have to face Suran Omari on my own terms. "No—that won't be necessary."

Jahla looks as if she wants to insist, but she nods instead.

The morning passes quickly, and as the hour approaches, I prepare to leave. Jahla and two of the craven guards join me. The remaining two stay behind to keep my chamber free of assassins waiting in the shadows. In the corridors, we pass attendants who whisper their congratulations and pledge their loyalty. I hope it will be better once we leave the Temple's halls, but the courtyard is even worse. Hundreds of people have camped out overnight for a chance to see me. I push down the doubts nibbling away at my confidence.

"The orishas are smiling upon you," I tell them to offer some semblance of hope. The gods may be petty at times, but they do love their creations in their own strange ways.

We encounter more loyalists as we descend from the Temple and cross the West Market. The craven guards push them back so we can reach the litter station leading up the mountain to the Almighty Palace. I show the letter to one of the gendars, who clears Jahla and me for passage to the palace. He insists that I can have only one companion with me. I don't argue. The other two cravens will shift into birds or something else. Likely, they'll arrive at the palace before us. Jahla and I ascend the mountain, and as soon as we step outside of our litter, her back goes rigid.

"Rudjek isn't here," she tells me. "Nor is Fadyi. Only your other guards." She nods at the pair we'd left only a moment ago, now strolling toward us, still disguised as gendars. But a set of actual gendars blocks their path and demand to know why they're not at their assigned posts.

At the same time, a palace attendant hurries over and bows briskly. "Welcome, *Ka*-Priestess. The Almighty One is finishing a meeting with one of the foreign delegations, but he will be with you shortly."

The attendant leads the way to a sunny salon overlooking one of the gardens. Jahla paces as we wait. I'm surprised to hear Princess Veeka's high-pitched voice drifting from the corridor outside the salon. I expected her to have returned to Galke after Rudjek informed his father that he would not marry her.

I poke my head into the hall just as she and her adviser, Prefect Clopa, are about to pass the salon. The princess startles, her violet-colored eyes going wide.

"I should've known that you'd be back, too," she says sourly. "Have you seen Rudjek today? No one will tell me where he is."

"No," I admit, uneasy. It seems too convenient that Suran Omari invited me to the palace while Rudjek is away.

"Then why are you here?" she asks pointedly.

I don't see how it's her business, but I answer anyway. "To see the Almighty One."

She considers me for a moment. "Can we have a word in private, Arrah?"

"Princess Veeka, that would not be advisable," Prefect Clopa whispers. I hear the unspoken subtext: *she's the enemy.*

"I insist," the princess says.

"Give us a moment," I tell Jahla. She and the Prefect wait in the corridor as Princess Veeka joins me in the salon.

The princess makes a tour of the room, examining the various trinkets and idols on display. "When I first came here, I believed that meeting Rudjek was only a formality. His father assured me that we would be a good match. Had I known he already loved another, I wouldn't have come."

I recall her words at the palace, where she declared that she didn't want to become a third wife like her mother.

"I find myself in a predicament," she admits. "I could return to Galke, where our customs dictate that I be gifted in marriage to one of my father's generals. It isn't the worst fate. But you see, I've grown accustomed to the freedom I enjoy in the Kingdom. No one tells me what I can and can't do or who I can and can't see. I like it here, and Rudjek is charming and handsome, but most important, he is kind."

I want to be patient with the princess, but I'm not fond of the direction this conversation is going. Still, I let her finish. I owe her that much after being incredibly rude the last time we met.

Princess Veeka sighs. "I don't think of you as my competition anymore. . . . I hope you can have all the things that I cannot."

"You don't . . ." I can't believe that I'm going to say this. "You don't have to go back to Galke, you know."

"I don't plan to. I will ask the Almighty One and Queen Serre to stay on as one of their advisers. I know Galkian politics as a matter of practice and can be of service to the Kingdom." Princess Veeka pauses. "But I need you to know that my reason for staying isn't because I secretly believe I have a chance with Rudjek."

I resist telling her not to count herself out. Soon, I'll be dead, and Rudjek will move on, eventually.

Two gendars push through the double doors of the salon, interrupting our conversation. Suran Omari trails behind them, every bit as self-assured as I remember. Gods. Rudjek is the spitting image of him with his curly hair, square jaw, and eyes black as oil pits. He wears a white-and-gold elara more suitable for ceremonies than everyday palace business. He's taken the precaution of adorning himself with craven bone. I spot the wristlet and the lion's head pendant pinned to his tunic. If he's wearing all those trinkets, then he must not know I gave up my magic after all. Good—I can use that to my advantage.

"Leave us, Princess Veeka," he commands, his voice not unkind. "I have business with our new *Ka*-Priestess."

"Of course, Almighty One," Princess Veeka says with a gracious smile. She bows, and the gendars escort her out, letting the doors close behind them.

Now Suran Omari and I are alone.

"I'm told that you dispatched my assassins with ease in the tribal lands," Suran says. I hadn't forgotten how he speaks with the arrogance of a man who always gets what he wants. "Burned them to ashes."

"That's true," I say without hesitation. "I hope this means that you have learned not to trifle with me."

Suran's lips curl in pure hatred. "You must understand why you and my son can never be—" His words cut off abruptly as if something more important has occurred to him. He frowns as he studies my face, and I know I'm in trouble. "I could feel your magic before, but something's changed." He breaks into a slow smile. "It's gone."

Dread fills my belly. He knows. Of course he does. He has craven blood. Even before Rudjek had awakened into his anti-magic, he had sensed my magic, too. "I'm simply better at hiding it," I say with forced ease. "Now to the point of why you summoned me here. If you want to atone for your crimes, you must release the people you imprisoned for using magic."

"I no longer see a reason to do that," he says, clearly not believing my lie. "It's just as I thought; you're nothing but another charlatan like your mother."

I'm burning with anger that he has the nerve to bring up my mother after everything he's done. "Then you leave me no choice. I will do everything in my power to make sure that Prince Derane unseats you and gets his throne back. He'll have the Temple's full support."

Suran pulls out a knife of craven bone, and I stumble in surprise. I expected him to fall back on his usual political scheming but nothing like this. I reach for Daho's dagger hidden beneath the sash around my waist but stop short of drawing it. If I use the blade, I'll die. I can't let that happen, not while Efiya is still a threat.

When Suran lurches for me, I duck and jam my elbow into his side. He grunts, barely slowing down. He's nimbler than he looks. Before I can call to Jahla for help, he yanks my head back, and then I feel the cold sting of his knife at my throat.

"Do this, and Rudjek will hate you for the rest of your miserable life," I say through gritted teeth.

"He'll never know the truth," Suran whispers next to my ear. "I called you to the palace to make peace, but it so happens that an attendant in my service had other ideas. Your mother fed his young daughter's soul to a demon, and he wanted revenge. It's all so unfortunate."

I shouldn't be shocked that he's already thought this out. He's despicable. Nothing will ever change that. I bite down on my lip hard enough to draw blood. I'm out of options, all except one. I can call magic, though that might kill me even faster. My fingers twitch. I'm on the verge of giving in.

"Goodbye, *Ka*-Priestess," Suran spits, but he falters when a great roaring fills the room.

Pulsing rings of light appear in the middle of the salon, and Daho is a flash of silver skin and white wings as he descends from the gate. In a blur, he disarms Suran and knocks him against a wall.

Despite everything, I'm relieved to see him. Part of me had wondered—*had worried*—that the next time we met he would be waging war on the orishas with Efiya by his side.

But Daho's attention isn't on me. I'm gasping for air, half in shock, as he stalks toward Suran. I can't let him kill Rudjek's father, no matter how much I despise him. "No," I wheeze. "Leave him."

"I should have done this a long time ago," Daho says, his teeth bared. He extends his hand, and Suran's discarded dagger flies to him, hilt first. Suran calls for his guards, a trickle of blood creeping down his forehead. They won't get here in time.

I race toward them, but Daho is too fast. He cuts off Suran's cry with one quick thrust. I stop short. Dread courses through me as Suran slumps to the floor, the dagger still in his chest.

"He had that coming." Daho gives him a final disgusted look, then he turns to me, the hard glint in his eyes gone. "I should have told you about Efiya."

I can't stop staring at Suran. He's really dead. I don't feel sorry for him, but I'm worried about what Rudjek will do. He already hates Daho, and this will only make things so much worse.

"She's my best friend's daughter." He sighs, his face twisted in anguish. "You must understand the position that puts me in."

"You won't be able to control her," I warn him. "She'll undermine you every chance she gets."

He glances at my waist, to the dagger made of Eluua's soul. "I'm afraid it's too late for that."

I retrieve the blade and offer it to him. Maybe it's a mistake. "You need it more than I do."

Just before he enters the mouth of the roaring gate, Daho says, "Keep it."

Then he's gone.

TWENTY-THREE
EFIYA

I've split myself in two again. I'm strolling through the palace halls with Tyrek. I'm also in the library with Papa and Evelyn as they nervously wait for the Demon King to return. He's run off through the gate. I suppose Arrah's gotten herself in more trouble. That could be the only reason why he left in such a hurry.

"I'm bored out of my mind," Tyrek complains. He's following me like a lost dog. "Perhaps I should go to Zöran to keep an eye on things there. I still have friends who could be of use."

"Or I could put you back in the dagger once I take it from my sister."

Tyrek stares at me with his mouth open until he breaks into a smile. He thinks that I am teasing him, but I'm dead serious. He's starting to get on my nerves. "Even that would be more entertaining than these mirthless people."

I roll my eyes. "What happened to the woman you've been spending all your time with?"

"That didn't work out so well." Tyrek sighs. "I like my lovers with a little more spice."

He says this as we arrive in front of the gilded doors of the great hall. I've visited the demons inside every day since Evelyn brought me here. I'm the only one who comes. Sometimes I talk to them, and sometimes I just sit and keep them company.

Tyrek grimaces when he sees them for the first time. "This is morbid even for my taste."

"I don't want them to feel forgotten."

"Why don't we have a little fun?" Tyrek steps so close to me that I can smell him. "It's been too long since you let me share your bed. This is as good a place as any. I do like an audience on occasion."

I glare at him. "Is that all you can think about? Can't you see that these people are suffering?"

His face sours. "Like you really care."

I have no interest in dealing with Tyrek right now. I shouldn't have brought him here. He doesn't understand what it's like to be lonely. He had a family that loved him, and he threw that away.

While in the library with Papa and Evelyn, I'm looking through the endless shelves of books. I'm not particularly in the mood for reading, but I like flipping through the pages. Papa is sitting at a small table beside the window, moving pieces around on a game-board with three tiers. I wish I had paid attention when he tried to teach me the rules. I'm regretting a lot of things lately.

"People have been talking," Evelyn says, perched on a windowsill. She's wearing black trousers and an orange blouse. "They're convinced Daho will betray us to the gods if it means getting Dimma back."

Papa says nothing. He doesn't even look up from the gameboard.

"And it's clear he's threatened by Efiya's power," Evelyn continues. "Who knows what he'll do if one day he decides that she is of no more use to him."

Papa winces like he's been struck by a blade. Evelyn's pulling all the right strings. I don't even have to lift a finger.

"We would follow you should you choose to act," she tells him.

Papa moves a game piece to the second tier. "I don't know what to think anymore."

"You have a child to protect, Shezmu," Evelyn says with so much yearning that I feel sorry for her. "That is all that matters now."

Back in the great hall, I pause by the demon whispering, "the end." Evelyn told me his name was Kalen. She should've said his name *is* Kalen. He isn't dead—none of them are. I squeeze his shoulder, and he shudders as my magic wraps around him. I can give these demons what no one else can: their freedom.

Both in the library and in the great hall, my skin tingles as the gate between worlds opens and closes again. Ah, the Demon King is back and so quickly, too. A moment later, he storms inside the library. He grimaces when he sees Papa's face and stops in the middle of the room.

"You went to Zöran alone after the gods almost killed you?" Shezmu accuses him. "Are you not thinking straight?"

"I'm thinking straight for the first time in ages, brother." The Demon King glances at Evelyn sitting on the windowsill, but he acts like I'm not even here. "Arrah was in trouble. I had to help her."

I clenched my teeth together so hard that they ache. Arrah, Arrah, Arrah. She's all he cares about, and I hate him for it. He used me to free himself from Koré's prison; now, I mean nothing to him. Just another pawn in his game.

"Where's your dagger?" Shezmu demands.

"I left it with her," the Demon King says like it should be obvious. "She needs it to protect herself."

"The girl has Dimma's soul—she's a god," Evelyn spits. "She doesn't need the dagger. But it was our only advantage over the Twin Kings."

I cross my arms and glare at him. He really is the most inconsiderate person I have ever met. "I guess it doesn't matter to you that my sister keeps trying to kill me with it. Maybe one day she'll succeed."

"If you find yourself at the end of the blade, it's your own doing," the Demon King says coldly. "You never can leave well enough alone."

Papa and Evelyn are speechless, but I don't know why his words come as a shock to them. The Demon King has made it clear that I could die tomorrow and he wouldn't so much as shed a tear.

Papa's shoulders sag as he slowly stands, the game forgotten. "I thought it a lie. I didn't want to believe the vision of the future that Iben showed me all those millennia ago. But it was true."

I frown. What vision is Papa talking about? This is the first I'm hearing of it. Before Arrah trapped me in the dagger, I could travel the threads of time, but I've lost that ability. Papa should've told me about this vision if it's so important. I hate that he's still treating me like a child.

The Demon King raises his chin defiantly. "Are you finally ready to tell me what he showed you, brother?"

"Are you?" Shezmu snaps.

The Demon King laughs, and it's a bitter, sarcastic sound. "I've made my decision. That is all you need to know."

Papa glances to the floor, and when he meets his friend's eyes again, his are glassy with tears. "I saw you standing with Arrah against your own people." He pauses as if to gather his courage. "You would choose her after everything we've been through together?"

The Demon King gives Papa an equally hurt look. Both wear their fraught emotions like moth-eaten clothes. "Yes, if you force my hand, but you already knew that. Arrah is my only path back to Dimma, and I will not let you or anyone else stand in the way of that." He cuts his eyes at me to make his meaning clear.

"You'd kill my daughter." It's a statement, not a question. He already knows the answer.

"If she gets in my way," the Demon King admits without a shred of remorse.

Tears rim Papa's bloodshot eyes. "I won't lose another child because of Dimma." He takes one uneven step toward his friend. "You don't want me as an enemy, brother."

"We've been through a lot together, Shezmu," the Demon King says, "but here is where our paths diverge."

Neither my father nor the Demon King notices Evelyn reaching behind her back. I could intervene, of course, but this is playing out perfectly. I hadn't expected things to go so fast. Now they finally see what I've been telling them all along: the Demon King will betray us the first chance he gets.

Evelyn looks like someone's ripped her heart in two as she flings a pair of daggers at him. They soar across the library in a flash, but a sword of light appears in the Demon King's hand. He deflects the daggers in one sweep. Evelyn is already on the move. She turns from flesh to smoke to flesh again. Then she's on top of him, shrieking and clawing at his eyes.

"Stop this before there is no turning back!" he growls.

"It's too late for that," she spits. "You are no longer the king we once knew."

"What's happening?" Tyrek asks me in the great hall, diverting my attention from the fight. "You have *that* look."

I grimace, annoyed, but the perfect opportunity has presented itself. "The Demon King is trying to kill Papa and Evelyn," I say, my voice filled with as much panic as I can muster on such short notice. "We have to help them."

"What do you mean 'we'?" Tyrek's eyes go wide. "I don't see how it's any of my business."

Ignoring him, I turn to the frozen demons in the great hall, my eyes pleading. "I can free you—but the Demon King has forbidden me to use my magic." It isn't exactly true, but it isn't precisely a lie, either. "You have to help Papa and Evelyn." According to Evelyn, Shezmu took care of the demons while their king was obsessed with getting Dimma back for centuries, so I'm willing to bet they're loyal to my father.

Back in the library, Papa's wielding his own swords of light. Although he looks miserable, he joins Evelyn against his former friend. Jasym runs into the library, followed by another dozen demons. None of them are as strong as the Demon King or Papa. How disappointing that more haven't come.

The Demon King is a blur of rage as he fights back. Papa parries, barely dodging a blow and delivering one of his own. His sword slices into the Demon King's belly, burning through his flesh with ease. But the Demon King only stumbles before recovering. He grits his teeth as he fends off Evelyn, Jasym, and the others who press the attack. It's a messy affair of mangled bodies that repair themselves almost immediately.

I decide to act when it's clear that Papa and the others can't end their king. I twitch my fingers, and two swords appear in my hands: shotels with curved blades. I like the way they sing as they cut through the air. They're fine weapons that I learned to wield with ease against my sister. That seems so long ago.

I am faster than the Demon King. It takes no time to shred his body with my swords. He crumples in a heap and looks down at his savaged chest, shocked that his vessel isn't healing. "Heka's gift is wonderful, isn't it? Remarkable, really." I cluck my tongue. "We gave you the chance to show your loyalty to your people, but you turned your back on us. What happens now is your fault."

"You've made a grave mistake, Efiya—one of many," the Demon King spits, blood staining his teeth.

The souls inside me twist and squirm, desperate to get out, but I don't mind them. Today they're about to be joined by one more. My mouth waters at the thought of how delectable the Demon King's soul will taste as it slips across my tongue. Once I have him, I'll be unstoppable. "You will live on inside me."

As I descend upon him, the Demon King uses the last of his strength to call forth the gate, but Papa raises his hand, and the gate closes instantly. "This is your end, brother. Don't make this harder than it needs to be."

Darkness bleeds across the library. Before I can react, an overwhelming sense of dread pours into my mind, seeping into every corner. The walls, the bookshelves, and even the windows ooze with writhing shadows.

Demon after demon falls. Their vessels begin to crack, revealing hollow insides filled with gray light—their souls. The shadows devour them.

"You would use Fram's children against your own people?" Shezmu howls with rage. It's his gravest weakness: underestimating the Demon King. "You'd better hope the reapers kill me before I can kill you."

Ah, these are the reapers he told me about. When the Demon King killed the orisha of life and death, he inherited control of their children. I will control them once I devour his soul, and I will control the gate between worlds. Things are shaping up quite nicely for me.

I redouble my efforts, fighting against the dread that binds me in chains. I can't free myself. I need to rejoin my two halves.

"Help me, please," I beg the frozen demons in the great hall. "He's killing us."

Tyrek startles next to me, alarmed, but then I take a chance. I pour my magic into the great hall. Ribbons of white light weave around the demons. It's taking all of my strength to do this, and I fall to my knees.

Tyrek is holding me, screaming my name. "Efiya, are you all right?"

The demons escape their bondage, melt into smoke, and disappear. I draw myself back into one place: in the library just as the freed demons arrive. Now I'm ready to end this. We close ranks around the Demon King. We have him where we want him. He bares his teeth, then the reapers bleed the life out of more demons with a quickness that shocks even me. It's pure carnage.

I back away, but the reapers suddenly surround me, ignoring the other demons. Their dread permeates the air. It's crushing, all-consuming, inescapable. My soul is unraveling. I won't be able to hold on for long.

"Papa!" I scream.

"Release the gate, or she dies," the Demon King demands.

Shezmu growls in anguish as the gate opens again. He hadn't even hesitated. "Leave her alone," he whispers. "Please."

I hate that he has to beg for my life, but I know now that my father truly loves me, despite all my faults and mistakes. He loves me, and I love him. I won't let the Demon King ruin that.

"Don't follow me." The Demon King stumbles toward the gate with the reapers at his back.

When he's gone, Papa wraps me in his arms and weeps. I'm safe, but some of the demons aren't so lucky. It's a shame, really. I just freed most of them. Now they're dead, and the reapers destroyed their souls.

Jasym comes to stand next to their sister. "I bet he's running straight to Dimma."

"Of course, he is," Evelyn spits. "He's a fool."

Papa stares at where the gate had been only a moment ago. "We have to finish what we started."

I'm in a foul mood as Tyrek walks into the library—I'd forgotten about him that quickly. He breaks into a slow clap. "Well done, Efiya," he says with fake admiration. "You overplayed your hand yet again. The Demon King has proven himself more cunning than you."

I whirl around to face the prince, giving him my most inviting smile, and then snap his neck. His beautiful face twists in surprise as the light fades from his eyes. This time I won't bring him back.

TWENTY-FOUR
ARRAH

I watch Suran Omari take his final breaths. Blood has soaked completely through his white and gold elara. It's too much to wrap my mind around, too surreal. The man who had my mother tortured—who helped create the monster she became—is dying. The man who banished my family from the Kingdom, who sent assassins after me and, when they failed, tried to kill me himself. I knew he was ruthless, but I never thought he'd stoop this low.

I've wanted him to pay for his crimes for a long time—yet, as much as I hate Suran, he's still Rudjek's father. He can't die because of me.

I kneel at his side, but in truth, I don't know what to do. The craven bone dagger is still lodged in his chest. It's the only thing that's keeping him from bleeding out faster. His dark eyes lock on mine. There's so much fear in them that it must've been there all along, simmering underneath his rage. I don't know if he's seeing my mother or me.

"Know that I'm doing this for Rudjek," I tell him angrily. "If not for him, I would let you die."

There's fighting in the corridor outside the salon, the clash of swords, calls for reinforcements, moans of agony. "Jahla!" I scream.

The fear slips away from Suran's gaze, and he settles into a look of regret. Another man might be pondering where he went wrong or regretting his misdeeds. Not Suran. He's only sorry he failed.

The door bursts open, and five red-clad gendars rush in with their swords raised. Anti-magic brushes against my skin, and I'm relieved they're cravens, not true soldiers of the Kingdom arriving to find me kneeling over their dying king. Jahla sweeps in after them, her silver hair trailing behind her. From the bloody scene in her wake, I surmise that Suran had ordered his guards to keep everyone from the salon. I still can't believe that he'd planned this. I almost reconsider letting him die.

"Help him," I plead.

Jahla stares at Suran's near lifeless body, her face set in a deep frown. She crouches at his side and presses two fingers to his throat. "I don't know if I should. He's caused so much trouble already."

Queen Serre races into the salon with another set of guards on her heels. When she sees Suran, she screams, the black veins along her forehead pulsing. For the first time, I realize she looks like an endoyan that Dimma once knew. Perhaps that woman had fled through the gate from Ilora to Zöran when Dimma unleashed her wrath on the endoyans for betraying the demon people. Some part of me realizes that my life—Dimma's life—is coming full circle. Serre rushes across the room, half stumbling.

Queen Serre glares at the gendars, who to her must appear apathetic to the king's predicament. "Don't just stand there—call for his physicians!"

Several of the human guards rush to carry out her order.

"I couldn't save Majka," Jahla says, her voice stilted. "Why should I save him?"

"Do it for Rudjek's sake," I tell her.

"Don't let him die like this," Queen Serre says, realizing there's still hope. "Perhaps he deserves it, but I beg you to show mercy to your king."

Jahla sighs in resignation. "I still think it's a mistake."

"Everyone except this gendar and Arrah, get out!" Queen Serre demands.

The cravens look to Jahla, who nods for them to leave. The human guards depart, too.

"Why have you done this, Arrah?" Queen Serre turns on me. "I know Suran and your mother had history. . . ."

"I didn't," I say, and offer no further explanation. I'm too tired to be furious with her. I know how this must look. I'm alive, and her husband is very much not. Had she known about his plans?

She looks from her husband back to me, considering. "Then who?"

"Arrah," Jahla interrupts. "If I proceed, he will be changed. He's too close to death."

I swallow hard, my heart racing. I thought that she'd be able to heal him. I hadn't expected this. "He'll . . . become like Rudjek?"

Jahla pulls the blade from his chest. "I'm afraid so."

"What does that mean?" Queen Serre asks.

He will become a craven, and no good could come of him having such power. He'd only use it to further his twisted agenda. "He will be alive," I say, hiding my true thoughts.

I pace the room until Queen Serre steps in front of me. Her eyes are troubled. She clearly has more than Suran's survival on her mind. "I've sensed a change in Rudjek since the first time he returned from the tribal lands." She stares at me a moment longer before turning away and going to the window. "But even before that, I noticed strange things about him, Jemi, and Uran," she says of her three sons. "When they were young, they hardly ever got hurt, and if one did, they'd heal exceptionally fast without help from a physician. I always thought it odd, but Suran just said it took a lot to make an Omari bleed." She glances back at me. "It's more than that, isn't it? Rudjek is different somehow."

"It's not my place to say," I answer, unable to hold her gaze.

"I fear this is much bigger than I ever understood."

To my relief, Rudjek bursts into the salon with Fadyi and Elder Ro on his heels. He skids to a stop, taking in the sight of his father, covered in blood, of Jahla and his mother and me. "Is he . . . ?"

"He is awakening." Jahla climbs to her feet. "It was the only way to save his life."

"This is an interesting turn of events," Elder Ro remarks, and I'm not imagining the trace of a smirk on her lips.

"My father can't be trusted with anti-magic," Rudjek says, his voice turning hard. "He'll claim the tribal lands if he knows magic can't affect him. I fear what else he'll do."

"That would be disastrous," Elder Ro assures him.

Queen Serre watches the two of them keenly. "Anti-magic?"

she repeats slowly. "Only the bones of a craven can protect against magic." She's finally connecting the pieces, but her face doesn't betray her feelings. "You're one of them. You're a craven. You all are." Queen Serre leans against a wall and stares at her husband, who still hasn't moved. "Does Suran know?"

Rudjek shakes his head. "There's much I need to tell you, Adé. I promise that I will explain everything in time."

"We'll follow your lead, whatever you decide." Elder Ro tells him, then lowers her gaze. "If you will excuse us . . . we will leave you to this Eldest Clan business."

Fadyi gives both Rudjek and Jahla a sympathetic look before he and Elder Ro depart. I don't pretend to understand the dynamics between the four of them. I hadn't even realized that Jahla was also of the Eldest Clan.

Rudjek crosses the room and takes my hands. "Are you okay?"

I nod, though I feel numb. "You haven't asked what happened to him."

Rudjek stares down at our interlaced fingers, sticky with blood. "I'm sure it was his fault."

"He attacked me." I don't want to tell him the rest, but I can't lie either. "The Demon King saved my life."

Shock appears in Rudjek's eyes. His body goes rigid. He isn't the only one. Every face in the salon is riddled with dread and fear. "The Demon King did this to my father?"

I bite my lip. "There's something you must see."

I show Rudjek the letter from his father. He skims it, then drops the paper as if it's burning a hole in his hand. He pulls me against him, and I let myself sink into his warmth, shaking, finally beginning to thaw. "Gods, he lured you here. . . . I'm so sorry, Arrah."

Queen Serre watches our embrace. Then she startles as Suran Omari inhales a breath that sends a chill down my spine. When he opens his eyes, they are two bottomless pits of darkness, and they are glaring straight at me.

DAHO

After Shezmu, Yacara, and I fail to consume the god of life and death's soul, the Twin Kings return to Ilora. We leave Iben's gate open as an invitation.

My army is waiting for them—stronger than ever, fat off the souls of the weaker gods. We will not fail this time, and I will take Dimma back from Fram even if I have to tear them apart with my bare hands. When Koré and Re'Mec ascend from the gate, thrice as many gods accompany them as did the day Fram stole Dimma's soul.

The Twin Kings shimmer into being from thin air in the center of Jiiek, in the market where vendors once sold curiosities imported from distant lands. It's bare dirt now. They have already caused so much destruction, yet they will do much worse before the end.

Shezmu and Yacara flank me, their swords ready. Evelyn, Jasym, and the others are at our backs. Together we have survived despite the gods' punishment. We have built some semblance of a life for ourselves. My heart aches with the knowledge that we will be enemies one day, if Iben's vision is to be believed.

"This is how you repay our mercy?" Re'Mec muses, taking in my army. "We could have killed every single one of you, but we gave you a second chance instead."

Shezmu scowls at the sun god. "You're not a very good liar, Re'Mec. You couldn't kill us, but we've found a way to kill *you*."

"What have you done with our siblings?" Koré demands. Her twin swords shift between silver moonlight and raging fire.

"You really haven't guessed yet?" I pat my belly and smile. "We ate them."

"Impossible!" Re'Mec spits, but Koré understands immediately that I am telling the truth. She's always been the smarter of the two.

"You fear me." I laugh as sweat stings my eyes. The irony of it is too much to fathom, too sweet to resist. "You fear me because I am a reflection of you. I am your greed, your insatiable hunger, your lust, your arrogance. *I am you.*"

Re'Mec's eyes blaze like twin suns growing more feverish. He spits on the ground, and the soil at his feet turns a sickly yellow. "You are nothing like us, boy," he says, his face splitting into a grimace. "We are what the Supreme Cataclysm intended, but you are an abomination forged by our sister's misguided love."

Koré seems less sure. She lets out a sigh, one that draws the heat from the air. I resist the urge to shiver—the act would be a falsity, a lie. I have no true sense of cold anymore. I have only memories of it. "That's not all we are, Daho," she says. "We can't deny ourselves, that in us, we are love, hate, pain, greed, revenge, compassion, joy, empathy . . . every emotion that can ever be experienced. That is the nature of what we are, but you see only the bad, only the worst. Your child put the universe out of balance. We had to try to correct that, though it seems we failed. In a sense, we killed him and Dimma in service of the Supreme Cataclysm and the continuation of all life."

I hold Fram's secret close. They cannot find out that Dimma is alive. "You killed them in service of yourselves." So long ago, when I was a boy, I revered the stories of our creator, how unwavering she'd been in her convictions. Now I despise her. "Don't try to convince me otherwise. You are afraid of your own mortality."

"Yes, that's true," Koré says as she starts to pace. "And Dimma and your child are gone now, but the universe is still dying."

I point the dagger at her. "You said my son was the reason the universe was dying, but you were wrong. Nothing has changed."

Re'Mec reaches his arm toward the sun. Flames streak across the sky and land on his fingertips. The sun dims, and shadows fall over Jiiek. An acrid smell burns my nose, and I realize with horror that he intends to kill our sun. "A god cannot be wrong," he says, and his voice is a clap of thunder.

The trees and grass wither before my eyes. The rich soil turns from black to ash. The other gods are helping Re'Mec destroy our world. I give the signal, and my army attacks, with Shezmu in command. He is a spark of brilliance as he shreds, tears, and cuts through the gods' ranks. His mouth becomes a black hole that consumes soul after soul.

I will take care of the Twin Kings myself. I extend my dagger into a sword of light and descend upon Re'Mec. The dagger cuts through his sword as easily as if it were ripe fruit. He staggers back, but his sister is there to block my next blow, and she is not so easily overpowered.

I strike again, again, again, cutting and slicing. I am tireless, but at best, it's a stalemate. Re'Mec becomes a streak of flame that my blade cannot touch. Koré is a mirage that shimmers in and out of sight. I follow them across Ilora until we land far away from the rest of the battle.

"True love always demands sacrifice," Koré whispers on the wind. "You must know that by now."

"I couldn't agree more," I say. "It's certainly worth sacrificing a few gods for."

There is a sudden dampness in the air, and gods . . . No, not gods, *people* converge on our position. They dress in white and hold long, slim blades. Their skin is constantly moving and shifting, and their faces are blank canvases with no features.

Re'Mec claps and laughs. "My newest children are impressive, aren't they? I call them cravens. My sister believed you would come to your senses after Dimma died, but I knew better. Now it's time to say goodbye." He gives me a mocking wave.

I rush at them, and immediately heat scorches my skin. The pain is incredible, but I keep pushing. The cravens move with such grace that I'm transfixed. I try to let go of my body, but I can't, nor can I repair it. These creatures have somehow bound me in flesh. It's not until I feel my soul begin to unspool that I understand what Re'Mec has done. The cravens were created solely for this purpose—to destroy us. They, too, are pawns in the gods' game.

I back away from the Twin Kings with the cravens in pursuit. I'm counting on them following me. I'm the one they want.

By the time I enter Iben's gate, I'm finally able to let go of my body. I search the threads for the one that will lead me to Fram. A dozen, a hundred, thousands of threads. Time is endless here, but I grow more and more frantic until, finally, I come upon the right thread. I can feel its pulsing with Fram's soul. I follow it, careening toward the end. I exit the gate in Zöran. Fram is waiting for me where Dimma and I once had a summer palace on top of a mountain. The palace and the mountain are gone, destroyed by the gods. There is only a valley of lush green here now.

"One can build a castle in the clouds and still not reach heaven," Fram says. "If there even is such a place."

I force calm into my voice, knowing I cannot fail this time. "Why did you spare Dimma only to keep her imprisoned?"

"I haven't yet decided that I *am* sparing her," Fram says after a long pause. "I am still thinking upon it. These decisions must be properly weighed and considered. I am not my siblings. I am not brash or impatient. I had all the time in the universe before you killed Iben."

"I'll strike a deal with you. I will stop killing the gods if you return Dimma to me," I say. "You already killed our child. You and your brethren got what you wanted."

"I did not kill your child." Fram stares at me, and something like sympathy creases their faces. "Dimma did that on her own."

I refuse to listen to their lies. I only see flashes of light as I attack the orisha of life and death, but an overwhelming rush of dread crushes my determination. My arms fall slack. Black bleeds from the corners of my eyes as Fram's two sides merge into one. They are a mass of writhing shadows with no discernible shape, bearing down on me. I fall to my knees, and the dagger drops from my hand.

"You shouldn't have come here," Fram's dual voices whisper. "My children are hungry."

"Let them devour me, then," I say, ready to give myself over to them. Fram's shadows crawl across my skin, draining my will to fight.

Dimma's soul is so close that I can almost reach out and touch her. She didn't kill our son. I refuse to believe that—it isn't true. Fram only wants to make me suffer more. "I'm sorry," I say. Or maybe I only think it. I can't tell the difference. I am melting, dying, and the pain is numbing. "I'm so sorry, Dimma. I couldn't protect you and our son."

I am nearing death when I see her on the bone throne. But the scene is all wrong. This throne—I built many years after she died. She never sat upon it. This is one of Iben's gifts, like the vision he showed Shezmu and me.

Dimma is staring at her empty hands with tears on her cheeks. Then she looks to my left. "You shouldn't be here," two voices say at once. One voice belongs to Dimma, and one is unknown to me.

At my side, I see a human girl with golden eyes. It's the girl that Iben showed me so long ago—the girl I would betray my people for. Who is she? None of this makes sense, but it feels real. *It feels right.* "I've . . . I've seen this before," I say, certain of it. But when is this happening—now, in the past, in the future? "I've seen this exact moment."

"Why are you here?" Dimma and the girl say at the same time.

"What happened to your son?" the girl asks solemnly. "Did you kill him?"

But before Dimma can answer, she fades, along with the throne, the girl, and everything else. The moment slips away.

I scream, pushing the images out of my head. Dimma did not kill our son, and she isn't dead—she's isn't. She's . . . she's . . . she's—

I sob, trapped inside my own mind, as half of my army pours through the gate. The battle starts anew, and Fram turns their attention to the onslaught. It's just enough distraction to let me break free of their hold. I retrieve the dagger. I've seen the human girl twice now in visions. She's important. She must be the key to getting Dimma back. Her presence fills me with hope that there is still a chance.

The Twin Kings emerge from the gate with their cravens—and Shezmu, chained between them. Fram's writhing ribbons shoot out with breathtaking speed and punch through Shezmu's chest; then, methodically, they cut down every soldier in my army. I scream in rage as their bodies turn into dust that scatters in the wind. The gods become streaks of light as they gather up my people's souls like farmers harvesting crops.

I've failed to free Dimma. Now I've failed them.

Some of the gods move to the gate. Their forms melt and flow inside, and the gate closes. I command it to open again to call forth the rest of my army, but it doesn't respond. I can feel the gods inside the gate resisting; they've forged a barrier between it and me.

Given time, I can break it. But I'm out of time.

There is a single moment of perfect stillness before Fram, Koré, and Re'Mec attack me from all directions. I am cut down by lightning, burned by fire, savaged by shadows.

I'm on my knees again. It's then that Koré approaches me with a box softly glowing. She opens it. "We can't kill you now that you've eaten our brethren," she says. "But I've found a way to stop you until we can free them."

My soul slips into the box, and I become lost in memories.

I pull Dimma into my arms. "Let me be the first to tell our child a story." I press my chin against the top of her head and inhale her scent. "Once, there was a broken boy who fell from the sky. A goddess, both terrifying and terrifyingly beautiful, saved him from death. The goddess had eyes the deep brown of night pearls and a heart bigger than the world." Dimma curls against me, contentedly listening to our story.

For countless millennia, I reside in a vast dark place, reliving my memories. I'm alone, save for a glimmer of light at the edges of the darkness. I am neither cold nor warm as I drift toward the light. But whenever I get close, it pushes me back into the dark.

This becomes my existence, this place where there is no day or night, no time. I question my choices, my mistakes, my regrets, my sanity. I think about every moment I had with Dimma and spend eternity missing her.

Now and again, I can sense her soul. The feeling is faint at first, like a dream, but it grows stronger over time. I slowly come to understand that I am in a prison. Koré is my jailer, and I am chained by the souls of other gods.

The core of Dimma's soul stays the same, but she's transforming into something else. It happens again and again, and in time I see a pattern.

There's always a brief moment when her soul is restored to its original condition. Every hundred years, she's transformed. She's . . . she's reborn.

One day I begin to reach beyond my prison. I scream at Koré until she finally relents and deigns to speak to me. We fall into a routine of hostile conversation.

"We're stuck in this world because of you," Koré hisses. "You have no idea how incredibly inconvenient it is to travel the old way. The universe is endless, and it takes much time."

"I'll open the gate if you let me go," I say out of spite.

"This box is your home for eternity," she says primly. "I am keeping you close, my child. This way, you will do no more harm."

But while she is talking, I discover a gap in my prison, and I home in on a people who possess magic but aren't gods. Curious. They call themselves the tribes of Heka.

Heka is one of the gods that I haven't met. He has given mortals magic for reasons of his own, much to the Twin Kings' annoyance. I eavesdrop as they debate what to do with him.

"He resists any effort I've made to talk," Koré says. "He dwells in the mouth of the Supreme Cataclysm."

"Calling himself the mother and father as if he made humans," Re'Mec fumes. "They are my children. *Mine.*"

"Calm yourself, brother," Koré says. "We should let him be unless he becomes a problem."

"Why until then?" Re'Mec is as impulsive as ever. "We waited until Daho became a problem. Look what that got us."

"We made a mistake with Dimma," Koré admits. "Let's not do the same with Heka."

I track the course of Dimma's soul. Fram has taken away her gifts and memories, but I can predict when she will be born again. I reach the mind of a Mulani named Arti among Heka's worshippers, who will become Dimma's next mother. She has immense magic, more than I've ever felt before in a mortal, and golden eyes . . . eyes like the girl from my visions.

The girl I saw in my vision . . . she isn't going to help me get Dimma back. She *is* Dimma.

PART IV

I am bound by my mother's hand.
Her last act of defiance against her siblings.
But the universe is full of sweet contradictions.
And I am full of tricks.
I cannot break my promise to her.
But I can bend it.
—Heka

TWENTY-FIVE
ARRAH

I'm only half listening as Rudjek explains the truth about his craven heritage to his mother. For her part, Queen Serre takes it stoically as she asks him questions. Jahla stays close to Suran Omari, who hasn't fully come to his senses yet.

"How could you keep such a secret from me for so long?" Serre demands. "Your father, I can understand, but I should've been the first to know."

"Adé," Rudjek pleads with her. "I've wanted to tell you so many times, but the moment never seemed right."

"It's a lot to take in," she says. "You're not completely human."

Rudjek smiles at his mother. "Neither are you."

As he tells her about her endoyan ancestry, I can't stop seeing the moment Daho plunged the craven-bone knife into Suran's heart. Only months before, he'd been desperate to get Dimma back—desperate to wake her. Yet, he's gone out of his way to save my life twice. After my conversation with Koré, Re'Mec, and the others, I'm starting to second-guess his intentions. They believe that I'm Dimma, but

Daho—the person who knew her best—isn't convinced. That should give me some solace, but I don't know what to think anymore.

Efiya has already started to seed dissent among his people. He only has himself to blame. He should've known that she would not listen to reason, nor would she be content with a second chance at life. My sister has our mother's unwavering ambition and cruelty. She's done unspeakable things, and I don't doubt she's planning worse.

Perhaps I'm a fool for caring about what happens to Daho. We could've been friends in another life. We *were* friends in this one for the short time he was pretending to be Sukar. After everything that's happened, my cousin's vision of him standing over my broken body seems less and less likely. If anything, that honor will go to my sister.

Jahla backs away from Suran as he comes to his feet, swaying unsteadily. His elara is torn and soaked in blood. For once in his life, his appearance matches his underhanded deeds. Rudjek and Serre abruptly stop their conversation as Suran's new anti-magic pulses around him in an invisible heat wave.

"By all means," Suran says, his voice raw, "continue to talk as if I am not present."

"You look well, Almighty One," I tell him, mostly for my own bitter enjoyment.

Suran groans and meets my eyes. "Everything I've done has been in service of protecting my family. Your mother proved herself to be dangerous time and time again. I could never trust someone of her blood."

"You speak of trust when you tried to kill Arrah twice!" Rudjek hurls the words at his father. "You're the one who can't be trusted.

You destroy everything you touch."

Queen Serre stands close to her son as if she could protect him. But she's careful to keep her face neutral.

"You sent Jemi away when he needed us," Rudjek continues relentlessly. "You knew he wasn't well, but you sent him to the deserts of Yöom because he embarrassed you. And even that's not enough for you. You have the attendants slip matay leaves into Uran's nightly tea to keep him docile. Didn't think I would find out about that, did you?"

Queen Serre stiffens, and I think perhaps she knew about the matay leaves.

"I had no choice!" Suran snaps, his face still faintly wan. "I cannot have my sons ruining the Omari reputation. While our Sukkara cousins sat in the palace feasting and drinking, the Omari have always run the Kingdom. We've expanded the borders, kept enemies at bay, brokered deals, made allies. It's our name that will ring in the halls of history. My sons will not stain that legacy."

The black veins pulse in Serre's forehead. "You have dishonored your family's name of your own accord, husband."

Suran flinches at his wife's words. "That's a matter of perspective."

"Let's talk about perspective," I say. "I am the *Ka*-Priestess of the Almighty Kingdom, and people are flocking to the Temple in droves. Despite what you believe, they will follow me. What do you think will happen if they find out that you attempted to murder me with your own hands?"

"You may have had magic before, but you have none now," Suran spits. "Your words carry no weight, nor do I fear the Temple loyalists."

"Perhaps this will hold weight." Rudjek steps between his father and me. "The *Ka*-Priestess, Arrah N'yar, is under my protection and the protection of the craven people. Should she receive even a scratch that I can trace back to you, there will be dire consequences."

"Are you threatening me?" Suran says, his eyes brimming with venom. "Think very carefully before you answer, son. I do not take kindly to threats—even from my children."

Rudjek smiles, his expression too calm to be genuine. "Of course not, Father. I am simply stating a fact."

I lay out my demands. "You will reverse your ban on magic and free the people you falsely imprisoned. No further lawmaking will happen without my vote, as is Kingdom custom."

"In case you were thinking of not listening to her"—Rudjek crosses his arms—"I already had those people released on your behalf as soon as I found out. The Crown Prince title does carry its privileges."

I'm surprised by this news, but I shouldn't be. Rudjek and I might not always agree on our approach, but he isn't anything like his father. It gives me hope that one day the Kingdom will be in better hands, even if . . . if I'm dead. I swallow the dread threatening to take over. It's hard to accept that after surviving my mother, my sister, Suran, and vengeance gods, I'm still going to die. It isn't fair, but I draw back my shoulders and hold my head high. The least I can do is get under Suran's skin while I'm still around. That and kill my sister.

Suran's entire body seems to sag. He looks from his son to his wife, then to me. "You've turned my entire family against me."

"You did that on your own," Rudjek tells him.

"I suppose you give me no choice," Suran says bitingly. "You win."

He's lying. I don't need magic to see that, but this impasse will do for now.

Suran storms out of the salon, and Serre squeezes my arm. "I will do my best to ensure that he honors that promise."

After his mother leaves, Rudjek gives me a huge smile. "You were brilliant—I'm pretty sure my father pissed his trousers." He steps close to me, and I glance at Jahla, who is staring conspicuously out a window. Rudjek shifts on his heels. "I have no right to ask this after my father has proven himself a treacherous ass yet again . . . but will you stay awhile?"

I hold up my hands covered in sticky blood. "Only if I have a place to clean up first."

Rudjek bites his bottom lip. "I can manage that. The whole west wing of the palace is the Crown Prince's domain."

I quirk an eyebrow. "The whole wing?"

A look passes between us, full of all the things we can't say here.

"I'll see about getting you a change of clothes," Jahla says, turning away from the window. She sounds almost relieved to have something to do.

"We'll be in my private quarters." Rudjek clears his throat, and after she's gone, he adds, "I promise I have no ulterior motives."

I smile at him coyly. "That's disappointing."

As we leave the salon, Fadyi and another two dozen cravens posing as gendars stand at attention. Fadyi falls in steps with us, his gaze briefly landing on my bloodstained sheath. "I spoke with Elder Ro," he tells Rudjek. "From now on, we'll have your father watched at all times. He will no longer be a problem."

"Thank you," Rudjek says, nodding to his friend.

"There is another matter," Fadyi says as we pass a terrace overlooking one of the gardens. "Our scouts have spotted several Fyaran ships en route. We expect them to arrive in time for the summit tomorrow afternoon."

"Finally," Rudjek sighs. "I had almost given up hope."

"I'm concerned about the number of ships," Fadyi says. "They've sent thrice as many as the other nations."

"Can't say I'm surprised," Rudjek tells him. "The Fyaran are our biggest military rival, and at last report, their forces were double the size of the Kingdom's. I suspect they want to remind us of that."

"I suggest not letting them all enter the bay," Fadyi advises.

"I agree." Rudjek's eyebrows knit together in concentration. "Take a message to my aunt, General Solar. Inform her that I recommend we let only the lead ship and one escort into the bay. Commandant Dakte will think of an appropriate excuse to give if the Fyarans protest."

"Will they take offense?" I ask, fascinated by how easily Rudjek has fallen into this strategic rhetoric.

He shrugs. "They would've found something to gripe about at the summit either way. A typical Fyaran move."

Rudjek's changed so much from the days he shied away from the responsibilities his father thrust upon him. I see glimpses of the king he'll be one day. I'm only sorry that I won't be here for it. I push down my thoughts. "How do you know so much about Fyaran policies?" I ask, truly interested.

"I have my sources." Rudjek winks at Fadyi, who nods as if to agree.

As we reach the west wing, Fadyi slows his pace. "I'll keep you informed."

"One more thing," Rudjek says. "Can you have attendants bring the evening meal to my private dining hall tonight? Enough for two."

"Of course." Fadyi bows and takes his leave.

We walk down another long corridor. "You're presuming much, Crown Prince."

"If I am ever out of line, I know you will put me in my place."

"I would indeed," I say, though he is most definitely not out of line.

My mind veers toward thoughts I have kept under lock and key, and a rising ache inside me matches the warmth of Rudjek's anti-magic against my skin. "Tell me about this summit," I say after a moment of awkward silence. "I'm assuming, as *Ka*-Priestess, I should attend."

"Yes, I was going to get around to that next," Rudjek says as two guards push open the double doors to his private quarters. "My father has been conversing with the delegates in my absence, but it's clear that some are wary of his approach. I think it best that you and I attend as a united front."

"I don't know what I will say to them," I tell him.

"The truth, or as much of it as you feel comfortable sharing," Rudjek suggests.

Soon Jahla comes with a change of clothes, a plain tunic with matching trousers. I thank her, and she quickly retreats. Rudjek shows me to the washroom and leaves me to it.

By the time I've returned, the table in the salon is laden with piping hot trays of food. Wisps of smoke curl in the air, filling my nose with aromatic spices that make my mouth water. But I see Rudjek standing at the window. He's changed into a loosely fitting elara made of soft gray fabric, and eating is the last thing on my mind.

"Kiss me," I say quietly, knowing that this might be one of the only chances we have left. "Kiss me like our lips are two suns colliding."

Rudjek laughs as he crosses the room in a few strides, then he does. His mouth is sweet and soft and warm. A fire burns inside me, aching and pulsing and throbbing, and I know it's always been there, waiting for this moment. Rudjek, my best friend. Rudjek, something more. We are both hungry and desperate, eager. I draw him closer, my fingers tracing the smooth skin beneath his tunic. His hands take liberties that send thrills through my body, which only makes me want him more. Tonight, I will have my fill of him and he of me.

"Are we moving too fast?" he says breathlessly against my collarbone.

"No," I moan. "Not fast enough as far as I'm concerned."

"My thought precisely."

I grimace in frustration when bells ring, like the ones that track the passage of time in the East and West Markets. I ignore them, not wanting anything to interrupt this moment, but the sound only grows louder. Light suddenly fills the room, and we both jump apart. To my horror, Daho stumbles from the gate between worlds, then he collapses at our feet.

TWENTY-SIX
ARRAH

Neither Rudjek nor I move as we stare at Daho. He's completely still, his wings broken and twisted in impossible ways. Shadows pool around him and snake across the salon like tentacles starved for life. I take a step forward, but Rudjek gently grabs my arm. This is my worst fear come true. If Daho's here in this state, that could only mean one thing. Efiya has control of his army.

Rudjek grimaces as the shadows coil away from his anti-magic. They stretch up the walls and across the table of uneaten food. "Is it too much to hope that he's actually dead?"

I don't expect Rudjek to feel any sympathy for him, but I remember the boy who fell from the sky. The boy who was on the verge of dying until Dimma nursed him back to health. His body is only a vessel, like mud shaped into something it was never met to be. He should be able to make a new one, so why hasn't he? Some part of me expects Dimma to wake, to push against her chains, but there is only stillness inside me. The dread pumping in my veins and the growing fear are my own.

Rudjek's anti-magic intensifies, filling the salon with almost unbearable heat. It pushes the shadows back until they disappear. Patches of Daho's silvery skin darken to ash and flake away.

"What are you doing?" I demand, turning on him.

"Finishing the job," Rudjek says, a determined glint in his eyes. "This might be our best chance to kill him."

"You can't," I say, but my voice is so small, broken. "Without Daho, we have no hope of defeating my sister. Don't you see that? Efiya's turned against him—and now we can use that to our advantage."

"How do you know for sure?" Rudjek asks skeptically. "You're making a lot of assumptions, Arrah."

"I know my sister."

Rudjek squeezes his eyes shut for a moment as his anti-magic cools. When he opens them again, the Crown Prince is back, already thinking ahead, calculating. "What's to stop Efiya and Shezmu from coming through the gate after him?" Rudjek shifts on the balls of his feet. "He's led them straight to *you.*"

"Efiya was always going to come for me," I snap. "I have the dagger. . . ." My voice trails off as the realization hits me. I have something much more valuable than the blade. "I have Dimma's soul."

Rudjek stares at me, his face twisted in anguish. "And why settle for the Twin Kings when she can have the master of souls herself?" He steps around Daho's body and grabs his sword belt. "We have to mobilize now—go on high alert."

"You can't tell anyone he's here," I say. "I've come to an understanding with the orishas—or more like a fragile truce—but if they learn that Daho's vulnerable, they might be tempted to break it."

Rudjek massages his forehead and looks down at Daho again, his eyes filled with disgust. "I think this is a bad idea, but I'll keep quiet for now."

I don't miss the uncertainty in his voice, but it's no more so than what I'm feeling myself. I could be making another mistake. "Help me get him to your bed."

"You expect me to help *him* into *my* bed?" Rudjek scowls. "He tried to kill me and my sorry excuse for a father. He's eaten countless souls—yet I'm supposed to trust him?"

"I never said anything about trusting him. But like it or not, it won't be long before Efiya attacks the Kingdom with his army."

"I would rather leave him on the floor," Rudjek says flippantly. "Actually, let's put him back in Koré's box for the rest of eternity."

"Rudjek," I say sharply.

"Fine," he relents. "They'll have to amend the songs about me from 'Mighty Rudjek Omari Slays the Demon King' to 'Mighty Rudjek Omari, um, Nurses the Demon King Back to Health.' It doesn't have quite the same ring to it."

"Think of it this way. You will forever be able to claim that the Demon King came to you quivering on his knees for your help."

Rudjek grimaces. "He's here for you."

"He's here because he has nowhere else to go." But I know that's only partly true. "And I have the only weapon that will stop my sister."

"This is not how I expected to spend my night," Rudjek moans.

We're both disheveled, our clothes wrinkled. And I can still feel the heat from his mouth against mine, his hands tracing up my thighs. "Neither did I."

As though he's reading my mind, he straightens his elara. "Let's get to it, then."

"Thank you," I say quietly.

It takes much effort to wrestle Daho's unconscious body from the floor, and more than once, his wings slap Rudjek in the face. "Perhaps you can convince him to make a vessel that's not as heavy as a boulder next time," Rudjek grunts as we half drag him through several rooms.

When we finally get him into the bed, Rudjek glances down at Daho again. "Will you be okay alone with him until I return?" He scratches his eyebrow irritably. "You know what, never mind. Don't answer that."

I wrap my arms around my shoulders, warding off a chill, and answer anyway. "I'll be fine as long as my sister doesn't come through the gate."

Rudjek lets out a deep sigh. "Let's hope she's in the same shape he is. That should buy us a little time."

Once he's gone, I pace back and forth in the bedchamber, unable to be still. Efiya has control of Daho's army. There's no way to stop her, to stop this war. Deep down, I've always known it would come to this. I'd been fooling myself to think otherwise. This is the end—the true end, and I can do nothing to prevent it. It's well past midnight when I finally tire myself out and slump on a chair across from the bed. Rudjek still hasn't returned, but I can feel anti-magic from the many craven guards he's stationed in the west wing.

I remember Heka's words on the crossroads. *There was a promise made; it binds me.* The gods are strange creatures with their own peculiarities. That much I understand. Heka was bound by the promise he made to the tribal people. But was he trying to tell me something else? Re'Mec and the others said that Heka came from the Supreme Cataclysm much later after Dimma died. Yet, time is slippery, ebbing and flowing to its own drum. A dull ache starts to build in my head, and the more I try to concentrate, the worse it becomes. I'm missing something, some connection. Then I blurt out: "Heka knows what happened to your son."

But Daho doesn't stir. The bedchamber is quiet as the first morning bell tolls. I can't keep my eyes open any longer, and I drift off into a haze.

When I wake, I'm buried in layers of crisp sheets and pillows that smell like lemon and lilac. Sunlight pours into the room, which is much smaller than the chamber where we'd left Daho. I climb out of bed and enter the salon. Rudjek is pouring over maps, and rough sketches of battle plans line the wall opposite the windows.

"Hello," he says without looking away from his work.

"Hello," I echo his greeting. "I don't remember coming here."

"I carried you," he says, his back still to me. His stance is rigid like he's struggling to hold himself together. "I thought you'd be more comfortable in a bed." Though his voice is light, there's no mistaking the hesitation beneath his words.

I touch his shoulder, and he finally meets my gaze. "Have I not made my feelings for you clear—have I not given you my heart?"

Rudjek cups my face, his eyes sad. "Yet, he's returned to steal you away from me."

"No one can change how I feel about you—not him, not even your father." I glance to my feet. "Time is our only enemy."

He lifts my chin to plant a sweet kiss on my lips. He looks like he wants to say more, but he doesn't.

"I take it that there have been no attacks," I say, knowing if there had, he would've told me already.

"None so far," Rudjek says. "Perhaps Efiya has grown more cautious and less impulsive. At the camp on the island, she seemed changed in some way. . . . I can't explain it."

"I can," I tell him. "It's the souls she's eaten. They have become a part of her. She might be strong enough to fight the nature of human souls, but the orishas would alter her in some way."

"Interesting," Rudjek muses. "Though it hasn't quelled her blood lust."

"Clearly not."

"I had attendants go to the Temple to fetch your ceremonial robes," Rudjek says. "Emere insisted on coming along to help you dress and escort you to the summit."

I nervously fidget with the wishing stone on the chain around my neck. The weight of it brings me some comfort. "Of course she did."

Only an hour later, I walk the palace corridors, surrounded by Temple attendants and craven disguised as palace guards. Rudjek left before us with his own entourage. I am wearing a rich gold kaftan trimmed in red, not much different from one my mother would've worn to a day of debating with Suran Omari at the coliseum.

We pass Sukkara and Omari family members in the halls. Some catch my eye as if to say they support me while others avoid meeting my gaze. We exit the main palace and cross rose gardens to enter a smaller version of the coliseum. The palace is a city in itself, with so many buildings and domes, all amply decorated in lapis lazuli, mother of pearl, gold, and precious gemstone. Even the cobblestones between buildings are carved into beautiful mosaic patterns that reflect the sun in brilliant patterns.

Emere is by my side, but I'd rather it be one of my friends. Rudjek would lean in close and utter something entirely inappropriate to calm my nerves. I would be reassured by Essnai's quiet strength, or Sukar might say that listening to politicians debate was like watching pigs wallow in mud. I push down a snicker, and Emere gives me a sidelong glance as if she thinks I'm already breaking under the pressure of my position. But she doesn't know that I broke a long time ago and learned how to put myself back together.

We are almost the last to arrive at the coliseum. There is no two-tiered elevated platform where the royal family can perch over the assembly in the shadows like the one in the West Market. Instead, it's all one level, circular, with the Omari family crest stained into all the windows.

Suran Omari has moved quickly to replace any signs of the Sukkaras' emblem on the palace grounds. Yet, Prince Derane Sukkara is here, lurking amidst the Kingdom delegates and the guildmasters. Kira's father, Guildmaster Ny of the Scribes Guild. Guildmaster Ohakim of the Laborers' Guild. Rudjek's aunt, General Solar of the Military Guild. The white-haired Guildmaster of the Scholars, Elrin Morra, the longest-serving head scholar in Kingdom history. I haven't forgotten that she and Guildmaster Ny had sided with me at Tyrek's trial. Though we were wrong in that case, they still strike me as the most reasonable and balanced of the guildmasters.

The delegates gather beneath where their banners hang from

the domed ceiling. Elder Ro and several craven representatives stand under a plain white flag that has drawn the attention of several other delegates. "If they're not from Siihi or Ghujiek, then who are they?" a diplomat from Estheria whispers to their colleague. Their flag is light blue stitched with a black shrike.

Princess Veeka, Prefect Clopa, and others from Galke are near a flag with a stallion. The Yöomi delegate's flag has a mountain. The Zeknorian has crossed swords above a shield. They're next to the Delenians with their sly fox. Though many smaller nations aren't present, most notably absent are the Fyarans, who haven't arrived in time after all. There are so many people here and countries represented, but I still fear it won't be enough against my sister.

I smile when I see my cousin Semma and the other chieftains. I wasn't sure if the tribes would decide to come. She waves at me, and I want to go to her, but we're playing our parts now, not in Grandmother's tent braiding each other's hair.

Rudjek and his father are at the front of the coliseum, standing side by side. The tension between the two is almost palpable. "Today, we have gathered the largest assembly of nations in the history of Zöran," Suran says, projecting his voice with ease. His dark eyes have a spark in them, a hunger. The anti-magic has given him a youthful glow. It's a subtle change but unmistakable. "Instead of bickering among ourselves, we have chosen to stand together against the greatest threat our world has ever seen."

"Why should this be our problem?" a bearded man from Zeknor with auburn hair says. He's tall and wears a stately uniform of soft blue and gray, his face weathered and scarred. "Had the demons not been plotting to lure your Crown Prince away, they would have never come to Zeknor. We have no personal quarrel with them."

"Yet, Commander Korr, the demons saw fit to kill an entire village in your country at a whim," Rudjek says with sympathy. "Do you think if they destroy the Kingdom, they will suddenly decide to spare you?"

"We do not believe in your gods," says someone from Delene. The woman pushes back her veil, revealing diaphanous skin with faint black veins streaking down her forehead. "Why should we fight for them?"

Suran Omari's jaw twitches ever so slightly, but my cousin speaks up. "We do not worship the gods of the Kingdom, either, and it did not stop the demons from invading our lands."

"We should be securing our own borders and concentrating our efforts at home," an Estherian delegate says, "not wasting time on an alliance."

Several of the delegates murmur their agreement.

A Yöomi with pale gray eyes, fanning himself, clears his throat. He's wearing a stiff tunic of a patchwork of vibrant colors. "The Demon King wants *her*." He pointed at me, and I go still. "Is it not true that she carries the soul of his dead wife?"

The outrage is immediate, and a chorus of opinions fills the coliseum. I have no doubt from the smug look on Suran's face that he'd somehow found out and shared the information in the hopes of undermining my position. I raise my chin, looking directly at the Yöomi. Once I had been ashamed that I carried Dimma's soul . . . that I *was* her. For a long time, I've thought that I was a piece and she was the whole, but that time has passed. I cannot move forward without accepting that her past is also mine.

"I do carry her soul, yes," I say as Emere and the other attendants bristle next to me. "Yet, that will not save you."

"You should lure the Demon King here alone, *Ka*-Priestess," Commander Korr suggests. "Surely he'll come if you ask him to. Then we kill him. That should give his army pause."

I dig my nails into my palms. Daho is already here, lying helplessly in Rudjek's bed. If these delegates got wind of that, they'd try to kill him and fail miserably. They still don't get it. If he were easy to kill, the gods would have done it long ago. "Some would say the Demon King has cause to hate the gods, but my sister is the real enemy. . . ." My voice falters, and I inhale a sharp breath. *My sister will destroy all of you to get to me.* "She alone would eat the souls of everything in this room if it suited her mood. She has no regard for life."

"You're the *Ka*-Priestess; you have magic," Princess Veeka says, surrounded by the Galkian delegation. "Why can't you stop her on your own?"

"She no longer possesses magic," Suran answers on my behalf, his voice seething with contempt. "It would seem that the orishas did not think her worthy of their gift."

Rudjek opens his mouth to speak, but I beat him to it. I match Suran's contempt with indifference. "I gave up my magic to save your son's life. Would you rather I'd let him die?"

Suran purses his lips, his eyes narrow, for once looking like he's lost for words. I turn to the delegates, fearful of how they might take the news. We're already so few against my sister and Daho's army. We can't afford to lose any support. "Magic alone can't save us—I should know that best," I say. I pause, dread eating at my confidence.

This delegation can't fail. It can't. If it does, Efiya will win. "Magic destroyed my family, and it almost destroyed me. Our best chance to defeat my sister is to work together."

"The *Ka*-Priestess is wise," Rudjek says, his expression holding nothing back. For the first time, his mask slips and he lets down his guard in public. He is the Crown Prince, but he's also the boy who went to the end of this world and entered another to save me. "If we are to defeat the demons, it will take the cravens from the Southern delegation and their anti-magic, and the magic of the tribal lands, combined with the forces of the rest of our nations."

"Cravens?" someone scoffs. "Have you lost your mind, boy? Those are not cravens. They're people. Burning fires, we've come here on the word of an Omari. The whole lot of them are mad if you ask me."

Rudjek doesn't even blink at the slight. He nods at Elder Ro, who steps forward. "Perhaps this form will be more familiar to you, but I can take many."

Before our eyes, Elder Ro shifts into the shape of the monster from the stories. Tall and lumbering with tree bark skin, a horned nose, and claws as sharp as newly forged blades. The delegates fall into chaos, but she changes back into a human form just as quickly.

"I have a confession to make," Rudjek admits. "I am human, but I'm also part craven." He quirks an eyebrow. "I'm nowhere as talented Elder Ro, sadly, so you're stuck gazing upon this handsome face."

Rudjek's attempt to lighten the mood in the hall fails miserably. "You're some kind of half-breed?" a Zeknorian next to Commander Korr spits.

"And so are you," Queen Serre says, hurrying to her son's side. "Have you not wondered why our skin is so thin and our veins so dark?" She pointedly stares at several delegates from the North. "We are the descendants of a people called endoyans who were cousins to the demons. So let's not get on the topic of purity."

"Serre!" barks one of the Delenian delegates from her country. "Enough with these lies—have you lost all sense living among these Tamarans? Father would be ashamed."

"I believe my son," Queen Serre says simply, her head held high.

"I haven't always seen eye to eye with Crown Prince Rudjek," comes a familiar voice. It's Commandant Dakte. He steps forward from the back of the hall in his formal gendar attire. "But he is honorable and a fierce warrior who fought bravely in Zeknor. We wouldn't have pushed the demons back without him."

Rudjek quirks an eyebrow at his former second-in-command, clearly enjoying that the older man has been forced to admit this in front of everyone.

"I grow tired of this conversation," says the Yöomi delegate. "Why should my people trust cousins of the very demons who are trying to destroy our world . . . ?" He grimaces at Elder Ro. "Or these monstrosities from the South?"

"Perhaps you should leave, then," says the Estherian delegate. "You can't even stop the Fyaran from stealing your people from right underneath your noses." He says this just as the Fyaran delegates march into the coliseum, their faces stern. They're two heads taller than most of the others in the room, and although they don't have pointed teeth, there's no denying they are also descendants of the endoyans.

"We come to hear of your plan to defeat the demons," the Fyaran general at the head of the delegation says in broken Tamaran. "But instead, we hear lies spoken against our great nation. Perhaps coming here was a mistake."

I grit my teeth. I'm so tempted to call magic right now. If only to use it to slap some sense into every one of the delegates who hasn't figured out that fighting among ourselves will get us nowhere. This bickering is a waste of time. And if it's true what the Estherian said about the Fyarans, then maybe I might just do worse to them.

"That's good to hear—since this alliance is built on friendship," Rudjek says to the Fyaran general. "If any nation should attack another or steal its people, as was claimed, then the rest of us would have to retaliate. Are we clear?"

Rudjek's words cut deep, and the hall goes silent enough to hear the birds chirping in the gardens. The Fyaran general casts him an icy stare and flexes his fingers in his leather gloves like he's itching to draw a sword that isn't there. For Rudjek's part, he doesn't back down.

"Whatever you say, Crown Prince," the Fyaran answers with a fake smile.

"Then let's turn to the real business at hand." Rudjek lays out his strategy for defeating the demons. "We divide our forces into battalions, each with a unit of cravens and tribal people in their ranks. Together they can keep the demons from shedding their physical forms and destroy their souls. These battalions will be concentrated on protesting each of your own countries, but I am planning to take the fight to the demons myself."

I hadn't expected that, but maybe I should've realized that his plans would change. He has access to the gate now, but Rudjek is assuming that Daho will help him. No, that isn't right. He's betting that Daho will open the gate for *me*.

"You know where they are?" the Fyaran general asks.

Rudjek meets my gaze, something shifting in his eyes. "Yes."

My belly flutters with nerves as the delegates argue over Rudjek's plan. It's our chance to strike at Efiya first, and he was right to think of it, but some of them don't seem convinced. On impulse, I pull Daho's dagger. "This is the only weapon that can trap my sister, and I am the only one who can use it." I let this information soak in. This isn't the time to hold back. "I'm going with Rudjek."

"As am I!" shouts Commander Korr of the Zeknorians. "The demons destroyed one of our villages. It's time that we taste our revenge."

One by one, the other delegates agree to send volunteers, though some still seem reluctant.

"How exactly are we supposed to get to Ilora?" the Fyaran general asks.

I stand a little taller. "Leave that to me."

"Gather your volunteers at the Southern docks at fourth morning bells," Rudjek says. "Arrah and I will be waiting."

He's assuming that Daho will be awake by then.

After the official talks are over, Emere pulls me aside. "I was concerned when you did not return to the Temple last night."

"I was with the Crown Prince," I admit.

She casts an embarrassed glance at Rudjek. "I hate to ask so much of you so soon, but I have invited candidates interested in becoming your seers to the Temple. I believe some of them to be more than capable."

The Temple has always had a *Ka*-Priestess and four seers—that is, until my mother almost destroyed it. But that's the last thing on my mind. I'm anxious to check on Daho. He's been in Rudjek's chamber alone for hours. I hope he doesn't wake up and do something brash.

Emere looks at me, her eyes almost begging. I cannot ignore my responsibilities to the Temple, especially knowing that I won't be *Ka*-Priestess for long. The least I can do is help her find suitable seers to run the Temple once I'm gone. "I'll come, but I can't stay long," I say.

Jahla and my craven guards accompany me back to the Temple. Nearly a hundred candidates fill the Hall of Orishas, and I'm overwhelmed by the sheer number of them. One by one, Emere introduces each candidate petitioning to become one of the next seers. From what I can sense, none are particularly talented in magic. Maybe in a different life, that would mean something. I've held on to Grandmother's words. *Our greatest power lies not in our magic, but in our hearts.* Though, I don't know if I've ever really understood what she meant until now.

I spend a few moments with a third of the candidates before Emere sees that I'm starting to lose focus. She sends the rest home, promising we will hold another gathering in the coming days, but I won't be here for it. A few had stood out from the others, and I recommend that Emere move forward with them. She leaves immediately to start preparations.

Once the hall is clear of everyone except Jahla, my craven guards, and attendants going about their duties, I take a moment to linger in the shifting shadows between the orisha statues. The first evening bells toll in the courtyard outside. Dimma never felt at ease among her brethren. They're fickle at best. Dangerous at their worst. Even after I came to a truce with them, I can't say I feel better. Perhaps things will change when I die and . . . she returns.

I shudder. I've been gone from the palace too long—and Daho might already be awake. I want to deliver the news of our plans. I don't think it'll go well if he hears it from Rudjek. I don't trust the two of them not to be at each's throats. "We should get back," I say, anxious to leave.

Jahla and I are on our way out of the hall when a wide-eyed man bursts through the doors. His clothes are covered in soot, and he has burns across half his face. "*Ka*-Priestess!" he cries. "We need the *Ka*-Priestess!"

The Temple attendants rush toward the man just as the Hall of Orishas explodes. I stumble as shards of glass and bits of stone hurtle toward us. Jahla spins me out of the way of the debris. I watch in horror as it tears through her, ripping and shredding her flesh. When the dust settles, she's balled up on the floor, gasping for air.

"Jahla," I say, clambering on my hands and knees to get to her.

She winces and drags herself to sit up next to Re'Mec's statue. "I'll live."

I glance around as we get to our feet. The other cravens are all right. The attendants haven't fared so well. They lay half-buried in jagged cuts of stone. I step toward them, but a familiar sickly-sweet voice stops me in my tracks. My head spins in a haze of sinking dread.

"This is a pleasant surprise," Efiya says. Gray smoke pools on the floor in front of the shattered wall until it coalesces into my sister. She is dressed in ice-blue silk that billows around her feet, and she has never looked more deadly.

"Go!" I yell to Jahla and the others.

They can't protect me, not from her. They'll only get themselves killed.

"Not a chance," Jahla says as her anti-magic stings my skin.

Shezmu and Evelyn land in the hall behind my sister, their wings backlit by the fires burning across the city. Shezmu is stone-faced, and Evelyn is pure rage as her glowing eyes land on me. She's mad, but she's the one who betrayed Daho, not the other way around. He trusted them, and they turned against him. This is my sister's doing.

I reach for the dagger against my waist. I can end this now. "Don't do this, Efiya." I hate how feeble and ridiculous I sound. I can't reason with my sister, and it's time to face the truth. "Stop this madness."

Efiya smiles, and it's like a warm summer day full of sweet lies. "Oh, I will, as soon as I take everything I want."

Her answer chills me to the bone. She wants the dagger, power, and Dimma's soul. The blade suddenly doesn't feel like enough—nothing will ever be enough against my sister.

"We can't have you going around taking everything, can we?" Re'Mec says in a thundering voice. I gasp as the statue beside me lifts its ram's head and turns toward Efiya. "That wouldn't be fair to the rest of us."

All around me, the last of the orishas take the place of their statue. Koré, Nana, Kiva, Mouran, Sisi, Kekiyé, Oma, Essi, and finally Re'Mec.

Koré stands opposite her brother, her glowing twin swords ready. "If you want Arrah, you must go through us first."

"That is . . . most . . ." Efiya glances down innocently, then she laughs. " . . . *fortunate*. I've been waiting for this day for a very long time."

Efiya strikes, and she, Shezmu, and Evelyn become streaks of light. Along with the orishas and the cravens, they move so fast that I can't discern what's happening. Someone tugs at my sleeve, and I startle. Kiva, the god of children and innocence, wraps his little hand around mine and looks up at me with big round eyes. "It's time for you to leave."

Before I can protest, he wraps me in a cloak of shadows.

"I'm good at hiding," he says in his child's voice. "I can hide you."

"I'll be fine," I say. "Protect the children."

"I am gathering them right now," he says, delighted.

Right. The orishas can be in multiple places at once.

I know what I have to do—where I have to go. "Send me to Rudjek's quarters."

Before I'm done speaking, Kiva gives me a shove. I land on my butt in the salon. It's empty until Daho stumbles out of the bedchamber, looking dazed. "Arrah," he croaks, voice hoarse.

Almost at the same time, Rudjek bursts into the salon from the antechamber, his elara soaked in blood, his shotels drawn. "Efiya and the demons are attacking the city."

My sister doesn't care about Tamar—it's a distraction. "She's come for me."

"We'll make our stand here," Rudjek decides, his expression hard and unrelenting.

Daho supports his weight against the doorframe. His skin is still so pallid. "And you'll die."

"Do you have a better plan?" Rudjek shoots back. "She's already beat you senseless."

"I can lure Efiya out of the city," I say, interrupting their argument.

Daho's eyes come into sharp focus. "What are you saying?"

I squeeze the hilt of the dagger. "We're going to play a little game."

TWENTY-SEVEN
EFIYA

I'm disappointed in my sister, but I can't say I'm surprised. How pathetic of her to hide in the orishas' temple. It's their fault that we're enemies. They turned her against me. I want things to be better between us, but it's too late for that now. I have no choice. I have to kill her.

The gods are in my way. And they clearly aren't going to make this easy. The hall expands until the space becomes immense and bottomless. It's almost as bad as the endless darkness inside the Demon King's dagger. I groan and push down my apprehension. This isn't the time for it.

"You're like a gnat that refuses to die," Re'Mec drawls. "I'm tired of playing this game."

"Really?" I smile at him. "I'm just getting started."

Evelyn's wings flutter open as she leaps at Koré with her daggers raised, but she cuts into thin air. Koré is a flash that shimmers in and out of my line of vision. Papa joins Evelyn and becomes a thing of nightmares. I have never seen him like this, and I'm impressed. His wings transform into writhing ribbons that shred Essi, the sky god's vessel. But he only slows the orisha down.

The souls inside me rage. Fayouma, the mother of beast and fowl, and Ugeniou, the god of the harvest, are furious that I am attacking their kin. Yookulu, the god of seasons, is a thousand insects eating away at my flesh. My belly burns as all three of them claw, bite, and push to get free. Too late, I realize I'm on my knees, and Nana, Re'Mec, and Sisi have surrounded me. Their magic begins to unravel my soul, but I resist. With a twitch of my fingers, I twist my own magic into sharp edges and fling it at the orishas.

It's not enough to kill them, but it gives them pause.

As I get to my feet again, Re'Mec is the first to recover. His swords clash with mine. I attack, swinging, slicing, cutting. My magic tears into him, but he keeps repelling my efforts. I scream in frustration. Try as I might, I'm not strong enough to defeat him. I need my sister's soul—or Dimma's, whoever she's calling herself these days.

"You're so pathetic," Re'Mec taunts me. I can almost hear an echo of my mother's voice. She always made me feel like a failure. I was never good enough for her. I wish she were here now to see me end the gods. She'd see that I'm not anyone's puppet anymore. Burning with rage, I slash my sword across Re'Mec's chest. Light pours from inside him. Finally, we're getting somewhere.

Re'Mec stumbles back and looks down at himself in disbelief. He's so arrogant, and now he knows that he isn't invincible. Nana and Sisi step in front of him protectively. How odd that they'd risk themselves for him. He hardly seems worth it.

Evelyn still has her hands full with Koré, and Papa is like a cyclone bearing down on the others. Three gods flee: Oma, the goddess of dreams; Kekiyé, the orisha of gratitude; and Kiva, the little one. Kiva's run off with my sister while Oma and Kekiyé descend upon the city, where my demons have begun their siege—but for every soul they take, I will add a century to their agony.

Thinking of that restores my determination. I grin as the orishas press their attack—Sisi with the force of a volcano and Nana whipping herself into a windstorm.

I focus all my magic on Sisi for the moment. Her fire cools, and her body turns to lava. Then when she is a solid chunk of rock, I shove her over. She shatters into a thousand pieces. She isn't dead, though she won't be putting herself back together anytime soon.

I want her soul, but the turmoil inside me won't make room for more. I hate that Heka was right. I should've been more careful with which souls I ate. It's nearly impossible to deny my hunger when it's burning inside me constantly. I must sate it.

"This is starting to get interesting, don't you think?" I shout to Re'Mec, who's backing away from me, holding his chest.

Mouran comes to help Nana, and I split myself in two. I fight them both at the same time, but I'm weaker in this state. I'm out of breath. Sweat stings my eyes. Blood, *actual* blood, pours from my wounds. Perhaps it wasn't a good idea after all. Nana gets in a lucky blow that I'd have easily deflected if I were at my full strength.

Her haunting laughter fills my ears. "The little girl is getting tired."

While I'm fighting Nana, my other half grabs Mouran's tail and throws him through the hole in the Temple wall. Within moments, a horde of demons converges on him and devours his soul.

To my delight, Re'Mec roars in anguish.

"One by one, the gods fall," Evelyn recites, her eyes wild. "One by one, they die in this very hall."

Papa joins her in the taunting. "What was that little song you liked to sing, Re'Mec? Ah, I remember it." He chants: "*One more demon on my sword. Another one dead, and I'm so bored.*"

"Are you bored now?" Evelyn coos.

Re'Mec growls, and the wound in his chest closes. We could fight until the universe collapses, and while that is appealing, I have to get to my sister.

My arms start to tingle. The Demon King's opening the gate. I suppose it was too much to hope he'd crawled in a hole and died. Somehow, he's still holding on to his pitiful life. And I'm willing to bet that Arrah's with him.

"Well, this has been fun," I say, "but I have somewhere that I have to be. Papa, you'll keep them busy, won't you?"

"Of course, daughter." He looks at me with such pride that I have to turn away. I love my father. I can't deny that. Sometimes I wonder what our lives would be like if we left all of this behind. We could've stayed in that world covered in the never-ending forest. That wouldn't be so bad, would it? I guess I'll never know.

I fold myself into the void between time and land in a bedchamber, the place where I sensed the gate opening. Arrah startles. I've interrupted her escape. I'm giddy with excitement as I move to block her path to the gate.

She's pulled the dagger from her waist. "Looking for this?" Arrah brandishes the blade. "It will never be yours."

I'm appalled that she would dare speak to me with so much disgust. I lunge forward, but my body passes right through her. Clever.

This is a trick. She is long gone. The gate disappears at my back.

The false Arrah smiles coldly. "You still like games, don't you, sister?"

I clap with delight. "How can I resist?"

"If you want the dagger, come find me."

Then the phantom disappears.

Arrah didn't bother setting up rules for the game. Perhaps she knows that I won't follow them. No matter. I need Papa to open the gate so I can find her, but someone bursts into the room and catches my attention. It's the new Almighty One, Rudjek's father and my mother's sworn enemy. He has a sword in his hand.

Suran Omari curses at the sight of me, then frowns, confused. His anti-magic smells rank. "You're not Arrah." He says my sister's name with pure hatred.

It doesn't take long for me to surmise that this sorry creature had intended to kill her. I almost laugh. He'd been our mother's greatest nemesis, yet I'd never gotten around to paying him a visit. "I'm Efiya." I offer him a smile. "It's nice to finally meet you."

The Almighty One spits on the floor. If he possessed good sense, he would flee or call for his guards. Instead, he advances. He's moving painfully slow. I could easily stop his heart or snap his neck, but I'm going to make an example out of him.

My magic coils around his mind. I haven't compelled anyone to do my bidding in a very long time. I miss my little playthings. His steps falter, and he drops his sword. His thoughts are wrapped in contradictions, lies, deception, love, lust, and greed. I frown, disgusted at what I discover. My army attacked his city, and his first thought was to use the distraction to come after my sister. He hates her as much as he hated our mother. Maybe even more so. He can't stand that Rudjek loves her.

"Come with me," I command him. "I want to show you something."

The Almighty One's black eyes shine with venom. He's completely under my control. I could take away his hatred, but it's a reminder that he's a servant of the gods I so despise.

He claws at the chain of magic, which I let him do for show. The doors to the salon fly open, and his guards rush forward. I crush their throats with a mere thought. It's a simple task that takes no effort at all. As I push ahead with Suran leading the way, we pass by soldiers issuing orders and racing to join the fighting on the palace grounds. They gawk or flee when they see me, too afraid to do more. They look to be from across Zöran—Northerners, Estherians, Yöomi, the tribal people, the cravens. They can do nothing to stop me.

Rudjek's mother is standing in the middle of the hallway. Her arms are limp at her sides. She looks at her husband with pity. I expect her to drop to her knees and beg me to spare him, but when I draw closer, she only ducks out of my way.

The Almighty One locks eyes with his queen, and there's no mistaking the hurt and pain in his gaze. For her part, she brushes away tears from her cheeks, but she doesn't even offer him a kind word. Good for her. He doesn't deserve it. He's a vile creature who must be taught a lesson.

Soon we're on the palace steps. Bodies, or parts of them, litter the gardens. Entrails lie in flower beds. Blood rains down from the skies. To my satisfaction, the demons are eating soul after soul, giving in to their truest nature. And why should they deny this gift from Dimma herself? But some of them have fallen, too. The tribal people have found a way to keep the demons from shedding their vessels while the cravens unravel their souls. It's most unfortunate, but I knew there would be casualties.

I walk with the Almighty One to look upon his precious city. Tamar burns bright against the horizon. I revel in the chaos. This is the end of the gods' legacy and the beginning of mine. Remembering how Arrah had brandished the Demon King's dagger, the spark of a new idea forms at the back of my mind.

"It will be worse than this before I'm done," I tell the Almighty One. "Nothing will be left of the Kingdom, not even a memory." I lean in close to him and whisper. "But you won't be here to see it."

The Almighty One cannot resist the seed I plant in his mind: he lurches and stumbles forward. He pauses only a moment, his eyes meeting mine. A single tear slips down his cheek before he throws himself over the edge of the mountain. His body breaks against the rocks. It's a quick death. No one can ever say I'm not merciful.

TWENTY-EIGHT
ARRAH

When I materialize on the other side of the gate, Rudjek touches my arm. His anti-magic is a gentle caress, and I lean into him, letting it ward off the chill in the air. In front of us, Daho hunches over, his face ghastly.

"Efiya will come," I tell them. "She can't resist a challenge."

"Let's hope that's the case." Rudjek grimaces. "Or could it be that *he* brought us here with an ulterior motive?"

"What motive would that be?" Daho growls, defiant despite his weakened state. "You think too highly of yourself, Crown Prince. If you want, I can send you back to Zöran."

"You would like that, wouldn't you?" Rudjek says. "You're so transparent."

Daho gives Rudjek a cutting smile. "Am I?"

I stumble away from them, too tired to listen to their bickering. We're alongside a shore on a sandy beach. Lightning cuts through a wall of gray clouds. There's neither sun nor moon in the sky, and it's impossible to tell what time of day it is here with the thick fog. The sand sinks under my feet as water laps at my ankles. An odd sense of awareness pricks at the back of my neck.

"Where exactly have you brought us?" Rudjek demands.

"Egrin," Daho says. "People lived here once, but they destroyed themselves."

"Uh-grin," I enunciate as I spot the slim tips of tentacles emerging from the water.

"Then what are those?" Rudjek asks.

"Mouran's first children," I recall from Dimma's memories. She had encountered them while searching for a cure for death, trying to save Daho. "They're harmless."

"Fascinating," Daho says. "I never knew they were here."

I kneel, and several tentacles reach for my outstretched hand. Their surface is cool, smooth, slick like an eel's. The creatures' collective voices speak as one, a chorus swelling in my head. "They remember you, though they never knew your name, so they called you 'It.' They say, 'It has come back, and it has brought new friends.'"

Daho smiles down at me, letting the tentacles crawl up his arms. "I'm honored that they remember me."

Rudjek lets out a guttural groan that shatters the moment. "While this is a riveting conversation, our *real* friends are dying in Tamar."

I glance away, ashamed for letting myself get so easily distracted by Dimma's memories. There is no way around it. I left behind Essnai, Kira, Jayla, Fadyi, and many more people I care about, knowing that the odds were insurmountable. If something happens to them, it will be my fault.

"We are all aware of the situation, *Crown Prince*," Daho says dismissively.

Rudjek grips the hilts of his shotels. "Had you not come to Zöran, our friends would be fine."

Daho draws his hand back, and the tentacles fall to the sand. "I had nowhere else to go."

Rudjek jabs a finger at him. "You had the entirety of the universe at your beck and call. Every death we suffer is on your head."

Daho comes to his feet and stares at the sea. A stiff wind ruffles through his feathers. "I plan to trap Efiya in the dagger again. It's the only way to stop her. She's too volatile." He pauses and meets my gaze. There's sadness and regret in his eyes. "I will have to kill Shezmu."

I cringe at the pain in his voice—and know that there is nothing I can do, no words I can offer to comfort him. Shezmu is his best friend—his brother. Now they're at odds. Nothing can fix that.

"If you hadn't bade him and Arti to make that monstrosity, none of us would be in this situation," Rudjek reminds him. "Arrah almost died trapping Efiya in the very dagger you're suggesting now—the one you released her from."

"We could do without your added cynicism." Daho jerks his head in Rudjek's direction. "As I said before, I can send you back to Zöran if you want."

"I'm staying," Rudjek says firmly. "I don't trust you."

Daho sighs, his features sharp against the gloom. "Ah, finally, we agree on something."

I rub my forehead—a dull ache pulses along my temples. I don't know how much of their bickering I can take. "We need to rest."

Daho trudges across the sand away from the shore. "I know a place."

"Are you okay?" Rudjek falls in step with me. "You don't look well."

"I'm just tired," I say, but it's more than that. Bone-gnawing fatigue has caught up with me. It's been days since Rudjek has had time to use his anti-magic to help me cope with the aches and pains from trading my years. Now I'm feeling the full brunt of my sacrifice.

We follow Daho through tall, golden clumps of grass that sway in the icy wind, giving way to a field of pink flowers. Worms wriggle in the soil beneath our feet. He leads us to a wall of vines shrouding a dimly lit cave. It's damp inside, and the sound of dripping water echoes against the stone. When we emerge on the other side, we're in a garden overgrown with vines and moss. It's quiet here, and the trees protect against the brunt of the wind.

"If I remember correctly," Daho says, "most of the vegetation is edible."

"Why here?" I ask as the leaves rustle against their branches.

Daho gingerly lowers himself to the ground. I'm surprised that he still hasn't healed after a full day. I realize just how close Efiya must've come to killing him. Only her magic could do this much damage. "Shezmu doesn't know this place," he explains. "That should buy us some time before we have to move on."

"So that's it?" Rudjek says, disgusted. "Keep running until we have nowhere left to go?"

"My immediate plan is to rest so I can recover my strength," Daho snaps at him. He spreads his wings and leans against a tree. "You still have no idea how powerful Efiya is."

Rudjek sits on a patch of grass, and I settle next to him. I should've expected that my sister would attack so swiftly. . . . I should've been ready. She's never been one for patience. I curl up against Rudjek, and he pulls me close. I'm thirsty and hungry, but I'm also too tired to think straight.

I watch as Daho struggles to find a comfortable position. "You had to know that Efiya would betray you."

Daho looks at Rudjek and me, then he closes his eyes. "Yes."

Rudjek's nostrils flare, and he bares his teeth. "You knew it . . . and still released her?"

"You wouldn't understand," Daho says. "It's complicated."

"We have nowhere to go. I'm all ears," Rudjek tells him.

"When Shezmu and I tracked down Iben—the god of time— he showed each of us a glimpse of the future." Daho fiddles with a tangle of moss, threading it between his fingers like a spider's web. "In the vision Shezmu betrays me for Efiya, but Dimma would once again be by my side. For many years, I thought about how I could change that version of the future. I didn't want to lose my best friend, but in the end, I couldn't risk not getting Dimma back."

Rudjek waits a beat. "So you decided to do nothing?"

Daho lets out a miserable sigh. "When Arrah and I went back in time to Dimma's last memory to find out what happened to my son—I'd already seen part of that particular moment a very long time ago. I realized I had to let events play out as they should."

"You knew I would agree even before you asked," I say.

"For me, you already had," Daho confirms.

I don't tell him of my suspicion that Heka has the answer he seeks. This isn't the time to be chasing after ghosts. It's best that he doesn't know. Rudjek's anti-magic curls around me, and I welcome the calm it brings. I sink into it, forgetting my hunger and thirst or that my whole body aches. The anti-magic is like a warm bath, and soon I'm drifting on the edge of sleep. I can't help but wonder if Rudjek's done this now so he can talk to Daho alone.

"Something still doesn't make sense to me," Rudjek insists. "You ate Iben's soul—you should know how to manipulate the outcome of your future."

"You clearly do not understand the gods, Rudjek," Daho says. "You're too enamored with the Twin Kings, but you haven't known them as long as I. They can't change their natures. Iben kept the secret of time, and it died with him."

"You know what I think?" Rudjek says. "You want the universe to burn, and you needed Efiya for that, but you got in over your head."

"I'm growing tired of you," Daho mutters. "You truly can't comprehend what's at stake here."

"I know that if Arrah keeps listening to you, you're going to get her killed," Rudjek says. "But that's exactly what you want, isn't it? To make her think you're helping when all along you're just waiting for Dimma to come back. That's the only thing you've ever cared about."

"For someone who talks so much, you're not very bright," Daho says. "Had I wanted to, I could have killed Arrah myself many times over. Clearly, that's not my intention."

"Forgive me if I don't believe you," Rudjek says. "You did try to kill me."

"I don't like you, Rudjek. You're a spoiled brat who's been

pampered all your life. You've never known true hardship, and you never will. If you survive Efiya's wrath, you'll become a pompous ass as petty and destructive as your father."

"You're one to talk when you're responsible for the death of countless." Rudjek laughs. "And for the record, you know nothing about me."

"I know you're not good enough for Arrah," Daho says. "Your father tried to kill her twice, and you didn't have the guts to put a knife in his heart." Rudjek starts to say something, but Daho cuts him off. "Did she tell you that she doesn't have much time left? Yet, she's still doing everything she can to stop Efiya."

"She wouldn't be dying if you had stayed where you belonged," Rudjek shoots back. "In Koré's box."

Some of the fire fades from Daho's voice. "Perhaps you're right."

"Of course I am." Rudjek, too, seems wary of their conversation. Neither of them speaks for a while, each lost in his own thoughts until Rudjek asks, "How . . . ?" He stumbles over the word. "How long does she have?"

Daho takes a long time before he answers. "A year, give or take a few months, with your anti-magic helping her."

One year . . . assuming that I survive my sister. I would give almost anything for a chance to live my life without fear, heartache, or another terrible thing waiting in the shadows. But that will never happen. I tell myself that at least I'll go on my own terms, but that doesn't bring me peace. Silent tears slide down my cheeks.

"Twenty-gods," Rudjek whispers, his voice choked. "It isn't fair."

"I know," Daho admits quietly before changing the subject. "I have something I must do. I will return soon."

"Right now?" Rudjek groans. "Can't it wait?"

"I need to find Heka," Daho says. "If Efiya has only a taste of his magic, then perhaps he is the key to stopping her, Shezmu, and the others."

"Arrah already asked him for help," Rudjek says. "He refused."

"I don't intend to ask," Daho grumbles. "I'll eat his soul if I have to."

DAHO

Now you understand why I've spent eons seeking revenge against the gods. They cannot be allowed to ruin more lives. Dimma may never forgive me for what I must do, but it's a risk I must take. I can no longer hide in the past, reminiscing on what I might have done differently. The moment has come. Heka is the only god that matters now. His power will give me the strength to stop Efiya and anyone else who gets in my way.

I glance at Arrah once more. Rudjek is cradling her in his arms. He's a thorn in my side, but I believe he cares for her. Though I would never admit it, he reminds me a little of my much younger self.

"Keep her safe," I say before drawing on Iben's power to open the gate.

Rudjek flicks me an obscene gesture that leaves nothing open to interpretation. He despises me, but I can't fault him for that. In fairness, I did try my best to kill him.

Iben's magic twists the fabric of the universe, removing space and time from the equation to mold it into a new purpose. Satisfaction and relief swell within me when I give in to the gods' natures—into *my* natures. They are a part of me.

The gate appears as dim stars set upon an indigo sky—it's a memory of a night that Dimma and I danced in the shadow of a star so hot that it cast a cerulean aura. I push the thought aside as I step into the gate, and it remakes me into tiny pulses that match the harmonics of the universe itself.

I'm driven by instinct coupled with determination. When I was on the edge of sleep, I heard Arrah say, *Heka knows what happened to your son.* I could leave well enough alone and wait for Dimma to tell me herself, but in this one thing, I have no patience. If the god of the tribal lands knows Dimma's secret, I will force him to tell me. I have my means.

I expect to search countless threads or have to journey to the mouth of the Supreme Cataclysm itself to seek out Heka, but he has left the essence of himself in plain sight. He wants to be found, which is peculiar for a god who spends most of his time hiding.

I come upon a world of snow and ice, and he is ribbons of white light billowing in the wind, almost invisible against the backdrop. When I retake my physical form and draw closer to him, he changes into a vessel that stops me cold. I stare in disbelief that he dares appear as Shezmu. His long white hair blows in the wind, and snowflakes fall upon his silver skin. Though he's mimicking Shezmu, there's something different about his eyes. Shezmu's are the color of emeralds, and Heka's are the lush green of a forest.

"When Dimma saved you beside the frozen lake, you had long pale hair like your friend," he says, a grin on his lips.

I frown. It's an odd thing to bring up, though it's true. "My barber liked to keep up with all the latest trends at the time." I swallow the lump in my throat. Shezmu has been my best friend and brother for an eternity, and now we are enemies. "Why him?" I manage to choke out.

"There are but only a few people you love deeply," Heka answers in Shezmu's voice. "He is one of them." The tribal god says this with so much conviction that I can't argue. "Dimma is the other."

I hover in front of him, my wings flapping against the snow. I'm not here to play games. I want answers. "Arrah believes that you know what happened to my son."

Heka looks amused, which only makes me boil with anger. "Does she?"

"Tell me what you know," I demand.

"I cannot." Strands of hair blow across his face. "I am bound by a promise."

"A promise you made to Dimma?" I say, surprised by this news. I don't know how old Heka is or when he came to be. When I was still in Koré's box, she and Re'Mec thought he must've been hiding in the mouth of the Supreme Cataclysm for a millennia, though they had never been quite sure.

Heka smiles at that, delighted that I have come to this conclusion. "She bid me not to interfere."

I frown. "Yet you let me find you now."

"Well, yes." He waves his hand with a flourish. "I can . . . bend the rules. I've done it on occasion."

Heka hasn't answered me directly, but I sense the truth in him. My son is alive. He is out there somewhere, hidden from the gods. That is why the universe is still dying.

"How could the gods not know?" I ask, searching for a question that he can answer.

"Those born first of the universe are not impervious to deception from each other." Heka's wings flutter irritably against his back. "Though you must already know this."

I don't miss that Heka does not call them gods. That is purposeful. I don't think he considers himself one of them, either. My son is alive, and Dimma will return soon. I have no reason to trust Heka, but I take his word without question. That in itself confuses me. Is it some trick of his magic?

"You have the power to stop Efiya. Why haven't you?"

Heka sighs impatiently. "As I have said, I cannot interfere."

"Yet, you helped create her."

"I was bending the rules," he admits, "but I did not break them."

I frown again, trying to make sense of this conversation, of him. "You were bending the rules to help *me*?"

Heka says nothing. Even though the wind howls around us, his hair falls still. I realize that despite his appearance and the strength of his magic, he's so very young. I am losing myself in his gaze . . . in eyes I know by heart. The illusion of Shezmu melts away.

He returns to his form of ribbons of light, but this is only the version of himself that he wants me to see. "Why do you cry?"

Tears sweep down my cheeks, chilled by the icy wind. I am speechless, babbling incoherently, sobbing uncontrollably. For all my plotting and scheming, all my murderous ways, I never saw what was right in front of me. Weren't the clues always there? *He* is my son . . . *Heka* is my son. His gift to the tribal people helped me find Dimma's soul, and that same gift freed me.

He reaches one of his ribbons of light to me. I don't want to wake from this dream and realize I'm in Koré's prison. I'm still the broken boy that Dimma found beside the frozen lake. I inhale a deep breath and find my courage. I need it now more than ever before.

My hand is heavy as stone as I finally take Heka's offer; then I know for sure. I close my eyes and remember the warm spark of life I once sensed inside Dimma. That spark has grown into a miracle. "Does Arrah know?" I ask.

"No," Heka answers.

I laugh through my tears. I laugh so hard that it hurts. I never dared hope to lay eyes upon my son, not after the gods stole everything from me. Soon my family will be together. "I have so many questions."

"They can wait for now," Heka says. "You are needed elsewhere."

A sharp pain tugs at the base of my neck, along with looming foreboding. No sooner had I thought things might be all right for once than I'm again proven wrong. Arrah's panic pulses through my head. She's in trouble. I haven't the time to say goodbye to Heka—to my son—as I open the gate again and race toward her. It can't end like this—not when I've come this far.

TWENTY-NINE
ARRAH

"Why didn't you stop him?" I ask as I pace back and forth in the mossy grass.

Rudjek sits against a tree, cleaning his swords. "I wasn't aware that I was his keeper and he, my ward. Last I checked, he was a five-thousand-year-old soul-eating bastard with the manners of a wild hog. He should be able to take care of himself."

"Rudjek!" I stare at him in disbelief. "This isn't the time to be joking."

He furiously strokes a rag down the length of his blade. "I'm dead serious."

I groan in frustration. I don't know how I ever thought he and Daho could put aside their mutual hatred for each other and work together. It was too much to hope for. "How long has he been gone?"

Rudjek rolls his eyes. "A full day."

I can't shake the sinking feeling in my gut. "You should have stopped him," I say again. "You don't understand. If Heka doesn't tell him what he wants . . . he might do something he'll regret."

Rudjek stands up and sheaths his swords. "The Demon King believes that Heka can help us stop Efiya, and as much as it pains me to admit it, he might be right."

I glare at him. Sometimes he can be so annoying. Doesn't he realize that Heka and Daho can't be at odds . . . they can't. . . . The very idea of it terrifies me.

"Why don't you face the fact that *Daho* cares about himself first and foremost?" Rudjek sighs. "He doesn't care about you. He only wants to ensure that Efiya doesn't eat your soul so he can get Dimma back. Other than that, you could be dead this very moment, and he wouldn't bat an eye."

"I *am* dying, Rudjek," I snap. "We both know I won't be around for another year."

He stops mid-stroke. "You heard?"

I pick at the hem of my tunic. "Yes."

"How can you be so nonchalant about it?" he says quietly.

I turn my back to him. I could scream. I could cry. I don't want to fight anymore. He acts like I'm just giving up, but in truth, I'm coming to terms with my fate. I could spend the rest of my short life lamenting my impending death, but death comes for everyone. I am not the first, and I won't be the last, to die young. I feel the weight of it dragging me down every day. I wake up and pretend that this will be the day I will discover that it all was a bad dream. But no amount of magic or anti-magic can restore what I have lost or change what I must become.

I've been clinging to the edge of a cliff, afraid of what I will find in the murky depth of my fall, refusing to let go. It'd been a mistake to fight Dimma's return. She must finish what she started; it's only with her rebirth that the universe will be able to heal again. I instinctively know it to be true, yet it's taken me far too long to come to this conclusion. I don't want to trust Dimma, but it's myself that I haven't trusted.

"I made my choices," I tell Rudjek, turning around to face him again. "As much as I wanted to see myself as separate from Dimma, we both know that isn't quite true. I am still a part of her. Her mistakes are mine, and mine are hers."

"You were the one who told me not to trust Dimma, and now you talk as if you want her to come back," Rudjek says accusingly.

"No matter what you or I want, she *will* come back," I try to explain, but I can tell it's going over his head. "Dimma and Daho are not innocent, but neither are the orishas. Who is considered good or bad depends on the one telling the story. Sometimes there are shades of gray. But sometimes . . . there are not. If Daho hopes to defeat Efiya, he'll need Dimma. She must finish what she started when she made him immortal."

"Arrah, what are you saying?" Rudjek steps closer to me. He already knows, but he's going to make me say it plainly.

"I must release Dimma's soul before Efiya can consume it." I am trembling as the words tumble from my lips. They sound strange spoken aloud. "I must die, Rudjek."

He laughs, but it's mirthless and bitter and cold. "You expect me to accept that and go on about my business like it's of no consequence?"

"I expect you to understand that I have not come to this conclusion lightly," I tell him. "I'm not giving up; I'm facing who I am for the first time. All of me, the good and the bad."

"You're impossibly stubborn. You know that?" Rudjek says.

I close the space between us. "So you've told me before."

He caresses my cheek, and I know it will be one of the last times I revel in his warmth. "I wouldn't have you any other way."

I will miss him dearly. "I want you to be the one to do it."

"You want me to end your life?" He's looking down at me through his fan of dark lashes.

"I figure that you'll make it painless. Will you help me?"

Rudjek's expression is tender, and it takes a long time before he answers. "Yes."

I rise on my tiptoes and kiss him. His lips eagerly latch on to mine, and we lose ourselves in the heat of the embrace—tongue, lips, and teeth. "I want so much more of you," I say against his mouth.

"And I of you," he whispers back.

I feel a tingle at the back of my neck that signals the gate's opening again. Rudjek and I both moan our disappointment. Daho has the worst timing. I start to pull away, but Rudjek holds on to me tightly.

"I rather like the idea of making the Demon King jealous," he says. "How about another kiss?"

I smile. "You enjoy antagonizing him a little too much."

"It's one of my guilty pleasures," he admits.

Someone yawns, and immediately I know it's not Daho. Dread courses through my chest. "You really could've made this a lot more difficult, sister," comes Efiya's sweet drawl. "This is a boring game. I found you too easily."

Rudjek pulls his shotels in one breath, but Efiya is already moving. She's a blur of fire, and she's not alone. Shezmu and Evelyn are with her. Rudjek is knocked aside, his shotels dislodged as they attack him. Efiya comes for me, and before I can fully draw the dagger, she has me pinned to a tree. Bark digs into my flesh.

"I'll be taking that." She pries the dagger from my fingers and thrusts it into her boot. "I'll make better use of it."

I grit my teeth, trying to free myself from Efiya's hold. "You will never win. There will always be people who will stand against you."

"And they will die." She leans so close that I can see a flash of every soul she's consumed in her gaze. "Starting with you."

"When you kill me, you'll only release a more powerful enemy," I tell her, stalling for time. Rudjek is on his feet again, his shotels silver flashes as he battles Shezmu and Evelyn. He's barely holding his own, but his anti-magic keeps them from coming in for the kill. "Dimma will destroy you."

"Dimma will become a part of me," Efiya says, then her face turns sad. "I will miss you, sister, truly." As she opens her mouth wide, I stare in horror. Her tongue rises, and a black, bottomless hole replaces her throat.

I feel a tug against my soul. It can't end like this. I can't be trapped inside her forever. My soul is uprooted, dragged from the depths of my body, leaving a trail of fire that would bring me to my knees if Efiya's magic were not holding me in place. I dig my nails into the tree, fighting for every breath. I imagine holding on to the tether between my soul and body. And somehow, by some miracle, my soul—*Dimma's soul, our soul*— does not slip from my mouth as easily as I have seen happen to so many others.

"Arghh," Efiya groans. She closes her mouth and wipes it with the back of her hand. "You always have to be so difficult."

I'm winded, but I allow myself a smile. "You are such a disappointment, sister," I say, echoing words my mother had uttered to her on many occasions. "All that power and no sense with it."

Efiya stumbles back, the insult hitting its mark. The one thing that we have always had in common is the desire for our mother's approval. Perhaps she came closer to it. "Take that back," she demands, almost pleadingly. "You don't mean it!"

"Why would I take it back when it's the truth?" I say. "Mother knew, and I know it, too. Why can't you admit it to yourself?" I cringe inside, hating this particular game. I see the hurt and pain in her eyes, and it's like twisting a knife through my own hand. The cut goes both ways.

Where are you, Daho? I need you. Doesn't he feel I'm in trouble through his connection with Dimma? He'd come so fast before when Suran threatened my life. Now I'm desperate to feel the gate open again.

Efiya must see the despair in my eyes. "You're very clever, sister, but your taunting will not work. Time for you to die." She strokes my braids gently, lost in thought for a moment until she takes a fistful of my hair and slams my head against the tree.

The world fades in and out, the trees swiveling and blending into the sky. When I regain my senses, I'm on my back on the ground, and Efiya is straddling me, my arms pinned to my sides. I moan, blinking through my blurry vision.

"Now, where were we?" she says as her mouth again opens wide.

The tug comes at once; this time, my soul begins to slip from my body more easily. I won't be able to resist much longer, and Dimma's magic is still locked away by her promise to me. Why hasn't she awakened? If she's not willing to save me then surely herself. But then I remember what Heka said, that he was bound by a promise. I realize the horrible truth at once. She can't break her own promise—not even to herself.

"I release you!" I scream. "I release you from your promise!"

I wait, expecting Dimma to do something—anything—but the silence inside me is deafening.

My shrieking does nothing to distract Efiya. I must seem like a madwoman to her, but she only leans in for the kill. Her mouth is so wide now that there's little left of her face. The abyss inside her is endless, and I can hear the echo of many voices coming from her throat. This is Dimma's curse, her gift to the demons turned against her.

"Arrah!" I hear Rudjek wail my name, but he sounds so far away.

I pour every drop of my strength into resisting the tug on my soul, but I'm losing. It won't be long now. I feel my grasp slipping when a sudden howling picks up. My sister is flung back.

I cough and taste blood on my tongue. Efiya is heaving on the ground with a sword of pure light through her belly. She gasps as she stares at the blade in shock and irritation. I don't let myself breathe a sigh of relief. This isn't over.

Shadows bleed into the corners of my eyes, and an unbearable sense of dread fills my belly. Fram's children descend upon the field, draining life from everything they touch. Rudjek stumbles to my side and falls to the ground. I reach for him, but a bout of dizziness overcomes me.

"Devour them," Daho commands of the reapers. His voice is grave, but there is no doubt lacing his words.

Dozens of reapers glide forward like nightmares come to life. They are impossibly long and thin, skeleton-like, cloaked in shadows. They sweep across the field, where Shezmu is pulling the sword from Efiya's belly. He quickly opens the gate with a sweep of his hand. His is a look of pure hatred as he meets Daho's eyes, then he lifts Efiya in his arms, and they escape with Evelyn.

Daho helps me to my feet. I lean against him until I think better of it.

Rudjek's chest heaves up and down. He's almost entirely covered in blood. Daho offers him a hand, but he slaps it away. "What took you so long?"

"I was occupied," he says without further explanation.

"Unbelievable," Rudjek groans.

"What happened with Heka?" I ask. I have to know.

"I'll explain later," Daho insists. "We must leave before they return with reinforcements." He opens the gate again, and I help Rudjek, whose wounds are already starting to heal.

The reapers pour into the gate first, and Daho follows behind them. Rudjek and I stand at the threshold, and I squeeze his hand. We were in the throes of death only a moment ago. Next time we won't be so lucky.

THIRTY
ARRAH

I'm exhausted by the time we arrive in the ruins of a city. We're assaulted by the acrid smell of recent death. Two black vultures hiss as they fight off a dog, or at least what vaguely resembles a dog, over a body singed beyond recognition. In every corner of the city, scavengers tear flesh from bone, trotting off with an arm, a leg, or another body part. The reapers disappear, spreading out across the land.

Daho looks around, just as shocked as Rudjek and me. "This was a thriving metropolis only a few months ago."

"It would seem that Efiya and your demons decided to pay it a visit." Rudjek sniffs the air. "The stench of their magic still lingers."

"She must've come here after I fled Ilora," Daho says in a daze. "These people weren't her enemies. Why would she do this?"

"She did it for the same reason she destroyed the tribes," I say. It's no different from the centuries he spent tracking down the gods. "The more souls Efiya and the others consume, the stronger they will become. You know that already."

Daho stumbles through the debris. "I can't believe Shezmu would go along with something this horrible."

"Well, start believing it," Rudjek spits. "This is your fault for releasing Efiya."

Daho turns away from us, his wings rustling. "I realize now it was a mistake."

"Twenty-gods—you're just realizing that?" Rudjek swipes at the blood and dirt caked on his jaw. "Perhaps you've also noticed that Efiya has your dagger, and she almost ate Arrah's soul. Neither would have happened had you not run off looking for Heka."

"Did you . . . ?" I pause. I'm almost afraid to ask. "What happened with Heka?"

Daho's shoulders tense. When he finally turns around, his expression is guarded. "I didn't eat his soul if that's what you think."

He's hiding something. It's written all over his face. I've lived my entire life shrouded in secrets, and I have no patience for another one. It's time for everything to come to light—it's time to face the truth, no matter the consequences. "But something *did* happen."

Rudjek shifts his weight and grasps the hilts of his swords. I know he's in pain, too, and I hate that he and I won't have our happy ending. I can only hope that after this is over, he'll have a chance at a real life. "I think I'll let you continue this conversation in private."

"You don't have to leave," I say, but he only smiles at me sadly and walks away.

"Arrah, I shouldn't be telling you this. . . . I don't know how or if it will change the future, but you deserve to know the truth." Daho's mood shifts almost immediately. His eyes glow with pure joy;

it radiates from his whole body. This is the Daho that Dimma fell in love with, the one she went to the ends of the universe to save. "Heka is my son."

Daho is beaming at me, lost in the revelation that his son is alive, but I'm in shock. Heka gave the tribal people magic and abandoned them when they needed him. Countless people have died because of his decisions. But he's also the reason Daho is free, and soon Dimma will be, too. It's a lot to process, and I can't help but feel bitter. Heka stood by while Efiya killed almost everyone I love. He's been manipulating events to get what he wants—to be reunited with his mother and father.

"There's so much I still don't understand, but he's alive," Daho says. "That's all that matters."

I swallow the bile on my tongue. "That brings little comfort when he's been willing to sacrifice so many lives to get to this point."

"You're right," Daho says. "I won't deny that, but none of this would've happened if the gods had left well enough alone. The Supreme Cataclysm made Dimma in its image, and who's to say that the universe isn't supposed to die by design? Who's to say that this hasn't happened before or that it won't happen again?"

"I don't know," I admit, my head spinning. "Nor do you. What you say is only conjecture to justify your decisions and those of your son and Dimma."

He smiles sheepishly. "Can you blame me for trying to make sense of the senseless?"

"I suppose not." I glance away. I remember what Koré told me about Dimma's nature—about *my* nature. *I've long thought your nature has something to do with transformation. You've become*

Arrah, haven't you? It's not like me—I'm only wearing a face. This is a vessel. It is not the essence of who I am, but you've become someone else completely. My heart is racing when I meet Daho's eyes again, and I hold myself very still so I don't lose my nerve. "After we visited Dimma's memory, you said that I wasn't her—that it was better than the idea that she'd fallen in love with someone else, but you don't believe that."

Daho rubs his hand across his head and shifts his position. The purple undertone in his skin deepens in color. He's embarrassed and trying to figure out what to say. "It's not for me to tell you who you are, Arrah," he finally utters. His voice is low and raw. "I'm only sorry that I didn't understand before that a god's nature cannot be denied."

"I will love Rudjek even after I die," I confess. "You must accept that."

He presses his lips into a hard line. "I know."

"Now that we've cleared the air," I say. "Let's move on to more important things."

He raises an eyebrow. "Go on."

I tell him about my truce with the orishas. "When the time comes, they will stand with us against Efiya. Koré and Re'Mec will make sure of it."

"I never thought I'd see the day when the Twin Kings and I were on the same side." Daho grimaces and shakes his feathers in indignation. "What assurances do I have that they won't turn on us at the first opportunity?"

"You have my word." I lift my chin. "That should be enough."

Daho nods. "It is."

"Good," I say. "Now, if we are to stop Efiya, we also need Dimma. We both knew that it would come to this."

"Arrah," he says. "I would never ask you to . . ." His words fall silent, washed out by the raspy hissing of the vultures.

I don't want to linger on this conversation yet again. "I've made my decision. Rudjek will help me; we'll do it today."

Daho's eyebrows shoot up. *"Him?"*

"Yes, him." I cross my arms.

Daho scratches his shoulder, looking so much younger than his years. "It's just that . . . I would never think him capable."

"You don't know Rudjek half as well as you think."

"So it would seem."

Rudjek clears his throat behind me. I know that he's been eavesdropping this whole time—those superior craven senses at play again. "I found a place to clean up," he says, his deep timbre ringing in my ears. "It's on the edge of the city and surprisingly not drenched in blood and mangled bodies. It would seem that there are people left outside the city. I saw a scouting party."

Daho backs away. "I'll be around if you need me."

Rudjek and I spent most of the day together alone. The modest cabin he found still has vegetables growing in the garden and smoked meat in a little shed on the edge of the property. Once we're clean, we decide to make a meal together. When we're done eating, we lie in the gardens next to vegetables that look like seashells and taste vaguely like plantains. I lay my face on his chest, and he tucks his chin against the top of my head.

"You know, you really were a spoiled brat the first time I met you," I say, listening to the steady rhythm of his heartbeat.

"And I thought you were so strange," Rudjek admits. "Seeing you and your father laughing as you pulled up weeds along the Serpent River."

"They were herbs for blood medicine!"

"I didn't know that at the time," he says, then inhales a sharp breath. "I wish that things could've been different between us. I should've told you how I felt long before now."

I rub my fingertips across the bristle of hair along his chin. "Tell me now."

He presses his mouth to my hair and whispers, "I love you, Arrah, and I will still love you even after you're gone."

I shift my position and meet his gaze, watching as he fights to push back his tears. "I will always love you, too." I bite my lip. We must do this before one of us loses our resolve. "Rudjek, it's time."

He sits up, hunching forward for a moment before reaching for the blade on the grass next to him. He'd found it in the cabin, not wanting to use his shotels. "It'll be quick."

"I understand," I say as he draws me close to him. I breathe in his smell of woodsmoke and lilac for the last time and sink into his embrace. I hate that I've asked him to do this, but if I am to die, I'd rather it be in his arms.

There is a moment of hesitation, and I see how his hand trembles. It's just enough time for me to draw in one more breath before he plunges the knife between my ribs. "Goodbye, Arrah."

Twenty-gods, it hurts. The pain is searing, but it doesn't last long. My head falls slack against him. I blink, and Daho is standing over us, peering down at me like in Semma's vision, but it's different, too. Rudjek. He's holding me until I feel nothing at all—until I am no more.

"Hello again."

Dimma stands across from me on a plane of stars, wearing a midnight blue dress that bleeds into the space around her. She's exactly how I remember: tall with golden brown skin, eyes as dark as night pearls, and slender black veins along her forehead.

Unlike the last time we met, I'm not angry. I know that we belong together. We always have. "Here we are again."

"We are one," she says, reading my thoughts. "Yet, we are different."

She extends her hand to me, and I accept her offer. Our two selves melt together. It's a blending of mind and body and soul. Her magic is immense, consuming, terrifying. With it, comes her great hunger, the curse that she passed on to the demons. But there is also beauty, wonder, nurture. It is the part of me that's been missing my entire life.

"We have some unfinished business," Dimma and I say in agreement.

When I open my eyes again, the world looks different. It's sharper, more detailed, as if everything is newly made. It's teeming with light, pulsing with energy. I'm still Arrah, and I am Dimma, too. I frown, confused. We are one, but still, a sliver of our consciousness remains apart. I search our mind, and I understand. This is a temporary arrangement, a small grace from Dimma.

I stroke Rudjek's chin, and he startles, smiling down at me, hopeful. "Thank you," I say, and his smile fades.

"Dimma," Daho croaks, his voice choked with tears.

My love is as beautiful as I remember. His face is perfect and so strange. His eyes glow as he takes me from Rudjek's arms. As he sobs against my shoulder, my vessel changes. I am once again the goddess he once called terrifying and terrifyingly beautiful.

"Arrah is with me." I pull away from my love and peer down at Rudjek, still on the grass, clutching the bloody knife. I extend a hand to him, and he seems to recognize what I mean. She is here, and she still longs for him.

Rudjek accepts my peace offering and comes to his feet. I take Daho's hand, too. The three of us have much to do.

THIRTY-ONE
EFIYA

I run my thumb along the edge of the dagger. There are no souls left inside, but it isn't an empty vessel. It hums with Eluua's boundless energy and her rage. I sit on the bone throne. I'm not used to losing or admitting that I need help. Papa, Evelyn, and the others won't be enough. Even after the demons filled their bellies with souls, they're still too weak.

I was so close to killing my sister. I could taste her soul. If the Demon King hadn't shown up, I would have had it. I'm sick of him getting in my way. I jab the blade into one of the skulls out of frustration. It cuts clean through the crystal.

It seems my sister has been busy. I can't believe she convinced Rudjek to fight by the Demon King's side. I can only assume this means that the orishas and the Demon King have come to a truce as well. I always knew he would betray us.

Papa steps onto the platform and sits on the floor next to the throne. His long white hair frames his face. His wings quiver against his back. He looks like someone swimming in regrets, and that's the last thing I need from him right now.

"I'm sorry he betrayed you, Papa," I say before he speaks. "I know it must be devastating, but we will have our revenge. My sister betrayed me, too."

"Silence, daughter," Shezmu snaps. "It's not the same. You've known Arrah for such a short time, but Daho and I have been friends for an eternity. We've always been there for each other." He gives me an inscrutable look and adds, "He was Ta'la's godfather."

A stab of jealousy swells inside me. Ta'la. The daughter who died. I'll always be second to her, the same way I was second to Arrah in our mother's eyes. Because Ta'la never got the chance to live a long life, she's everything Papa thinks a daughter should be. So very perfect when clearly, I am not.

If she weren't dead already, I would consider killing her myself.

I sigh, searching for words to comfort him. "You're right, Papa. It's so much worse. You were like brothers, and he still turned his back on you." I do sympathize with him, but it isn't like any of this should be a surprise.

"Did he betray me, or did we both let Iben play us against each other?" Shezmu says with tears in his eyes. "He planted the seed."

"The gods are always pulling strings. That is what they do."

"We need to end this," Shezmu mumbles to himself. "I'm tired of this war. I'm tired of living forever."

I sit up straighter. "I will end it, but with half the demons refusing to fight the Demon King, I need more help."

Papa massages his forehead. He can't see beyond his own misery. "We might change their minds in time, but that's the one thing we don't have."

"I'm not talking about those cowards," I say through clenched teeth. I will always be bitter that they chose not to side with me. I hold up the dagger, and the sunlight catches on the blade. "I need Eluua."

Papa's face twists in horror. I know what he must be thinking. Eluua helped the endoyans attack his people. She's the reason Ta'la is dead. Though he should've learned by now that people change, even the gods. I've changed, too. "You can't be serious."

"I came to understand Eluua when I was inside the dagger," I say stubbornly. "She knows the gods could have freed her long ago, but they left her in this state as punishment. She hates Koré, Re'Mec, and Dimma, which means she's useful to us."

Papa lurches to his feet, and his whole body is trembling. "She's a monster, Efiya."

I'm losing patience with him, but he deserves to know my reasoning. I owe him that much. "Unlike you and Evelyn and the others, she doesn't have ties to the Demon King and Dimma. Nor will she hesitate to destroy everything the other gods stand for."

He stares at me like he's opened his eyes for the first time. Maybe I've pushed him too far, but he needs to get over his sense of loyalty to his friend and let go of the past. "I didn't want to see you for who you are, Efiya." He chokes back tears. "You are what I became after Ta'la died. Angry, vengeful, manipulative, insatiable."

"Is that a compliment?" I ask cautiously. It feels like a trap.

"It is simply a statement of fact, daughter." Shezmu inhales a weary breath. "I wish I could have given you a different life."

That makes me think again about our visit to the forest world. It was nice walking barefoot under the lush trees, listening to the animals foraging. A part of me longs to go back there. But it's only a small part that I refuse to let win. I'm not about to give up now, not when I'm so close to beating my sister at her own game.

The only other time I felt such peace was in Kefu when I curled up next to Arrah in her bed, smelling her clean skin. She was very fragile then, almost broken when I first saw her. For a short time, she was my whole world. I can never get those moments back, and I miss them. I still loved Arrah even after she betrayed me, but love is why we're in this mess. I'd much rather cut it out of my heart.

"I know this is difficult for you to understand, Papa," I say. "But I like my life exactly the way it is. I will never be like Ta'la or Arrah. I will always do things the way I want. You can either accept me as I am or crawl back to the Demon King while he plans to kill your daughter."

Papa glances up at the sky dome and the shimmering light dancing on its surface. "I hope you know what you're doing."

"Oh, I do," I say. "I always do."

I hold the dagger flat against my hand, and my magic wraps around it in brilliant sparks. I can feel it resisting, thanks to Dimma's curse. Sweat trickles across my brow, and I clutch the throne with my other hand. It takes all my concentration before the blade begins to melt. When it's done, it's a shimmering puddle in my palm. I peer into it, admiring my own reflection and smile. The puddle slips between my fingers and takes shape on an identical throne across from me.

Eluua begins to appear with my face, eyes, and collarbone, but she changes her vessel when I frown in disapproval. Good. She already knows who's in charge. She becomes a creature with a thin, elongated face and gaunt cheekbones. Her skin is smooth gray marble, and her hair is a shade darker than midnight. "Where . . . is . . . Dimma?" She croaks out each word. Her wretched voice is a scrape against my ears.

Papa stands beside me, poised to strike. She doesn't seem to notice him, or me for that matter. Her eyes are hollow sockets.

"You may help me kill Dimma, but her soul is mine." I state what should be obvious. "Is that clear?"

"Clear," Eluua echoes mockingly, though I'm not at all reassured.

"You will also help us destroy the gods and the Demon King," Shezmu says sharply.

"Yes," she hisses, still not focused on either of us. "The others can help, too."

I lean forward on my throne, my interest piqued. "What others?"

Eluua breaks into a smile that fills out her face and rounds her cheeks. She radiates a warm, inviting light, but I am not fooled. She is every bit as dangerous as I am. I like that about her. It keeps things interesting. "The children of the Supreme Cataclysm that the Twin Kings deemed undesirable."

"In other words, gods they couldn't control?" Shezmu deduces.

She grips the skulls on the arms of her throne so hard that they shatter. "Yes."

I'm not sure Eluua is in her right mind. Who knows if it's the result of being trapped in the dagger or if she was unhinged even before then. No matter: I need her only for a little while, and if she becomes a problem, I will take of her.

"Take us to them," I say in my most gentle voice as if it's a request, not a demand.

Eluua clicks her teeth, and it sounds like metal clinking against metal. Then the throne disappears as she stands up. "Open the gate, and I shall be at your command."

Papa calls for reinforcements to accompany us: a dozen of the most powerful demons in our ranks, including Evelyn. She hasn't been the same since the Demon King betrayed us. I don't think she will ever be herself again. The sparks of joy and life once in her eyes have dulled. He stole those from her, and I intend to repay him by ripping his soul from his body.

When we've gathered on the palace steps, Papa opens the gate. Eluua stands next to me. Her impossibly thin fingers wiggle anxiously at her sides, and her gray skin practically glows. She's buzzing with energy that's waiting to be unleashed. She will do nicely.

I smile. "Show us the way."

We follow Eluua into the gate and travel the strands for longer than I ever have done before. Wherever we're going must be very far. I lose all sense of time as I pulse along the path she sets until we arrive at the edge of a world surrounded by a storm. I can feel the pull of the Supreme Cataclysm stronger here.

We float in the stars. The clouds are so thick that you can't see the surface. Thunder crackles and lightning cuts through the dark, giving the world its only source of light. When I try to use my magic to peer into the haze, it rebounds. "Where are we?"

Eluua stares down at the swirling clouds. "The place where Re'Mec and Koré imprisoned those of our brethren who refuse to abide by their rules. Our siblings that they deem too destructive." Eluua's eyes blaze fire. "We are all made in the image of the Supreme Cataclysm. What gives them the right to say which of us can express our nature freely and which must temper our hunger?"

"What did they do to deserve imprisonment?" Shezmu asks.

"No worse than treat mortal kind like the pests they are," Eluua answers dismissively. "Before Dimma trapped me, I used to come here and try to break the wards, but I couldn't do it alone." Eluua gives me a wide-eyed smile. "Now I have you. Help me free my brethren, Efiya, and we will help you destroy your enemies."

This is more than I could've ever dreamed—finally, a true advantage over the Twin Kings, my sister, and the Demon King. Eluua and I float side by side and pour our magic into the raging storm. The dark clouds roll at a dizzying speed, resisting our combined effort. Papa, Evelyn, and the others add their magic.

Soon the clouds lighten from dark to gray to milky white before thinning out. It's perpetual twilight in this world, and I watch as a creature crawls its way from the bowels of the earth. Moments later, another appears at the mouth of a cave. A third rises from a murky swamp.

I laugh at the irony of the moment. I'm going to make the gods destroy each other.

THIRTY-TWO
ARRAH AND DIMMA

There isn't much time now that we have reached the beginning of the end. Daho has taken Rudjek through the gate to gather his forces from Zöran, leaving me alone. As I walk barefoot through the ruins, I am reminded of my last days on Ilora after the endoyans and Eluua had almost destroyed the demon people. I had walked through the ruins then, too, taking in the layers of death. Mortal kind can and do destroy themselves, but we are often the catalysts to their destruction.

I do not regret my choices or the past, but I regret not having the foresight to understand the consequences.

Before Daho left, he told me that our son was alive. I wept at the news, for the last memory I have before my first death was of mourning him. The universe is still dying, but this time it will be different. How different, I do not know.

My brethren pour from the mouth of the gate one by one: Koré, Re'Mec, Nana, Sisi, Oma, Essi, Kekiyé, and Kiva. Some of them I am meeting for the first time. Some had come to the summer palace on Zöran to speak with Daho and me before I died. They are much fewer in number. There is some hostility, yes. Apprehension and suspicion thread in the space between us. But there is also kinship and recognition as well as regret. Though I can't say there is love, there is a certain affection.

Koré and Re'Mec are the first to come closer, as always. They take their roles seriously as the oldest of our kind. Koré has returned to her demon vessel with black wings, her hair writhing against her shoulders in an invisible storm. Re'Mec is human, golden-haired and bronze-skinned, though he's made himself taller. Essi is a shadow. Nana is clay, molded into a person. Sisi is fire. Oma is shrouded in ribbons of light. Kekiyé appears as one of his children, his face covered in many eyes. Kiva is a child with floating balls of all sizes circling him.

"It's been a long time, Dimma," Koré says.

Re'Mec scoffs and gives her a sidelong glance. "That's the first thing you have to say to her. 'It's been a long time.' Really, sister?"

"I supposed you have something cleverer to say?" Koré lets out an exaggerated sigh, but it's all pretend with them. They love this banter. They thrive on it.

I find myself longing to have that relationship with my siblings, to have that connection, but after so much time, they are enigmas to me, as I must be to them.

"Shall we go to Ilora now and finish what we started?" Re'Mec quirks an eyebrow at me. "Put down the abominations you created."

I bristle at that as the hem of my sheath catches in the wind. "They could easily put you down." I can't resist the urge to strike back at him, if only in words. Ours will be an uneasy truce forged by a mutual desire to survive. "No matter. They are coming here."

Koré narrows her eyes as she tunes into the vibrations echoing from the gate. Then she trembles at a new revelation. "Efiya has freed Eluua and the *undesirables*."

Some of my siblings hiss and curse at this news, but I do not find it surprising. "Perhaps it's time to come to terms with what we are."

"You are so young and so naive, sister," Koré says. "There are those among us with an affinity for great destruction. Those who seeded hundreds of worlds with life, only to spend their own lives torturing their children in the most awful ways. *That* is who Efiya released from their prison."

"I told you that we should have hauled them back to the Supreme Cataclysm to unmake them." Re'Mec throws up his arms. "Instead, you insisted upon giving them time to change. Gods don't change."

"You have," Sisi says through her vessel of flames. "A thousand years ago, you would not be conversing with Dimma, would you?"

"We can change," Nana adds, "but it is a slow process."

"Not all of us can change," Koré says sadly. "We are about to see that for ourselves."

She says this as Efiya and Eluua slip from the gate.

Anger and regret fill my vessel as I lay eyes upon my sister. I still remember when she curled up against my side and pretended to sleep—the way she buried her nose in my hair or the nape of my neck. But when I see Eluua, my feelings shift to rage. They both have done horrible things, but I don't have a history with Eluua the way I have with Efiya. Who would Efiya be had she not been born to free Daho? It is a question that I cannot answer.

"Good, you're all here." Eluua claps her hands. "This is every-thing we could have hoped for."

Efiya grimaces at her side as if annoyed that Eluua has taken it upon herself to speak first. Theirs is an alliance that could never last. They both crave to be the center of attention. Efiya peers around, perhaps noting that Daho and Rudjek are absent; then her eyes land on me. She sees Dimma only, not her sister, but I am both. "All of this trouble to bring you back," she says, looking down her nose at me. "You're nothing special."

"Efiya," I say, and my voice is Arrah's, the one she would recognize. "You still have a chance to end this before—"

"Don't bother," she snaps as two shotels appear in her hands. "I'm done with this game."

Efiya attacks. They all do. Efiya, Eluua, and a dozen of my brethren. They are blurs of smoke and rain and tentacles and barbs and flashes of light. We converge, clashing and shredding each other's vessels. Efiya strikes her sword across my chest, and I stumble, only for Eluua to dig her claws into my back.

Eluua moves close to my ear, her breath so hot that it peels flesh away from bones. "I thought about you often over the millennia, *Dimma*. I must admit that when Daho discovered that you were alive, I was thrilled. I wanted to be the one to kill you, and now I get that chance."

I turn to face Eluua while I hold up a hand to stop Efiya from advancing. From the corner of my eyes, I see Efiya go still but not completely. She writhes against my power, struggling to break free. She's strong—stronger than I had expected. I won't be able to hold her for long.

I let go of my physical form, and Efiya pitches forward, but I am already ascending into the sky with Eluua in my grasp. We become ribbons of crackling energy lashing at each other, tearing, seeking an advantage. Her soul pulses against me—so bright and so full of fire. I can't risk letting Eluua live this time.

I can sense my growing hunger, the part of me that I passed on to Daho and the demons. Her soul is unspooling, and all I can think about is how I want to weave it into my own, how badly I want to taste it. I'm losing myself to this hunger. This is my nature—to consume and transform. I cannot deny it. I am the master of souls. I can do with them as I please, but there are consequences even for my kind. I shiver as I push down my urge. If I consume Eluua, I will add her endless thirst for destruction to my own endless hunger, and that would be very bad. Instead, I will drag her soul to the mouth of the Supreme Cataclysm. Eluua must be unmade. She must meet her final death.

Before I get very far, there is a pull against my soul, followed by excruciating pain. I hear screams and wails and curses and clashes of weapons. Re'Mec and Koré are back-to-back fighting off four of our siblings. Nana is on the ground, shredded into a thousand pieces and unable to pull herself back together. Sisi's fire has dimmed, her movements languid as she cools. Oma is backing away from her attackers. Kekiyé rushes to protect Kiva, who tries to fend off two of our brethren, both bearing down on him.

We are losing. We're too few, and they are too many. I send a call for help through my bond with Daho, but he doesn't answer. I don't sense him. Our connection is gone. How could that be possible . . . unless . . . unless. I realize then that none of the other demons have come through the gate: Shezmu, Evelyn, or the others. If Daho and Rudjek aren't here, they must be under attack, too. *Is he . . . ?* No,

I can't allow myself to think it. After all this time, waiting for each other, desperately hoping. He can't be *gone*.

It can't end this way.

I am falling into a black abyss, my soul adrift. I try to pull myself free, but the strain is too great. I'm halfway down Efiya's throat, and I hear the echoes of the other trapped souls inside her, begging to be let go. The souls are familiar. My father and my mother from my life as Arrah. My siblings Ugeniou, Yookulu, and Fayouma. So many others trapped inside of this one girl.

I latch on to Efiya's throat, clinging to her flesh. She is screaming now—a horrible, horrible sound. I crawl my way back up, my hooks piercing deep inside her. Soon she's heaving, bent over on the ground, and I am oozing from her lips.

"I hate you so much," she cries, her shoulders shaking. "Why should you be the special one? Why should everyone care about saving you?"

She sounds so very young, so confused. I was young once, and I made mistakes even if my intentions were pure. I don't condone Efiya's actions, but I sympathize with her. She thinks she wants to kill us, but what she wants is to be seen, to be loved, to be nurtured, to be the center of her own story. I would hold her if I thought it would do any good, but it's too late for that now.

"I do not hate you, Efiya," I tell her. "I see you for who you are."

Something passes between us, and Efiya looks up at me, silent. Her glowing eyes shine with unshed tears, and her lip trembles. "You really are my sister, aren't you?" she asks.

I nod. "Even in death."

Our moment is cut short when Eluua attacks again. She claws

and bites my newly reformed vessel. But this time, I am ready for her. I disburse into a thousand tiny lights and buzz around Eluua in a frenzy. I force her to ascend into the sky. She resists, but it's no matter. We keep ascending and ascending until we are enveloped in darkness. No one comes to help her. They are too busy with their own conquests, all except Efiya, who is still on her knees, weeping.

The roaring call of the Supreme Cataclysm is a reassuring sound. All places lead to our creator, our destroyer. The need to reunite with it is so strong that Eluua stops fighting me. I drag her the rest of the way. We're both lulled into a state of peace. This is why my brethren made worlds so far away from the Supreme Cataclysm. They fear the temptation of this call, for one day, we all will have to answer it. We are immortal, yes, but we too shall be unmade. I stare into the pit of fire, knowing now that everything eventually runs its course. Everything comes to an end.

I am thinking these things as Eluua and I stand on the edge of the Supreme Cataclysm and peer down into the turmoil that is its mouth and womb.

Vines blossom from Eluua's vessel and root her in place. "I won't go."

But in the end, the call is too strong, and she steps forward, falling into the abyss.

DAHO

As expected, I am unwelcome at the Almighty Palace. Rudjek explains quickly to his people that I am here to help, but their animosity is palatable. I find it amusing that several of the cravens stay close, presumably to protect him from me, when it is *I* who need protecting from his insufferable arrogance. He's been a pain in my ass since the moment I returned.

The craven who looks Tamaran, Fadyi, and Jahla, the one whose hair sometimes appears white and sometimes pale silver, flank him as we cross the palace grounds. I keep my distance. Their anti-magic cuts into my skin, but I have endured much worse. Essnai and her heartmate, Kira, are also with us, along with a host of soldiers gathered from across Zöran.

I rather like Essnai. She's an excellent dancer and a good friend to Arrah. Or shall I say, she *was* a good friend. Even I'm having a hard time adjusting to the change. While the others are conferring, she comes to me without hesitation. I do my best to push back my uneasiness. "What of Arrah?" Essnai asks quietly. From her look, I can tell that she already suspects.

I'm relieved that Dimma is back, but I feel Arrah's absence. Perhaps it is out of some sense of obligation or guilt. These past months, I got to know Arrah, and in some strange way I had come to think of her as my friend, too. "Arrah is a part of Dimma now." I find myself wanting to justify, to explain, but how can I? I got what I wanted.

Essnai's gaze travels across my face, probing. When she speaks again, her voice is choked with tears. "She deserves better than to be a memory in someone's else life."

Nothing that I could ever say will soothe her or lessen her grief. "Be well, Essnai." I dip my head and touch my hand to my heart in the Aatiri tradition.

"Take care of my friend." She walks away. "Or else."

I wince at her command. She doesn't seem to understand fully that Arrah is gone.

"Kira, you will stay in Zöran to help Elder Ro," I hear Rudjek command. "Work with Semma from the tribes and split the craven forces across our key strategic points, as discussed. Fadyi, Jahla, and I will lead a force back through the gate."

"And why do they get to go while I stay behind?" Kira says, affronted, her hands on her hips. "I've saved your life many times over."

Rudjek gives her a cheeky grin. He really thinks he can sweet-talk everyone around him. "And I am grateful for that, but I need someone the gendars trust to help lead efforts here. My father would appoint Commandant Dakte, and we know how that will go."

Kira glances away, and Rudjek frowns. Ah, there is a secret here. I see it on every face. Something they're not telling him.

Queen Serre, who'd slipped down from the palace steps, finally speaks. "Your father is dead, Rudjek." She pauses, gathering her courage, her throat bobbing beneath her sheer veil. "Efiya killed him. After it happened, I sent soldiers to fetch you, but you were nowhere to be found."

Rudjek stares at his mother, his emotions sealed behind hollow eyes. Everyone watches him. I wonder if they know that his father was a royal ass. He deserved to die ten times over for his deeds. "May the king rest in peace," Rudjek declares, almost as if rehearsed. "I shall have my revenge against Efiya, I assure you."

It isn't that his words are empty, but they don't ring true, either. He's saying what is expected of him, learning to be a politician. If he survives, perhaps, he will become a better king than I. It never really suited my temperament.

"If it's all the same to you, Crown Prince"—I interrupt the solemn moment—"we should not tarry long." I'm anxious to get back to Dimma, then to take the fight to Efiya before she can make her next move.

Ignoring me, Rudjek bids for his craven guardians to gather the rest of the forces that will accompany us through the gate while Kira and Essnai return to the city proper. I search for the bond between Dimma and me, but it's not there. Something's wrong.

Before I can reach for Iben's gift, I know it's too late. A familiar itch scrapes against the back of my neck. I turn as Shezmu and Evelyn emerge from a ring of light so bright that it washes out my vision. I'm flung backward, and I hit the ground. A piercing pain spreads through my chest. I'm desperate for air. Anti-magic burns through my vessel.

My mind is lost in a fog and stringing my thoughts together to make sense of the situation is immensely difficult. Anti-magic. Rudjek. No. Not Rudjek. Shezmu. I writhe in agony as my army pours through the gate, but they're not my army anymore. They belong to Efiya. They fan out like a plague bleeding across the sky. *Where is Efiya? Where is she? Where?* When the gate closes, my heart sinks. She's gone after Dimma. I should never have left her.

I grapple with the craven bone lodged in my chest, but my hands are slicked with blood. I cannot shed my body. The anti-magic has made that impossible. I attempt to call forth the reapers, who are always on the edge of my consciousness, teeming inside me, but they remain asleep.

I'm assaulted by screams, clashes of swords, the pungent smell of death. My people are relentless as they tear through Rudjek's forces. They're much stronger than before, much faster, having recently consumed so many new souls.

Evelyn peers down at me with another craven-bone dagger in her hand. Shezmu stands opposite her with one of his own. "Efiya said that these would come in handy," she says, brandishing the knife. "I intend to make your death quick. I suppose I owe you that much."

I remember when she'd nursed me back to health after the Collector had almost destroyed my soul. The look of hope in her eyes when we kissed in the arboretum. The way she forced a smile after I found out that Dimma wasn't dead. In truth, I'd been awkward around her. Now her eyes are full of rage. I don't begrudge her for it. I killed many of her friends.

It's more painful to gaze upon Shezmu, his face twisted in anguish. He grasps his dagger so tightly that his knuckles are pale. I blink back tears. His betrayal cuts the deepest. "You were never good at strategy, brother," he says sadly. "That is why I always beat you at Paradigm when we played. I used to admire your single-mindedness when I thought you had our best interests at heart."

"You mean until you had your own agenda." I choke on the blood pooling in my throat. "Once you fathered Efiya, you did not care about freeing Dimma. Your only concern was that you had a replacement for Ta'la."

"No one can replace Ta'la," Shezmu spits. "You should know that after having lost a child of your own."

Not so long ago, Shezmu would have been the first person I told after discovering my son was alive, but I'm desperate to keep it a secret from him. He must never know. I switch my tactics. "Efiya wants to kill your queen, who you swore you would avenge. How can you come to terms with that?"

Shezmu doesn't answer, but Evelyn has plenty to say. "Dimma isn't our queen. She's just another terrible god that we must rid ourselves of."

"I won't allow it." It's taking too long to expel the craven bone, and I can stall them only so much.

Evelyn twitches her fingers at her sides, and I rise from the ground, stiff, under the control of her magic. She plunges her bone dagger into my belly and twists. I scream as more anti-magic flares inside me. It's destroying my flesh from the inside out. I will give Re'Mec credit. He's made an efficient weapon in the craven people. Their ability to counter magic is masterfully done. I would wring his neck right now if he were here.

"Efiya has released Eluua and joined with several gods to attack Dimma and the Twin Kings," Shezmu says. "When she's done with them, we'll destroy whatever gods are left. Then it will finally be over. All of it. No more games, no more endless suffering. We will live our lives freely."

"You mean freely until Efiya gets bored again," I say. "Then perhaps you'll be lucky if she kills you as quickly as she killed her human parents."

Evelyn frowns at that. She didn't know. I suppose not. It wasn't something that I had mentioned to her nor had I heard Shezmu share.

"Efiya has a long history of betraying those closest to her," I add, seeing an opportunity. "It's only a matter of time."

"Shut up!" Evelyn roars as she drives the blade between my ribs, burning another hole through my flesh. "You do not know her."

I spit out the bitter blood on my tongue. "You are right about that. None of us really know her, do we? She's so unpredictable. Perchance it's because she hasn't embraced the souls inside of her."

Shezmu swipes his blade across my throat, splitting my flesh with one stroke. As I fall to my knees, I know one thing for certain. I will die today if I cannot escape this vessel. "I will miss you, brother." He raises the craven-bone dagger again, intending to deliver his final blow, but his face twists in pain.

A sword pierces through his chest, the strike quick and true. A second blow takes his head. Shezmu shrugs off his decapitated body like a snake shedding its skin. His soul is a wisp of gray smoke, unharmed, as he rises above the carnage.

Rudjek stands over me while Jahla, Fadyi, and Elder Ro close in on Evelyn. She backs away from them, but I can feel their anti-magic undoing her soul. She screams, and it sounds as terrible as a mountain collapsing in on itself.

Jasym races to their sister's side and wraps their arms around her protectively. "We surrender!" they scream. "We surrender!"

"Never!" Evelyn snarls. "I'd rather die than bow to the gods."

"This isn't who we are . . ." Jasym pulls their sister closer. "Maybe . . . maybe there's another way."

I don't expect the cravens to show my people mercy, but I'm proven wrong. Jahla, Fadyi, and Elder Ro cease their attack, and Evelyn leans her face into her sibling and begins to cry.

Rudjek reaches down and pulls out the bone dagger still lodged between my ribs. What I wouldn't do to wipe that smug look from his face. "The mighty Demon King," he sneers. "Not so mighty anymore."

What he doesn't see is Shezmu slipping into the gate behind him while he's acting like an arrogant prick. I can't speak until my body's pushed back the anti-magic enough to heal my neck. I climb to my feet, my breath labored.

"You fool." I glare at Rudjek. "Shezmu has escaped."

Rudjek grimaces as he takes in the battle across the palace grounds and the city beyond. I see the moment that something shifts inside him. "I can't go with you. I need to protect my people." It must be a difficult decision for him, but it's for the best. The Arrah he knew is gone, no pretending otherwise.

"Maybe I was wrong about you," I admit. "One day you might just pull your head out of your ass."

Rudjek narrows his eyes into a cutting smile. "And perhaps you won't always be a soul-eating bastard."

"Don't count on it," I say, leaving him behind.

I enter the gate and race to save Dimma. Shezmu thinks he always beat me at Paradigm, but the truth is I let him. It was never about winning for me. I played because he was my best friend and I enjoyed listening to him talk about his family and the petty palace gossip. He was my link to mortality when I thought I had lost it. But Shezmu and I have been locked in a different game since Iben revealed our diverting paths, and now it must finally end.

PART V

What will satisfy this hunger inside me
Despite feeding it, I am still starving
It grows and grows and grows
Refusing to be sated or appeased
Soon there will be nothing left to offer it
But my own flesh.
—Efiya

THIRTY-THREE
DIMMA AND ARRAH

When I return to the battle, Efiya is curled up on her side on the ground, cradling her belly. She is crying and babbling incoherently. I ache for her, but this was always inevitable. The souls of my siblings are very powerful, and she has not sated their natures. Fayouma, Ugeniou, and Yookulu refuse to be still, as do Efiya's human victims. Arti, Oshhe, the witchdoctors from the tribal lands. It won't be long now before they either kill her or she becomes like the demons once frozen in a moment in time. She has the strength to let the souls go, but I will not force her to do it. It has to be her decision.

Iben's gate opens, and Shezmu appears in the mouth of a firestorm. I have not seen him through these eyes in a very long time, not since the nights he used to sit across from Daho in the library, playing their favorite board game. They will never have that life again or their friendship, and that makes me sad. He immediately goes to Efiya and pulls her into his arms. "I can't lose you, too," he cries as he gently rocks her. "Please don't die."

"Papa?" Efiya murmurs, frowning up at him. "Who am I?"

I remember how he carried Ta'la on his hip when she was young. She was always so curious about the world, and he obliged her every question. Now Shezmu is speechless, giving no answer, which only makes Efiya burst into fresh tears.

Soon Daho descends from the firestorm that is Iben's gate, and some small part of me laments that Rudjek is not with him. I am glad that we had a chance to say our goodbyes. Daho takes in the sight of Koré, Re'Mec, and the others at a standstill with our recently freed brethren. I take his hand, and he stares into my eyes. Our is a language that does not need words. He knows what I want, what must be done.

He nods his consent, and I reach inside his belly, my hand passing through flesh. He drops to his knees in agony. There is no other way. I search through the souls of my siblings inside him, and my fingers brush against the one I seek. I sigh, relieved to find that it is undamaged. I untangle Fram's soul from his, and Daho screams. He's breathing hard and sweating by the time I'm done with the task. He'll be weak for a while, but he will recover eventually.

I look down at the custodian of life and death. Their soul appears as twin balls of fire and ice. I have missed them. When they slip from my hand and retake physical form, I gaze upon their beautiful faces. Twin bodies of light and dark and the gray space between them. I should feel resentful that they have caused me so much pain, but that emotion has no purpose for me now.

"Sister," Fram says in their two voices, both warm and inviting. "Did your time as a mortal serve you well? For I hoped that it would help you truly understand your nature."

What I understand about my nature is that it is ever-changing and without boundaries. This was the Supreme Cataclysm's gift to all of us if we chose to embrace it. I sense a change in Fram, too. "Perhaps it has served me as well as your time in Daho's belly has served you," I offer with a raise of my eyebrow.

"Indeed," Fram says as they take in the world again. "It would appear that our siblings need our help."

"It would appear so."

There is so much left unsaid between us, but time is not in our favor. Fram and I join the battle, though I keep some of my attention on Daho. He is watching Shezmu cradling Efiya, perhaps waiting for his next move, but I do not think his friend has any fight left in him.

I take no pleasure as, one by one, my brethren's numbers dwindle again. Even my kind is not eternal. Everything that begins must end, or if not end, it must start again.

When it's all over, Daho stands at my side opposite Koré, Re'Mec, Fram, Nana, Kiva, and Sisi. The rest have perished in the battle. Shezmu has called upon Iben's power to create a bubble to slow down time around him and Efiya in an attempt to delay her death. I do not doubt that he intends to live that way for as long as possible, holding her while she is forever dying. He has created a new purgatory for himself, one that will destroy him in time.

"I need another very long nap," Re'Mec says with a yawn. This is his way of hiding from the pain and sadness we all feel after losing so much. "But I can't do that until you fix the mess you've made, *Dimma*."

He means my gift of immortality to the demons. He wants me to take it back. But I sense that Rudjek and the cravens have defeated the demons in Zöran. Some of them have returned to the Supreme

Cataclysm while some have chosen to stop fighting. And there are those still on Ilora. I will not take my gift from any of them unless the demon themselves ask me to.

"No," I say. "Our time is passing, brother, but theirs has only begun. They are not abominations as you once claimed. They are children of this universe, same as us."

"You can't expect that we will let them live," Nana says. "They pose too much of a threat."

"The demon left either chose not to fight or put down their arms—that ought to count for something," I say. "They've changed. Let's not also forget that they've done nothing but suffer under our petty scrabbles. It's time to give them back what we stole: a chance to live their lives."

"And what of the universe?" Koré asks. "It's still dying."

"In a few million years, give or take," Kiva volunteers, perched upon a floating ball with his legs crossed.

"We must accept the nature of the Supreme Cataclysm," I say. "It is the creator and the destroyer, and the universe is only another one of its children."

"You think the universe was always going to die . . . that it has nothing to do with you stealing the gift of immortality when you changed my children and bore a son of your own?" Koré surmises.

We've lost so many of our siblings and so many of our children. All senseless deaths that have been for nothing. But if I've learned one thing from Arrah, it's that in the darkest hours, there are always glimmers of hope. In this moment, I dare hope my siblings will come to terms with the inevitable. "When I stood in the mouth of the Supreme Cataclysm with Eluua, I almost answered its call," I tell my brethren. "One day, I will do so without regret, as is meant to be. The Supreme Cataclysm, too, will die eventually and be reborn. That is its nature. We have always known that, whether or not we chose to accept it."

Nana toils over the idea. "Then that will be the end of us."

"For a long time, I was obsessed with curing death to save my love." I glance at Daho. "But we mustn't be afraid of our own mortality."

"Best to live fully in the time we already have," Sisi adds, her flames burning brightly.

"It is a difficult thing to admit when I'm wrong—as such is my nature to be arrogant and sometimes foolish, I suppose," Koré says after some consideration. "I need to say this before I change my mind. I am sorry, Dimma, for all the suffering we caused with our stubbornness. Had we listened to you long ago, we could've found another way." She glances at Daho. "I'm sorry to you as well, my child. I have failed you and your people."

Daho rustles at my side and grumbles. It will take more than an apology for him to forgive her. I don't know that he ever will. Only time will tell.

"Oh, this is *so* wonderful," Re'Mec cheers. "While we're all having revelations of some sort, I want to remind you that I was the first out of the Supreme Cataclysm's womb. Koré and I shaped worlds millions of years before any of you were born. That should count for something." He paces in circles. "Whatever happened to minding your elders? And as your elder, I say, dying is overrated."

Koré pats his shoulder sympathetically. "Perhaps you should take that nap, brother. We shall talk about this in a few hundred years."

"And for the record," Re'Mec says, ignoring his twin, "I don't have anything to apologize for. The whole lot of you would still be aimlessly clinging to the mouth of the Supreme Cataclysm if not for me. I carried each and every one of you out of the inferno with my bare hands."

He's such a pompous ass, Arrah says inside my mind, and I smile. My brother will never change, of that I'm sure. But he isn't wrong. I remember the care he took in those first moments of my life. "We are grateful for you, brother," I say. "I'm sorry if we've never shown any gratitude."

"Well, that's something, at least." Re'Mec scoffs, but it doesn't hide the satisfaction beaming in his blue eyes. "I will take that nap after all."

As my siblings depart and go their separate ways, Kiva beckons for me to bend forward so that he can whisper in my ear. "I have always known that Heka was your son," he says conspiratorially, "but I never told anyone."

I'm surprised by this—but maybe I shouldn't be. Kiva is very clever. The others underestimate him. "Thank you—I suppose it's no longer a secret."

Kiva smiles at me and glances up at Fram, the only other one of my brethren to remain. "Good. I don't like secrets anyway." At that, he floats away on his ball and disappears inside a cloud.

"It seems that we are more alike than we are different, sister," Fram tells me. "I hope that we can start again."

"Anything is possible," I say before they depart.

Now only Daho and I are left, with the question of what to do with Shezmu and Efiya. He stares at them, shadows behind swirling mist. "Shezmu is as vengeful as I, if not more so. He could be dangerous if we leave him to his own devices."

"I'm inclined to agree, but I also believe they deserve to decide their own fates."

Daho's eyebrows shoot up. "Even after everything they've done?"

"Especially after everything they're done," I say. "We have made mistakes, too, and we have a second chance."

I take Daho's hand, and we shed our vessels and ascend into the endless night of the universe. We might not have eternity together, but we have a good long while left. "Let's go wait for our son," I tell him. "I know where he likes to hide."

"And where is that?" Daho asks as our souls intertwine.

"I'll show you."

When Daho sees the Supreme Cataclysm for the first time, he lingers on the edge, listening to its song. Arrah once saw an image of the Supreme Cataclysm in the Almighty Temple depicted as a tornado on its side. I find that rendition accurate. *I haven't forgotten you. You are woven into my soul, and our experiences have given me a new perspective. For that, I am grateful.*

Daho creates himself a new vessel and sits on top of one of the many caverns that make up the outer shell of our creator. I sense that not all of them are empty. There is new life brewing inside, not yet ready to emerge. "I have a great desire to rest here for a spell. How about you, Dimma?"

I settle next to him, my feet dangling over the edge. His wings brush against my back as he draws me closer. I recall the days we sat beside the frozen lake, quietly watching as the world slowly changed. I had asked him about Ilora and what it was like to be mortal. Now, after my many rebirths and deaths, I find that I have even more questions. "Sounds like the perfect chance to get to know each other all over again."

"Is this our end, Dimma?" Daho asks as I lean my head against his shoulder.

"Yes, but it is also our beginning."

THIRTY-FOUR
HEKA

My mother and father are waiting for me, but I have unfinished business that I must attend to before joining them. I have been patient for a very long time, and I can be patient a while longer. I suspect the same of them. For now, sit a spell, and I will tell you some of my secrets.

First, you must know this: I am very good at bending rules, and I have been very busy since my mother bid me to hide from her siblings. I am my parents' child, yes, but I am also an agent of the Supreme Cataclysm. I am no cosmic miracle. I am here by design. The Supreme Cataclysm is sentient, but it is a creature that understands only at a subatomic level. The ideas of life and death are meaningless to it. It creates and consumes so that it might create again, and that is the core of what you call magic.

But that is changing. Through me, it is gaining a deeper understanding of the universe that it birthed. Re'Mec, Koré, and the others are also agents of the Supreme Cataclysm, but they have forgotten. That is a side effect of living too long. It's easy to forget the meaning of life when you do not fear death. But you are mortal; you will not make such a mistake. You know that your life (that every life) is precious.

After I was born, I watched as the first of the Supreme Cataclysm's children imprisoned my mother and father. I wanted to help, but I was unable to break free of my promise to her. Her gift to manipulate souls is extensive, perhaps even more than she knows. Had Fram brought my mother to the Supreme Cataclysm, I could have saved her, and my father would not have spent his existence seeking revenge against their brethren. But then again, there wouldn't have been a story.

I travel to where Shezmu and Efiya are locked in a moment in time. They appear to be sitting very still, shrouded in mist, but once I slip past that illusion, both of them startle. "Hello, Efiya," I say, appearing as her lost sister Arrah.

By now, you should know that I have no true physical form. I am more at ease when I am free of such burdens, but I have found that most people prefer the familiar. I become a comforting or a discomforting sight, depending on the person's mind. Shezmu frowns, for he sees me as my father, his former friend.

"What do you want, Heka?" Efiya wipes tears from her cheeks. "Did you come to gloat?"

I am not accustomed to gloating, but I warned Efiya that the souls she had consumed would eventually kill her. I offered to carry them away. My mother may be the master of souls, but I am their custodian. It is my responsibility to collect them. Efiya has been using my gift in a way that goes against my nature.

"I am here to see if you have changed your mind," I say in Arrah's voice.

The souls rumble in her belly again, and Efiya doubles over. She's a sickly shade of gray, and her hair has fallen out in patches. Her fingernails have yellowed, her teeth splintered, but I am not concerned about superficial appearances. I'm more worried about what will happen to this girl I helped to create for my own selfish reasons.

I am not innocent in the chaos of this story. My father devised a plan with Arti of Tribe Mulani to free himself. I knew that her magic, along with Shezmu's in his weakened state, would not be enough, so I nudged her in the right direction. Efiya would not exist if not for me, so I am responsible for every life lost because of her. That is why I have taken such care to collect those souls.

"You would like that, wouldn't you?" Efiya glares at me, her green eyes turning dull. "You want me to be weak and dependent on others, but I will no longer be a pawn in your game or Dimma's or the Demon King's." She laughs, sweat beading on her forehead. "You said I would beg you to take away these souls. You were wrong. I would rather die!"

Efiya has always been proud—that dimension of her personality does not come from the souls inside of her asserting themselves. But pride can make us foolish or oblivious or reckless, all of which she has demonstrated over her very short life.

Shezmu clutches her hands. "He's offering you a chance to live."

Efiya peers up into her father's eyes, and for once, I see the little girl she should have been, had she been left to her own devices. "What will become of me if I can't protect myself or you?"

"There will always be dangers in the universe, Efiya," Shezmu says. "Haven't you seen by now that not even the gods are infallible? Together, let us put this life behind us and try again. I know I'm not the perfect father, but I'll do my best."

Shezmu glances up at me for confirmation, and I nod. It is within my power to take away the pain of their past. Some would say that people like Efiya do not deserve a second chance, but I am not here to judge.

"Will you love me, Papa, even when I fail or make a mistake?" Efiya blinks back her tears. "What if I cannot be perfect like Ta'la?"

Shezmu grimaces. "Ta'la wasn't perfect, Efiya. No one is. My heart is big enough to love the both of you equally."

After another moment, Efiya looks up at me, resigned. "Do it, then! Take them all away. Take everything—my memories, your magic, everything. Please, just make it all stop!"

I do not give her a chance to regret her choice. I untether her soul from her vessel and set to work, scraping away everything that has happened since her birth. Her memories are stubborn, but when I'm done, she's unmarred by her past. She is also a baby again.

Shezmu cradles her in his arms tenderly. "We'll go back to the world of endless forests, daughter. You liked it there." Shezmu glances up at me with tears in his eyes. "Will you grant me a favor, Heka?"

I nod again.

"I want you to take the souls that I have consumed," he says, then he pauses and glances down at his daughter. "And . . . and take away my immortality so that I may live my life and die one day."

I come with them to their new home, and Efiya's little eyes go wide as she beholds the trees towering over them. I carry out Shezmu's wishes. He is mortal again. For now, he and Efiya are alone, but one day perhaps they'll meet the people who live in the heart of the never-ending forest. What happens after that will be up to them.

I return to Zöran to complete my final task. With the demons gone, the tribal people have left their hiding place. They travel the crossroads to find the earth awakening in their lands. Tender plants push through the soil, and rain has come after a long drought.

Semma and the other chieftains have set up a camp near my destroyed temple in the valley. I had almost forgotten that it was time for the Blood Moon Festival. Though I will not give magic to the people this year, I have prepared a better gift.

I walk through the camp disguised as one of them. It's only in physical form that I can appreciate the rustling of cloth in the wind, the smell of spices, the laughter. I pass the Zu tents covered in animal hide, the white tents of the Mulani tribe. I step between vibrant tents of quilted silk and tents that are little more than sheets draped on wire. In my wandering, I release souls. The few sparks of magic left in the tribal lands dance in the air in delight, as does my heart.

I do not decide which souls will return to the Supreme Cataclysm to be unmade or stay to get a second chance. Though I will admit this. There are some souls that I did not bother collecting when they died. I think you know who they are. They have already passed into the Supreme Cataclysm. For the rest, each soul determines its own path. Unlike with Efiya, I do not take away their memories. History should not be buried or sanitized. It must bear the bluntness of truth so that people can learn from it.

Sparks of magic alight on each soul and remake their bodies one by one. I release everyone into the valley, whether they are from the North, Estheria, the Kingdom, or the tribes. Let them enjoy the festivities before they make their final journeys home.

"This is the work of the mother and father," someone cheers. "Praise Heka! He has returned."

I have returned, yes, but only for this moment. I owe these people a great debt. Without them, my dream of seeing my own mother and father again would not have been possible.

A Zu with tattoos covering his skin pushes his way through the growing crowd. He's confused until he comes upon a familiar face. "Majka, is that you?" he asks in disbelief, coming to a halt. "Of all the rotten people I could run into . . . I must be cursed."

"You are blessed, dear Sukar, to gaze upon my beautiful face." Majka beams at him and presses his hand against his heart. "But how have I come to be back in the tribal lands? The last I recall, I was dying in the North."

Sukar scratches his head. "I think I died here."

"Well, we both look very much alive to me," Majka says, slapping Sukar on the back. "I think a celebration is in order."

The souls that choose to move on float into the sky, following the call of the Supreme Cataclysm. In the end, there are thousands of people crowding the valley and thousands more that ascend into death.

Have I done enough? That I cannot say. I have done what I can in a tribute to Arrah, Rudjek, and their friends. And to honor all the sacrifices every person in this valley made. The people of this world will face other threats and conflicts, but for now, they will enter an age of peace.

"Goodbye," I say for the final time as I let go of my human vessel. It dissipates into countless sparks of magic that spread throughout the valley, drifting aimlessly through the air. Though some of that magic lands on people, imbuing them with my gift. There again, I have gone back on my word.

Now I'm ascending into the depths of the universe on my way to my mother and father. I am nervous. It will be the first time that we are all together since before my birth. What should be my first words? I have so many questions.

When I arrive, they are sitting on the edge of the Supreme Cataclysm, with a space left between them. I settle there, surrounded by their warmth. For the first time in my life, I know that I am home.

THIRTY-FIVE
RUDJEK

I stifle a yawn as my advisers drone on about a dispute between two families in the Southern province. Both heads of households have laid claim to a fertile strip of land that borders their properties. One wants to graze his cows there, and the other wants to expand his bamboo crop. The two advisers, both career politicians, present cases on behalf of the petitioners with a vigor that is wearing on my patience.

"Why have you not taken this dispute before the Vizier to pass judgment?" I ask, interrupting their passionate argument over the benefits of cow manure. Not that either of them has ever experienced working in a field. "This hardly seems worth my time."

I had gone against the tradition of handpicking a new Vizier in favor of an election, much to the guildmasters' protests. The people had voted for a fish merchant from the East Market, who held weekly assemblies in the coliseum. He's been more than adept at handling these quarrels.

One of the advisers straightens his shoulders and purses his lips like I have just asked him to solve the mysteries of the universe. "My king, these are very important families with significant influence in the Southern province. Wouldn't it be more discreet to ensure their privacy?"

"They would not want to be treated like common folk, Almighty One," chimes the other adviser.

"If that is so, then maybe they shouldn't act like petulant children," I say sharply, but then I catch Adé's eyes. My mother is sitting in the small audience scattered about the throne room, surrounded by her advisers, mostly women from her home country and the former Queen Estelle. She quirks an eyebrow at me, conveying so much in one small gesture.

I've been Almighty One for a little over two years now. After I led the battle against the demons while Prince Derane hid in his countryside villa, the public pressured him to concede his claim on the throne. I thought that he would fight it, but in the end, he decided that he liked a life of leisure too much to take on the responsibilities of running the Kingdom. Adé says that my position is precarious because I'm so young and advises that I work harder to endear support.

"I do employ you to make a fair and just judgment," says the first adviser. "We do not want to make an enemy of either of the families. They are valuable to the throne."

"I've heard enough," I utter, exasperated, "I rule that they split the land by season. When it's not time for planting and growing bamboo, then the cows should provide excellent fertilizer."

"You are most wise, Almighty One," the second adviser says. "That is a most amicable decision."

"Most impressive," says the first adviser. "I'm sure the families will agree."

I've come to understand that a lot of these informal sessions are to appease the people of influence's need for attention, and when there is nothing of importance to discuss, they send their petty grievances. "Now, if we're done for today," I say, rising to my feet.

"Almighty One," I hear Princess Veeka's saccharine voice perk up from the audience. "I have a trade opportunity to present on behalf of my father, King Qu'setta of Galke."

I put my butt back on the throne and gesture to the princess. "By all means, you have the floor."

Princess Veeka has proven to be an excellent ambassador for Galke and a skilled negotiator. More than that, she's become a close friend. Shortly after I took the throne, the guildmasters pushed me to reconsider an engagement between us, but neither Princess Veeka nor I was interested. Recently, she told me she was seeing a person she met during the Fire Festival, and before that, it has been one of my Sukkara cousins.

For now, I have been able to stave off the conversations about potential marriage arrangements. I remember when I asked Fadyi if Caster of the Eldest Clan, my craven ancestor, had foreseen a queen by my side, and the answer had not been encouraging. The only queen I would want is gone now, and not a day goes by that I don't think of Arrah. The Demon King and Dimma got their happy ending, and I get to have riveting conversations about cow manure and whale oil.

It's well into the late afternoon when I finally dismiss the session for the day. Everyone slowly files out of the hall while I stay put, reveling in the silence that follows. I inhale a deep breath and close my eyes.

"I have heard news that your brother will arrive in the morning," Adé says quietly. "I am relieved that you've convinced him to return home."

I smile. "That was supposed to be a surprise. Can I keep no secrets from you?"

"Uran doesn't know, so it shall be a surprise for him and the children," she says. "It will be good to have the three of you together again."

Jemi, Uran, and I had been inseparable when we were boys, though I was always the annoying little brother they wanted to go away. Instead, my father had sent Jemi to a desert and kept Uran mostly under lock and key. I vowed to change that when I took the throne. Though Uran still has his moments when he needs to retreat from the world, he's been more open to talking recently. None of us have seen Jemi in many years, and I must admit, I'm a bit nervous. Our correspondence over the past few months hasn't given me much insight into his state of mind.

"You look tired, my son," Adé says, coming to my side. "Are you not sleeping well?"

The question is a formality. She already knows that I hardly ever sleep. There is no herb or remedy to quell my nightmares. I don't need much sleep either way, so most nights, I walk the palace grounds or practice shifting my form with Fadyi and Jahla, to no avail. Perhaps one day I will master that particular craven skill, but it seems unlikely.

I stand and gently squeeze her shoulders. "I'm fine, Adé. You don't need to worry. I am getting along the best I can."

"Perhaps you, Majka, and Kira should take back to sneaking down to the docks at night to gamble like you did when you were younger," she says. "I'm sure you can perfect a disguise so no one recognizes you."

"You know about that, too?"

"There isn't much that doesn't make it to my ears." She cups my face. "I am here if you ever want to talk, Rudjek."

"I know." I kiss her forehead. "I'll see you at the evening meal. I will retire in my chambers until then."

"Of course," she says with a nod. "I hope your rest is fruitful."

Though she hasn't said anything directly, clearly she knows that I still sometimes leave the palace in the afternoons. Fadyi, Jahla, and Majka are waiting for me in my salon. Well, Fadyi is staring out the window at the gardens while Jahla and Majka are making good use of their free time. I've changed into a faded tunic, dark trousers, and don a cloak fashioned out of burlap.

"What adventure shall we seek today?" Fadyi turns away from the window. "Shall we go fishing again or attend a match at the arena?"

He's starting to loosen up a bit. The sun god would say that I'm a bad influence on him, but it's nice to see the change. We attended a private concert earlier in the season, and he tapped his feet the entire time.

"I was thinking about perusing the East Market," I say, dashing his hope. "I'm not in the mood for anything else."

"As you wish," Fadyi says.

"And I suppose I have to stay here and guard your wing of the palace while you three go have fun?" Majka says as he and Jahla finally end their embrace.

"Well, that or you can climb down the mountain with us," I say. "I'm sure Jahla can shift into a creature that can carry you."

"You know what?" Majka stretches his legs out on the couch. "I think I *will* stay here."

"You don't know what you're missing," Jahla tells him.

"Oh, I know exactly what I'm missing," he says, closing his eyes.

I smile, still amazed that he's back, along with Sukar, Raëke, and the craven twins Ezaric and Tzaric, though the latter three decided to return to the Dark Forest. The tribal people say it's Heka's doing, which sounds about right. The last I heard from Re'Mec and Koré is that the demons would no longer be a threat. They had returned to Ilora to rebuild their lives. Re'Mec had mentioned something about needing a nap.

Fadyi, Jahla, and I sneak out of the palace through the secret attendants' passageways and head to the edge of the mountain, behind the animal stalls. I can't leave by litter, or my human and craven guards alike would insist upon accompanying me when all I want is a reprieve from my responsibilities, if only for a little while.

We hike down the almost vertical rock face. My fingers and toes adjust to become sticky, adhering to the surface. I have a superb center of gravity, if I may say so myself. Jahla scuttles along beside me in the form of an albino lizard. Fadyi is a black-and-gray eagle, ever circling like a nervous mother hen.

Once we're at the bottom of the mountain, we duck between the trees and come out in the West Market. I lift my hood to shroud most of my face, though it's much too hot for it. Fadyi and Jahla keep their animal forms and watch from a distance. They know that I want to be alone.

I cross through the pristine cobblestone streets of the West Market, dip alongside the row houses, and enter the East Market. It's pure chaos here, with merchants and patrons shouting each other down, haggling and posturing. I can see why Arrah used to like this market so much. It's so easy to lose yourself here, forget about your troubles. Sometimes, as I weave through the crowds, I spot a girl of Arrah's complexion with golden eyes, and my knees go weak. But everything else is all wrong, and I feel like a fool.

After I killed her, I watched her face transform before my eyes. She became Dimma, the terrible goddess, *ama* to the Demon King. But there's a part of me that still thinks I'm going to find her waiting for me in the market. She'll be looking at trinkets or watching the street performers, just the way she liked to do before . . . before everything went to hell.

I am close to Essnai's new dress shop, which she set up next to her family's. She's bustling around the entrance, with spools of colorful cloth draped across her arm. Patrons flock to the rows of sheaths, asking about fitting and prices. Kira is sitting under the shade of the shop's eave, poring through a box of scrolls.

"Tomorrow's lesson plans," she says, holding one of the scrolls. She glances up at me, squinting against the sunlight. "Wandering again?"

"Just taking a walk," I tell her. "It's nice out."

Kira has been teaching at the Almighty Temple since the new seers opened the school again. I miss having her around, but it's clear that being a scribe is her true calling. We still occasionally go to the arena to practice our fighting skills. To no one's surprise, I remain the best swordsman in all of Tamar, and across the Almighty Kingdom.

"We should all get together some time soon," Kira says. "It's been a while since I've had the chance to pester Majka."

I smile. "He misses it greatly."

Kira says something else, but I get a tingling at the back of my neck. There's magic nearby, not the small sort I sense from some people of tribal descent. It's strong, commanding—the magic of a god. I sniff the air, looking for the source, and my senses point me in the direction of the docks.

I utter an incomprehensible apology to Kira and set off at a sprint, easily slipping through the dense crowd. My heart is beating so fast that it feels like it's going to break free of my chest. It can't be *her*, can it? I arrive at the docks, but the magic is pulling me farther. I laugh deliriously and keep running—to the secret spot by the river where Arrah and I used to meet.

EPILOGUE

I stare into a face that used to belong to me. I'm confused by this. How could it belong to me and now belong to someone else? I am in a dark place, but it's warm and comforting, and beyond the edge of where I lie, there is a pit of swirling silver mist like a brewing storm. Sometimes I stare into it, too, losing myself in its rhythmic motion. It calls to my soul, beckoning for me to join with it, but I resist its pull. I'm not ready to answer its call. I yearn to do so much more with my life. There is no time here, no day or night. I do not get thirsty or hungry.

I am sure that I am dead, for I have no sensation at all. Is this what ascension into death feels like? Is my soul undergoing the unmaking, returning to the mother and father or the Supreme Cataclysm? Are they one and the same? Is this one long dream? I wonder about the swirling silver mist. It seems important somehow, but I don't know why.

I don't believe that I'm supposed to be here. I'm supposed to be wearing the face of the one who peers down at me with a curious expression. She is me, and I am her, but no, that isn't right. We are separate beings, but we once shared the same body. My memories are hazy. Is this part of the unmaking—a washing away from the past, a cleansing, a fresh start? Will my flesh be stripped away, too?

"I did not think it possible," says a deep voice. "Will she be all right?"

A second face appears next to the first one. This face is silver, and the first is brown. They both have black lines along their foreheads.

"It's too early to tell," the woman says. "She is missing parts of herself that are still within me. Untangling them is proving to be more delicate work than I expected. It will take some time."

"I hope not too long," Daho says. "Time might be near limitless for us, but that is not the case for her."

There. I remember. His name is Daho. Her name is Dimma. I do not yet have a tongue or a mouth, so I can't ask them the questions burning in my mind. *Who am I? Why am I here?*

Dimma and Daho are always near, either in my line of sight or within earshot. There is another one with them, and they talk in words that do not make sense to me. The third is named Heka. He is their son. I stare down at my hands in the weak light. My fingers are webbed. My body is changing rapidly, growing toward the version of myself that I remember.

I sleep for a very long time. I do not know how long. A few days, an eternity? When I wake again, I have a mouth, teeth, a tongue. My fingers wiggle freely. There are so many faces spinning in my mind as my memories piece themselves back together. Little by little everything becomes clearer.

Dimma smiles at me. "Are you feeling better now, Arrah?"

Arrah, yes, that's my name. I am Arrah. She is Dimma. We are not the same—not anymore. I nod as I finally sit up. "Aren't I supposed to be a part of you? How is this possible?"

"I found a way to separate us," Dimma says. "I'm only sorry that it has taken so long to give you back all your memories."

I realize what she's saying and begin to weep. "I'm going home?"

"Yes," she says, reaching for my hand. "I will take you."

My first steps are uneasy, but the reflex of walking comes back to me quickly. I root around my mouth with my tongue and find that my missing teeth have returned. Dimma has made me over from scratch. I am the same as I was before I started to trade my years for magic.

"I must warn you that things may be different from what you remember," she says. "Some time has passed."

"It doesn't matter," I say. "I'm ready."

She's still holding my hand when we peer over the ledge of the Supreme Cataclysm into the blackness around it. I glance back to see Daho and Heka watching. Heka is again ribbons of light. Though I am separate from Dimma now, I still remember her love for Heka and in a strange way, I will always care for him, too.

Dimma and I take one step, and we're gliding through the endless void of space surrounding the Supreme Cataclysm. It feels like we've been traveling for days when we reach Iben's gate. She tells me that this is the closest it can open to the Supreme Cataclysm without being consumed by it. Then we travel as pulses of light until we land in Zöran.

We stand on the banks of the Serpent River, overlooking the docks to the south and the boats as they float lazily on the water. A breeze rustles the grass, and the smell of mint fills the air. This is home. This is where I belong.

"I owe you much more than I can ever repay, Arrah," Dimma says at my side. "But in growing you a new body, I have given you back the years you traded for magic. You will live a full life."

I am choked up with tears. How can I live a full life without all the people I lost? My father, Grandmother, Sukar, and so many others. I'm thankful to be alive, but it doesn't stop me from feeling sad. "Thank you for giving me a second chance."

Dimma smiles down at me, and she looks more hopeful than I've felt in a long time. I hold on to a piece of that hope as she lets go of my hands and disappears back into the gate between worlds.

I wonder if I will have the same gift for seeing magic or if that will be gone as well. I find myself not caring as I sit cross-legged on the grass. It makes my backside itch, but it feels glorious to have any sensation again. I press my hand to my chest, tuning into the rising and falling of my breath. It is something that I will never take for granted again. There is magic in living, in waking up each day. I will never forget that.

I stay at the river for a long time, watching as the boats come and go, remembering that Rudjek and I used to meet here. How much time has passed since I went away? Dimma warned me that things would be different. Maybe one day, I'll build up the courage to look for him, but not today. Today, I am content to have my life back and have this quiet moment.

I hear footfalls approaching from behind, and I go very still. Some part of me is afraid that if I move, someone will take this away from me, that I'll realize I'm dreaming in the belly of the Supreme Cataclysm as its slowly unmakes me, that this is all a cruel joke.

The person stops and exhales a deep sigh. Only then do I know. I whirl around, not believing it's true, but I lift my gaze from his feet to his long limbs to his beautiful face. His skin is the most perfect shade of ebony, his head shaven. He's smiling down at me with tears in his eyes, and I am so overcome with joy that my body has become useless.

"Hello, little priestess," my father says, smiling broadly at me.

I know that it's really him. I feel it in my bones. He is alive. He's here with me.

"Father," I utter, trying to climb to my feet, but he slips down beside me. "How?"

He pulls me into his arms. "Heka."

We both are sobbing now, holding each other like it's the end of the world. We stay that way for a long time, and I think that I hear another set of footsteps come and go. Perhaps someone saw us and decided not to interrupt.

"Your grandmother, the great Aatiri chieftain, told me to be patient," Oshhe says.

"Grandmother's alive, too?" I ask, stunned.

"Yes—she and many more," he confirms. "She foresaw your return."

I swallow, dread filling my chest. "What about Arti and Efiya?"

My father shakes his head. "They were not returned with the others."

I don't know how I feel about this news. My relationship with my mother had always been difficult. I craved her love and affection, her respect. I wanted to make her proud of me. But in that desire, I lost something of myself. I hope that Arti finds the peace in death that eluded her in life. As for Efiya, I will hold on to my memory of when she was a little girl curled up next to me in bed. That is the Efiya that never got to be.

"What shall we do, Father?" I ask.

"We still have the shop," he says with a shrug. "I could use your help with cleaning bones and crushing herbs for my blood medicines. And Ty is at our old villa, running the household. We'll get through this one day at a time."

My father pulls a bag of milk candies out of his pocket, and I can smell the sweet aroma of cinnamon and nutmeg. He takes a candy for himself and hands the bag to me. I pop one into my mouth, then another, savoring the taste as they melt on my tongue. They taste like heaven, if there is such a place.

"It's been a long time since you last told me a story," I tell my father.

He smiles as he riffles through the bag and takes another candy for himself. "Has it been? I was under the impression that I had told you all my good stories, but perhaps there's one left to tell."

I perk up at that, ready to hear this yet untold story. My father settles in next to me, rocking until he's gotten in a more comfortable position. The sun starts to set over the mountain at our backs, casting an ethereal amber glow across the river. Frogs croak at the water's edge and torchlight flares to life at the docks farther downriver. The mood couldn't be more perfect.

It doesn't matter what story my father is telling as I tune into his words, listening to the timbre and pitch of his voice. I slip into a deep state of peace.

This isn't the end of our story; it is just the beginning.

ACKNOWLEDGMENTS

I am immensely thankfully to have completed the Kingdom of Souls series surrounded by my very own cast of characters, who wore multiple hats and played such important roles every step along the way. I couldn't have written Arrah's story without their support, love, encouragement, and the occasional kick in the pants.

Always thankful to my mother, who encouraged my love of reading. To my brothers, I will always be grateful for your support and our lively conversations. To my sweet baby J, you make everything I do worth it. To Cyril, your dedication to your passion inspires me to never give up.

To my literary agent, Suzie Townsend, you continue to be a tireless advocate and cheerleader, and I am so thankful for your insight. Thanks to Joanna Volpe, New Leaf Literary Agency's fearless leader. Pouya Shahbazian, the best film agent in the known world. Veronica Grijalva and Victoria Henderson for shopping Master in the international markets. Meredith Barnes, for your wealth of advice. To Sophia, for keeping me organized and on track. To Hilary, Joe, Madhuri, and Kelsey, thank you for your support.

To my amazing editors, Stephanie Stein at HarperTeen and Vicky Leech at HarperVoyager UK. I am thankful for your thoughtfulness, sharp eyes, and our brainstorming sessions. I am especially thankful for your patience and your passion. Always appreciate that you support my incessant need to never take the easy route in my stories.

To the team behind Stephanie at HarperTeen—Sophie Schmidt, Jon Howard, and Robin Roy, couldn't do it without your expertise—many thanks. To Jenn Corcoran for publicity, Shannon Cox for marketing, and Kristen Eckhardt for production, thank you. I'm so grateful for the school and library team, Patty Rosati, Mimi Rankin, and Josie Dallam. Another round of applause for Jenna Stempel-Lobell for brilliant designs.

Much respect and admiration to cover artist, Adeyemi Adegbesan, for a series of beautiful covers. Keisha, thank you for becoming the face of Arrah and channeling her perfectly.

Natasha Bardon, thank you for being a champion of this book at HarperVoyager UK. To the marketing team, Rachel Quin, Fleur Clarke, and Hannah O'Brien, thank you. Jaime Frost, thank you for publicity. To the design team, you created a magical cover for the UK market. Thanks to Robyn Watts, for working tirelessly on production and organizing the special edition.

To my wonderful friend Ronni Davis, I'm so proud of you. I adore your energy, kindness, friendship, and humor. Thanks for being exactly who you are.

Alexis Henderson, one of these days when we're not on endless deadlines we're going to finish all the secret projects we've been cooking up.

To my wonderful writing family: Samira, Gloria, Lizzie, Ronni,

Kat, Anna, Zetta, Ebony, Cathy, Nancy, Irene, Reese, Mia, Lane, Rosaria, and Jeff. To the Speculators: David S., Antra, Nikki, Axie, David M., Nikki, Liz, Erin, Alex, Helen, Amanda. Thank you for inspiring me to keep at it.

Many thanks to the booksellers and librarians for championing *Master of Souls*. And to the readers who have offered me encouragement and support throughout the years.